VINTAGE
SCIENCE
FICTION

VINTAGE SCIENCE FICTION

EDITED BY
PETER HAINING

CARROLL & GRAF PUBLISHERS, INC.
NEW YORK

First Carroll & Graf edition 1999

Carroll & Graf Publishers, Inc.
19 West 21st Street
New York, NY 10010-6805

Library of Congress Cataloging-in-Publication Data is available.
ISBN: 0-7867-0647-3

Manufactured in the United States of America

CONTENTS

Contents

Note: This is a list of film titles. The original works on which these films were based may have had different titles from those listed above. The original title for each story is given in its introduction.

PERMISSIONS

The Editor and publishers are grateful to the following authors, their agents and publishers for permission to include copyright stories in this collection: International Scripts for the extract from Rocketship Galileo by Robert A. Heinlein; Fleetway Publications and MGN Newspapers Group for "It Came From Outer Space", based on an outline by Ray Bradbury, and "The Conquest of Space" by Werner von Braun; Fantasy House Inc. for "Lot" by Ward Moore; Scott Meredith Literary Agency for "Sentinel of Eternity" by Arthur C. Clarke and " We Can Remember It For You Wholesale" by Philip K. Dick; William Nolan for the extract from Logan's World; Bantam Books Inc. and Desilu Productions for "The Unreal McCoy" by James Blish; New English Library for "The Lawnmower Man" by Stephen King; and Little, Brown for "The Forbidden" by Clive Barker; Random House Group for "The Adventures of Superman" by George Lowther; King Size Publications Inc for "What Price Venus?" by Evan Hunter; HarperCollins Publishers Ltd for "Enderby and the Sleeping Beauty" by Nigel Kneale; Bantam Books for "The Monsters Are Due on Maple Street" by Rod Serling; Michael Joseph Ltd for "Dumb Martian" by John Wyndam; BBC Enterprises for "The Lair of the Zarbi" by Bill Strutton; Greenleaf Publishing Company for "The Invisible Enemy" by Jerry Sohl; *Astounding Science Fiction* for "Liar!" by Isaac Asimov; Abner Stein Ltd for "I'll Not Look For Wine" by

PART I

PROLOGUE

The Cinema of Possibilities

There still exists in the vaults of the American Film Institutes in New York a faded print of a short, black and white movie with the intriguing title, *Dream of a Rarebit Fiend*. Shot in a single day during the Spring of 1906, this five-minute silent would probably have long since been forgotten but for the fact that its maker employed a technique so revolutionary that it would be used again – though few people are aware of the fact – over sixty years later in one of the most famous of all Science Fiction movies, *2001: A Space Odyssey*.

Dream of a Rarebit Fiend concerns a man who has dined rather too well on the famous cheese snack and afterwards falls into a restless sleep. Suddenly, he sits up in bed to find his room full of a nightmare assembly of huge pieces of food. These objects – all quite clearly actors dressed in rudimentary costumes – then proceed to chase the hapless, pyjama-clad fellow around the bedroom.

What startled audiences who watched the film back in the first decade of the Twentieth Century – and can still amaze any viewer lucky enough to be given a screening today – is the way the man and his weird pursuers run across the room, up a wall, over the ceiling and then back down the far wall to the floor again. There is no pause in the action, no suggestion that the sequence had been filmed in anything other than one continuous take. And so, indeed, it had. For subsequent research has established that what the unknown director did was to have all his actors run on the spot while

1

the entire set of the room turned through a complete circle in front of his camera!

Whether Stanley Kubrick the producer-director of *2001* ever saw this little piece of film history is not known. Certainly he has never admitted to the fact. But it was precisely this same technique he employed while filming an equally impressive scene in his 1968 spectacular when a stewardess on the lunar space station, unhampered by gravity, walks from the floor to the ceiling and through a doorway in the ceiling, as if it were the most natural thing to do. In order to film this effect, Kubrick duplicated the idea of the revolving set just as his unheralded forerunner had done in 1906.

Such are the facts of what surely deserves to be at least a footnote in cinema history. Yet I am using the evidence here for no other purpose than to underline the longevity of special effects in the making of pictures – in particular in the creation of Space Movies: those pictures in which man either travels beyond his natural confines on Earth or else confronts the possibility that there might be other life forms in the universe of which our world is only a tiny fragment.

In actual fact, film makers have been creating pictures about space travel almost since the advent of the cinema. One of the earliest pioneers was the French magician-turned-cinematographer, George Melies, who shot his 16-minute production, *A Trip To The Moon*, in his tiny Paris studio as early as 1902. He was followed by the German expressionist, Fritz Lang, with his dystopian masterpiece, *Metropolis* (1926), and *The Girl in the Moon* (1929) which is generally credited with inaugurating the space travelling tradition in Science Fiction cinema.

In the following pages I have assembled a selection of short stories which represent several of the landmark pictures in the genre, together spanning half a century of film history and technological development. Through them it is possible to note how the special effects that began as mere trick photography have progressed and now reached a kind of apogee in Virtual Reality. Of the stories themselves, each I believe lives up to the definition that "the father of modern Science Fiction", H.G.Wells himself, once offered to describe his books – and which, equally, might be used to define Space Movies themselves. For all are, surely, "Fantasias of possibility".

PETER HAINING,
London, 1995.

DESTINATION MOON

> (Eagle-Lion Pictures, 1950)
> Starring: John Archer, Warner Anderson & Tom Powers
> Directed by Irvin Pichel
> Screenplay based on *Rocket Ship Galileo*
> by Robert A. Heinlein

Destination Moon, **the American film which effectively initiated the boom in Space Movies, owed its production and subsequent success to the vision of one man, George Pal. A Hungarian-born, former film animator, Pal had fled from Nazi Germany at the outset of World War Two and moved to America where he became one of the most inventive and influential makers of fantasy pictures. Indeed, it was thanks to his pioneer work that the SF film became one of the hottest commercial properties in Hollywood in the Fifties – in turn encouraging the publication of many more science fiction novels and the belated entry of SF onto the television screen. Determined to make** *Destination Moon* **as authentic as possible, Pal enlisted a team of experts: the former German rocket scientist, Hermann Oberth, who now lived in the US; astronomical expert Chesley Bonestell who painted the backdrops for the space ship's journey through space; and the rising star of SF, Robert A. Heinlein (1907–1988). Heinlein, today regarded as one of the major figures in twentieth-century science fiction, based the screenplay on one of his own novels,** *Rocket Ship Galileo* **(1947). In this, a scientist Donald Cargraves and three young assistants, Ross Jenkins, Art Mueller and Maurice Abrams, make an eventful journey to the moon only to find they have been beaten to it by a group of renegade Nazis who have escaped from Earth! Although this element of the book** was omitted from the movie, Heinlein's description of the flight to the moon which he wrote years before it actually occurred proved remarkably accurate, as did the starkly authentic reconstruction of the moon's surface devised by the art director, Ernst Fegte, also way ahead of the real thing being seen in close-up. The sum total of all this was a picture with an almost documentary feel that enthralled large audiences and opened a new era in cinema history. In the following episode, Cargraves and his companions make their "cinematic" touchdown in the year 1950 in a manner that would be almost exactly duplicated by Neil Armstrong and the crew of Eagle twenty years later on July 21, 1969 . . .

The *Galileo* continued her climb up from earth, toward that invisible boundary where the earth ceased to claim title and the lesser mass of the moon took charge. Up and up, out and farther out, rising in free flight, slowing from the still effective tug of the earth but still carried on by the speed she had attained under the drive of the jet, until at last the *Galileo* slipped quietly over the border and was in the moon's back yard. From there on she accelerated slowly as she fell toward the silvery satellite.

They ate and slept and ate again. They stared at the receding earth. And they slept again.

While they slept, Joe the Robot stirred, consulted his cam, decided that he had had enough of this weightlessness, and started the jet. But first he straightened out the ship so that the jet faced toward the moon, breaking their fall, while the port stared back at earth.

The noise of the jet woke them up. Cargraves had had them strap themselves down in anticipation of weight. They unstrapped and climbed up to the control station. "Where's the moon?" demanded Art.

"Under us, of course," Morrie informed him.

"Better try for it with radar, Morrie," Cargraves directed.

"Check!" Morrie switched on the juice, waited for it to warm, then adjusted it. The moon showed as a large vague mass on one side of the scope. "About fifteen thousand miles," he declared. "We'd better do some checking, Skipper."

They were busy for more than an hour, taking sights, taking readings, and computing. The bearing and distance of the moon, in relation to the ship, were available by radar. Direct star sights out the port established the direction of drive of the ship. Successive radar readings established the course and speed of the ship for comparison with the courses and speeds as given by the automatic instruments showing on the board. All these factors had to be taken into consideration in computing a check on the management of Joe the Robot.

Minor errors were found and the corrections were fed to the automatic pilot. Joe accepted the changes in his orders without comment.

While Morrie and Cargraves did this, Art and Ross were preparing the best meal they could throw together. It was a relief to have weight under their feet and it was a decided relief to their stomachs. Those organs had become adjusted to free fall, but hardly reconciled. Back on firm footing they hollered for solid food.

The meal was over and Cargraves was thinking sadly of his ruined pipe, when the control alarm sounded. Joe the Robot had completed his orders, his cam had run out, he called for relief.

They all scrambled up to the control station. The moon, blindingly white and incredibly huge was shouldering its way into one side of the port. They were so close to it now that their progress was visible, if one looked closely, by sighting across the frame of the port at some fixed object, a crater or a mountain range.

"Wheel!" Art yelled.

"Kinda knocks your eyes out, doesn't it?" Ross said, gazing in open wonder.

"It does," agreed Cargraves. "But we've got work to do. Get back and strap yourself down and stand by for maneuvering."

While he complied, he strapped himself into his chair and then flipped a switch which ordered Joe to go to sleep; he was in direct, manual command of the rocket. With Morrie to coach him by instrument, he put the ship through a jockeying series of changes, gentle on the whole and involving only minor changes in course at any one time, but all intended to bring the ship from the flat conoid trajectory it had been following into a circular orbit around the moon.

"How'm I doin'?" he demanded a long time later.

"Right in the groove," Morrie assured him, after a short delay.

"Sure enough of it for me to go automatic and swing ship?"

"Let me track her a few more minutes." Presently Morrie assured him as requested. They had already gone into free flight just before Cargraves asked for a check. He now called out to Art and Ross that they could unstrap. He then started the ship to swinging so that the port faced toward the moon and switched on a combination which told Joe that he must get back to work; it was now his business to watch the altitude by radar and to see to it that altitude and speed remained constant.

Art was up at the port, with his camera, by the time he and Morrie had unstrapped.

"Goshawmighty," exclaimed Art, "this is something!" He unlimbered his equipment and began snapping frantically, until Ross pointed out that his lens cover was still on. Then he steadied down.

Ross floated face down and stared out at the desolation. They were speeding silently along, only two hundred miles above the ground, and they were approaching the sunrise line of light and darkness. The shadows were long on the barren wastes below them, the mountain peaks and the great gaping craters more horrendous on that account. "It's scary," Ross decided. "I'm not sure I like it."

"Want off at the next corner?" Cargraves inquired.

"No, but I'm not dead certain I'm glad I came."

Morrie grasped his arm, to steady himself apparently, but quite as much for the comfort of solid human companionship. "You know what I think, Ross," he began, as he stared out at the endless miles of craters. "I think I know how it got that way. Those aren't volcanic craters, that's certain – and it wasn't done by meteors. *They did it themselves!*"

"Huh? Who?"

"The moon people. They did it. They wrecked themselves. They ruined themselves. *They had one atomic war too many.*"

"Huh? What the – " Ross stared, then looked back at the surface as if to read the grim mystery there. Art stopped taking pictures.

"How about it, Doc?"

Cargraves wrinkled his brow. "Could be," he admitted. "None of the other theories for natural causes hold water for one reason or another. It would account for the relatively smooth parts we call 'seas', They really were seas; that's why they weren't hit very hard."

"And that's why they aren't seas any more," Morrie went on. "They blew their atmosphere off and the seas boiled away. Look at Tycho. That's where they set off the biggest ammunition dump on the planet. It cracked the whole planet. I'll bet somebody worked out a counterweapon that worked too well. It set off every atom bomb on the moon all at once and it ruined them! I'm sure of it."

"Well," said Cargraves, "I'm not sure of it, but I admit the theory is attractive. Perhaps we'll find out when we land. The notion of setting off all the bombs at once – there are strong theoretical objections to that. Nobody has any idea how to do it."

"Nobody knew how to make an atom bomb a few years ago," Morrie pointed out.

"That's true." Cargraves wanted to change the subject; it was unpleasantly close to horrors that had haunted his dreams since the beginning of World War II. "Ross, how do you feel about the other side of the moon now?"

"We'll know pretty soon," Ross chuckled. "Say – this is the Other Side!"

And so it was. They had leveled off in their circular orbit near the left limb of the moon as seen from the earth and were coasting over the mysterious other face. Ross scanned it closely. "Looks about the same."

"Did you expect anything different?"

"No, I guess not. But I had hoped." Even as he spoke they crossed the sunrise line and the ground below them was dark, not invisible, for it was still illuminated by faint starlight – starlight only, for the earthshine never reached this face. The suncapped peaks receded rapidly in the distance. At the rate they were traveling, a speed of nearly 4000 miles per hour necessary to maintain them in a low-level circular orbit, the complete circuit of the planet would take a little over an hour and a half.

"No more pictures, I guess," Art said sadly. "I wish it was a different time of the month"

"Yes," agreed Ross, still peering out, "it's a dirty shame to be this close and not see anything."

"Don't be impatient," Cargraves told him; "when we start back in eight or nine days, we swing around again and you can stare and take pictures till you're cross-eyed."

"Why only eight or nine days? We've got more food than that."

"Two reasons. The first is, if we take off at new moon we won't have to stare into the sun on the way back. The second is, I'm homesick and I haven't even landed yet." He grinned. In utter seriousness he felt that it was not wise to stretch their luck by sticking around too long.

The trip across the lighted and familiar face of the moon was delightful, but so short that it was like window shopping in a speeding car. The craters and the "seas" were old familiar friends, yet strange and new. It reminded them of the always strange experience of seeing a famous television star on a personal appearance tour – recognition with an odd feeling of unreality.

Art shifted over to the motion-picture camera once used to record the progress of the *Starstruck* series, and got a complete sequence from *Mare Fecunditatis* to the crater Kepler, at which point Cargraves ordered him emphatically to stop at once and strap himself down.

They were coming into their landing trajectory. Cargraves and Morrie had selected a flat, unnamed area beyond *Oceanus Procellarum* for the landing because it was just on the border between the earth side and the unknown side, and thereby fitted two plans: to attempt to establish radio contact with earth, for which direct line-of-sight would be necessary, and to permit them to explore at least a portion of the unknown side.

Joe the Robot was called again and told to consult a second cam concealed in his dark insides, a cam which provided for the necessary braking drive and the final ticklish contact on maneuvering jets and radar. Cargraves carefully leveled the ship at the exact altitude and speed Joe would need for the approach and slipped over to automatic when Morrie signaled that they were at the exact, precalculated distance necessary for the landing.

Joe took over. He flipped the ship over, using the maneuvering rockets, then started backing in to a landing, using the jet in the tail to kill their still tremendous speed. The moon was below them now and Cargraves could see nothing but the stars, the stars and the crescent of the earth – a quarter of a million miles away and no help to him now.

He wondered if he would ever set foot on it again.

Morrie was studying the approach in the radar scope. "Checking out to nine zeros, Captain," he announced proudly and with considerable exaggeration. "It's in the bag."

The ground came up rapidly in the scope. When they were close and no longer, for the moment, dropping at all, Joe cut the main jet and flipped them over.

When he had collected himself from the wild gyration of the somersault, Cargraves saw the nose jets reach out and splash in front of them and realized that the belly jets were in play, too, as the surge of power pushed the seat of the chair up against him. He felt almost as if he could land it himself, it seemed so much like his first wild landing on the New Mexico desert.

Then for one frantic second he saw the smooth, flat ground ahead of the splash of the plowing nose jets give way to a desolation of rocky ridges, sharp crevasses, loose and dangerous cosmic rubble . . . soil from which, if they landed without crashing, they could not hope to take off.

The sunlight had fooled them. With the sun behind them the badlands had cast no shadows they could see; the flat plain had appeared to stretch to the mountains ahead. These were no mountains, but they were quite sufficient to wreck the *Galileo*.

The horrible second it took him to size up the situation was followed by frantic action. With one hand he cut the automatic pilot; with the other he twisted violently on the knob controlling the tail jet. He slapped the belly jets on full.

Her nose lifted.

She hung there, ready to fall, kept steady on her jets only by her gyros. Then slowly, slowly, slowly, the mighty tail jet reached out – so slowly that he knew at that moment that the logy response of the atomic pile would never serve him for what he had to do next, which was to land her himself.

The *Galileo* pulled away from the surface of the moon. "That was close," Morrie said mildly.

Cargraves wiped the sweat from his eyes and shivered.

He knew what was called for now, in all reason. He knew that he should turn the ship away from the moon, head her in the general direction of the earth and work out a return path, a path to a planet with an atmosphere to help a pilot put down his savage ship. He knew right then that he was not the stuff of heroes, that he was getting old and knew it.

But he hated to tell Morrie.

"Going to put her down on manual?" the boy inquired.

"Huh?"

"That's the only way we'll get her down on a strange field. I can see that now – you've got to be able to see your spot at the last half minute – nose jets and no radar."

"I can't do it, Morrie."

The younger man said nothing. He simply sat and stared ahead without expression.

"I'm going to head her back to earth, Morrie."

The boy gave absolutely no sign of having heard him. There was neither approval nor disapproval on his face, nor any faint suggestion.

Cargraves thought of the scene when Ross, blind and bandaged, had told him off. Of Art, quelling his space sickness to get his pictures. He thought, too, of the hot and tiring days when he and Morrie had qualified for piloting together.

The boy said nothing, neither did he look at him.

These kids, these damn kids! How had he gotten up here, with a rocket under his hand and a cargo of minors to be responsible for? He was a laboratory scientist, not a superman. If it had been Ross, if Ross were a pilot – even where he now was, he shivered at the recollection of Ross's hair-raising driving. Art was about as bad. Morrie was worse.

He knew he would never be a hot pilot – not by twenty years. These kids, with their casual ignorance, with their hot rod rigs, it was for them; piloting was their kind of a job. They were too young and too ignorant to care and their reflexes were not hobbled by second thoughts. He remembered Ross's words: "I'll go to the moon if I have to walk!"

"Land her, Morrie."

"Aye, aye, sir!"

The boy never looked at him. He flipped her up on her tail, then let her drop slowly by easing off on the tail jet. Purely by the seat of his pants, by some inner calculation – for Cargraves could see nothing through the port but stars, and neither could the boy – he flipped her over again, cutting the tail jet as he did so.

The ground was close to them and coming up fast.

He kicked her once with the belly jets, placing them thereby over a smooth stretch of land, and started taking her down with quick blasts of the nose jets, while sneaking a look between blasts.

When he had her down so close that Cargraves was sure that he was going to land her on her nose, crushing in the port and killing them, he gave her one more blast which made her rise a trifle, kicked her level and brought her down on the belly jets, almost horizontal, and so close to the ground that Cargraves could see it ahead of them, out the port.

Glancing casually out the port, Morrie gave one last squirt with the belly jets and let her settle. They grated heavily and were stopped. The *Galileo* sat on the face of the moon.

"Landed, sir. Time: Oh-eight-three-four."

Cargraves drew in a breath. "A beautiful, beautiful landing, Morrie."

"Thanks, Captain."

IT CAME FROM OUTER SPACE

(Universal, 1953)
Starring: Richard Carlson, Barbara Rush
& Charles Drake
Directed by Jack Arnold
Based on a screen treatment,
"The Meteor" by Ray Bradbury

Another of the film-makers who helped to establish the Space Movie in cinema history was Jack Arnold – a man whom critic John Baxter has gone so far as to call "the great genius of American fantasy film". Writing in 1970, Baxter said: "From 1953 to 1958 reaching across the boom years, Arnold directed for Universal a series of films which, for sheer virtuosity of style and clarity of vision, have few equals in the cinema." Arnold, who began as an actor but learned his trade as a film-maker during the Second World War making training films for the Army Signal Corps, was specifically signed by Universal to get them into the SF boom. His first choice of subject was a treatment by Ray Bradbury (1920–), then one of the fastest rising young stars in American fantasy fiction. Ray's story of an alien space craft which crash lands in the desert and releases its occupants into a nearby town where they "borrow" human forms, had originally been entitled, *Ground Zero (The Atomic Monster)* but was changed to *The Meteor* before finally appearing on the screen as *It Came From Outer Space*. Arnold and his team took full advantage of the handy Arizona desert for much of their location shooting, and the picture was further enhanced by some outstanding special effects featuring the shape-changing aliens created by Clifford Stine and David S. Horsley. Another unique element of *It Came From Outer*

Space **was the fact it was filmed in 3-D, thereby enabling it to be released as "the world's first 3-D science fiction film" – with special glasses handed to each member of the audience as they entered the cinema. Jack Arnold's brilliant camerawork and the sense of hostility the film generated from being set in a real environment that all viewers could relate to, made the picture unlike anything that had been seen on the screen before and once more suggested whole new areas of possibilities for the makers of Space Movies. The director himself went on to film several more SF classics including *Creature From The Black Lagoon* (1954), *Revenge of the Creature* (1955) and *The Incredible Shrinking Man* (1957). The reputation of author Ray Bradbury was also assured, and among his later works to be filmed have been *The Beast From 20,000 Fathoms* (1953), *Fahrenheit 451* (1966), *The Illustrated Man* (1969) and *The Martian Chronicles* (1980). The following adaptation of Ray's treatment is taken directly from the film.**

A ship hurtled through airless space. It was a strange speck of alien geometry, moving almost at the speed of light. Behind it streaked the glow of ions – the atomic particles that flung it with world-splitting force across the gulf between the stars.

It was a survey ship from the planet Ool in the system of Sirius.

In the control room a puddle was talking to a cloud. Somewhere between the pair two eyes floated, egg-sized, luminous, yellow. Now and then a swirl of vapour passed across the delicate quartz of the instrument panel; a liver-coloured tentacle would appear as if from nowhere, make an adjustment and dissolve, leaving on the surface a trail like the slime of snails.

No words passed; but the thoughts went back and forth.

"We are about to pass a small star with nine planets."

"It's on the chart. Only one planet with life-forms – the third from the star."

"Intelligent life?"

"Our people have never mixed, but the planet has been surveyed from missiles. There are many forms of life. The leading type has developed language and tools. It stands on two legs, and it has only one body from birth to death . . ."

"That," said the cloud with a vibrating eye, "must be inconvenient."

"Yes. To be unable to change form is . . . unimaginable. Those beings are very strange."

"How much science have they?"

"Not much. They've only just discovered atomic energy."

The eye grew; the cloud spiralled and became a column. "Astrogator!"

A thing that looked like a spilled jelly stirred. "Sir?"

"We'll reduce speed to one light-unit and find a path between the second and third planets. I will take a look at them with the visorscope."

"You'll see their cities," said the puddle confidently.

*

Sand Rock, Arizona. A small town, now almost invisible from above in its blue-black blanket of evening. A spot of winking lights on the cold floor of the night-time desert, from which came a tiny sound of humanity as someone crossed Main Street, lurching from bar to bar.

There, under a spangle of stars, a mile out of town along the desert highway, Putnam's shack showed two rectangles of homely lamplight. The light spent itself in the emptiness of the surrounding desert, but just managed in its passing to gild the tube of a big telescope which stood near the door.

A tiny house and a tiny telescope, stuck drunkenly on the surface of the turning globe that is the planet Earth. Far away beyond the atmosphere – beyond, even, the far-flung orbit of the moon – something was happening that would soon bring terror to this patch of Arizona.

But this moment was one of peace; the coyotes cried in the outer ring of dark as they had always done; the stars whee'ed overhead. And John Putnam, struggling science-journalist, was talking about marriage.

"Maybe it's my money you're after?"

The girl looked startled.

"Money?"

"Well, I got a cheque to-day . . ."

"Johnny, you've sold another article!"

"That's right. Now I've got enough to finish building the house."

He grinned at her. She smiled back; spread her arms to include the room, the desk, the photographs of moonscape and nebulae on the wall.

"All this and heaven, too!"

"Let's go outside and take a peep at heaven," he said.

Ellen Fields followed him outside to the telescope. She was the local schoolteacher, and young for her job. John was young as well – amazingly so for one whose articles on astronomy were already piling up a reputation with the leading scientific journals. It was natural that the two best brains in Sand Rock should be engaged to be married.

"What are you working on?" Ellen said.

"Perturbations in the orbit of Jupiter Twelve."

"Oh, John, wouldn't it be wonderful if you found another Jovian moon."

"I'd call it *Ellen* after you."

"I'd never be able to live up to that," she laughed.

"Everyone would think you were a Greek goddess. But, after all, they wouldn't be far – "

He broke off.

"Look!"

She clutched him. They stood swaying, gazing upward, following the long arc of the metor-like object that was blazing across the sky.

At one moment the glittering stars had been hanging in

their old positions against the blue-black night; in the next they had been blotted out in the sudden flare of the visitor. It was as if some cosmic giant had drawn a careless line of fire across the firmament with a huge and terrible pencil; but before the first shock of surprise had faded the pair saw the meteor itself like a glowing fruit vanish behind the top of a nearby range. There followed a ground tremor which rattled the casements of the shack and moved sickeningly into their stomachs like the impact of a bomb.

In a flash John was at the telescope.

"What was it?"

"Meteor!" he snapped. "One of the biggest . . ."

"Can you see anything?"

He had the telescope at horizontal.

"Yep . . . plenty. Look."

She peered through the eyepiece; saw fiery, billowing smoke which obscured the view.

"That," he said, "is about four miles away. Somewhere by the old Excelsior Mine. Get your wrap!"

*

Diamond-hard, the alien metal had buried itself deeply in the crumbly rock. Clouds of heated dust swirled upwards. Rocks ran bouncingly down the steep sides of the crater, piling up against the red-hot thing at the bottom.

The thing was six-sided and the size of a large house. The odd second or so of passage through the atmosphere had heated its surface by friction to a dull glow.

Minutes passed. The smoke cleared slightly; the fall of rock paused as if the shaken ground had reached an uneasy balance. For a moment there was almost silence. Then in the hot hull a six-sided panel moved inwards; there was suddenly a hole of precise and accurate geometry in the side of the visitor. A black hole.

Slowly the blackness moved, as if touched by the mist of

dawn. A white, damp vapour gathered at the entrance, and in the midst an eye.

An eye yellow as saffron, with a cold, questing pupil like the yolk of an egg!

And then the creature poured slowly after its eye. It was at once liquid, solid and gaseous; it half-walked, half-floated. It was never still; at one instant it spread itself like the sensitive, oozy passage of a sea-squid; at another it would be a mere wraith that left a glittering wake of slime on the piled rocks; yet when a fall of earth in its path spelled manual work it seemed with some queer chemistry of its own to grow actual tentacles, whipcord-like and brown, which sucked and lifted, and then, the task done, withered into gas as if their owner had forgotten them.

Slowly the creature oozed up towards the crater rim.

Near the top a rabbit, petrified, lay under flat ears, quivering.

*

The car hummed along the desert road, John at the wheel, Ellen beside him.

The Excelsior was an old gold mine, a relic of the nineteenth century, but was still worked by casual prospectors who sometimes found there a streak of poor but marketable dirt. The entrance lay against the side of the shallow hill, the top of which had now been transformed into the still smoking crater that glowed faintly in the darkness.

They left the car near the shaft and toiled up to the crater rim. Breathlessly they peered over . . .

Mist and smoke and tumbled rock.

"It's really something," Ellen said.

"Honey . . . the biggest thing that's happened around here. I'm going to take a look."

"Be careful, John."

The Meteor

He picked his way down the slope. On a ledge below the level of her feet he turned to wave, but the rising smoke had already hidden her from view. It was a smoke that, strangely, did not attack the throat; nothing seemed to be burning, and he got the impression that rock and metal – the world itself – had been scorched beyond endurance, and that the smoke was the pure and angry energy of the wound that had been death. He touched a rock; it stung his fingers, and he followed the ridge downwards gingerly, his heart beating fast . . .

On the lower slope it was a craziness of boulders. He paused, blinded, not knowing for a moment the direction of up or down. Then the smoke cleared a little and the starlight began to gain over the blackness and chaos around him.

Or had the chaos been followed by something worse? Were his eyes playing tricks?

The bottom of the crater opened out into a wide and nearly horizontal shaft that must have been part of the old workings, now opened to the starlight. And half blocking the shaft was something huge and regular in shape, lathe-smooth and . . .

Yes, by heck! A door!

John Putnam knew no fear at that moment – only an immense interest. He started forward, stumbling slightly; it was only when the corner of his eye caught the strange glitter of slime on the rocks that he paused again, and the first quake and shudder went through him. He knelt and touched the slime with his finger.

Cold, cold . . .

He stood up; looked again at the smooth, half-buried object below. Then the fear took shape and leaped.

What he had mistaken for a door was no door. There was only a smooth surface.

Or . . .

A well-fitting door that had been open and was now shut? The thought brought out prickles all over him.

How long he stood there still and silent he never knew.

Suddenly he felt that he must regain the top at any cost. He turned, his boots scrabbing furiously at the rocks – and in the same instant there came a deep baritone rumble and a trickle of stones – a rumble that grew to a roar . . .

Landslide!

Above him the ridge . . . somehow he managed to wade upwards against the accelerating fall and press himself against its overhang. Soon boulders bigger than his head were pouring past; his shoulder went numb as a blow sent him sideways, he had a vision of chunks like automobiles plunging past him into the shaft as the dust took his throat, spots danced in front of his eyes and he lost consciousness.

*

"John! Oh, John!"

There was immediate gladness as he opened his eyes. He was lying on the gravel of the crater rim, and Ellen was rubbing his forehead and his eyes were full of stars – real ones.

"I'm okay." He got up, staggered, and an arm caught him.

"Guess you was almost a gonner."

He recognised Pete Davis, a truck driver from the town.

"Walloped over here soon as I saw that thing falling. Started down myself when the landslip took on. Just in time to yank you over the top of that overhang. How yuh feelin'?"

"Guess I wasn't really hurt."

"But your arm . . ." Ellen said, watching him as he rubbed it tenderly.

"Forget it. There was something down there . . ."

"Sure," Pete said. "A million tons of rock that nearly hit you."

"No, that's not what I . . . I mean something else. Some kind of ship."

"A what?"

"What kind of a ship?" Ellen asked.

"Like a huge ball, rammed into the old shaft at the bottom. And . . . and I saw an open portway."

"And inside," Pete went on triumphantly, "there was a bug-eyed monster!"

"Well . . . something. Next thing I knew the door was shut; and then the landslide started."

"Well, here come folks," Pete grunted, as headlamps appeared and car doors were slammed at the foot of the hill. "You're not gonna tell those people you saw Martians runnin' around down there?"

"Ellen! You don't believe me either."

"I . . . I don't know," she whispered.

The three were squatting on their heels. They did not get up as two tall figures strode slowly up the slope and stood over them.

"Resting?"

It was big Matt Warren, the Sheriff, bulky, self-confident, like the personification of a world in which nothing ever happened that had not taken place a billion times before. With him was a lanky reporter from the local newspaper, one Kenn Loring.

"Just washed up," Pete said. "We been down there, and there was a landslide."

"Tell us what happened," Loring asked.

"Meteor. Johnny here says it's the biggest ever."

"It was no meteor," John Putnam said; and he felt the girl's hand suddenly tighten in his as if restraining him. "There's some kind of ship down there. I don't know what kind."

"Sure, *I* know," Loring said. "A spaceship! Straight out of one of those stars you write about!"

"Listen," John told him. "It's really there – it's buried right down there. We'll have to get this whole area sealed off until we know what we're up against."

The Sheriff lighted a cigarette with a calculated slowness, as if he had all the time in the world. He ignored Putnam.

"Did you see it, Ellen?"

"No . . . but if John says he saw it . . ."

"C'mon," he said. "I'll take you home, Ellen."

"No, thanks. Johnny'll take me home."

Once more Putnam felt the pressure of her hand.

"Let's get out of here," she pleaded.

*

The convertible sped toward Sand Rock.

"You're driving too fast," she told him.

"Sorry, honey – it's the way it gets me."

"You can't really blame them."

"Tell you I saw it! I even saw some kind of slimy tracks . . . Listen, I'm going to phone Doctor Snell at the Wayne Observatory. Ask him to get over first thing in the morning. Not to mention the army – it'd be awful wrong not to tell the army . . ."

"Aren't you taking on a lot, Johnny? All that's really Matt's job – he's sheriff. Why, I've known him all my life, and I just wouldn't like Matt to get angry at you, Johnny . . ."

"We're not exactly like brothers as it is," he said grimly.

"What's that?"

His foot came off the accelerator. He stopped at the side of the road.

"Some sort of bird, I think, front of the windscreen. I sure am jumpy."

"It wasn't a bird," she said. "I don't know what it was. It looked like an egg or something . . . an egg that glowed, up in the air. And a kind of mist around it. Oh, Johnny – I'm scared! What do you mean, thinking up all this stuff about Martians . . ."

But Putnam was out of the car, staring back along the dim road. Like the tail-end of a dream captured on waking, he had almost fancied a thin, diaphanous stuff vanishing into the almost-tangible background of the night . . .

He felt the girl beside him as he took two or three paces along the road.

"Johnny, let's go . . ."

He stopped. Something was beside the road. It was a Joshua tree. Just an ordinary . . .

The tree froze his eyeballs. His whole body was held in an agony of tension; on the one hand the grip of curiosity, of manhood, and the presence of the girl told him to stay; on the other, the whole weight of ancestral terror, kept deep down in human kind since caveman days, pressed him to be gone. For there was something unutterably creepy about the tree – something impossible to define – a fleshiness, a sense of horrific intelligence.

He jumped as Ellen screamed.

"It's just a Joshua tree!" he mouthed as he half carried her to the car.

"Let's get away . . . quickly . . ." she sobbed.

*

The convertible faded away – became a faint pencil of headlamps on the desert road and a hum. And then nothing. The desert spoke to itself with a coyote's howl, and the stars seemed to drip from the sky.

The Joshua tree started to ooze away into the night.

*

Luckily John Putnam had the good sense to avoid a clash with the Sheriff by leaving that official to contract the military. He contented himself with a late call to Wayne Observatory and a brief account of his adventure. Doctor Snell already knew about the meteor. Yes, he would be along in the morning. Yes, he would bring geiger counters;

he would also test for metal and electromagnetism. But what was this about spaceships?

He had no doubt (he said) that a night's rest – an hour or two of forgetfulness of that landslide – would cure John of *that* hallucination!

In the morning John called for Ellen, got her to cut school, and set off for the crater. On the way Ellen shoved a newspaper beneath his nose.

STAR-GAZER SEES MARTIANS

"Huh . . ." he said, and kept his eyes on the road.

There was a notice up at the crater: "No Admittance Without Authorization." From the jeeps strewn about at all angles it was clear that the army was in control. A grey-haired, bespectacled man came down the slope, wrung John's hand, and kissed Ellen's cheek.

"Well, Doctor Snell, this is nice!"

"John, I'd never have guessed that my star pupil was going to join the saucer-spotters – the spaceship fans!"

John's spirits fell at once; a deep depression stole over him.

"But Doctor Snell, I *did* see it! If only we could get together quietly and talk about it . . ."

"I'd quit talking here, at any rate. The place is thick with reporters, all hot after The Man Who Saw The Monsters. How about you, Ellen? See any bug-eyes yourself?"

"No," she answered. "I didn't. But listen here, Doctor Snell, if John says a thing it's true."

John stole a grateful glance at her. This was sheer love and loyalty; he knew only too well the doubts she really felt.

"I can prove there's a spaceship down there," he said at length," if I can get you to help me dig it out."

"My poor dumb dope! There's a meteor down there – it all checks – the metallic dust, the fusion from heat, the angle of contact. It's a very big one – maybe as big as the famous one that fell in prehistoric times in Arizona. Someday we'll dig it out. But not until we've been able to raise half a million bucks from somewhere. For, boy, that meteor's in plenty deep; since you got out of the pit last night there's been another fall, and it's now got enough stuff on top of it to bury the White House."

"I've been hoping I'd run into·you, Putnam!"

It was the Sheriff, who came scrambling from the crater and dusted himself down.

"What's the matter, Matt? Have I been breaking the law?"

"You might call it that. Ellen's supposed to be teachin' school. If you want to drive yourself crazy seeing Martians, that's your lookout; but leave Ellen out of it – she's got her job."

"Listen, I – "

"No, you listen. I knew Ellen when she was a crawler. I also knew her pop. I was his deputy – "

He broke off as a crowd of reporters and camera men came from the pit.

"There's the guy!"

"That's John Putnam!"

"Say, Mr Putnam, what about this monster you saw last night?"

"Quick!" Ellen said. She grabbed his arm. "He's nothing to say, boys!" she yelled; and together they ran down the slope to the car.

John drove savagely. "What do you know? Snell agrees with the Sheriff that I'm crazy."

"I just wish we'd found one of them!" she sighed. "Just one little monster to toss into the Sheriff's office, and maybe another for dear Doctor Snell's bedroom!"

The road was a long, smooth rib in the desert. The telegraph poles danced past tirelessly. Suddenly the blankness ahead contained life; a friendly reminder that other people existed. A work truck stood by the road; two figures were perched and busy on one of the poles.

John stopped the car.

"Hiya, Frank! George!"

Frank was an elderly engineer; George his young assistant. Both had called in the first place at John's shack to fix the telephone, and had often been there since as guests to squint through the telescope and talk science-fiction.

"Well, where'd you two come from?" Frank grunted. "Thought you'd be all day back at that crater."

"I don't much like the show over there."

"Heard they'd got you going, John. Don't let 'em ride you, boy."

"Have you two seen anything unusual this morning?" John asked.

George said: "You mean like another meteor?"

"No, I don't mean that."

"Well, we ain't, have we, Frank? Although I sure have been hearing things."

"Hearing what things?"

"Like this," George said. He was strapped right on the top of the telegraph pole with a handphone plugged in. "Come up and listen."

"Darndest noise ever," he added, as John swarmed up the ladder and took the phone. "Any ideas?"

John did not answer. The noise was not music, but it might have been a kind of chant. It hovered between the boundaries of low and high frequency, so that some of it was a faint rumble almost too deep for the ear, and some of it again was so high that only a bat could have registered it properly. Of sound on the normal audio-band between these extremes there was none.

It was like an utterly alien creature – an other-worldly creature – talking to itself! The thought smote John softly between the eyes; but he said nothing except: "Now it's gone."

"Well, that's the way – comes and goes. Had enough?"

"Yes. Didn't know what it was, anyway."

Frank said: "Sounded to me like someone was pluggin' in. George, why don't we drive up the line and take a squint?"

"Anything you say, boss."

"We'll have a look the other way," John told them. "I'll let you know if we spot anyone."

*

The creature was half a Joshua tree, half a rivulet of slime.
There was no one about. It was relaxing!

Mimicry, although as natural to its race as running to a hare, was still a conscious effort. It was pleasant, when events allowed, to let the acquired shape melt – to allow it to relapse a little into the running glob of mist and mucus that was its natural self.

It had experimented. It had been for a short time a coyote. Then a rabbit. Then a telegraph pole. But those were mere sports. There was only one form which could manipulate the repair and digging-out of the spaceship, and that was the useful arrangement of a central trunk with two extensions, the whole mounted on a pair of legs, which was the property of this strange planet's ruling race – Man! But first it had to catch and study Man. Even a mimic had to know his subject.

The Joshua tree dissolved completely as a work truck, full of ladders and wire, came into sight. A pool and an eye and a few tentacles strewed themselves across the road and waited.

*

The car stopped.

"Did you see something, John?"

"No, there's nothing. Only . . . I had a strange feeling." He shrugged. "I'd better get back to Frank and George and tell them we saw nothing."

"Oh, but they won't need . . ."

"We promised."

He backed and turned. Soon, far ahead like a toy, the works truck came and went in the lakes of heat-haze that flowed from the desert. As he drew nearer a tight core of foreboding grew in John's chest. He braked the convertible beside the truck. It was empty; both doors were flapping open, and he stumbled out on to the road, scanning the flat horizons . . .

Ellen, beside him, said: "Perhaps . . . perhaps they went off into the desert."

"And left both doors open?"

There was an outcrop of rock a quarter of a mile into the desert. John took her hand, tensely leading her towards it. Yes – the haze and dancing bands of light had been playing tricks – there *was* a man beside the rock.

"George!"

"Hello."

"Where's Frank?"

"He . . . went off to look around."

"I couldn't see you at first. The sun . . ."

"Yes," George said. "The sun. The beautiful sun."

And he lifted his head and stared, stared at the sun. Unblinking!

*

The Sheriff was sitting in his office. He had left the army men and the scientist and the reporters to talk and scramble at the crater; it had been time for him to go back and attend to the peace of Sand Rock.

The door from the sunlit street burst open. John and Ellen came in breathlessly.

"You're coming right out with us, Matt. Bring your gun!"

"Listen," he said patiently. "The school principal's been here. You're supposed to be teachin' school, Ellen."

"Oh, cut it out, Matt! You listen to John – it's important."

Putnam was gabbling out the story of the two telephone engineers. ". . . And then we found George," he finished. "Yet somehow he wasn't like George. He was like a man so shocked . . . a man shocked right out of his personality. He talked like someone else, not George – his voice was lifeless. And . . . and . . ."

"Something had happened to his eyes," Ellen put in. "He kept staring at the sun and didn't blink!"

"We tried to ask him where Frank was. He said, 'Just around.' Imagine saying that in the desert! Then we tried to get him to come with us, but he wouldn't. We left him standing there like crazy – the sun beating down and him staring at it, unblinking!"

Matt Warren tilted back his chair.

"Has this anything to do with your Martian monsters? If so, I ain't buying."

"How do I know? It's utterly queer, that's all. Seems to me George went nuts. There was no sign of Frank. Maybe George had knocked him out and he was lying on the sand somewhere – you can't see far in that dazzle. But if so, what was it sent George nuts?"

"Only one answer to that!" the Sheriff said. "Your monsters!" He was grinning and looking at the window.

"Do you really think so?" Ellen asked.

"Oh, sure! But before we discuss it, Putnam, would you mind opening that door and just look over them two guys passing down the street?"

"What . . .?" John crossed to the street-door and opened it.

"Hi!" he yelled. He was out of the door in an instant, chasing after the two figures.

George and Frank! Just turning the corner . . . but their backs were unmistakable.

He reached the corner. It was the entrance to a narrow alley leading off Main Street; there was a lot of scaffolding where a new building, finished except for the paintwork, stood flush with the alley. The clean, unpainted door was the only one ajar. He pushed it.

George and Frank were standing in the hall.

Their eyes glowed!

He said: "George! Frank!"

"Keep away," Frank said.

"Where've you been? What happened back there? If anything's wrong I want to help."

"Stand back."

The voice – was it Frank's or George's? – was like a diaphragm fed with an air pump; there was nothing in it of flesh and blood. The voice of a robot telling someone's weight in return for a coin in a slot.

Two pairs of eyes glowed . . .

"Whoever you are," John whispered, ". . . whatever you are . . . I want to help you."

"Then keep away. We do not want to hurt you – or anyone. Your friends are alive. They will not be harmed if you keep away – give us time . . ."

"Time for what?"

"Or terrible things will happen," said the voice, ignoring his question. "Terrible to you, because undreamed of. Undreamed of because never experienced. Never experienced because not of your world."

Putnam's muscles relaxed, seemed to obey an impulse not of his body or mind. He stepped back dutifully to let the pair come out. They passed him without a sideways glance and walked like marionettes to the head of the alley. Then they turned the corner.

With a half sob he flung his stupefied self into action – sprang after them. He saw them walking the centre of the street, left right! left right! Sinister toy men! The dazzle swallowed them – the bright mouth of Main Street where the buildings finished and the desert almost instantly began.

The Meteor

*

The voice of the radio announcer was self-satisfied and hearty.

"Well, folks! No one has yet turned up any bug-eyed monsters . . . so it must be set down as another of those hoaxes . . . another case of saucers on the brain . . . this time by a young publicity-seeking astronomer. Of course, if he *should* bring a Martian to your favourite radio station, this network would be only too pleased to give our visitor the freedom of the air – even if he could only honk . . ."

John cut the radio so savagely that the set rocked.

"Don't let it get you, John dear."

"We sit!" he snorted. "We wait! Things are happening – folks are disappearing – everyone *knows* there's something queer going on – and nothing's done! There's no money to clear a few tons of rock and settle doubts for good!"

Two days had passed since his strange encounter in the alley. Although it was still possible for radio announcers to treat the whole matter as light entertainment, the climate of the town itself was somewhat more tense.

George's wife had already been to the Sheriff to say that her husband was missing. Frank's mother had come forward with the same story. Two prospectors, who had been working at the Excelsior Mine for the past week, had not shown up at their lodgings in town. The army, it was true, had pulled out that afternoon, uninterested and intact; only Doctor Snell still remained at the mine.

The telephone rang.

"Putnam speaking."

"This is Matt. Putnam, I apologise!"

"What goes on?"

"Doctor Snell's car is still at the crater. But Snell's missing."

"Now are you ready to believe me?"

"I'm trying, or I wouldn't have called you."

33

"You've got to believe there's a ship buried out there – that at least some of our visitors from space got out before the ship was covered over."

"Sure, I'm trying to believe just that. There's another thing, Putnam – the hardware store's been raided. Nothing taken except electrical gear."

"It all adds up! What happened to George and Frank's telephone truck? That's never been found, has it? Don't you see? – they want electrical spares."

"Listen, Putnam, I'm coming round to your way of thinking, but other folks aren't. They'd think I was crazy like you if I spilled this stuff around. So it's just you and me together. I'm coming out to your place right away and we'll get up to that crater and pry a bit."

Five minutes later the Sheriff's car braked outside and there came the sound of an impatient horn.

"Ellen, you stay here. I guess we'll both have room for some ham and eggs when we get back."

"John! There's danger out there . . ."

"I'm glad someone's realising that at last; but I'll be careful, don't worry."

He kissed her.

*

The rim of the crater shimmered. The bodywork of the empty car at the foot of the hill was too hot for the hand; visible heat made the background move like jelly; vultures wheeled in the hot blue bowl of the sky.

"Well, he's not here," Matt said, "and it's a cinch he wouldn't leave without his car. I'd give a lot to have things back to what they were yesterday, with me calling you a fool!"

Together they crossed the rim and climbed down into the jumble of boulders within the crater. The heat seemed to pulse slowly as in an oven; it was the driving blood in their own bodies that gave the impression.

"There's nothing here," Matt grunted. "At least, whatever's here is buried too deep for any gear in Sand Rock to tackle. But where in heck is Doctor Snell? Another thing – " He turned to John almost fiercely. "If these monsters of yours *have* kidnapped Doctor Snell, not to mention two prospectors and a coupla telephone linesmen, what they done with 'em? There just ain't no place to hide in this county 'cept Sand Rock; the desert's got a way of frying a guy by day and freezing him by night. It sure is a poor break for those guys."

They searched; they poked among the rocks while the heat blistered their feet through the soles of their boots. And at last they had to admit that the crater contained no clue. Sorrowfully they got into the Sheriff's baking hot car and drove away, leaving the scientist's empty car behind.

"Stop a moment," John said.

He had caught a glimpse of something black against the crumbly hill. The Sheriff backed the car and he jumped out.

It was a small heap of burnt-out chassis parts.

"I'd bet my bottom dollar that *that* was George and Frank's telephone truck!"

"Could be," Matt frowned, sucking his teeth. "The plot thickens."

*

"What now?" John asked as they sped back towards his shack.

"It's not a local job. I got my duty, and that's to tell police headquarters in Flagstaff; and if I didn't do that today I'd be all set for losing my badge."

"Whew! The monsters from space are in for some publicity, after all."

"Aw, people don't take to that stuff, even if you give 'em real monsters with their cornflakes."

They drew up outside John's shack.

"So long, Matt. Call me if there's anything."

"I sure will. Give my love to Ellen and tell her I apologise for being snooty."

John watched the car rattle off towards town. He turned with a sigh to his front door; and then he remembered the ham and eggs.

"Darn! Hey, Ellen . . ."

There was no answer.

The room was a shambles. There was a glistening trail of filmy stuff on the carpet.

Slime.

*

"Hello! Matt? Listen, they've got Ellen!"

"What's that? How? Where?"

He babbled the story into the phone. "Come back here right away! We must go up to the crater . . ."

"But that's crazy! Nothing passed us on the road."

"Everything's crazy. We're just not dealing with things of this world."

"I'll be right over – soon as I've got a deputy and posse."

"Matt, listen to me. For heck's sake – no posse. Just you and me."

"Now you're nuts."

"It's something that struck me. What if those creatures mean no harm? What if they kidnap people for some reason we haven't guessed – like for study, the way we catch zoo animals? See? Violence might be the worst line at present . . ."

"I don't see," Matt answered, "but in case there's a thousandth chance of you being right I'll come alone for Ellen's sake."

Again the arrival of the Sheriff's car; again the rush over the grey, hot road towards the crater. A white-faced Putnam; a scowling Sheriff who said, as he wrenched the car around a bend: "It's enough to send a guy bat-dreams.

What'll we find when we get there? Just the crater – a hole full of rock to the brim. And what'll we be able to do? Nothing!"

"While I was waiting for you I thought of something. Something a kid could have thought of but we didn't. The Excelsior Mine! I guess th're must be a way through the workings, and that's where we'll find Ellen and the others."

"The mine's a long way from the crater. They think the main tunnels all fell in years ago. Besides, the workings are down to be searched tonight if those two prospectors haven't shown up by then."

Away to the left, where the low hill petered out in the flatness of the desert floor, was the entrance to the old mine. Matt drove towards it and braked where the black hole of the tunnel could be seen.

"It doesn't go in very far," he said. "I've got a flash-lamp – come on . . ."

"I'm going in alone," John told him.

"But listen . . ."

"I want you to do this for me, Matt. I've a hunch it would be best for Ellen. So will you stay here?"

"Well, if that's the way you want it . . ."

*

The alien world pressed against the beings from Ool and was terrifying. Space itself was a lesser horror. Out there between the worlds it was like a cocoon; a spaceship did not seem to be anything but a speck, hanging for ever against a multitude of changeless stars, and it was possible to fall into the illusion of timelessness. But here on this hostile planet all was hideous labour and emergency Labour made the more bitter because of homesickness for the vaporous and lightweight world of Ool.

That the ship had buried itself beneath a huge quantity of the dense material of this world had been at first a matter for despair. The beings were built entirely differently from any living form on the Earth. Their bodies were mere globs of molecules surrounding a fixed and yellow eye. And whilst an Earth-type creature – man or beast – would adapt *the body for certain actions, such as flexing the muscles or arching the spine, the beings from Ool would actually change theirs. To watch such a creature at work would be to see bits of it flow from a liquid to a gaseous state or from solid to jelly according to the work in hand!*

The beings had plenty of brain but little strength. The civilisation of Ool was rich in science, but here, lost and broken on an alien planet, there was nothing to use against the stubborn mass of rock except their frail bodies and a few ray guns, the use of which might easily start another landslide.

It had been the Commander who had thought of the idea of changing their bodies into those of men. It seemed clear that a body native to the planet would be the right sort to deal with a problem like the landslide – with the massed rocks which were so hard and heavy compared with the vapours and light soils of Ool.

It had also been the Commander who had ordered the crew to strike out horizontally from the buried ship with the ray guns in order to clear working space around it. In that way they had found a link with the galleries of the old mine.

And now, having probed and seeped into the bodies of the few humans who had come their way, a gang was at work, slowly raying a space around the ship, renewing the circuits of the electronic computor that formed its heart, testing the superstructure . . .

A strange gang . . .

Three Georges. A half-dozen Franks.

Two Ellens . . .

*

John poked the flashlight into the mouth of the mine and followed its beam. His feet crunched on hard flint; his movements sent tiny pebbles down the walls and on to his head. Soon he had to bend; later came a time when he was on all fours, pushing the beam into impenetrable darkness. He shivered, although the sweat was running into his eyes. Obviously this was a place for coyotes and rabbits; nothing else could find lodging in here . . .

Then his ears caught the rumblings.

A muffled thunder, turning into minute ground tremors; and at the same time – more continuous, if fainter – a tap, tap, tap.

He scrambled forward, to bring his forehead crashing against the roof. The gallery had narrowed to a mere warren. He kept his head down and crawled a few more yards, until his torch showed a blank surface, which he felt with his hands and knew for the end of the passage.

For minutes he lay there in his torn, dusty clothing, listening to his own breathing and the distant tapping and occasional low rumble. Then he turned gingerly, sensing that his knees were bruised and sticking through tears in his pants, and started back the way he had come. At once came a pitter-patter of flints and dust on the crown of his head; a small cascade that grew until, with a sick apprehension, he put his head down, covered it with his hands and waited in the blackness for the inevitable.

It came. It was as if someone had hit him heavily with a baseball bat, and his lungs were full of dust, and over his body ran like liquid fear the thought of being buried alive. He heaved – more in panic than anything else – and the loose stuff slid off his back, and he wriggled in his yearning for light and air and freedom to move freely wherever he wanted to go.

But there was light. He went for it like a moth, ignoring in his frenzy the fresh torrent of earth and rock that bounced against his ears. He remembered butting with his head, wrenching his legs away from a weight that would have pinned them down; and then he found himself lying half in and half out of a gaping hole, and the sky was above with vultures weaving.

He stood up, feeling weak. He had come right through the hill and he shuddered at the recollection.

A figure was standing halfway up the slope, staturesque amongst the boulders.

"Ellen!" he yelled, and plunged forward.

*

Up the hillside he ran, a scarecrow figure, breathless and nearly spent, the rocks bruising his legs, the yearning of thirst on his tongue.

"Ellen!"

The figure had gone.

He reached the spot. Leathery growths of cactus – stones jagged as glass.

The vultures overhead were silent witnesses as he sat down suddenly, sweat cold and prickly on him, feeling the silence like something tangible.

Then he saw the hole.

It was a rectangle half the height of a man, and the timber shoring told him what it was. Another entrance to the mine!

He had lost his torch. He blundered into the hole shouting "Ellen! Ellen! Ellen!"

The darkness met him like black water, and the sound of his own voice dwindled as if he were shouting into a thick curtain of cotton wool . . .

And suddenly he froze, transfixed by something un-guessed – the never-experienced. His mind was free, the muscles of his body unfettered and ready to move him on; yet a voice was telling him to stop.

A voice inside his head; but the voice of someone else.

A voice that spoke to him without sound, without words.

A voice of pure *thought*, intruding into his own brain.

"Stay where you are," the voice said.

In the stunned depths of his mind he knew that he was meeting the strange science of telepathy. Some other brain was thinking directly into his mind!

He heard his own physical voice croak: "Where's Ellen?"

"Safe," said the voice inside him.

"Come out into the open – out where I can see you!"

"No."

"What do you want? What are you really doing?"

"We are repairing our ship to leave your world. We need to be left alone."

"You've kidnapped and stolen," he thought. And he felt the answering thought of the other as if he had spoken aloud.

"But we meant no harm. By nightfall we will have left your planet, upon which we crashed by chance. We are living forms like yourselves . . ."

"Then why are you hiding?"

"Yours is an isolated world. You have never met any type of intelligence other than yourselves. Nearer the centre of our star-galaxy all types of intelligence meet and co-operate, but you have always been alone. You would be horrified at the sight of us . . . you would want to kill us, because we are so very different from yourselves."

"All I understand is that you've taken my friends . . . and now the woman."

"We make use of their bodies, but they are safe. They will return to you when we have freed our ship. But if you bring your people here to destroy us the captives will be destroyed, too."

"Stand out in the sun!" John signalled.

"In time perhaps . . ."

"Let me see you now!"

"No, let us stay apart."

"I've got to see you as you really are. Come out – or I can't take the responsibility of protecting you."

A pause.

"Very well."

John backed into the sun. The hole gaped black. And then he screamed . . .

*

The Sheriff milled around his car, mopping his neck frequently with a handkerchief. He made off suddenly towards the hill; thought better of it; came back and sat for a moment in the sparse shade of the car. All the time he was shooting anxious glances towards the mouth of the mine and his foot was scrabbing impatiently in the dust.

Then he started up and began to run. He met John fifty yards from the jalopy and grabbed the reeling body in time to prevent it from falling.

"Where's Ellen?"

"She's . . . safe . . ." John panted.

"Where? What have they done to you?"

"Nothing."

"Men don't look the way you look for nothing."

"I . . . I saw them, Matt! Horrible!"

"And you left Ellen with them?" Matt was shouting into the white face.

"She's safe . . . as long as we don't interfere."

Haltingly he poured his story into the incredulous ears of the other. "You see?" he finished. "They're mad to get away because they know we'd kill them if we could. And we would! We'd kill them because they're different. Like when we squash spiders – but this time it would be with even more cause! We're just not advanced enough to stand the impact of other types of living beings with better brains than ourselves!

"That," he added, "is why they've been hiding behind other people's faces."

He had told all he knew. Now he looked into Matt's face, expecting to find some understanding there; but what he saw was a typical human face – the face of a lord of creation, brave, stubborn . . .

"All I know is this," Matt grunted." They've got five people over there, and it's up to us to get 'em out."

"When are you going to stop being a badge and do some thinking?"

"A thing's wrong – so someone's got to set it right. Okay! You won't set it right! But I will, see?"

"Matt, listen to me! They weren't fooling! They need a few more hours. If you go to them with violence now . . . they'll kill Ellen!"

He lunged with two tired and would-be restraining hands. Matt's hand flashed up and caught the front of his shirt.

"Look at you – you're all washed up. You're hysterical. Remember what I am? I'm the Sheriff – someone responsible for the law around here. And the law says there's to be a posse to clear those devils out!"

John's despairful fist caught Matt's chin a glancing blow. Matt had expected it and was ready. John was dimly aware of hitting the dust, of being lifted and dumped into the car. When he came to himself in the rattling car he knew a stupefying feeling of contempt for himself.

The rushing air revived him; the guilt inside him blossomed into an intolerable growth; here in Matt was truly boneheaded conduct – conduct asking for disaster – and he was letting himself be pushed around.

Matt was concentrating on his driving. John advanced his hand slowly to the shaking door of the car and stole a glance at the road. He knew the spot ahead where there was a bank of soft, crash-breaking sand . . .

When the time came he was out of the speeding car like an acrobat and turning over and over on the soft sand; and then he staggered up and began to run across the desert at right angles to the road.

When he was out of breath he turned. Far away stood the car with Matt beside it waving both arms at him. He waved his arms back, almost grinning . . .

*

It was a long way back to the hills. The sun was low in the sky by the time he reached the spot where the collapsed gallery gave on to the hillside. Passing the pile of earth, from which he had emerged earlier that day like a crushed and frightened rabbit, his foot struck something metallic. The torch! He pocketed it thankfully

Higher. Here was the real entrance to the mine. He went into the blackness, holding the beam in front of him, trying not to think of the nightmare thing he had seen there, trying not to open his mind to the voices he expected to sound within it at any moment. His brain cringed!

But nothing happened; and the passage seemed to be widening.

Suddenly it was an almost circular chamber hewn out of rock; and at the same time he heard the sounds of work around the buried spaceship – the tapping and scraping, like the activities of underground dwarfs in fairy tales.

And then he heard a sound like an intake of breath. He swung the torch.

"Who's there?"

His beam flashed across the space.

"Ellen!"

She stood there, ten yards from him, unhurt, cool.

"Ellen! Are you all right? I . . ."

Then she spoke. Or didn't speak. The voice was not a sound – not words – but a set of questionings popping thought-like into his head:

"Why have you come back? Who have you brought with you? Why do you wish to destroy us?"

He felt weak. He had lost her. This was not Ellen; or if it

was Ellen's body in front of him, something else was in possession.

He said: "I came back to warn you. Some men of my world are on their way here . . ."

"I know" – her thought-voice said inside him – "there are a dozen cars on the road from the town this minute."

"I tried to stop them . . ."   ·

"We are not yet ready. Not quite ready."

"Take me to . . . to your friends. I want to help."

"Come."

He followed her; and soon the ground sloped, the walls widened and the work-sounds became a roar. There was light, blue and vibrant – the naked light of energy – and a prickling went over him as he breathed an air like the aftermath of storm, all washed clean with electricity.

For the second time in his life he saw the spaceship, the six-sided globe with its hull aglow, as if the contained force of its motors was a sort of lifeblood making its plates flush like flesh.

Around the ship the rock and earth had been cleared; above it the massed debris shut out the sun. Busy round the open port, through which strange mechanisms could be glimpsed, were a dozen figures familiar as home. He recognised the backs of Doctor Snell, of Frank . . . and then one of the figures turned and came towards him. He nearly collapsed . . .

He stared open-jawed at *himself*!

*

The other-John – the man with the face he had never seen except in mirrors – came swiftly to him and gazed without curiosity. The sad thought of the other-John came to birth in his head:

"So the men of your world are on their way, and will destroy us?"

He answered with another statement. "You are not *me* . . . and *that* is not Ellen."

"All we took are safe. But if those others of your world come to destroy us they will be destroyed themselves. There is enough power here to tear your world apart."

"Listen to me," John said. "There's still a way."

"Is there? All we need is time."

John gazed past his double to the saffron-glowing spaceship, which seemed to leap and tremble as if ready that instant to break its bonds of rock and thunder into the sky; at the busy figures – so like his friends and yet so obviously not his friends – at the brilliantly-lit port with its strange glimpse of a motive-force fit to hurl this massive thing to the outer stars. And his inner ear almost heard the sound of arrival of Matt's car and the cars of the posse. But that was impossible; it was his time-sense that told him they must by now be at the foot of the hill . . .

"Give me back the people of my world," he said. "– the girl and the men; between us we shall stop those others, and you will fly away in peace."

"How can I trust you?"

"Didn't you say you could tear the earth apart? If we attack you, you could reach out and destroy us. Why are you so . . . so afraid of us?"

"Because you might force us to kill. Our world is very old; our memories are longer than yours; and we have grown out of the habit of killing and don't like such a thing forced upon us."

"You are wiser than the best of us," John said: and then a longing struck him, and he added: "Will you change into your natural form and let me see you as you are?"

Before his eyes he watched the image of himself melt drooling into gas and liquid; watched the great yellow eye materialise, the whipcord tendons and liver-coloured tentacles wave. He smiled in the sudden, sure knowledge that all his loathing, his small-town horror, had vanished and would never come back.

"Remember us when you get to the stars," he said, "and come back in a thousand years. And now, there's no time to lose – give me my friends and let me get out of here!"

Thoughts in this place ran like speech. John was dimly aware that the human forms about the ship had vanished; instead were the now familiar glob-creatures, some already slithering into the open port. The vibrations of the ship shook the earth; but when he heard an actual human voice the sound shook him to the depths of his being.

"John! Oh, John!"

Ellen had darted, released from the rocky spaces behind the ship. She was in his arms, and the unmistakably solid and human forms of Snell, the two telephone men and the pair of missing prospectors were about him.

"Quick!" he said. "No explanations – we've to get back up the shaft – or we'll all be dead!"

*

The posse climbed the hill – Matt, his deputy, a crowd of the grim and worthy citizens of Sand Rock.

"Hear anything?"

"Sure, Matt – kind o' vibrations."

"Matt, I'm sure scared – don't mind admittin'."

"Well," Matt grunted, "guess none of us feel so good."

"What's best to do?"

"We goin' to the crater, or to the old workings?"

"I reckon we might look at the crater first," Matt said.

"What's that?" The deputy was pointing into the heavy dusk.

With a crunch of rock a whole crowd of people came diagonally down the hill.

"Matt, stop! Don't go near that crater!"

"Putnam! What in jeepers . . . and Ellen! Why . . ."

"It's all right! We're all here. But we've got to clear off quickly, because – "

He dragged Ellen down – everyone dropped down – as a dull, deep explosion heaved the ground beneath them and made the hill shake and dance and throw bits of itself overside like droplets.

The explosion ended in a loud, continuous blare too deep to be called a scream – a noise that grated inside the very bones of their bodies and made every face grimace.

"Are *they* down there?" Matt gasped. "Well, I guess that takes care of 'em!"

"Yes," John repeated. "That takes care of them. But don't get up . . ."

There came a sound like the ground being sick, and they all sensed rather than saw that the piled rocks which had lain in the crater were now being flung into the night sky like dust. They lay cowering, expecting the crushing blows. Not far away the ground-rocks splintered as the stuff came down.

Seconds seemed like years as they waited.

And like a whirlwind the great bright thing came rushing from the core of the hill, vertically upwards, and shot in dwindling fire into the starbright air, printing a fiery and fast-fading streak against the background of the hills.

The humans lay there for minutes.

Matt rose to his feet and spoke soberly.

"They've gone."

"For good, John?" It was Ellen, whispering.

"Not for good," John said. "It wasn't quite the right point in history for us to meet. But they'll be back a thousand years from now."

*

Far above the atmosphere, speeding from the planet, the Commander spoke to the Astrogator:

"Sometime we'll go back."

"In a short time they'll have space-travel themselves. They might come to us."

The Commander gave the Oolean version of a shudder. He said: "It's easier to make spaceships than friends."

THE CONQUEST OF SPACE

(Paramount, 1955)
Starring: Walter Brooke, Eric Fleming
& William Hopper
Directed by Byron Haskin
Screenplayed based on "Life On Mars"
by Werner von Braun

Not to be outdone by the other major studios, Paramount Pictures in 1955 bought the rights to a story by a man who was then actually involved in helping to make space flight a reality, Werner von Braun (1912–1977), a German-born rocket scientist who had earlier designed the infamous V2 rockets which bombed London at the end of the Second World War. Von Braun had, in fact, turned his youthful enthusiasm for the works of Jules Verne and H.G. Wells into practical research, but after the fall of Germany he was recruited by the Americans to work with their own scientists on space exploration. The V2 which he had seen used with such destructive purpose now became the prototype for a whole new generation of rockets which would later take men to the moon and launch probes to the other planets. The film-maker charged with bringing to the cinema screen Von Braun's vision of a journey to Mars was the resourceful George Pal who, just as he had done when making *Destination Moon*, again surrounded himself with experts including Chesley Bonestell, Will Ley and designers Hal Pereira and J. McMillan Johnson – all of whom now had the added benefit of working in technicolour. To direct, Pal hired Byron Haskins, who likewise brought a special skill to the job having previously been the head of the Special Effects department at the rival Warner Brothers studios. In the movie, the journey of the rocket ship through space was brought to life by Haskins

with a series of notable effects sequences – including a space burial with the corpse falling slowly towards the sun – and culminating in an evocative red landscape which had been specialy envisioned by Chesley Bonestell to represent the surface of Mars. Sadly, the pictures subsequently sent back to earth by NASA's orbiting spacecraft have shown the reality to be rather different. This, however, does nothing to spoil a viewing of the picture today, or of reading the story on which it was based by the man who probably did more than anyone else to realise man's long dream of conquering space . . .

Mckay sat easily in his seat on the flight deck, watching Bill Squire beside him at the controls of *Goddard*, the big rocket-nosed glider which had launched them from the expedition's cargo ship orbiting 620 miles out from the surface of Mars. The glider was following a free-coasting spiral around the red planet, and McKay felt a slight forward pull on his shoulder straps with the retarding effect of air drag in the weak Martian atmosphere.

He glanced down through binoculars from their present height of ninety-six miles at the multicoloured spectacle beneath, then back at Squire whose eyes were fixed on the dials in front of him. This was no longer space flight. He was using aircraft controls.

The long ellipse carried them out of the Martian day and into night as *Goddard* winged downwards. But half an hour later the night sky became a dusky cyclorama shaded to purple, and from purple to blue. At last the glider emerged into full sunlight.

McKay looked around at the ten astronauts who had been his companions on the deep-space voyage of 260 days from the artificial satellite *Lunetta*, poised in orbit above Earth. With the exception of Sterling, the brilliant young archeologist, these men were all experienced pioneers of the space age.

No emotion showed in their faces, but McKay, leader of this first expedition to explore a distant planet, guessed that all of them shared the same apprehension. A landing on unknown terrain without a prepared runway was tricky business. No better man for it than Bill Squire, but who knew what the surface of Mars would be like? Pulverized rock? Sand? Lava dust? How would the skis of the tandem landing gear behave when they touched down? Would the surface hold, or would the treads break through brittle crust, bringing them to a catastrophic stop?

They were on course. The altimeter showed 2,500 feet, and McKay studied the terrain, picking out features from the pilot's contour map.

The ground was coming up fast now, and Squire was turning the nose of the glider south. McKay reached up to tighten the shoulder straps and turned to nod at the men behind him. Then he braced for contact, which would come at 120 miles an hour.

Dust rose in a cloud outside *Goddard's* windows with the first impact and there were two or three stunning jolts as the skis bumped over the surface. But the great glider gradually rumbled to a stop, steadied by its outrigger skids. Squire grinned – he'd put the first ship down on Mars!

McKay unbuckled his straps and stood up. "Nice landing, Bill," he said, and turned to face the others. "Now don't get excited. We'll try some knee bends before we go outside. Quickest way I know to shake out the after-effects of weightlessness. And we are going to need our strength."

He put the crew through calisthenics and then had them close the helmet visors of their pressure suits. One by one they worked their way through the airlock and assembled on the wing, twelve adventurers in space suits, the first Earthmen to scan Mars' desolate landscape. For their base they had picked the area called Libya, south of Moeris Lacus and directly athwart the Martian equator.

"It's like desert country in our southwest," said Duncan Ross, their geologist, into his helmet microphone.

"Rugged," McKay agreed. "Surface seems to be mostly reddish-yellow sand." He turned to the pilot. "You got us here, Bill, so you should be the first man to touch down. Jump, boy!"

"Not with my legs as weak as they are," Squire protested. "I'm going to slide." He dropped to the trailing-edge flaps and coasted part of the eighteen feet to the ground. "Nothing to it," he said into his microphone. "Gravity's too weak to let you drop hard." McKay could see him grinning. "Hey!" Bill called. "That was the first message from Mars!"

McKay laughed and turned to John Berger, the radio operator. "Get inside and flash *Oberth*," he said to the radio operator. *Oberth* was the mother ship with a crew of three, which would continue to orbit above the planet until the expedition was ready to return to earth, 449 days from now. "Tell Phil Boyer it was a perfect landing with all personnel and equipment intact," he said. "Tell him we're proceeding now to set up camp."

The others were on the ground when McKay jumped to join them. Spottswood and Burke, the engineers, had opened the cargo bay and were lowering two tractors from the yawning belly. The others were erecting the hermetic tent which contained light cots, chairs and cooking equipment. The tent would be inflated by the standard "spaceman's atmosphere" of forty per cent. oxygen and sixty per cent. helium in which space suits could be replenished.

"Let's get the return rocket erected," McKay said. "Detach the forward section of *Goddard* from the wings," he ordered.

Under Spottswood's skilled direction the tractors hooked on, and soon a gap appeared between the slim fore part of the glider's body and its thicker rear section. Cables were attached to the bullet-shaped nose, and the tractors drew it upright, settling it on four levelling jacks. Guy wires secured the sleek return rocket against heavy winds.

McKay inspected the job with satisfaction.

"Now we know we can get away fast in case of trouble," he said. "Not that we'll find any." But this was an intrusion into unexplored territory, and George McKay remembered the tales he had read since childhood about hostile monsters on Mars.

Herbert Breitstein, the chemist, was preparing dinner when they entered the pressure tent. This would be the first food they would eat normally with knives and forks since they left *Lunetta* nearly nine months before. But the others were too tired to care much. They took off their space suits in the air-conditioned interior, ate a quick meal around the table and then, after McKay had detailed the order in which they would stand watch during the night, the men lay down on their aluminium cots. McKay breathed a quick prayer of thanks for their safe landing and then he was asleep . . .

.

They were up shortly after dawn, and at breakfast McKay gave orders for the day. "I'll take the Number One tractor and look around a bit. Departure in half an hour," he said. "Sterling, Ross and Burke will go with me. Spottswood, I want you and the others to make a thorough check of *Goddard's* communication equipment. We'll keep in touch with the base by radio, and Berger will relay every message back to *Oberth*. All clear ?"

Two hours later their lumbering tractor was approaching a conical out-cropping of the bright yellow mountain range which formed one side of the valley where they had set up their base. McKay was at the controls. Suddenly Sterling called from the back seat, "Colonel, would you stop a minute while I put my glasses on that ridge?"

McKay braked the treads, and Sterling stood up in the pressurized interior. "It *is* – I swear there's a spidery-looking ancient temple up there," he said excitedly. "It's like a Grecian ruin."

The others brought up their glasses. "You're right," Duncan Ross said. "That thing was built! Funny – the columns are so thin that any good breeze would bring the whole thing down."

"I guess Martian gravity's your answer to that," McKay said. "It didn't take long to prove there was life on this planet once." He felt a tingle of excitement. Was there still life around here? For a moment he wondered if they had been foolhardy not to bring any weapons along with them.

They churned forward, Sterling trying desperately to keep his binoculars steady against the pitching and yawing. Then he almost shouted. "Behind that ruin and to the right – there's something shaped like an oversized army hut."

McKay changed course and put on more speed till they had come within fifty yards of the structure. All of them surveyed the curving walls.

"It looks remarkably unlike anything ancient," McKay said. "We'll investigate." He reached for his space helmet and nodded to Sterling and Ross. "Burke, you guard the tractor," he ordered, "while the three of us do a reconnaissance. If there's trouble, radio the base and start back immediately to report what's happened."

He dropped through the airlock, with Sterling and Ross close behind, and they approached the odd structure cautiously. Ross tapped the material of the exterior with his geologist's hammer.

"Hard as granite," he said.

They continued around the building. After a short distance the three explorers stopped. A set of perfect steps was cut at the point where the building's end curved away from the semicylindrical main portion.

"Stay here," McKay said. "I'm going up."

They saw him climb the steps to the rim of a rounded roof. Suddenly he stopped abruptly. For over a minute they saw him stare down, motionless. Finally, his staccato voice resounded from their helmet earphones. "Sterling and Ross, come up at once," he said. "I'm standing beside a heavy glass roof. There are machines below, I think – fourteen big red casings that could be turbine housings. The interior seems covered with silvery-white metal." Suddenly his voice recovered from the excitement, and he inquired in the tone of an experienced radio operator: "Burke, do you read me? Over."

"Loud and clear," came back Burke's awed voice.

"Good, just keep the tape-recorder running. This is something for keeps."

Sterling and Ross were beside him now, peering into the interior. "Over by that furthest casing," Sterling said hoarsely. "There's someone moving. See him, Ross?"

The figure came slowly towards them, unaware of the Earthmen. He appeared to be checking the gauges which were visible on the machines. There was not only life on Mars – they had run into an outpost of a highly developed Martian civilization! But McKay kept his voice steady as he droned out a description of the subterranean installation into his helmet microphone, which was heard not only by Burke but by the party at the base camp.

". . . an undersized, dark-haired man – repeat 'man'. Definitely human in appearance. Fair, white skin, beardless, dressed in an oriental-looking long white tunic with gay coloured stitching."

Ross broke in as the creature came into full view. "Look at the size of that head," he muttered. "If what's inside is all brains we can learn plenty here!"

"Suppose he sees us?" Sterling whispered.

"We want him to," McKay answered. "We're bound to run into Martians sooner or later." He looked sharply at the others. "Anybody worried?"

"No, sir," Ross said stolidly, while young Sterling swallowed dryly and shook his head.

"Let's make him see us," McKay said. He rapped gently on the glass with the hasp of his knife. Below them the man stopped and looked up, momentarily startled. Then he waved his hand in what seemed a friendly gesture. McKay talked constantly into his microphone so that every detail would be recorded by both Burke and the party at the base. He waved back at the Martian, pointed to himself and his companions, then towards the level where the figure stood. The Martian considered for a moment, then he smiled and pointed to the end of the building where the three explorers stood. He walked in that direction and disappeared through a door.

"Seems friendly enough," Ross said. "But will he let us in?"

The answer came a moment later when a panel slid back beside them at the top of the steps. The opening widened rapidly until it became a rectangular door within which they could see the Martian behind a curving sheet of glass. He beckoned them to come through the opening.

McKay nodded, spoke a final, full message into his microphone to tell the others what was happening. Then the three men stepped inside, and the door slid rapidly shut behind them.

"I don't like this," Sterling began apprehensively, as the Martian continued to stare at them through the glass.

McKay cautioned him sharply. "Steady, Pete. We'll take it as it comes. Look at your pressure gauge. We're in an airlock."

The indicator showed four-sevenths of their space-suit pressure, and Ross drew a gas-analyzer from his belt: 39 per cent, oxygen, .3 per cent. carbon dioxide. The remainder was some sort of neutral gas.

"I hope it's nitrogen," Ross muttered.

McKay hoped so, too.

The hissing of the entering pressure ceased, and the glass partition slid out of sight. The man smiled, bowed and placed his hand over the left side of his chest. The three explorers repeated the gesture and went in. The glass partition closed at the push of a button, and the platform began to sink. Presently they stepped out on to the floor of the red machines.

The Martian led them the length of the great hall. As they strode along, McKay glanced anxiously at his pressure indicator and decided to risk the atmosphere. He depressurized his suit, took off his helmet and gulped a deep breath. Nothing happened, and he made a gesture to the others that everything was all right and for them to do the same.

They now entered a long corridor. It glowed with soft light which seemed to come evenly from the walls, roof and floor, for there were neither visible artificial light sources nor windows.

"They've found the secret of the firefly!" Sterling said wonderingly. "Light without heat."

The corridor ended in a large room hung with crimson textiles. Seated at a long, ebony-coloured table was an elderly Martian, dignified and imposing. Beside him was a younger man. They both rose as the little party entered. They placed their hands over their left chests and bowed solemnly, motioning the newcomers to be seated.

Their guide now began to talk to his chief, in a low, musical voice, occasionally interrupted by what were obviously questions. McKay was no linguist, and he glanced at Sterling who spoke a dozen languages easily. But the young archeologist shook his head and smiled nervously.

"Do you suppose they're talking about what to do with us?" he asked.

McKay shrugged his shoulders. "We'll know soon," he said. As he spoke the elderly Martian turned to look at him questioningly across the table. McKay drew a pencil from his pocket and made motions of writing.

The Martian twisted a knob at the edge of the table, and a white, luminescent rectangle appeared in front of McKay. McKay began to sketch the solar system, and the Martians watched as he traced the ellipse of the space-ship's flight. Then they smiled, indicating that they understood, and the young Martian opened a cabinet door and turned a dial. There was a low-pitched hum, interrupted by a recording of Phil Boyer's voice as the party in *Goddard* left *Oberth* the day before, and McKay's reply, "Happy orbiting, Phil."

Instantly the Martians looked at McKay questioningly. There was something impenetrable about their politeness. No wonder they had greeted their visitors calmly. They had listened in on the expedition's radio traffic and recorded it!

McKay wondered if they caught the meaning of the messages. "You understood?" he asked in English.

All three looked blank. Then the chief Martian brought out a large sheet which contained a schematic drawing marked in circled symbols and shaped like a pyramid. He pointed to one of the circles on the baseline and then to himself. Next he indicated a large circle at the apex of the pyramid and made a sweeping gesture, uttering a word which sounded like "Ahla". He pointed to his visitors and again said "Ahla."

"That's a government organization chart if I've ever seen one," Sterling said. "To think that we've come all the way across the solar system only to get tangled up in red tape! I think Ahla's the head man, and our ancient friend plans to send us to him – through channels, of course!"

McKay produced an astronomer's map of Mars that he had brought along and spread it on the table. McKay guessed it must seem pretty crude, but he pointed to Libya, where they had landed. The Martians nodded. Then he handed the pencil to the white-haired Martian and said, "Ahla," in a questioning tone.

His host took the pencil and drew a circle in the very centre of Lacus Solis. "Ahla," he repeated firmly. He placed his finger on Libya and drew it across the map till it paused at the circle. Then he pointed to the Earthmen.

"Ahla must be the chief city, not the name of the head man," McKay said to Ross and Sterling. "His attitude is so positive I think he's got some kind of transport. It's a good two thousand miles from here."

He stepped forward and made a gesture of speaking into a microphone. Instantly the young Martian handed McKay an instrument like any standard microphone.

"McKay to Tractor One and base," McKay droned. "Over."

John Berger's voice cut in. "Base to Colonel McKay – just a moment, sir." And then there was Bill Squire. "Are you all right, George? Over."

"Everything's fine," McKay said. "We're in this big building you've heard about. There are three Martians down here. We've had a map exercise, and they want us to go to Ahla, which seems to be the name of their capital. It's in Lacus Solis. Over."

Squire was obviously agitated. "That's two thousand miles from here. How are you going to get there? Over."

"I haven't the slightest idea, but so far these people seem remarkably friendly. No evidence of coercion or hostility. No weapons about. They're fantastically advanced technologically. And, Bill, they're wonderfully impressive people. There's a calmness about them that makes me think this civilization is old – very old. Over."

"But suppose they're just luring you to visit their king – or whatever he is. Leaving the rough stuff to high authority. Have you thought of that one? Over."

"I've thought of that one – and a lot more," said McKay crisply. "I don't see what else there is to do but go to Ahla. Our directive from Washington was to explore Mars. There are millions of dollars riding on this expedition, and I think we're on the edge of a magnificent discovery. We'll see it through. Burke, you're to return to base. All of you will wait till I can communicate again. Better post a double guard tonight. The Martians know where you are now. That's all, Bill. You're in command."

While McKay was speaking, the chief Martian had been giving instructions to their guide. Now the younger man stepped forward and signified they were ready. McKay and the others followed their guide into an elevator.

Down they went into the mass of Mars. But at last the car came to a gentle stop, and they were ushered into a gleaming, vault-like chamber about seventy feet long and ten feet high. Along one wall was a series of round windows, their lower rims touching the floor. They peered through.

Duncan Ross laughed excitedly. "This is enough to make any New Yorker feel at home," he said. "It's a subway!"

"But no rails," objected Sterling. "Same firefly illumination as upstairs. How do you suppose they do it?"

Behind one of the windows they saw a compartment equipped with fixed, comfortable chairs. The Martian turned a small handle, and the glass rose into the ceiling. They went inside, and the Martian motioned them to the chairs, which were equipped with seat belts.

Their guide seated himself in the forward end of the compartment before a small control panel. They heard his voice against the microphone, then a buzzer sounded, and the platform door slid down silently, followed by the compartment door itself.

They could see over the Martian's shoulder through another round window into the gleaming white tunnel ahead. The Martian flipped a few switches on the control panel and listened to a voice which came back through his radio telephone. Then he moved back, smiling reassuringly, to strap himself into a seat beside them.

Presently there were three bright flashes from the panel, followed in a few moments by a bright orange-red flash, and they were pressed into their seats by an acceleration like the effect of a rocket blast-off. But there was no noise whatsoever.

McKay punched his stop watch. His experienced feelings told him that he was undergoing not less than three G's pressure, and it continued for twenty seconds. This meant that they were moving at supersonic speed. But the question was – how?

His engineering mind could guess part of the solution. The compartment was pressurized, but the tunnel had been emptied of all atmosphere. *They were moving through a vacuum*!

There was absolutely no sound – no clicking of rail joints, no motor hum. Maybe the Martian could enlighten him further, in spite of the language barrier.

McKay took out a notebook and quickly sketched a streamlined train. Then he touched the Martian's arm, pointed to the sketch, indicated the wheels and rails. He waved his arm and pointed ahead. The Martian nodded and took the notebook and pencil. He worked rapidly, and on the opposite page appeared an engineering drawing. A wheel was sketched and crossed out. No wheels! A rail appeared under the wheel and was also crossed out.

The Martian's sketch then showed the secret of the transportation system. At each end of their car was an electric magnet with its poles on either side of a supporting rail in the roof of the tunnel. They kept their car magnetically suspended without bodily contact between magnet and rail. McKay was overcome with admiration at the device which provided such a free-floating frictionless support. Electronically the magnetizing current was so controlled that the width of the gap remained constant, regardless of load or forward motion.

He nodded to show that he had understood, for the sketch also explained what gave their car its propulsion. It was an application of the solenoid gun principle which ballistic experts on Earth had dreamed of for years, but had never succeeded in putting to practical use. A never-ending chain of coils one ahead of the other was energized in programmed succession. Surrounded by the coils, but attached to the roof of their car was a string of permanent magnets which was pulled through the coils as they were energized. This was substantially an electric motor's armature moving in a straight line instead of rotating. They were travelling almost as fast as a space rocket, but with a minimum expenditure of power as there were no friction losses.

McKay turned to Ross. "The minds that could develop this subway system could have put a space ship on earth years ago," he said. "I wonder why they didn't."

Far down the tunnel McKay saw the lighted windows of what must be a station appear and pass them so rapidly that the flash of light was almost imperceptible. There must be an automatic block-signal system of unparalleled efficiency, for no operator, however smart the Martians were, could cope with this enormous speed. Yes, their voyage was obviously controlled by some mechanism outside. Occasionally they slowed, then went on as the next block opened up.

McKay wondered how long it would take them to reach Lacus Solis. He glanced at the stop watch. They had been in motion one hour and fifty-three minutes. But who knew just how fast they were travelling?

Sterling had been dozing but now he woke up and leaned forward. "I wonder what this Ahla is like," he said. "Maybe our friend can show us." He took out his own notebook and, remembering the spidery temple, drew a city of thinly columned buildings and houses, with wide, tree-lined streets. Martians in fanciful spacesuits walked about. He showed it to their guide. "Ahla?" he said. "Ahla?"

The Martian looked in bewilderment for a moment. Then he laughed and shook his head. He took the notebook and worked busily for ten minutes, then handed it back.

"Ahla's underground!" Sterling cried. "See? A big vertical city with central squares in layers and parks at the top open to the sky but enclosed with domed glass roofs. Do you suppose the whole Martian population lives underground?"

"I've suspected it," McKay said. "I think Mars once had atmosphere enough to breathe, which explains that Grecian ruin. The change came gradually so that there was time to prepare technologically for an underground existence."

Sterling shivered. "It's uncanny," he said, "and we're going to be on Mars for more than a year. How do you two manage to keep calm with what we're going through? I don't mind admitting I'm scared."

McKay put a hand on his shoulder. "All right, Sterling," he said. "Just don't sound off. We're all a little scared in space. We keep it to ourselves so we don't infect others with our own fears."

It was twenty minutes later when the car gradually slowed, and the Martian signalled that their journey was to end. They were gliding soundlessly through a maze of switch-points. Outside they could see a marshalling yard with cars like their own, and bigger, windowless cars apparently designed for freight.

They moved to the windows to look out on the scene. Ahead, they saw a brightly lit area and a platform on which a crowd was clustered. They were still too far away to tell, but it seemed to McKay that they were all wearing tunics or robes.

"Ahla?" he said to their guide, who nodded vigorously.

McKay smiled and the guide smiled back. McKay could see no trace of guile in his face, but he found himself tense as the car slid along the platform.

"I'll go first," he said to Sterling and Ross. "Wait inside the car. If everything goes all right, follow me out."

Sterling moved up to his side.

"I'm not disobeying an order, Colonel," he said, "but if the Martians intend to clobber you, there's nothing to prevent them from clobbering us. Let's go together."

McKay smiled. "Good man, Pete," he said.

The inner door slid upwards. There was a hiss, and the outer door opened. The noise of many voices and of strange unearthly music swelled from the platform. Their guide jumped out and stood, bowing deferentially.

For just a moment McKay hesitated on the threshold of this climax to adventure. Then the three explorers stepped out into Ahla, the subterranean capital of Mars.

As the Earthmen left the car which had sped them 2,000 miles to Ahla through the subterranean tunnels of Mars, McKay's eyes swept the crowd of men and women on the platform. There might have been a hundred Martians, all dressed in some form of Grecian garment. McKay read eager curiosity in their faces – also calmness and complete absence of hostility.

"It's going to be okay," he said to Sterling and Ross. "We've got a reception committee!"

The music and voices ceased as an elderly Martian stepped forward. McKay advanced to meet him, with his companions just behind. When the Earthmen bowed and placed their hands over their hearts, a quick look of pleasure lighted the Martian's face, and he repeated the gesture. At the same time, a soft, welcoming "Ah" swelled from the crowd.

The Martian held out a handsome jewelled chain, similar to one he was wearing. McKay leaned down, and the dignitary hung it round his neck. Then, smiling warmly, he embraced the Earthman. The moment called for a token of goodwill in return. McKay wore a wrist watch, and he offered it now. The Martian seemed delighted and indicated that the Earthmen were to accompany him.

The three explorers, followed by their guide from the Libya station, advanced through the crowd. McKay studied the faces on each side. The tallest of the men was no more than five-feet-five, the women much smaller. They were by no means an unattractive race. They were slim and graceful and, except for the size of their heads, would have attracted no special notice on Earth if they wore conventional clothes. The dark hair of the men was close-cropped, but the women wore theirs long and pinned in a thick, heavy coil which covered the back of the head. They appraised their visitors calmly and talked softly among themselves.

From the station the party walked down a broad corridor which opened on a huge circular plaza, surrounded entirely by a window-studded wall some thirty storeys high. A solid roof covered the area at a height of perhaps 300 feet. The plaza was packed, and their host signalled a halt and spoke to the crowd. The people clapped, and again the sound of their massed "Ahs" swelled up, while the explorers bowed and stretched out their hands in greeting.

"They're wonderful!" Ross murmured.

Young Sterling said eagerly, "Their features are almost early Roman. And you know, some of these girls are really attractive. I'm sure you'd soon get accustomed to the size of their heads."

There were no vehicles of any sort in the plaza, and they could see no streets leading from it as the official who had become their host conducted them to a big gate leading into one of the "buildings" which surrounded it. There he spoke to the Martian from Libya and left them with gestures of farewell.

They passed through a sort of lobby. Then their guide took them down a corridor and, before they knew what had happened, they found themselves in the living room of a small apartment. A pretty maid appeared almost immediately with a tray of unfamiliar dishes and smilingly indicated that the explorers were to seat themselves.

"Tastes good anyway," Ross said. "I'd forgotten how hungry I was."

Sterling said, "I bet it's synthetic food of some sort – but not bad." He frowned a little. "First thing tomorrow I'm going to start learning Martian. It's a terrible handicap not to be able to talk with these people."

"With these girls, you mean," laughed McKay.

While they were eating and joking, their guide reappeared and motioned McKay to follow him. He took him into a small room and made him sit down in front of a table covered with green velvet. Then the guide left. Suddenly McKay saw Bill Squire sitting across the table from him.

"What on Mars are you doing here?" McKay shouted.

"I am not here at all, Colonel," Squire replied. "We are just talking over the Mars telephone."

It was a stunning experience. There was a life-size Bill Squire, in full colour and 3-D, sitting at the same velvet-covered table just four or five feet away speaking to him, yet it was nothing but an electronic illusion.

"The guys from the pumping station – that's what that subterranean installation in Libya really is – came over to our camp and indicated you had a message for us," Squire went on. "We decided you'd be unable to get in touch with us through anything but their own communication system and might need some assistance. That's why I left camp and took the chance of entering the pumping station."

McKay smiled. "These people must have figured you'd like to know what happened to us. Well, we're in Ahla, and you can cancel the guard duty, Bill. These are the friendliest people I've ever met. Pass this to *Oberth* for transmission to Earth. Tell them that tomorrow we'll begin a daily half-hour broadcast. Over and out."

When McKay opened the door of the telephone room, Sterling called excitedly from one of the bedrooms. "Look, Colonel," he said, pointing to a small disc. "Pillow-speakers. There's one with every bed. I'll bet they are going to give us a lesson in first-grade Martian while we're asleep."

"I hope it works," McKay said. "I've never used one of these things, but they're being tried out on Earth by some researchers to cram information through the subconscious.

I wonder how they are going to do it though, since they can't speak English. Anyway, I have confidence that they know what they're doing. This could cut down the language barrier in no time . . ."

When McKay awoke the next morning, the guide came into the bedroom. The man spoke, and sounds which had been gibberish the day before translated instantly in McKay's startled mind.

"Good morning," the Martian said. "I am Karis. Do you understand me?"

McKay astonished himself by replying in simple Martian. "Yes, I understand you. My name is George McKay. My companions are Peter Sterling and Duncan Ross."

"Thank you," said Karis politely. "I will wake them now. I am to be your personal aide while you are on Mars." He smiled. "You speak Martian very well," he said, "but we are using only easy words. In a few nights the pillow-speaker will teach you all of our language."

After breakfast, the Earthmen were taken on a sightseeing tour of the capital. Everywhere they met with unfailing courtesy. Karis explained the layout of the city as they stood before a model in the Municipal Building. A cutaway section showed that Ahla was twenty miles in diameter and exactly circular. The depth in the city centre was just under a mile, and its hub was composed of fifteen circular plazas, layered one above the other, and each a thousand feet in diameter.

Ahla had no streets, but from the rim of each plaza tubes of the radial metropolitan transit system extended to residential sections in all directions and to the many parks. These, they could see from the model, were vast subterranean open spaces in the top floor of the city, with transparent plexidomes to let in the sun.

The cleanliness of Ahla astounded the visitors. There was no dust, Karis explained, because it was removed by the central air-conditioning system, which also controlled the temperature and humidity. There were no streets, automobiles, pedestrian problems or crowded trains.

All that week, the Earthmen were kept busy with inspections and receptions. At a hospital they witnessed an operation in which a man whose arm had been destroyed in an accident was given another.

"We have a stock-pile of all parts of the body," explained a doctor matter-of-factly. "They are willed to us."

The Earthmen found the school they visited that afternoon more exhilarating. In one classroom six-year-olds were studying chemistry. A lecturer was rushing through the subject at terrifying speed. Within thirty minutes he covered the periodic system of elements and the mystery of electrical cohesion of atoms when forming molecules.

"We don't expect them to remember all this," the teacher explained as they left the room. "We just give them a grasp of the fundamentals. Learning in detail takes place at night through the pillow-speakers."

Each day McKay spent half an hour broadcasting a report to the base for transmission to Earth via the orbiting ship, *Oberth*. Each night their knowledge of Martian was increased through more advanced language tapes fed into their pillow-speakers. Sterling busied himself creating tapes in English at the request of the professors, so that Martians could learn one of the languages of Earth.

On the fifth day of their visit, McKay was amused to have two little girls greet him on Plaza 12 with "Good morning, Earthman." There was hardly a trace of Martian accent.

The other members of the expedition were being brought to Ahla that afternoon, leaving only the radio operator and two engineers at the base. But they had not arrived before McKay, Sterling and Ross had to leave the hotel.

That evening, Karis had arranged to take them to the house of Oraze, the leading astronomer of Mars. The Earthmen followed him into a subway station across the plaza. It was their first experience with the local transit system. They entered one of the small cars passing the platform at a walking pace, and Karis dialled a three-digit combination on a panel. They moved slowly to a point where unused cars were rotated back to the platform, but their own car flew down a straight tunnel until it reached a circular gallery. The number of this gallery, Karis explained, was controlled by the first digit he dialled.

"Now, you see, the car is being detached from its track and raised to the level where Oraze lives," he said. "The floor level is what the second digit of the dial directs."

The Earthmen watched out the window as their car passed nine levels till it came to Plaza 15.

"This is the top level," Karis pointed out. "Oraze lives here because as an astronomer he must be able to look out at the sky. His observatory is in the nearby park."

The car shot off to the left down the circular gallery and came to a stop at the location indicated by the third digit. As they left the car, its doors closed, and it started automatically on the return journey.

Oraze greeted them at the subway door of his spacious, modern-appearing apartment, and through a window in the entrance hall McKay could see the unblinking stars bright in the dark velvet firmament. The astronomer appeared to be a man in his fifties. He introduced his wife Linnith, his son Omi and his pretty daughter Arum.

Entering the dining room, the Earthmen and the Martians seated themselves at a table which was bare except for a dark red tablecloth. Omi handed each of them a small disc, and Linnith dimmed the illumination. A colour television screen lighted, and upon it in slow procession passed the dishes that were available. Each person pushed the buttons of his disc when he saw something he liked. The Earthmen were now familiar with Martian food, though this was their first try at selecting it electronically.

Presently there was a clicking sound. Linnith opened a door in the wall behind which were seven shining trays with the dishes each person had ordered. Spoons, forks, knives and napkins were also provided.

"It is a tubular delivery system," Arum explained, "which reaches every house in Ahla. I like it because there is no dish-washing. We return everything by the tubes."

Later Oraze produced a globe of Earth and talked astronomy with the Earthmen, while Linnith and the young people listened.

The Earth, moving around the sun through an orbit inside that of Mars, appeared to Martians as the Morning or Evening Star, Oraze explained, just as Venus appears to inhabitants of Earth. This, he added apologetically, makes observation by Martians more difficult than for Earth's astronomers when they study Mars.

Yet Martian observation, in spite of this and the curtain caused by Earth's more extended cloud cover, was remarkably advanced. They had determined seasonal, climatic and temperature data quite accurately, and their estimate of the composition of Earth's atmosphere was vastly superior to the information McKay had been given about Mars.

Martian science had conceived no very high opinion of the intelligence of Earthlings, the explorers learned, though Oraze added politely that this was probably because they had no knowledge of the kind of lives people on Earth led.

"Our conclusions," he said, "were based mainly on the fact that we saw you have our scarcest commodity – water – in ample supply. We couldn't conceive of a civilization which would permit deserts to exist when so much water is available to make them bloom like the many fertile areas on Earth we observed through our telescopes."

"Well, it's true that we are still stupid enough to have deserts," McKay said. "But you must admit, Oraze, that we know enough technology to put men on Mars."

"This seems a good time to clear up a mystery," Duncan Ross said. "Have you Martians ever visited Earth?"

"You may put your mind at rest," Oraze replied. "Martians feel no urge to storm the heavens. The centuries have dulled us in our subterranean burrows, and we are few who direct the attention of our fellow citizens to the stars."

"But how can that be," Ross pursued, "when all your people are so religious – so illuminated by a light that seems to come from heaven itself?"

"Our Martian God does not live in heaven," Oraze said softly. "A few of our better folk still keep Him in their hearts. But, in the minds of the majority, He has gradually been forgotten."

"But this whole planet is bursting with creative energy!" Peter protested. "Don't the easier living conditions on Earth tempt some of your adventurous souls?"

"Ah, but where are the adventurers?" asked Oraze resignedly. "You Earthmen have been impressed by superficialities. All our technological refinements are a screen for an age-weary, languid, satiated culture.

"You have told me that a few pioneering races civilized your globe a few centuries ago. The same thing happened here tens of thousands of years ago. Wars and revolutions preceded the present stable planetary government. Then came a long period of advancing civilization and culture. Living standards improved despite the inroads of erosion and drought. The fine arts advanced to unheard-of perfection. Mass production of consumer goods almost wiped out the differences between rich and poor.

"When we had to go underground five thousand years ago, our technology was advanced to the point where it could provide all these marvels you have seen. But when this subterranean paradise was completed, the mainspring of Martian endeavour, divine discontent, began to flag. The adventurous spirit died, and we are now a planet of peace-seeking and easeful people, content to rest on the laurels of our ancestors. The spirit of adventure has been drowned in a sea of organization."

He paused contemplatively and then went on. "There is no escaping the laws of nature," he said. "The demands of millions of beings can be fulfilled only by the production of millions of articles, each from an identical mould. Standardization and yet more standardization is necessary. Eventually that means standardization of tastes and desires – and, yes, even of opinions.

"Our food this evening was available to all five million Ahlans. Our tablecloth is one of the ten types you can buy on this planet. Our clothes, our shoes, our habits – all are the same. This is the major tragedy of our lives. It presses upon all of us like a horrible nightmare. Inwardly we constantly battle the dull, grey uniformity our civilization imposes upon us.

"The advance of technology is primarily responsible for our planetary peace and plenty. But with it has come a soul-destroying equivalence of everything by which we live, and a conformity that makes it very unappealing for a young Martian to become different or outstanding."

McKay and the others were deeply moved by the emotion which had stirred Oraze out of his Martian calm as he spoke.

"Do you feel that something of this sort will happen to Earth's civilization in time?" McKay asked.

Oraze looked up and spoke slowly. "Yours is still a young planet and vast parts of it are still untouched deserts or jungles," he said. "If you can preserve your pioneering spirit and develop these areas, you still have several hundred years of creative activity ahead of you. But thereafter the Law of Nature will catch up with you, too." He paused. "How can you escape it? Your global population is increasing alarmingly, you tell me. How can the people be fed and clothed except by mass production?"

"And must mass production always lead to standardization?" Ross asked.

"I can only say that it has seemed so to us," Oraze observed. "Maybe we made a grave mistake when we built that TransMars Subway System. It made global transportation so cheap and so fast that our people, regardless of their cultural origin and heritage, migrated to the big cities where they found it easiest to make a living. Within a few generations this development destroyed the old values of home-grown customs and beliefs, for most newcomers were only too eager to abandon their old standards and embrace the glib, conformist, big-city culture in their place. Perhaps, if we had not promoted this trend, we would not have lost the spirit of adventure and life would be different here." Oraze laid his hand on McKay's arm. "If your visit could inspire our people, stir their laggard spirits – what a blessing you would have brought!"

The Earthmen were thoughtful on their trip back to the centre of Ahla. Even Karis seemed sad.

"Oraze is right in saying that your coming here may give us a rebirth of adventure," he said. "People talk about nothing but your expedition. It is as though you had come in an enchanted ship."

McKay laughed. "When are you going to produce my other men from your enchanted subway?" he asked.

"I think we shall find them at the hotel now," Karis said.

He was right. And McKay immediately set up a schedule so that their observation of every phase of life on Mars would be stored in notebooks before their departure. Before, the 449 days they would have to spend on a barren Mars, or at least in orbit around Mars, had seemed a lonely prospect. The date of departure was fixed by the necessity of leaving Mars when the Earth was at a certain point on its orbit. Now, when they had made the amazing discovery that Mars was bustling with life, a year and three months seemed too short a span.

"The only way we can carry out our mission," McKay said, "is to split up. Every man will do the jobs his field of knowledge fits him for. We'll want to do some surface exploration, too."

"That is easy," Karis said. "But you will find the exhibits and museums in our big parks have a complete record of what life was like before we were driven underground."

They spent most of the weeks that followed studying elaborate exhibits. Answers to all the questions which Earth's scientists had asked since Mars was first sighted in space went into their notebooks.

Interspersed with their studies of Martian history were visits to Martian industrial cities where they saw the underground factories that provided the population of 800 million with food and consumer goods, as well as the nuclear power stations which energized the technological wonders of the planet.

But the Earthmen were impatient to get their own surface exploration started. McKay, Sterling, Ross and Karis made up the party.

They took the tractor up to Plaza 15, then transferred it to the last-stage freight elevator, which was equipped with an airlock at the summit, where they donned spacesuits for the first time in weeks. Karis opened the big hatch, and they looked out on rugged mountain terrain. There was a small level area in front of the exit and then the land rose sharply on all sides to a small plateau.

"Tough going," McKay said doubtfully. "You three go ahead on foot. I'll follow in the tractor."

He went through the tractor's airlock and started the reactor-powered turbine drive, while Sterling, Ross and Karis set out for the rise, loping easily in the weak Martian gravity McKay could hear them talking through his helmet receiver. Ross called back that the surface was volcanic.

"Seems hard enough," he said.

Sterling and Karis had already disappeared over the rim when the tractor began the climb. McKay lumbered to the top and braked to survey the scene around him. Far over to the left were the ruins of the ancient surface city, an enormous pile of jumbled masonry on a desolate plain.

McKay moved forward gingerly. He reached the edge of the plateau and, as he eased the big machine over, the crust gave way with a sudden crunch. The tractor plunged through the volcanic surface, jolted hard on solid rock and slid crazily downwards.

McKay braked hard, but the treads refused to grip on the scurrying stones. The controls were almost ineffective, and he fought them with all his intelligence. Unless he could stop the tractor or turn it aside in a few seconds, the ponderous machine would crash through the dome of the park, and plunge into the city of Ahla.

Dust from the avalanche rose in a yellow cloud around the tractor, and McKay could see only dimly that Karis was braced in front of him with an enormous boulder. As the wind blew the dust aside, McKay saw the nearness of the park's canopy and he alternately braked and released the brake, hoping to stop the slipping treads, praying they would catch traction.

Then he saw Karis bend down suddenly and he felt the right tread of the tractor lift. For a moment it balanced there uncertainly. Then the machine slowly turned in spite of its locked controls. It skirted the rim of the plexidome by no more than a yard. Then it was free and out on the open plain, and McKay cut the power. Karis came running up as McKay dropped through the air lock and shook his hand gratefully.

"You are quite safe now," the Martian said simply. "I am glad."

McKay wondered if these people ever lost their Olympian calm.

"Karis, you did the only thing that could save me," he said. "Marvellous how you handled that huge rock. You put it at the right side of the tread so the tractor was forced to the left."

Karis smiled. "A simple enough decision," he said. "It is not difficult to move large boulders in our Martian gravity."

Peter Sterling came running to join them, and they lumbered three miles across the plain to the ruins of ancient Ahla, which had been built on the surface thousands of years before. But all they could see were columns, foundations and a few reasonably intact but completely bare buildings.

"The people had plenty of time to strip the city," Karis said. "Anything of value and all the records were taken underground. Mars was already in a high state of civilization so, contrary perhaps to your expectations, you will find nothing primitive here.

"Over there to the right used to be an airport and you can still see the shells of some of our ancient jet aircraft. Oh yes, Martians used to fly a great deal. When we went underground, aviation was abandoned because our underground transport system was so much more efficient. The only flying machines we use now are a fleet of duct-fan aircraft from which the engineers observe the progress of the polar melts. But they are assigned to pumping stations near the poles."

One of the great belts of vegetation extended on both sides of the abandoned city as far as they could see. It was these fields, the explorers learned, which Earth's astronomers had called "canals".

"One thing we haven't thoroughly understood," McKay said, "is just how your water cycle works. I can see that, when the snow in the polar zones melts, you pump the water to the cities. But how do you return the water to the atmosphere so that new snow can fall at the poles?"

"Why, it's quite simple," Karis said. "Under each of these fields there are porous tile pipes. Into them our great cities pump their sewage and interior condensation. You see, they must get rid of exactly the same amount of water as we supply to them. Otherwise they would soon be flooded. Well, the waste water is absorbed by the roots of the plants and drawn up into the stems and leaves. This moisture escapes into our parched atmosphere, and strong winds of autumn carry it to the poles. There it is precipitated as snow, and in the spring the snow melts. The water is caught in big basins and flows through conduits to reservoirs situated all over the planet."

A sudden shadow darkened the sun. Karis looked up quickly. "It is one of our dust storms," he said. "I think we should return now so that we are back in the city before it strikes."

Already they could feel the wind rising as they re-entered the tractor and started back. Swirls of reddish-yellow dust eddied across the plain, and they saw Ross looking anxious behind his space helmet as they approached the plateau. The geologist had found an easier route up the jagged side, and there was no trouble getting back to the summit hatch.

As they emerged on Plaza 15 and drove the tractor to the freight elevator, Peter Sterling laughed suddenly.

"I must be going Martian," he said. "I've just realized I'm glad to be underground."

The fact was that they had all come to feel very much at home in the subterranean life of Mars. As the weeks sped by, McKay felt a great sense of accomplishment in the amount of information they had stored in their notebooks. Their research had covered the entire complex of Martian science, technology and history. Detailed descriptive blueprints and pictures were microfilmed for easy storage on the return rocket, *Goddard*, so that Earth's scientists could study and evaluate their findings later.

Now that he felt less pressed, McKay increased his broadcast time to Earth. From messages relayed to him by their orbiting interplanetary passenger ship, *Oberth*, Earth was insatiable in its appetite for every scrap of information he could send. And the most insistent of

Earth's demands was that the expedition bring back some of the marvellous Martians.

This was a subject McKay had not discussed with any of his Martian hosts. He tried it out on Karis one afternoon when they were on their way to the sports stadium to watch an athletic event.

"How would you like to come back to Earth with us, Karis?" he said.

"I should like that very much," the Martian said. "But I would not suggest it until you expressed the wish yourself."

"We're having lunch with Ansanto, the head of your Academy of Science, tomorrow," McKay said. "I'll bring it up then."

"Ansanto will be pleased," Karis said, as they left their car and joined a stream of Martians moving towards the stadium.

They entered the great oval amphitheatre and found their seats. McKay looked around the packed arena, then down at the young men and women who would be competing in a programme of field events. Their tanned bodies were almost naked and beautifully knit.

Karis explained that athletic superiority combined with physical symmetry made up the Martian ideal. "We strive to develop the whole body to achieve perfection in our men," he said. "It is true of our women, too."

McKay could believe they had succeeded. He watched the contests in growing wonder as the athletes jumped, threw weights and ran faster than he had ever seen before. He knew that the feeble Martian gravity had a lot to do with it, but it still astonished him to see a handsome young Martian maiden with the body of a goddess soar more than forty feet to win the high jump. Looking around the stadium at the spectators, dressed in their Grecian costumes and raising their "Ahs" of approval, he could imagine himself back in Earth's Golden Age in Greece, when the Olympic games were young.

Making notes for tomorrow's broadcast to Earth, McKay wrote: "We were impressed by the inner pride and enthusiasm with which the women presented their perfections. Despite their costumes, which verged upon nudism, there was not the slightest suggestion of that over-emphasis of the sensual which on Earth so frequently accompanies exposure of the female body. These women had beautiful bodies and they exhibited them in athletic excellence with no other purpose."

Next morning McKay went to the station of the trans-planetary system with Karis, and they took one of those supersonic subway cars for Laroni, a small town beneath the moss fields of Lacus Lunae. It turned out that Laroni was largely inhabited by artists, writers and philosophers whose individualities were expressed in what was, for Mars, a wide variety of decorative schemes and furnishings in their dwellings.

McKay was much impressed by Ansanto's breadth of mind and extensive historical knowledge as they talked during luncheon. He realised that here was a man with a perspective on the development of the planet such as few possessed.

After luncheon, the Earthman lost no time in proposing that the return flight include three Martians chosen by the Academy.

Ansanto's benign countenance lit up. "We have been hoping there could be such an invitation," he said quickly. "Yes, of course, Martians will go with you. You have reborn in us the spirit of adventure."

They discussed the type of men best suited for the Earth journey.

"I leave that to you, sir," McKay said, "but it would give us great pleasure if Karis might be one of the three."

Ansanto looked at the young Martian in some surprise.

"Karis is not a scientist," he began, "and yet – yes, I think Karis must go with you. He reflects the thoughts of our people." He smiled at Karis. "We shall discuss at the Academy our other two space pioneers. Their names will be announced at the dinner we plan in your honour before you leave us."

Time was growing short now, but McKay was confident that he and his companions had completed their studies. The Earthmen shuttled frequently between Ahla and their base camp, carrying the records of their observations, containers of microfilm and the samples of Martian life – clothing, shoes, packages of synthetic food, specialized tools, and reels of exposed film they had taken of life on Mars.

Martian engineers and mechanics had been assigned to help Spottswood and Burke in checking *Goddard* against the day of departure. Spottswood reported a week before take-off that they were ready.

Riding back to Ahla in one of the supersonic cars late that afternoon, McKay turned to Karis.

"What would you say was the most important achievement of your Martian technology?" he asked.

"Limitless electric power," Karis answered promptly. "Without this, our existence would be impossible." He drew from a pocket of his tunic some Martian currency and pointed to the symbols on the notes of different denominations. In very much the same way as the value of a dollar is based on the gold standard, Karis' bills were based on varying amounts of the Martian equivalent of kilowatt hours. "You see," Karis said, "electrical energy units are the standard of value on Mars. They are responsible for our material welfare – the clothes we wear, the food we eat, the air we breathe. It is electrical power which has reduced our standard work day to only four hours."

It occurred to McKay that, in an advanced technological civilization, where physical labour is virtually non-existent and the total production level is directly related to the total level of available electrical power, a kilowatt currency seemed to have a built-in mechanism against inflation: when a new generating station was built, more money would go into circulation to keep balance with the increased productivity.

"I am really impressed by what you have accomplished with electrification, Karis, but I have even greater respect for the intelligent way your people use their leisure," McKay said. "Everyone I meet seems to be following a creative hobby – painting, sculpture, sports activities, music, writing. Our folks back home could really learn a lot from you in this respect, too. You know, our scientists and engineers knock themselves out making life more comfortable, but all too many people just don't know what to do with their spare time."

"I think your people will improve in the art of cultured leisure as technology continues to free them from manual work," Karis said. "There is something eminently satisfying in working with your hands, but after centuries of enslavement to manual work many people have to learn to be proud of their hands again. Here on Mars there is practically no manual labour any more. Our machine tools are perfected to the stage where there is little more to making new machines than feeding instructions into a computer. We no longer have stenographers on Mars. You have seen our offices where we use mechanical transcription direct from the voice. Yes, we need to be creative with our hands again to make us forget what Oraze told you that night and what Ansanto repeated today – the greyness of standardization."

"Did you go to one of the universities, Karis?" McKay asked.

"My examination results were not good enough," Karis said, "and our testing system indicated that I should be more useful if I went through a technical school. I do not regret it. I have a good life. I am twenty-five now, and I am the deputy supervisor of the pumping station where you found me. It is not bad for one ten years out of technical school."

"I sometimes wonder," McKay said, as he watched a station flick past, "whether your Martian system is wise in racing children through school as fast as it does. We are much slower on Earth. Our children begin school at five, yours at three. But we do not feel that so young a child is able to understand all the advanced science you teach your youngsters by the time they are eight. And it seems incredibly young for boys and girls to enter the university or technical school at the age of twelve."

"But you do not use pillow-speakers, I believe," Karis said. "As you found when you learned Martian, all the drudgery of memorization is performed by the pillow-speaker. When the process of cramming knowledge is handled mechanically, then the child is free to think – to understand."

That evening, back in Ahla, McKay assembled all the Earthmen who were not at the base. One by one McKay questioned them and was relieved to find that none of the scientists felt his observations were incomplete.

The interesting thing was that none of these men appeared particularly eager to leave Mars. Their year and three months had created friendships for all of them among the Martians and developed a fascination for this technologically-driven life.

The 449th day when they must leave Mars was a Saturday, and on Thursday evening the Earthmen went up to Plaza 40 on their last trip through Ahla's transport system. The entire party of twelve had been summoned to this final banquet, and *Goddard*, the return rocket, was left in the care of Martian engineers.

The explorers entered the magnificent Academy of Science Building where they were received by Ardri, the Martian chief of state, and his ministers, as well as the principal intellectuals of the planet. After dinner, there was a programme of speeches. Ardri welcomed them to this final ceremony and called on McKay, who tried to express the thanks of all the Earthmen for the hospitality of the Martians.

Then Ansanto rose to give the address of the evening. "Brothers from Earth," he said, "the inspiration behind your daring journey across the solar system was far more than the urge to perform a technical feat, magnificent as it was. That inspiration brought you here so you might fulfil a mission that must have been planned by the Creator Himself.

"The meaning of that mission can only be that God willed that the living beings He has formed after His image and spread throughout the universe shall establish contact and learn to work together for His greater glory.

"Your voyage is indeed a great technical accomplishment that has made a profound impression on millions of Martians. But you have told us that people on Earth have been even more impressed by the messages that you have sent them about what you found here. So let me give you a word of warning and advice from an old man who is a citizen of an even older planet.

"The history of this planet has taught us that idolatry of our technical accomplishments constitutes the worst evil with which we threaten our race and our civilization. Worshipping those accomplishments renders man sterile and incapable of meeting the demands of the future. If we worship scientific achievement, we kill humility, and of humility alone can be born any further progress, scientific or otherwise.

"Man should worship none but God, if he would fulfil his mission in this life. Thus, and thus only, can we create the ethical foundation on which a technological civilization can be built from which all mankind can benefit."

Ansanto then called the roll of the Earthmen and, as each walked to the rostrum, Ardri hung about his neck Mars' highest decoration for scientific achievement. He then called up Granat and Koras, the two scientists who had been nominated to accompany the expedition back to Earth, and with them he summoned Karis, who walked proudly to receive the accolade of this man.

When they were all seated again, Ansanto called loudly, "Roll back the canopy!"

The ceiling slid away soundlessly and, as they looked through the transparent dome to the star-studded firmament, they saw a light brighter than the brightest star move slowly across the heavens.

"I have the honour to report," said Ansanto, "that, inspired by your visit, Mars has made its first venture into space. That light you see up there is an artificial satellite that was launched only this afternoon. When you Earthmen return to Mars, there will be a space station up there in orbit waiting to receive you."

It was all over then, and they said farewell. Oraze came up to McKay. "So it is good-bye for now," he said as he embraced McKay. "But we shall meet again. I feel sure of it."

A few hours later the Earthmen were in the subway cars, speeding down the straight tunnel, on their final journey to the base camp in Libya.

Karis woke them in the morning. The two Martian scientists had arrived and the party set out in the transplanetary cars.

In a little more than two hours they were back at the station under the floor of the red machines. The elevator carried them to the level where they had first glimpsed life on Mars. Their old friends, the superintendent and his assistant greeted them. McKay and his men donned their pressure suits, walked to the elevator, were lifted to the airlock and soon the little party was back on the surface of Mars.

At 0651 next morning McKay felt the blast and the acceleration which lifted their rocket ship into the clear, rarified Martian atmosphere. *Goddard* rose smoothly, and soon the flight track tilted into an easterly direction. After a little over two minutes the roar of the rocket engines subsided and an hour later the orbiting interplanetary ship *Oberth*, which would carry them back to Earth, slid into view . . .

A few days after that they were counting down the last minutes as *Oberth* was readied for the long return voyage across the solar system. McKay lay in his contour chair and, between careful checks of his instrument board, took a last glimpse at the vast reddish and greenish disc with the great white south polar cap that had been their second home for over a year.

Down there was an exciting civilization, undreamed of till their expedition found it.

He felt an immense sense of satisfaction, a deep assurance of what would come from this conjunction of intelligence between the planets Mars and Earth.

John Berger, at the radio, tore a sheet from his pad and passed it up to McKay. "Message from Radio Ahla," he said.

McKay read it to the expedition:

"Mars sends its blessings to your flight, its greetings to all people of Earth. Carry in your ship our remembrance and our promise of swift reunion. – Ardri."

PANIC IN THE YEAR ZERO

(American International, 1962)
Starring: Ray Milland, Jean Hagen & Mary Mitchell
Directed by Ray Milland
Based on the story "Lot" by Ward Moore

The exploding of the Atom Bomb at Hiroshima in 1945 not surprisingly inspired a whole group of novels and films of varying degrees of conviction and paranoia in which the Earth was threatened with cataclysmic destruction. The first of these was *The Beginning or the End* (1946) in which Brian Donlevy (who would later star in the film version of *Quatermass*) played a troubled scientist involved in building the Bomb in the Manhattan Project. This was followed by the "Red menace" of *Invasion U.S.A.* (1952) starring Gerald Mohr and Dan O'Herlihy, and Stanley Kramer's *On The Beach* (1959) based on Nevil Shute's novel about a world destroyed by radioactivity, with Gregory Peck, Ava Gardner and Anthony Perkins. For a number of critics the best picture of this kind was *Panic In The Year Zero* which focused on a typical American family and how they came to terms with life after an atomic war. Though to some others it was a cynical and particularly violent film for its time, it can now be seen as a forerunner of today's no-holds-barred extravaganzas such as *The Terminator* in which the central character abandons all the traditional ideals of humanity and shoots first and asks questions afterwards. *Panic in the Year Zero*, which was directed by its star, was starkly photographed in a grainy black and white style that added to the harshness of the ruined landscape of Los Angeles brilliantly created by special effects designer Daniel Heller. Ward Moore (1903–1978), the author of "Lot", the story on which the film was based, was curiously not credited for his contribution, although he was already well

**known as a writer of a number of best-selling mainstream
novels and the creator of a pair of classic SF books, *Greener
Than You Think* (1947) about a mutated grass that overruns
the world, and *Bring The Jubilee* (1953), a time travel story in
which a man from the future has the chance to change the
course of the American Civil War. First published in *The
Magazine of Fantasy and Science Fiction* in 1953, "Lot" has
been described by Brian Aldiss as "one of the most notable
stories describing nuclear holocaust and its consequences",
and it is perhaps therefore not so surprising that it should also
have inspired a landmark movie.**

Mr Jimmon even appeared elated, like a man about to set
out on a vacation.

"Well, folks, no use waiting any longer. We're all set. So
let's go."

There was a betrayal here; Mr Jimmon was not the kind
of man who addressed his family as "folks".

"David, you're sure . . .?"

Mr Jimmon merely smiled. This was quite out of character; customarily he reacted to his wife's habit of posing
unfinished questions – after seventeen years the unuttered
and larger part of the queries were always instantly known to
him in some mysterious way, as though unerringly projected
by the key in which the introduction was pitched, so that not
only the full wording was communicated to his mind, but the
shades and implications which circumstance and humour
attached to them – with sharp and querulous defence. No
matter how often he resolved to stare quietly or use the still
more effective, Afraid I didn't catch your meaning, dear, he
had never been able to put his resolution into force. Until this
moment of crisis. Crisis, reflected Mr Jimmon, still smiling
and moving suggestively towards the door, crisis changes
people. Brings out underlying qualities.

It was Jir who answered Molly Jimmon, with the adolescent's half-whine of exasperation. "Aw furcrysay Mom,

what's the idea? The highways'll be clogged tight. What's the good figuring out everything heada time and having everything all set if you're going to start all over again at the last minute? Get a grip on yourself and let's go."

Mr Jimmon did not voice the reflexive, That's no way to talk to your mother. Instead he thought, not unsympathetically, of woman's slow reaction time. Asset in childbirth, liability behind the wheel. He knew Molly was thinking of the house and all the things in it: her clothes and Erika's, the TV set – so sullenly ugly now, with the electricity gone – the refrigerator in which the food would soon begin to rot and stink, the dead stove, the cellarful of cases of canned stuff for which there was no room in the station wagon. And the Buick, blocked up in the garage, with the air thoughtfully let out of the tyres and the battery hidden.

Of course the house would be looted. But they had known that all along. When they – or rather he, for it was his executive's mind and training which were responsible for the Jimmons' preparation against this moment – planned so carefully and providentially, he had weighed property against life and decided on life. No other decision was possible.

"Aren't you at least going to phone Pearl and Dan?"

Now why in the world, thought Mr Jimmon, completely above petty irritation, should I call Dan Davisson? (Because of course it's *Dan* she means – My Old Beau. Oh, he was nobody then, just an impractical dreamer without a penny to his name; it wasn't for years that he was recognized as a Mathematical Genius; now he's a professor and all sorts of things – but she automatically says Pearl-and-Dan, not Dan.) What can Dan do with the square root of minus nothing to offset M equals whatever it is, at this moment? Or am I supposed to ask if Pearl has all her diamonds? Query, why doesn't Pearl wear pearls, only diamonds? My wife's friends, heh heh, but even the subtlest intonation won't label them when you're entertaining an important client and Pearl and Dan.

And why should I phone? What sudden paralysis afflicts her? Hysteria?

"No," said Mr Jimmon. "I did not phone Pearl and Dan."

Then he added, relenting, "Phone's been out since."

"But," said Molly.

She's hardly going to ask me to drive into town. He selected several answers in readiness. But she merely looked towards the telephone helplessly (she ought to have been fat, thought Mr Jimmon, really she should, or anyway plump; her thinness gives her that air of competence), so he amplified gently, "They're unquestionably all right. As far away from it as we are."

Wendell was already in the station wagon. With Waggie hidden somewhere. Should have sent the dog to the humane society; more merciful to have it put to sleep. Too late now; Waggie would have to take his chance. There were plenty of rabbits in the hills above Malibu, he had often seen them quite close to the house. At all events there was no room for a dog in the wagon, already loaded to within a pound of its capacity.

Erika came in briskly from the kitchen, her brown jodhpurs making her appear at first glance even younger than fourteen. But only at first glance; then the swell of hips and breast denied the childishness the jodhpurs seemed to accent.

"The water's gone, Mom. There's no use sticking around any longer."

Molly looked incredulous. "The water?"

"Of course the water's gone," said Mr Jimmon, not impatiently, but rather with satisfaction in his own foresight. "If It didn't get the aqueduct, the mains depend on pumps. Electric pumps. When the electricity went, the water went too."

"But the water," repeated Molly, as though this last catastrophe was beyond all reason – even the outrageous logic which It brought in its train.

Jir slouched past them and outside. Erika tucked in a strand of hair, pulled her jockey cap downward and sideways, glanced quickly at her mother and father, then followed. Molly took several steps, paused, smiled vaguely in the mirror and walked out of the house.

Mr Jimmon patted his pockets; the money was all there. He didn't even look back before closing the front door and rattling the knob to be sure the lock had caught. It had never failed, but Mr Jimmon always rattled it anyway. He strode to the station wagon, running his eyes over the springs to reassure himself again that they really hadn't overloaded it.

The sky was overcast; you might have thought it one of the regular morning high fogs if you didn't know. Mr Jimmon faced south-east, but It had been too far away to see anything. Now Erika and Molly were in the front seat; the boys were in the back lost amid the neatly packed stuff. He opened the door on the driver's side, got in, turned the key and started the motor. Then he said casually over his shoulder, "Put the dog out, Jir."

Wendell protested, too quickly, "Waggie's not here."

Molly exclaimed, "Oh, David . . ."

Mr Jimmon said patiently, "We're losing pretty valuable time. There's no room for the dog; we have no food for him. If we had room we could have taken more essentials; those few pounds might mean the difference."

"Can't find him," muttered Jir.

"He's not here. I tell you he's not here," shouted Wendell, tearful voiced.

"If I have to stop the motor and get him myself we'll be wasting still more time and gas." Mr Jimmon was still detached, judicial. "This isn't a matter of kindness to animals. It's life and death."

Erika said evenly, "Dad's right, you know. It's the dog or us. Put him out, Wend."

"I tell you – " Wendell began.

"Got him!" exclaimed Jir. "Okay, Waggie! Outside and good luck."

The spaniel wriggled ecstatically as he was picked up and put out through the open window. Mr Jimmon raced the motor, but it didn't drown out Wendell's anguish. He threw himself on his brother, hitting and kicking. Mr Jimmon took his foot off the gas, and as soon as he was sure the dog was away from the wheels, eased the station wagon out of the driveway and down the hill towards the ocean.

"Wendell, Wendell, stop," pleaded Molly. "Don't hurt him, Jir."

Mr Jimmon clicked on the radio. After a preliminary hum, clashing static crackled out. He pushed all five buttons in turn, varying the quality of unintelligible sound. "Want me to try?" offered Erika. She pushed the manual button and turned the knob slowly. Music dripped out.

Mr Jimmon grunted. "Mexican station. Try something else. Maybe you can get Ventura."

They rounded a tight curve. "Isn't that the Warbinns'?" asked Molly.

For the first time since It happened, Mr Jimmon had a twinge of impatience. There was no possibility, even with the unreliable eye of shocked excitement, of mistaking the Warbinns' blue Mercury. No one else on Rambla Catalina had one anything like it, and visitors would be most unlikely now. If Molly would apply the most elementary logic!

Besides, Warbinn had stopped the blue Mercury in the Jimmon driveway five times every week for the past two months – ever since they had decided to put the Buick up and keep the wagon packed and ready against this moment – for Mr Jimmon to ride with him to the city. Of course it was the Warbinns'.

"*. . . advised not to impede the progress of the military. Adequate medical staffs are standing by at all hospitals. Local civilian defence units are taking all steps in accordance . . .*"

"Santa Barbara," remarked Jir, nodding at the radio with an expert's assurance.

Mr Jimmon slowed, prepared to follow the Warbinns down to 101, but the Mercury halted and Mr Jimmon turned out to pass it. Warbinn was driving and Sally was in the front seat with him; the back seat appeared empty except for a few things obviously hastily thrown in. No foresight, thought Mr Jimmon.

Warbinn waved his hand vigorously out the window and Sally shouted something.

"*. . . panic will merely slow rescue efforts. Casualties are much smaller than originally reported . . .*"

"How do they know?" asked Mr Jimmon, waving politely at the Warbinns.

"Oh, David, aren't you going to stop? They want something."

"Probably just to talk."

"*. . . to retain every drop of water. Emergency power will be in operation shortly. There is no cause for undue alarm. General . . .*"

Through the rear-view mirror Mr Jimmon saw the blue Mercury start after them. He had been right then, they only wanted to say something inconsequential. At a time like this.

At the junction with U.S. 101, five cars blocked Rambla Catalina. Mr Jimmon set the handbrake, and steadying himself with the open door, stood on tiptoe twistedly, trying to see over the cars ahead. 101 was solid with traffic which barely moved. On the southbound side of the divided highway a stream of vehicles flowed illegally north.

"Thought everybody was figured to go east," gibed Jir over the other side of the car.

Mr Jimmon was not disturbed by his son's sarcasm. How right he'd been to rule out the trailer. Of course the bulk of the cars were headed eastward as he'd calculated; this sluggish mass was nothing compared with the countless ones which must now be blocking the roads to Pasadena; Alhambra, Garvey, Norwalk. Even the northbound refugees were undoubtedly taking 99 or regular 101 – the highway before them was really 101 Alternate – he had picked the most feasible exit.

The Warbinns drew up alongside. "Hurry didn't do you much good," shouted Warbinn, leaning forward to clear his wife's face.

Mr Jimmon reached in and turned off the ignition. Gas was going to be precious. He smiled and shook his head at Warbinn; no use pointing out that he'd got the inside lane by passing the Mercury, with a better chance to seize the opening on the highway when it came. "Get in the car, Jir, and shut the door. Have to be ready when this breaks."

"If it ever does," said Molly. "All that rush and bustle. We might just as well . . ."

Mr Jimmon was conscious of Warbinn's glowering at him and resolutely refused to turn his head. He pretended not to hear him yell, "Only wanted to tell you you forgot to pick up your bumper-jack. It's in front of our garage."

Mr Jimmon's stomach felt empty. What if he had a flat now? Ruined, condemned. He knew a burning hate for Warbinn – incompetent borrower, bad neighbour, thoughtless, shiftless, criminal. He owed it to himself to leap from the station wagon and seize Warbinn by the throat . . .

"What did he say, David? What is Mr Warbinn saying?"

Then he remembered it was the jack from the Buick; the station wagon's was safely packed where he could get at it easily. Naturally he would never have started out on a trip like this without checking so essential an item. "Nothing," he said, "nothing at all."

". . . *plane dispatches indicate target was the Signal Hill area. Minor damage was done to Long Beach, Wilmington, and San Pedro. All non-military air traffic warned from Mines Field . . ."*

The smash and crash of bumper and fender sounded familiarly on the highway. From his look-out station he couldn't see what had happened, but it was easy enough to reconstruct the impatient jerk forward that caused it. Mr Jimmon didn't exactly smile, but he allowed himself a faint quiver of internal satisfaction. A crash up ahead would make things worse, but a crash behind – and many of them were inevitable – must eventually create a gap.

Even as he thought this, the first car at the mouth of Rambla Catalina edged on to the shoulder of the highway. Mr Jimmon slid back in and started the motor, inching ahead after the car in front, gradually leaving the still uncomfortable proximity of the Warbinns.

"Got to go to the toilet," announced Wendell abruptly.

"Didn't I tell you – ! Well, hurry up! Jir, keep the door open and pull him in if the car starts to move."

"I can't go here."

Mr Jimmon restrained his impulse to snap, Hold it in then. Instead he said mildly, "This is a crisis, Wendell. No time for niceties. Hurry."

". . . the flash was seen as far north as Ventura and as far south as Newport. An eye-witness who has just arrived by helicopter . . ."

"That's what we should have had," remarked Jir. "You thought of everything except that."

"That's no way to speak to your father," admonished Molly.

"Aw heck, Mom, this is a crisis. No time for niceties."

"You're awful smart, Jir," said Erika. "Big, tough, brutal man."

"Go down, brat," returned Jir, "your nose needs wiping."

"As a matter of record," Mr Jimmon said calmly, "I thought of both plane and helicopter and decided against them."

"I can't go. Honest, I just can't go."

"Just relax, darling," advised Molly. "No one is looking."

"*. . . fires reported in Compton, Lynwood, Southgate, Harbour City, Lomita, and other spots are now under control. Residents are advised not to attempt to travel on the overcrowded highways as they are much safer in their homes or places of employment. The civilian defence . . .*"

The two cars ahead bumped forward. "Get in," shouted Mr Jimmon.

He got the left front tyre of the station wagon on the asphalt shoulder – the double lane of concrete was impossibly far ahead – only to be blocked by the packed procession. The clock on the dash said 11.04. Nearly five hours since It happened, and they were less than two miles from home. They could have done better walking. Or on horseback.

"*. . . All residents of the Los Angeles area are urged to remain calm. Local radio service will be restored in a matter of minutes, along with electricity and water. Reports of fifth column activities have been greatly exaggerated. The FBI has all known subversives under . . .*"

He reached over and shut it off. Then he edged a daring two inches further on the shoulder, almost grazing an aggressive Cadillac packed solid with cardboard cartons. On his left a Model A truck shivered and trembled. He knew, distantly and disapprovingly, that it belonged to two painters who called themselves man and wife. The truckbed was loaded high with household goods; poor, useless things no looter would bother to steal. In the cab the artists passed a quart beer bottle back and forth. The man waved it genially at him; Mr Jimmon nodded discouragingly back.

The thermometer on the mirror showed 90. Hot all right. Of course if they ever got rolling . . . I'm thirsty, he thought; probably suggestion. If I hadn't seen the thermometer. Anyway I'm not going to paw around in back for the canteen. Forethought. Like the arms. He cleared his throat. "Remember there's an automatic in the glove compartment. If anyone tries to open the door on your side, use it."

"Oh, David, I . . ."

Ah, humanity. Non-resistance. Gandhi. I've never shot at anything but a target. At a time like this. But they don't understand.

"I could use the rifle from back here," suggested Jir. "Can I, Dad?"

"I can reach the shotgun," said Wendell. "That's better at close range."

"Gee, you men are brave," jeered Erika. Mr Jimmon said nothing; both shotgun and rifle were unloaded. Foresight again.

He caught the hiccuping pause in the traffic instantly, gratified at his smooth coordination. How far he could proceed on the shoulder before running into a culvert narrowing the highway to the concrete he didn't know. Probably not more than a mile at most, but at least he was off Rambla Catalina and on 101.

He felt tremendously elated. Successful.

"Here we go!" He almost added, Hold on to your hats.

Of course the shoulder too was packed solid, and progress, even in low gear, was maddening. The gas consumption was something he did not want to think about; his pride in the way the needle of the gauge caressed the F shrank. And gas would be hard to come by in spite of his pocketful of ration coupons. Black market.

"Mind if I try the radio again?" asked Erika, switching it on.

Mr Jimmon, following the pattern of previous success, insinuated the left front tyre on to the concrete, eliciting a disapproving squawk from the Pontiac alongside. ". . . *sector was quiet. Enemy losses are estimated . . .*"

"Can't you get something else?" asked Jir. "Something less dusty?"

"Wish we had TV in the car," observed Wendell. "Joe Tellifer's old man put a set in the back seat of their Chrysler."

"Dry up, squirt," said Jir. "Let the air out of your head."

"Jir!"

"Oh, Mom, don't pay attention! Don't you see that's what he wants?"

"Listen, brat, if you weren't a girl, I'd spank you."

"You mean, if I wasn't your sister. You'd probably enjoy such childish sex-play with any other girl."

"Erika!"

Where do they learn it? marvelled Mr Jimmon. These progressive schools. Do you suppose . . .?

He edged the front wheel further in exultantly, taking advantage of a momentary lapse of attention on the part of the Pontiac's driver. Unless the other went berserk with frustration and rammed into him, he practically had a cinch on a car-length of the concrete now.

"Here we go!" he gloried. "We're on our way."

"Aw, if I was driving we'd be half-way to Oxnard by now."

"Jir, that's no way to talk to your father."

Mr Jimmon reflected dispassionately that Molly's ineffective admonitions only spurred Jir's sixteen-year-old brashness, already irritating enough in its own right. Indeed, if it were not for Molly, Jir might . . .

It was of course possible – here Mr Jimmon braked just short of the convertible ahead – Jir wasn't just going through a "difficult" period (What was particularly difficult about it? he inquired, in the face of all the books Molly suggestively left around on the psychological problems of growth. The boy had everything he could possibly want) but was the type who, in different circumstances drifted well into – well, perhaps not exactly juvenile delinquency, but . . .

". . . in the Long Beach-Wilmington-San Pedro area. Comparison with that which occurred at Pittsburgh reveals

98

that this morning's was in every way less serious. All fires are now under control and all the injured are now receiving medical attention . . ."

"I don't think they're telling the truth," stated Mrs Jimmon.

He snorted. He didn't think so either, but by what process had she arrived at that conclusion?

"I want to hear the ball game. Turn on the ball game, Rick," Wendell demanded.

Eleven sixteen, and rolling northward on the highway. Not bad, not bad at all. Foresight. Now if he could only edge his way leftward to the southbound strip they'd be beyond the Santa Barbara bottleneck by two o'clock.

"The lights," exclaimed Molly, "the taps!"

Oh no, thought Mr Jimmon, not that too. Out of the comic strips.

"Keep calm," advised Jir. "Electricity and water are both off – remember?"

"I'm not quite an imbecile yet, Jir. I'm quite aware everything went off. I was thinking of the time it went back on."

"Furcrysay, Mom, you worrying about next month's bills *now*?"

Mr Jimmon, nudging the station wagon ever leftward formed the sentence: You'd never worry about bills, young man, because you never have to pay them. Instead of saying it aloud, he formed another sentence: Molly, your talent for irrelevance amounts to genius. Both sentences gave him satisfaction.

The traffic gathered speed briefly, and he took advantage of the spurt to get solidly in the left-hand lane, right against the long island of concrete dividing the north from the southbound strips. "That's using the old bean, Dad," approved Wendell.

Whatever slight pleasure he might have felt in his son's approbation was overlaid with exasperation. Wendell, like

Jir, was more Manville than Jimmon; they carried Molly's stamp on their faces and minds. Only Erika was a true Jimmon. Made in my own image, he thought pridelessly.

"I can't help but think it would have been at least courteous to get in touch with Pearl and Dan. At least *try*. And the Warbinns . . ."

The gap in the concrete divider came sooner than he anticipated and he was on the comparatively unclogged southbound side. His foot went down on the accelerator and the station wagon grumbled earnestly ahead. For the first time Mr Jimmon became aware how tightly he'd been gripping the wheel; how rigid the muscles in his arms, shoulders and neck had been. He relaxed part-way as he adjusted to the speed of the cars ahead and the speedometer needle hung just below 45, but resentment against Molly (at least courteous), Jir (no time for niceties), and Wendell (not to go), rode up in the saliva under his tongue. Dependent. Helpless. Everything on him. Parasites.

At intervals Erika switched on the radio. News was always promised immediately, but little was forthcoming, only vague, nervous attempts to minimize the extent of the disaster and soothe listeners with allusions to civilian defence, military activities on the ever-advancing front, and comparison with the destruction of Pittsburgh, so vastly much worse than the comparatively harmless detonation at Los Angeles. Must be pretty bad, thought Mr Jimmon; cripple the war effort . . .

"I'm hungry," said Wendell.

Molly began stirring around, instructing Jir where to find the sandwiches. Mr Jimmon thought grimly of how they'd have to adjust to the absence of civilized niceties: bread and mayonnaise and lunch meat. Live on rabbit, squirrel, abalone, fish. When Wendell grew hungry he'd have to get his own food. Self-sufficiency. Hard and tough.

At Oxnard the snarled traffic slowed them to a crawl again. Beyond, the juncture with the main highway north kept them at the same infuriating pace. It was long after two when they reached Ventura, and Wendell, who had been fidgeting and jumping up and down in the seat for the past hour, proclaimed, "I'm tired of riding."

Mr Jimmon set his lips. Molly suggested, ineffectually, "Why don't you lie down, dear?"

"Can't. Way this crate is packed, ain't room for a grasshopper."

"Verry funny. Verrrry funny," said Jir.

"Now, Jir, leave him alone! He's just a little boy."

At Carpenteria the sun burst out. You might have thought it the regular dissipation of the fog, only it was almost time for the fog to come down again. Should he try the San Marcos Pass after Santa Barbara, or the longer, better way? Flexible plans, but . . . Wait and see.

It was four when they got to Santa Barbara and Mr Jimmon faced concerted though disorganized rebellion. Wendell was screaming with stiffness and boredom; Jir remarked casually to no one in particular that Santa Barbara was the place they were going to beat the bottleneck oh yeh; Molly said, Stop at the first clean-looking gas station. Even Erika added, "Yes, Dad, you'll really have to stop."

Mr Jimmon was appalled. With every second priceless and hordes of panic-stricken refugees pressing behind, they would rob him of all the precious gains he'd made by skill, daring, judgement. Stupidity and shortsightedness. Unbelievable. For their own silly comfort – good lord, did they think they had a monopoly on bodily weaknesses? He was cramped as they and wanted to go as badly. Time and space which could never be made up. Let them lose this half-hour and it was quite likely they'd never get out of Santa Barbara.

"If we lose a half-hour now we'll never get out of here."

"Well, now, David, that wouldn't be utterly disastrous, would it? There are awfully nice hotels here and I'm sure it would be more comfortable for everyone than your idea of camping in the woods, hunting and fishing . . ."

He turned off State; couldn't remember the name of the parallel street, but surely less traffic. He controlled his temper, not heroically, but desperately. "May I ask how long you would propose to stay in one of these awfully nice hotels?"

"Why, until we could go home."

"My dear Molly . . ." What could he say? My dear Molly, we are never going home, if you mean Malibu? Or: My dear Molly, you just don't understand what is happening?

The futility of trying to convey the clear picture in his mind. Or any picture. If she could not of herself see the endless mob pouring, pouring out of Los Angeles, searching frenziedly for escape and refuge, eating up the substance of the surrounding country in ever-widening circles, crowding, jam-packing, overflowing every hotel, boarding-house, lodging, or private home into which they could edge, agonizedly bidding up the price of everything until the chaos they brought with them was indistinguishable from the chaos they were fleeing – if she could not see all this instantly and automatically, she could not be brought to see it at all. Any more than the other aimless, planless, improvident fugitives could see it.

So, my dear Molly; nothing.

Silence gave consent to continued expostulation. "David, do you really mean you don't intend to stop at all?"

Was there any point in saying, Yes I do? He set his lips still more tightly and once more weighed San Marcos Pass against the coast route. Have to decide now.

"Why, the time we're waiting here, just waiting for the cars up ahead to move would be enough."

Could you call her stupid? He weighed the question slowly and justly, alert for the first jerk of the massed cars all around. Her reasoning was valid and logical if the laws of physics and geometry were suspended. (Was that right – physics and geometry? Body occupying two different positions at the same time?) It was the facts which were illogical – not Molly. She was just exasperating.

By the time they were half-way to Gaviota or Goleta – Mr Jimmon could never tell them apart – foresight and relentless sternness began to pay off. Those who had left Los Angeles without preparation and in panic were dropping out or slowing down, to get gas or oil, repair tyres, buy food, seek rest rooms. The station wagon was steadily forging ahead.

He gambled on the old highway out of Santa Barbara. Any kind of obstruction would block its two lanes; if it didn't he would be beating the legions on the wider, straighter road. There were stretches now where he could hit 50; once he sped a happy half-mile at 65.

Now the insubordination crackling all around gave indication of simultaneous explosion. "I really," began Molly, and then discarded this for a fresher, firmer start. "David, I don't understand how you can be so utterly selfish and inconsiderate."

Mr Jimmon could feel the veins in his forehead begin to swell, but this was one of those rages that didn't show.

"But, Dad, would ten minutes ruin everything?" asked Erika.

"Monomania," muttered Jir. "Single track. Like Hitler."

"I want my dog," yelped Wendell. "Dirty old dog-killer."

"Did you ever hear of cumulative – " Erika had addressed him reasonably; surely he could make her understand? "Did you ever hear of cumulative . . ." What was the word? Snowball rolling downhill was the image in his mind. "Oh, what's the use?"

The old road rejoined the new; again the station wagon was fitted into the traffic like parquetry. Mr Jimmon, from an exultant, unfettered – almost – 65 was imprisoned in a treadmill set at 38. Keep calm; you can do nothing about it, he admonished himself. Need all your nervous energy. Must be wrecks up ahead. And then, with a return of satisfaction: if I hadn't used strategy back there we'd have been with those making 25. A starting-stopping 25.

"It's fantastic," exclaimed Molly. "I could almost believe Jir's right and you've lost your mind."

Mr Jimmon smiled. This was the first time Molly had ever openly showed disloyalty before the children or sided with them in their presence. She was revealing herself. Under pressure. Not the pressure of events; her incredible attitude at Santa Barbara had demonstrated her incapacity to feel that. Just pressure against the bladder.

"No doubt those left behind can console their last moments with pride in their sanity." The sentence came out perfectly formed, with none of the annoying pauses or interpolated "ers" or "mmphs" which could, as he knew from unhappy experience, flaw the most crushing rejoinders.

"Oh, the end can always justify the means for those who want it that way."

"Don't they restrain people – "

"That's enough, Jir!"

Trust Molly to return quickly to fundamental hypocrisy; the automatic response – his mind felicitously grasped the phrase, conditioned reflex – to the customary stimulus. She had taken an explicit stand against his common sense, but her rigid code – honour thy father; iron rayon the wrong side; register and vote; avoid scenes; only white wine with fish; never re-hire a discharged servant – quickly substituted pattern for impulse. Seventeen years.

The road turned away from the ocean, squirmed inland and uphill for still slower miles; abruptly widened into a divided, four lane highway. Without hesitation Mr Jimmon took the southbound side; for the first time since they had left Rambla Catalina his foot went down to the floorboards and with a sigh of relief the station wagon jumped into smooth, ecstatic speed.

Improvisation and strategy again. And, he acknowledged generously, the defiant example this morning of those who'd done the same thing in Malibu. Now, out of re-established habit the other cars kept to the northbound side even though there was nothing coming south. Timidity, routine, inertia. Pretty soon they would realize sheepishly that there was neither traffic nor traffic cops to keep them off, but it would be miles before they had another chance to cross over. By that time he would have reached the comparatively uncongested stretch.

"It's dangerous, David."

Obey the law. No smoking. Keep off the grass. Please adjust your clothes before leaving. Trespassers will be. Picking California wildflowers or shrubs is forbidden. Parking 45 min. Do not.

She hadn't put the protest in the more usual form of a question. Would that technique have been more irritating? Isn't it *dangerous*, Day-vid? His calm conclusion: it didn't matter.

"No time for niceties," chirped Jir.

Mr Jimmon tried to remember Jir as a baby. All the bad novels he had read in the days when he read anything except *Time* and the *New Yorker*, all the movies he'd seen before they had a TV set, always prescribed such retrospection as a specific for softening the present. If he could recall David Alonzo Jimmon, junior, at six months, helpless and lovable, it should make Jir more acceptable by discovering some faint traces of the one in the other.

But though he could recreate in detail the interminable, disgusting, trembling months of that initial pregnancy (had he really been afraid she would die?) he was completely unable to reconstruct the appearance of his first-born before the age of . . . It must have been at six that Jir had taken his baby sister out for a walk and lost her. (Had Molly permitted it? He still didn't know for sure.) Erika hadn't been found for four hours.

The tidal screeching of sirens invaded and destroyed his thoughts. What the devil . . .? His foot lifted from the gas pedal as he slewed obediently to the right, ingrained reverence surfacing at the sound.

"I told you it wasn't safe! Are you really trying to kill us all?"

Whipping over the rise ahead, a pair of motor-cycles crackled. Behind them snapped a long line of assorted vehicles, fire-trucks and ambulances mostly, interspersed here and there with olive drab army equipment. The cavalcade flicked down the central white line, one wheel in each lane. Mr Jimmon edged the station wagon as far over as he could; it still occupied too much room to permit the free passage of the onrush without compromise.

The knees and elbows of the motor-cycle policemen stuck out widely, reminding Mr Jimmon of grasshoppers. The one on the near side was headed straight for the station wagon's left front fender; for a moment Mr Jimmon closed his eyes as he plotted the unswerving course, knifing through the crust-like steel, bouncing lightly on the tyres, and continuing unperturbed. He opened them to see the other officer shoot past, mouth angrily open in his direction while the one straight ahead came to a skidding stop.

"Going to get it now," gloated Wendell.

An old-fashioned parent, one of the horrible examples held up to shuddering moderns like himself, would have reached back and relieved his tension by clouting Wendell across the mouth. Mr Jimmon merely turned off the motor.

The cop was not indulging in the customary deliberate and ominous performance of slowly dismounting and striding towards his victim with ever more menacing steps. Instead he got off quickly and covered the few feet to Mr Jimmon's window with unimpressive speed.

Heavy goggles concealed his eyes; dust and stubble covered his face. "Operator's licence!"

Mr Jimmon knew what he was saying, but the sirens and the continuous rustle of the convoy prevented the sound from coming through. Again the cop deviated from the established routine; he did not take the proffered licence and examine it incredulously before drawing out his pad and pencil, but wrote the citation, glancing up and down from the card in Mr Jimmon's hand.

Even so, the last of the vehicles – *San Jose F.D.* – passed before he handed the summons through the window to be signed. "Turn around and proceed in the proper direction," he ordered curtly, pocketing the pad and buttoning his jacket briskly.

Mr Jimmon nodded. The officer hesitated, as though waiting for some limp excuse. Mr Jimmon said nothing.

"No tricks," said the policeman over his shoulder. "Turn around and proceed in the proper direction."

He almost ran to his motor-cycle, and roared off, twisting his head for a final stern frown as he passed, siren wailing. Mr Jimmon watched him dwindle in the rear-view mirror and then started the motor. "Gonna lose a lot more than you gained," commented Jir.

Mr Jimmon gave a last glance in the mirror and moved ahead, shifting into second. "David!" exclaimed Molly horrified, "you're not turning around!"

"Observant," muttered Mr Jimmon, between his teeth.

"Dad, you can't get away with it," Jir decided judicially.

Mr Jimmon's answer was to press the accelerator down savagely. The empty highway stretched invitingly ahead; a few hundred yards to their right they could see the north-bound lanes ant-clustered. The sudden motion stirred the traffic citation on his lap, floating it down to the floor. Erika leaned forward and picked it up.

"Throw it away," ordered Mr Jimmon.

Molly gasped. "You're out of your mind."

"You're a fool," stated Mr Jimmon calmly. "Why should I save that piece of paper?"

"Isn't what you told the cop." Jir was openly jeering now.

"I might as well have, if I'd wanted to waste conversation. I don't know why I was blessed with such a stupid family – "

"May be something in heredity after all."

If Jir had said it out loud, reflected Mr Jimmon, it would have passed casually as normal domestic repartee, a little ill-natured perhaps, certainly callow and trite, but not especially provocative. Muttered, so that it was barely audible, it was an ultimate defiance. He had read that far back in pre-history, when the young males felt their strength, they sought to overthrow the rule of the Old Man and usurp his place. No doubt they uttered a preliminary growl or screech as challenge. They were not very bright, but they acted in a pattern; a pattern Jir was apparently following.

Refreshed by placing Jir in proper Neanderthal setting, Mr Jimmon went on, "– None of you seem to have the slightest initiative or ability to grasp reality. Tickets, cops, judges, juries mean nothing any more. There is no law now but the law of survival."

"Aren't you being dramatic, David?" Molly's tone was deliberately aloof, adult to excited child.

"I could hear you underline words, Dad," said Erika, but he felt there was no malice in her gibe.

"You mean we can do anything we want now? Shoot people? Steal cars and things?" asked Wendell.

"There, David! You see?"

Yes, I see. Better than you. Little savage. This is the pattern. What will Wendell – and the thousands of other Wendells (for it would be unjust to suppose Molly's genes and domestic influence unique) – be like after six months of anarchy? Or after six years?

Survivors, yes. And that will be about all: naked, primitive, ferocious, superstitious savages. Wendell can read and write (but not so fluently as I or any of our generation at his age); how long will he retain the tags and scraps of progressive schooling?

And Jir? Detachedly Mr Jimmon foresaw the fate of Jir. Unlike Wendell, who would adjust to the new conditions, Jir would go wild in another sense. His values were already set; they were those of television, high school dating, comic strips, law and order. Released from civilization, his brief future would be one of guilty rape and pillage until he fell victim to another youth or gang bent the same way. Molly would disintegrate and perish quickly. Erika . . .

The station wagon flashed along the comparatively unimpeded highway. Having passed the next crossover, there were now other vehicles on the southbound strip, but even on the northbound one, crowding had eased.

Furiously Mr Jimmon determined to preserve the civilization in Erika. (He would teach her everything he knew (including the insurance business?)) . . . ah, if he were some kind of scientist, now – not the Dan Davisson kind, whose abstract speculations seemed always to prepare the way for some new method of destruction, but the . . . Franklin? Jefferson? Watt? Protect her night and day from the refugees who would be roaming the hills south of Monteray. The rifle ammunition, properly used – and he would see that no one but himself used it – would last years. After it was gone – presuming fragments and pieces of a suicidal world hadn't pulled itself miraculously together to offer a place to return to – there were the two hunting bows whose steel-tipped shafts could stop a man as easily as a deer or mountain lion. He remembered debating long, at the time he had first begun preparing for It, how many bows to order, measuring their weight and bulk against the other precious freight and deciding at last that two was the satisfactory minimum. It must have been in his subconscious mind all along that of the whole family Erika was the only other person who could be trusted with a bow.

"There will be – " he spoke in calm and solemn tones, not to Wendell, whose question was now left long behind, floating on the gas-greasy air of a sloping valley growing with live-oaks, but to a larger, impalpable audience, "– there will be others who will think that because there is no longer law or law enforcement – "

"You're being simply fantastic!" She spoke more sharply than he had ever heard her in front of the children. "Just because It happened to Los Angeles – "

"And Pittsburgh."

"All right. And Pittsburgh, doesn't mean that the whole United States has collapsed and everyone in the country is running frantically for safety."

"Yet," added Mr Jimmon firmly, "yet, do you suppose they are going to stop with Los Angeles and Pittsburgh, and leave Gary and Seattle standing? Or even New York and Chicago? Or do you imagine Washington will beg for armistice terms while there is the least sign of organized life left in the country?"

"We'll wipe Them out first," insisted Jir in patriotic shock. Wendell backed him up with a machine gun "Brrrrr".

"Undoubtedly. But it will be the last gasp. At any rate it will be years, if at all in my lifetime, before stable communities are re-established – "

"David, you're raving."

"Re-established," he repeated. "So there will be many others who'll also feel that the dwindling of law and order is license to kill people and steal cars 'and things'. Naked force and cunning will be the only means of self-preservation. That was why I picked out a spot where I felt survival would be easiest; not only because of wood and water, game and fish, but because it's nowhere near the main highways, and so unlikely to be chosen by any great number."

"I wish you'd stop harping on that insane idea. You're just a little too old and flabby for pioneering. Even when you were younger you were hardly the rugged, outdoor type."

No, thought Mr Jimmon, I was the sucker type. I would have gotten somewhere if I'd stayed in the bank, but like a bawd you pleaded; the insurance business brought in the quick money for you to give up your job and have Jir and the proper home. If you'd got rid of it as I wanted. Flabby, *flabby*! Do you think your scrawniness is so enticing?

Controlling himself, he said aloud, "We've been through all this. Months ago. It's not a question of physique, but of life."

"Nonsense. Perfect nonsense. Responsible people who really know its effects . . . Maybe it was advisable to leave Malibu for a few days or even a few weeks. And perhaps it's wise to stay away from the larger cities. But a small town or village, or even one of those ranches where they take boarders.

"Aw, Mom, you agreed. You know you did. What's the matter with you anyway? Why are you acting like a drip?"

"I want to go and shoot rabbits and bears like Dad said," insisted Wendell.

Erika said nothing, but Mr Jimmon felt he had her sympathy; the boys' agreement was specious. Wearily he debated going over the whole ground again, patiently pointing out that what Molly said might work in the Dakotas or the Great Smokies but was hardly operative anywhere within refugee range of the Pacific Coast. He had explained all this many times, including the almost certain impossibility of getting enough gasoline to take them into any of the reasonably safe areas; that was why they'd agreed on the region below Monterey, on California State Highway I, as the only logical goal.

A solitary car decorously bound in the legal direction interrupted his thoughts. Either crazy or has mighty important business, he decided. The car honked disapprovingly as it passed, hugging the extreme right side of the road.

Passing through Buellton the clamour again rose for a pause at a filling station. He conceded inwardly that he could afford ten or fifteen minutes without strategic loss since by now they must be among the leaders of the exodus; ahead lay little more than the normal travel. However, he had reached such a state of irritated frustration and consciousness of injustice that he was willing to endure unnecessary discomfort himself in order to inflict a longer delay on them. In fact it lessened his own suffering to know the delay was needless, that he was doing it, and that his action was a just – if inadequate – punishment.

"We'll stop this side of Santa Maria," he said. "I'll get gas there."

Mr Jimmon knew triumph: his forethought, his calculations, his generalship had justified themselves. Barring unlikely mechanical failure – the station wagon was in perfect shape – or accident – and the greatest danger had certainly passed – escape was now practically assured. For the first time he permitted himself to realize how unreal, how romantic the whole project had been. As any attempt to evade the fate charted for the multitude must be. The docile mass perished; the headstrong (but intelligent) individual survived.

Along with triumph went an expansion of his prophetic vision of life after reaching their destination. He had purposely not taxed the cargo capacity of the wagon with transitional goods; there was no tent, canned luxuries, sleeping bags, lanterns, candles, or any of the paraphernalia of camping midway between the urban and nomadic life. Instead, besides the weapons, tackle, and utensils, there was in miniature the List For Life On A Desert Island: shells and cartridges, lures, hooks, nets, gut, leaders, flint and steel, seeds, traps, needles and thread, government pamphlets on curing and tanning hides and the recognition of edible weeds and fungi, files, nails, a judicious stock of simple medicines. A pair of binoculars to spot intruders. No coffee, sugar, flour; they would begin living immediately as they would have to in a month or so in any case, on the old, half-forgotten human cunning.

"Cunning," he said aloud.

"What?"

"Nothing. Nothing."

"I still think you should have made an effort to reach Pearl and Dan."

"The telephone was dead, Mother."

"At the moment, Erika. You can hardly have forgotten how often the lines have been down before. And it never takes more than half an hour till they're working again."

"Mother, Dan Davisson is quite capable of looking after himself."

Mr Jimmon shut out the rest of the conversation so completely he didn't know whether there was any more to it or not. He shut out the intense preoccupation with driving, with making speed, with calculating possible gains. In the core of his mind, quite detached from everything about him, he examined and marvelled.

Erika. The cool, inflexible, adult tone. Almost indulgent, but so dispassionate as not to be. One might have expected her to be exasperated by Molly's silliness, to have answered impatiently, or not at all.

Mother. Never in his recollection had the children ever called her anything but Mom. The "Mother" implied – oh, it implied a multitude of things. An entirely new relationship, for one. A relationship of aloofness, or propriety without emotion. The ancient stump of the umbilical cord, black and shrivelled, had dropped off painlessly.

She had not bothered to argue about the telephone or point out the gulf between "before" and now. She had not even tried to touch Molly's deepening refusal of reality. She had been . . . indulgent.

Not "Uncle Dan", twitteringly imposed false avuncularity, but striking through it (and the façade of "Pearl and")

and aside (when I was a child I . . . something . . . but now I have put aside childish things); the wealth of implicit assertion. As yes, Mother, we all know the pardonable weakness and vanity; we excuse you for your constant reminders, but Mother, with all deference, we refuse to be forced any longer to be parties to middle age's nostalgic flirtatiousness. One could almost feel sorry for Molly.

. . . middle age's nostalgic flirtatiousness . . .

. . . *nostalgic* . . .

Metaphorically Mr Jimmon sat abruptly upright. The fact that he was already physically in this position made the transition, while invisible, no less emphatic. The nostalgic flirtatiousness of middle age implied – might imply – memory of something more than mere coquetry. Molly and Dan.

It all fitted together so perfectly it was impossible to believe it untrue. The impecunious young lovers, equally devoted to Dan's genius, realizing marriage was out of the question (he had never denied Molly's shrewdness; as for Dan's impracticality, well, impracticality wasn't necessarily uniform or consistent. Dan had been practical enough to marry Pearl and Pearl's money) could have renounced . . .

Or not renounced at all?

Mr Jimmon smiled; the thought did not ruffle him. Cuckoo, cuckoo. How vulgar, how absurd. Suppose Jir were Dan's? A blessed thought.

Regretfully he conceded the insuperable obstacle of Molly's conventionality. Jir was the product of his own loins. But wasn't there an old superstition about the image in the woman's mind at the instant of conception? So, justly and rightly Jir was not his. Nor Wendell, for that matter. Only Erika, by some accident. Mr Jimmon felt free and lighthearted.

"Get gas at the next station," he bulletined.

"The next one with a clean rest room," Molly corrected.

Invincible. The Earth-Mother, using men for her purposes: reproduction, clean rest rooms, nourishment, objects of culpability, *Homes and Gardens*. The bank was my life; I could have gone far but: Why, David – they pay you less than the janitor! It's ridiculous. And: I can't understand why you hesitate; it isn't as though it were a different type of work.

No, not different; just more profitable. Why didn't she tell Dan Davisson to become an accountant; that was the same type of work, just more profitable? Perhaps she had and Dan had simply been less befuddled. Or amenable. Or stronger in purpose? Mr Jimmon probed his pride thoroughly and relentlessly without finding the faintest twinge of retrospective jealousy. Nothing like that mattered now. Nor, he admitted, had it for years.

Two close-peaked hills gulped the sun. He toyed with the idea of crossing over to the northbound side now that it was uncongested and there were occasional southbound cars. Before he could decide the divided highway ended.

"I hope you're not planning to spend the night in some horrible motel," said Molly. "I want a decent bath and a good dinner."

Spend the night. Bath. Dinner. Again calm sentences formed in his mind, but they were blown apart by the unbelievable, the monumental obtuseness. How could you say, It is absolutely essential to drive till we get there? When there were no absolutes, no essentials in her concepts? My dear Molly, I.

"No," he said, switching on the lights.

Wendy, he knew, would be the next to kick up a fuss. Till he fell mercifully asleep. If he did. Jir was probably debating the relative excitements of driving all night and stopping in a strange town. His voice would soon be heard.

The lights of the combination wayside store and filling-station burned inefficiently, illuminating the deteriorating false-front brightly and leaving the gas pumps in shadow. Swallowing regret at finally surrendering to mechanical and human need, and so losing the hard-won position; relaxing, even for a short while, the fierce initiative that had brought them through in the face of all probability; he pulled the station wagon alongside the pumps and shut off the motor. About half-way – the worst half, much the worst half – to their goal. Not bad.

Molly opened the door on her side with stiff dignity. "I certainly wouldn't call this a *clean* station." She waited for a moment, hand still on the window, as though expecting an answer.

"Crummy joint," exclaimed Wendell, clambering awkwardly out.

"Why not?" asked Jir. "No time for niceties." He brushed past his mother who was walking slowly into the shadows.

"Erika," began Mr Jimmon, in a half-whisper.

"Yes, Dad?"

"Oh . . . never mind. Later."

He was not himself quite sure what he had wanted to say; what exclusive, urgent message he had to convey. For no particular reason he switched on the interior light and glanced at the packed orderliness of the wagon. Then he slid out from behind the wheel.

No sign of the attendant, but the place was certainly not closed. Not with the lights on and the hoses ready. He stretched, and walked slowly, savouring the comfortably painful uncramping of his muscles, towards the crude out-house labelled "Men". Molly, he thought, must be furious.

When he returned, a man was leaning against the station wagon. "Fill it up with ethyl," said Mr Jimmon pleasantly, "and check the oil and water."

The man made no move. "That'll be five bucks a gallon." Mr Jimmon thought there was an uncertain tremor in his voice.

"Nonsense; I've plenty of ration coupons."

"Okay." The nervousness was gone now, replaced by an ugly truculence. "Chew'm up and spit'm in your gas tank. See how far you can run on them."

The situation was not unanticipated. Indeed, Mr Jimmon thought with satisfaction of how much worse it must be closer to Los Angeles; how much harder the gouger would be on later supplicants as his supply of gasoline dwindled. "Listen," he said, and there was reasonableness rather than anger in his voice, "we're not out of gas. I've got enough to get to Santa Maria, even to San Luis Obispo."

"Okay. Go on then. Ain't stopping you."

"Listen. I understand your position. You have a right to make a profit in spite of government red tape."

Nervousness returned to the man's speech. "Look, whyn't you go on? There's plenty other stations up ahead."

The reluctant bandit. Mr Jimmon was entertained. He had fully intended to bargain, to offer $2 a gallon, even to threaten with the pistol in the glove compartment. Now it seemed mean and niggling even to protest. What good was money now? "All right," he said, "I'll pay you $5 a gallon."

Still the other made no move. "In advance."

For the first time Mr Jimmon was annoyed; time was being wasted. "Just how can I pay you in advance when I don't know how many gallons it'll take to fill the tank?"

The man shrugged.

"Tell you what I'll do. I'll pay for each gallon as you pump it. In advance." He drew out a handful of bills; the bulk of his money was in his wallet, but he'd put the small bills in his pockets. He handed over a five. "Spill the first one on the ground or in a can if you've got one."

"How's that?"

Why should I tell him; give him ideas? As if he hadn't got them already. "Just call me eccentric," he said. "I don't want the first gallon from the pump. Why should you care? It's just five dollars more profit."

For a moment Mr Jimmon thought the man was going to refuse, and he regarded his foresight with new reverence. Then he reached behind the pump and produced a flat-sided tin in which he inserted the flexible end of the hose. Mr Jimmon handed over the bill, the man wound the handle round and back – it was an ancient gas pump such as Mr Jimmon hadn't seen for years – and lifted the drooling hose from the can.

"Minute," said Mr Jimmon.

He stuck two fingers quickly and delicately inside the nozzle and smelled them. Gas all right, not water. He held out a ten-dollar bill. "Start filling."

Jir and Wendell appeared out of the shadows. "Can we stop at a town where there's a movie tonight?"

The handle turned, a cog-toothed rod crept up and retreated, gasoline gurgled into the tank. Movies, thought Mr Jimmon, handing over another bill; movies, rest rooms, baths, restaurants. Gouge apprehensively lest a scene be made and propriety disturbed. In a surrealist daydream he saw Molly turning the crank, grinding him on the cogs, pouring his essence into insatiable Jir and Wendell. He held out $20.

Twelve gallons had been put in when Molly appeared. "You have a phone here?" he asked casually. Knowing the answer from the blue enamelled sign not quite lost among less sturdy ones advertising soft drinks and cigarettes.

"You want to call the cops?" He didn't pause in his pumping.

"No. Know if the lines to L.A." – Mr Jimmon loathed the abbreviation – "are open yet?" He gave him another ten.

"How should I know?"

Mr Jimmon beckoned his wife around the other side of the wagon, out of sight. Swiftly but casually he extracted the contents of his wallet. The 200 dollar bills made a fat lump. "Put this in your bag," he said. "Tell you why later.

118

Meantime why don't you try and get Pearl and Dan on the phone? See if they're okay?"

He imagined the puzzled look on her face. "Go on," he urged. "We can spare a minute while he's checking the oil."

He thought there was a hint of uncertainty in Molly's walk as she went towards the store. Erika joined her brothers. The tank gulped: gasoline splashed on the concrete. "Guess that's it."

The man became suddenly brisk as he put up the hose, screwed the gas cap back on. Mr Jimmon had already disengaged the hood; the man offered the radiator a squirt of water, pulled up the oil gauge, wiped it, plunged it down, squinted at it under the light, and said, "Oil's OK."

"All right," said Mr Jimmon. "Get in Erika."

Some of the light shone directly on her face. Again he noted how mature and self-assured she looked. Erika would survive – and not as a savage either. The man started to wipe the windshield. "Oh, Jir," he said casually, "run in and see if your mother is getting her connexion. Tell her we'll wait."

"Aw furcrysay. I don't see why I always – "

"And ask her to buy a couple of boxes of candy bars if they've got them. Wendell, go with Jir, will you?"

He slid in behind the wheel and closed the door gently. The motor started with hardly a sound. As he put his foot on the clutch and shifted into low he thought Erika turned to him with a startled look. As the station wagon moved forward, he was sure of it.

"It's all right, Erika," said Mr Jimmon, "I'll explain later." He'd have lots of time to do it.

2001: A SPACE ODYSSEY

(MGM, 1968)
Starring: Keir Dullea, Gary Lockwood
& William Sylvester
Directed by Stanley Kubrick
Script by Arthur C. Clarke from his story
"Sentinel of Eternity"

Few other films have had quite such an impact on movie history in general or been more influential on the Space Movies genre in particular than Stanley Kubrick's visually overwhelming *2001: A Space Odyssey* which, a quarter of a century after it was made, still remains the benchmark against which all pictures of this kind are judged. It was by far the most ambitious SF film of its time and by spanning human history from prehistoric times to the year 2001 emphasised that man was still very much in the infancy of his development and was, in all probability, the "property" of vastly superior alien intelligences. But human beings were not actually at the core of the story – that distinction belonged to a space ship's super-computer, HAL 9000, which increasingly ran amok during the course of the journey, killing all the astronauts bar one before it reached the appointed rendezvous with an alien sentinel. HAL's demise during the climax to the picture has been called "one of the longest and most poignant death scenes in film history" (*The Times*) and actually won the superbrain – whose voice was that of actor Douglas Rain – an Oscar. Although *2001* was very much Kubrick's vision and he was responsible for many of the picture's remarkable innovations, the special effects owed a great deal to the team of Douglas Trumbell, a veteran of space documentary, and his fellow film technicians, Wally Veevers, Con Pederson and Tom Howard. This monumental film actually

**originated from a brief story, "The Sentinel of Eternity" by
Arthur C. Clarke (1917–), the English-born SF writer who
has been lavished with awards for his best-selling novels and
praised by scientists for the prescience of his ideas. Clarke
used the tale – which he had originally published in *10 Story
Fantasy* in September 1951 – as the basis for his script which
he worked on in 1966; but he was thereafter little involved in
the lengthy and extremely costly filming of the picture during
the next two years when Kubrick gave full vent to his
imagination and skill as a film maker to create a wholly
believable space voyage to Jupiter. Audiences around the
world had seen nothing like the wonders he brought to the
screen – and movie special effects, also, have never been the
same since.**

The next time you see the full moon high in the South, look
carefully at its right-hand edge and let your eye travel
upwards along the curve of the disc. Round about 2
o'clock you will notice a small, dark oval; anyone with
normal eyesight can find it quite easily. It is the great walled
plain, one of the finest on the Moon, known as the Mare
Crisium – the Sea of Crises. Three hundred miles in
diameter, and almost completely surrounded by a ring of
magnificent mountains, it had never been explored until we
entered it in the late summer of 1996.

Our expedition was a large one. We had two heavy
freighters which had flown our supplies and equipment
from the main lunar base in the Mare Serenitatis, five
hundred miles away. There were also three small rockets
which were intended for short-range transport over regions
which our surface vehicles couldn't cross. Luckily, most of
the Mare Crisium is very flat. There are none of the great
crevasses so common and so dangerous elsewhere, and very
few craters or mountains of any size. As far as we could tell,
our powerful caterpillar tractors would have no difficulty in
taking us wherever we wished.

I was geologist – or selenologist, if you want to be pedantic – in charge of the group exploring the southern region of the Mare. We had crossed a hundred miles of it in a week, skirting the foothills of the mountains along the shore of what was once the ancient sea, some thousand million years before. When life was beginning on Earth, it was already dying here. The waters were retreating down the flanks of those stupendous cliffs, retreating into the empty heart of the Moon. Over the land which we were crossing, the tideless ocean had once been half a mile deep, and now the only trace of moisture was the hoarfrost one could sometimes find in caves which the searing sunlight never penetrated.

We had begun our journey early in the slow lunar dawn, and still had almost a week of Earth-time before nightfall. Half a dozen times a day we would leave our vehicle and go outside in the spacesuits to hunt for interesting minerals, or to place markers for the guidance of future travellers. It was an uneventful routine. There is nothing hazardous or even particularly exciting about lunar exploration. We could live comfortably for a month in our pressurized tractors, and if we ran into trouble we could always radio for help and sit tight until one of the spaceships came to our rescue. When that happened there was always a frightful outcry about the waste of rocket fuel, so a tractor sent out an SOS only in a real emergency.

I said just now that there was nothing exciting about lunar exploration, but of course that isn't true. One could never grow tired of those incredible mountains, so much steeper and more rugged than the gentle hills of Earth. We never knew, as we rounded the capes and promontories of that vanished sea, what new splendors would be revealed to us. The whole southern curve of the Mare Crisium is a vast delta where a score of rivers had once found their way into the ocean, fed perhaps by the torrential rains that must have lashed the mountains in the brief volcanic age when the Moon was young. Each of these ancient valleys was an invitation, challenging us to climb into the unknown uplands beyond. But we had a hundred miles still to cover, and could only look longingly at the heights which others must scale.

We kept Earth-time aboard the tractor, and precisely at 22.00 hours the final radio message would be sent out to Base and we would close down for the day. Outside, the rocks would still be burning beneath the almost vertical sun, but to us it was night until we awoke again eight hours later. Then one of us would prepare breakfast, there would be a great buzzing of electric shavers, and someone would switch on the short-wave radio from Earth. Indeed, when the smell of frying bacon began to fill the cabin, it was sometimes hard to believe that we were not back on our own world – everything was so normal and homey, apart from the feeling of decreased weight and the unnatural slowness with which objects fell.

It was my turn to prepare breakfast in the corner of the main cabin that served as a galley. I can remember that moment quite vividly after all these years, for the radio had just played one of my favourite melodies, the old Welsh air, *David of the White Rock*. Our driver was already outside in his spacesuit, inspecting our caterpillar treads. My assistant, Louis Garnett, was up forward in the control position, making some belated entries in yesterday's log.

As I stood by the frying pan, waiting, like any terrestrial housewife, for the sausages to brown, I let my gaze wander idly over the mountain walls which covered the whole of the southern horizon, marching out of sight to east and west below the curve of the Moon. They seemed only a mile or two from the tractor, but I knew that the nearest was twenty miles away. On the Moon, of course, there is no loss of detail with distance – none of that almost imperceptible haziness which softens and sometimes transfigures all far-off things on Earth.

Those mountains were ten thousand feet high, and they climbed steeply out of the plain as if ages ago some subterranean eruption had smashed them skywards through the molten crust. The base of even the nearest was hidden from sight by the steeply curving surface of the plain, for the Moon is a very little world, and from where I was standing the optical horizon was only two miles away.

I lifted my eyes towards the peaks which no man had ever climbed, the peaks which, before the coming of Terrestrial life, had watched the retreating oceans sink sullenly into their graves, taking with them the hope and the morning promise of a world. The sunlight was beating against those ramparts with a glare that hurt the eyes, yet only a little way above them the stars were shining steadily in a sky blacker than a winter midnight on Earth.

I was turning away when my eye caught a metallic glitter high on the ridge of a great promontory thrusting out into the sea thirty miles to the west. It was a dimensionless point of light, as if a star had been clawed from the sky by one of those cruel peaks, and I imagined that some smooth rock surface was catching the sunlight and heliographing it straight into my eyes. Such things were not uncommon. When the Moon is in her second quarter, observers on Earth can sometimes see the great ranges in the Oceanus Procellarum burning with a blue-white iridescence as the sunlight flashes from their slopes and leaps again from world to world. But I was curious to know what kind of rock could be shining so brightly up there, and I climbed into the observation turret and swung our four inch telescope round to the west.

I could see just enough to tantalize me. Clear and sharp in the field of vision, the mountain peaks seemed only half a mile away, but whatever was catching the sunlight was still too small to be resolved. Yet it seemed to have an elusive symmetry, and the summit upon which it rested was curiously flat. I stared for a long time at that glittering enigma, straining my eyes into space, until presently a smell of burning from the galley told me that our breakfast sausages had made their quarter-million mile journey in vain.

All that morning we argued our way across the Mare Crisium while the western mountains reared higher in the sky. Even when we were out prospecting in the spacesuits, the discussion would continue over the radio. It was absolutely certain, my companions argued, that there had never been any form of intelligent life on the Moon. The only living things that had ever existed there were a few primitive plants and their slightly less degenerate ancestors. I knew that as well as anyone, but there are times when a scientist must not be afraid to make a fool of himself.

"Listen," I said at last, "I'm going up there, if only for my own peace of mind. That mountain's less than twelve thousand feet high – that's only two thousand under Earth gravity – and I can make the trip in twenty hours at the outside. I've always wanted to go up into those hills, anyway, and this gives me an excellent excuse."

"If you don't break your neck," said Garnett, "you'll be the laughing-stock of the expedition when we get back to Base. That mountain will probably be called Wilson's Folly from now on."

"I *won't* break my neck," I said firmly. "Who was the first man to climb Pico and Helicon?"

"But weren't you rather younger in those days?" asked Louis gently.

"That," I said with great dignity, "is as good a reason as any for going."

We went to bed early that night, after driving the tractor to within half a mile of the promontory. Garnett was coming with me in the morning; he was a good climber, and had often been with me on such exploits before. Our driver was only too glad to be left in charge of the machine.

At first sight, those cliffs seemed completely unscalable, but to anyone with a good head for heights, climbing is easy on a world where all weights are only a sixth of their normal value. The real danger in lunar mountaineering lies in overconfidence; a six hundred foot drop on the Moon can kill you just as thoroughly as a hundred foot fall on Earth.

We made our first half on a wide ledge about four thousand feet above the plain. Climbing had not been very difficult, but my limbs were stiff with the unaccustomed effort, and I was glad of the rest. We could still see the tractor as a tiny metal insect far down at the foot of the cliff, and we reported our progress to the driver before starting on the next ascent.

Hour by hour the horizon widened and more and more of the great plain came into sight. Now we could look for fifty miles out across the Mare, and could even see the peaks of the mountains on the opposite coast more than a hundred miles away. Few of the great lunar plains are as smooth as the Mare Crisium, and we could almost imagine that a sea of water and not of rock was lying there two miles below. Only a group of crater-pits low down on the skyline spoilt the illusion.

Our goal was still invisible over the crest of the mountain, and we were steering by maps, using the Earth as a guide. Almost due east of us, that great silver crescent hung low over the plain, already well into its first quarter. The sun and the stars would make their slow march across the sky and would sink presently from sight but Earth would always be there never moving from her appointed place, waxing and waning as the year and seasons passed. In ten days' time she would be a blinding disc bathing these rocks with her midnight radiance, fifty-fold brighter than the full moon. But we must be out of the mountains long before night, or else we would remain among them forever.

Inside our suits it was comfortably cool, for the refrigeration units were fighting the fierce sun and carrying away the body-heat of our exertions. We seldom spoke to each other, except to pass climbing instructions and to discuss our best plan of ascent. I do not know what Garnett was thinking, probably that this was the craziest goose-chase he had ever embarked upon. I more than half agreed with him, but the joy of climbing, the knowledge that no man had ever gone this way before and the exhilaration of the steadily widening landscape gave me all the reward I needed.

I don't think I was particularly excited when I saw in front of us the wall of rock I had first inspected through the telescope from thirty miles away. It would level off about fifty feet above our heads, and there on the plateau would be the thing that had lured me over these barren wastes. It was, almost certainly, nothing more than a boulder splintered ages ago by a falling meteor, and with its cleavage planes still fresh and bright in this incorruptible unchanging silence.

There were no hand-holds on the rock face, and we had to use a grapnel. My tired arms seemed to gain new strength as I swung the three-pronged metal anchor round my head and sent it sailing up towards the stars. The first time, it broke loose and came falling slowly back when we pulled the rope. On the third attempt, the prongs gripped firmly and our combined weights could not shift it.

Garnett looked at me anxiously. I could tell that he wanted to go first, but I smiled back at him through the glass of my helmet and shook my head. Slowly, taking my time, I began the final ascent.

Even with my spacesuit, I weighed only forty pounds here, so I pulled myself up hand over hand without bothering to use my feet. At the rim I paused and waved to my companion, then I scrambled over the edge and stood upright, staring ahead of me.

You must understand that until this very moment I had been almost completely convinced that there could be nothing strange or unusual for me to find here. Almost, but not quite; it was that haunting doubt that had driven me forwards. Well, it was a doubt no longer, but the haunting had scarcely begun.

I was standing on a plateau perhaps a hundred feet across. It had once been smooth – too smooth to be natural – but falling meteors had pitted and scored its surface through immeasurable aeons. It had been levelled to support a glittering, roughly pyramidal structure, twice as high as a man, that was set in the rock like a gigantic, many-faceted jewel.

Probably no emotion at all filled my mind in those first few seconds. Then I felt a great lifting of my heart, and a strange, inexpressible joy. For I loved the Moon, and now I knew that the creeping moss of Aristarchus and Eratosthenes was not the only life she had brought forth in her youth. The old, discredited dream of the first explorers was true. There had, after all, been a lunar civilization – and I was the first to find it. That I had come perhaps a hundred million years too late did not distress me; it was enough to have come at all.

My mind was beginning to function normally, to analyze and to ask questions. Was this a building, a shrine – or something for which my language had no name? If a building, then why was it erected in so uniquely inaccessible a spot? I wondered if it might be a temple, and I could picture the adepts of some strange priesthood calling on their gods to preserve them as the life of the Moon ebbed with the dying oceans, and calling on their gods in vain.

I took a dozen steps forward to examine the thing more closely, but some sense of caution kept me from going too near. I knew a little of archaeology, and tried to guess the cultural level of the civilization that must have smoothed this mountain and raised the glittering mirror surfaces that still dazzled my eyes.

The Egyptians could have done it, I thought, if their workmen had possessed whatever strange materials these far more ancient architects had used. Because of the thing's smallness, it did not occur to me that I might be looking at the handiwork of a race more advanced than my own. The idea that the Moon had possessed intelligence at all was still almost too tremendous to grasp, and my pride would not let me take the final, humiliating plunge.

And then I noticed something that set the scalp crawling at the back of my neck – something so trivial and so innocent that many would never have noticed it at all. I have said that the plateau was scarred by meteors; it was also coated inches deep with the cosmic dust that is always filtering down upon the surface of any world where there are no winds to disturb it. Yet the dust and the meteor scratches ended quite abruptly in a wide circle enclosing the little pyramid, as though an invisible wall was protecting it from the ravages of time and the slow but ceaseless bombardment from space.

There was someone shouting in my earphones, and I realized that Garnett had been calling me for some time. I walked unsteadily to the edge of the cliff and signalled him to join me, not trusting myself to speak. Then I went back towards that circle in the dust. I picked up a fragment of splintered rock and tossed it gently towards the shining enigma. If the pebble had vanished at that invisible barrier I should not have been surprised, but it seemed to hit a smooth, hemispherical surface and slid gently to the ground.

I knew then that I was looking at nothing that could be matched in the antiquity of my own race. This was not a building, but a machine, protecting itself with forces that had challenged Eternity. Those forces, whatever they might be, were still operating, and perhaps I had already come too close. I thought of all the radiations man had trapped and tamed in the past century. For all I knew, I might be as irrevocably doomed as if I had stepped into the deadly, silent aura of an unshielded atomic pile.

I remember turning then towards Garnett, who had joined me and was now standing motionless at my side. He seemed quite oblivious to me, so I did not disturb him but walked to the edge of the cliff in an effort to marshal my thoughts. There below me lay the Mare Crisium — Sea of Crises, indeed — strange and weird to most men, but reassuringly familiar to me. I lifted my eyes towards the crescent Earth, lying in her cradle of stars, and I wondered what her clouds had covered when these unknown builders had finished their work. Was it the steaming jungle of the Carboniferous, the bleak shoreline over which the first amphibians must crawl to conquer the land — or, earlier still, the long loneliness before the coming of life?

Do not ask me why I did not guess the truth sooner — the truth that seems so obvious now. In the first excitement of my discovery, I had assumed without question that this crystalline apparition had been built by some race belonging to the Moon's remote past, but suddenly, and with overwhelming force, the belief came to me that it was as alien to the Moon as I myself.

In twenty years we had found no trace of life but a few degenerate plants. No lunar civilization, whatever its doom, could have left but a single token of its existence.

I looked at the shining pyramid again, and the more remote it seemed from anything that had to do with the Moon. And suddenly I felt myself shaking with a foolish, hysterical laughter, brought on by excitement and over-exertion: for I had imagined that the little pyramid was speaking to me and was saying: "Sorry, I'm a stranger here myself."

It has taken us twenty years to crack that invisible shield and to reach the machine inside those crystal walls. What we could not understand, we broke at last with the savage might of atomic power and now I have seen the fragments of the lovely, glittering thing I found up there on the mountain.

They are meaningless. The mechanisms – if indeed they are mechanisms – of the pyramid belong to a technology that lies far beyond our horizon, perhaps to the technology of para-physical forces.

The mystery haunts us all the more now that the other planets have been reached and we know that only Earth has ever been the home of intelligent life. Nor could any lost civilization of our own world have built that machine, for the thickness of the meteoric dust on the plateau has enabled us to measure its age. It was set there upon its mountain before life had emerged from the seas of Earth.

When our world was half its present age, *something* from the stars swept through the Solar System, left this token of its passage, and went again upon its way. Until we destroyed it, that machine was still fulfilling the purpose of its builders; and as to that purpose, here is my guess.

Nearly a hundred thousand million stars are turning in the circle of the Milky Way, and long ago other races on the worlds of other suns must have scaled and passed the heights that we have reached. Think of such civilizations, far back in time against the fading afterglow of Creation, masters of a universe so young that life as yet had come only to a handful of worlds. Theirs would have been a loneliness we cannot imagine, the loneliness of gods looking out across infinity and finding none to share their thoughts.

They must have searched the star-clusters as we have searched the planets. Everywhere there would be worlds, but they would be empty or peopled with crawling, mindless things. Such was our own Earth, the smoke of the great volcanoes still staining its skies, when that first ship of the peoples of the dawn came sliding in from the abyss beyond Pluto. It passed the frozen outer worlds, knowing that life could play no part in their destinies. It came to rest among the inner planets, warming themselves around the fire of the Sun and waiting for their stories to begin.

Those wanderers must have looked on Earth, circling safely in the narrow zone between fire and ice, and must have guessed that it was the favorite of the Sun's children. Here, in the distant future, would be intelligence; but there were countless stars before them still, and they might never come this way again.

So they left a sentinel, one of millions they have scattered throughout the universe, watching over all worlds with the promise of life. It was a beacon that down the ages has been patiently signalling the fact that no one had discovered it.

Perhaps you understand now why that crystal pyramid was set upon the Moon instead of on the Earth. Its builders were not concerned with races still struggling up from savagery. They would be interested in our civilization only if we proved our fitness to survive – by crossing space and so escaping from the Earth, our cradle. That is the challenge that all intelligent races must meet, sooner or later. It is a double challenge, for it depends in turn upon the conquest of atomic energy and the last choice between life and death.

Once we had passed that crisis, it was only a matter of time before we found the pyramid and forced it open. Now its signals have ceased, and those whose duty it is will be turning their minds upon Earth. Perhaps they wish to help our infant civilization. But they must be very, very old, and the old are often insanely jealous of the young.

I can never look now at the Milky Way without wondering from which of those banked clouds of stars the emissaries are coming. If you will pardon so commonplace a simile, we have broken the glass of the fire-alarm and have nothing to do but to wait.

I do not think we will have to wait for long.

LOGAN'S RUN

(MGM/United Artists, 1976)
Starring: Michael York, Jenny Agutter & Peter Ustinov
Directed by Michael Anderson
Based on *Logan's Run* by William F. Nolan
& George C. Johnson

Logan's Run is another SF story which now enjoys an international cult reputation because of the movie it inspired, the TV series which followed, and the literary sequels which co-author William F. Nolan has written. The story is also set in the twenty-first century where the computer is all-powerful – now it actually rules the population and has solved the problem of over-population by ordering the mandatory death of men and women as soon as they reach the age of 21. To enforce this ruling, there exists a crack force of Sandmen who hunt down and kill anyone who tries to escape, those referred to as "runners". Logan, when first met, is a Sandman: cunning, efficient and a crack shot. But his ideals are put to the test when he reaches the fatal age just at the time when he has fallen in love with a beautiful girl, Jessica. The couple decide to become runners – and Logan soon comes to realise that he needs all his old resourcefulness to outwit the elite corps of killers to which he once belonged. According to his American creator, the respected and prolific author William F. Nolan (1928), the unique concept for *Logan's Run* came to him by simply reversing the old saying, "Life begins at Forty". Bill, who was formerly a commercial artist, worked on the original story with his friend, George Clayton Johnson, and although their novel was published in 1967, almost a decade passed before it was finally brought to the screen. But patience has been rewarded, and Bill has subsequently watched Logan (whom he named after the phone exchange of the Kansas City home where he grew up) become a "pop culture" hero with his own fan club, magazines, books and even games and puzzles inspired by the Sandman's world. The original novel has been followed by two sequels – both solo efforts by Bill – *Logan's World* (1977) and *Logan's Search* (1980), which together complete the trilogy. In order to represent the original movie and the TV series (which starred Gregory Harrison and Heather Menzies), the author has selected the following episode from *Logan's World*, and also provided these notes by way of introduction . . .

"*Logan's World* is, of course, a direct sequel to *Logan's Run*. Ten years have passed and the great computer that ruled the youth society, The Thinker, with its system of compulsory death at 21, has been destroyed and the force of Sandmen (DS or Deep Sleep operatives) have been disbanded. Logan and Jessica are now living with the Wilderness People beyond the destroyed cities and have a young son, Jag. When the boy becomes ill, Logan sets out to find a proper medicine for him, but while he is away, a gypsy band kill Jag and kidnap Jessica. When Logan discovers the dead boy he is convinced that Jess is also dead and is plunged into a deep depression. He decides to go to New York to obtain a large dosage of the drug R-11 as a way to recapture the love of his wife and son – despite being warned that the drug is extremely dangerous and he might never 'come out' or even die. He rejects the warning, declaring that without Jess and Jag, 'I'm dead already.' In this episode of Logan's extraordinary saga he again meets Dia, a young blind girl, who is a telepath, and Jonath, the leader of the Wilderness People. Now read on . . ."

Logan had taken a mazecar to the New York Complex on leave from DS school when he was sixteen to pairmate with a female who lived there. She was an older woman of twenty, a year away from Sleep and into young Sandmen. Gonzales 2 had told Logan about her, told him she was something really special. Chinese. Sexually astonishing.

Gonzales had been correct. Her voracious sensual appetites had drained Logan, left him anxious to return to duty. The pleasure with her had been so intense it was akin to pain. New York was different then: glittering, swarming with citizens, a world mecca for exotic living.

Now it was dark ruins.

But it had something Logan wanted far more than he had wanted the Chinese girl. It had R-11.

In 2010, when Mayor Margaret Hatch had ordered the Central Park fill-in, construction of the Green Giants had begun. Taking their name from the fact that they were replacing the last bit of open greenery in New York City, the Giants were designed to accommodate three million, a bold step in reducing the city's acute housing crisis. In height, they were taller than the Empire State and each was a self-contained miniature city, with every comfort and convenience. To get space in one, you hocked your soul, and signed a lifetime lease.

The first three-mile complex was a converted Giant. But, eventually, the outdated skytowers were torn down and replaced.

Nostalgia prevailed. As a memorial to the past, one of the Green Giants was allowed to remain standing, dwarfed by the three-mile city dwellings around it.

Yet it lived again when the Thinker died. Its precomputerized, self-contained power units were quickly utilized, and it became the hub in cross-state Market operations, a mighty storehouse-headquarters, humming with activity. After more than a century of obsolescence, it was now the only living structure in a dead city.

Logan came to the Giant for R-11.

Jonath had told him that he would have no trouble with Scavengers in New York. This was one city they did not control. "The Marketers are in charge there," Jonath had said.

"Who are they exactly?"

"Mostly ex-DS. A few key merchantmen. They keep the Scavengers in line. The city's wide open."

Flying over it at night, Logan got the impression of a vast, lightless range of man-made mountains, upthrusting peaks of steel and glass. Dominating the interior of the city, with flamebright gaudiness, standing two thousand feet above street level, light flooding out from its metal pores, stood the Green Giant.

As he swept over the shining structure, pinlights found his craft. Two Market patrolships soared up from the roof of the building to circle Logan, guiding him to a setdown on the Giant's illumined skyport.

Logan cut power, exited to the roof.

"No weapons allowed," a tall man in gray said to him. The Market guard carried a belted Fuser. His eyes were humorless.

Logan nodded, placed his holstered Gun inside the paravane, sealed the magnetic lock. "How long can I leave my ship here?" he asked.

"As long as you have business inside," said the guard. "We'll keep an eye on it."

"Thanks," said Logan.

Another gray-clad guard walked up to him as he neared the entrance shaft. "Name?"

"Logan 3."

"Seeing who?"

"Lacy 14."

"You'll need a contact pass."

Logan handed him the foilslip he'd obtained from Rawls. The guard studied it for a moment, notched one corner with a foilpunch, handed it back.

"Go ahead," he said, activating the shaft release.

Logan stepped inside.

The interior corridors shimmered with light; this intensity of artificial illumination stunned Logan. He'd seen nothing like it since the days of Arcade. Because the Giant was able to generate its own electricity, and had never depended on the Thinker for power, the death of the great computer had not affected it. Restoration had been relatively simple – and now this city-within-a-city was functioning at peak efficiency after long years of darkness. Indeed, a sleeping Giant had awakened to serve new masters.

Although the outer surface of the building glowed beacon-bright, the majority of its two hundred floors were dark; the Market occupied only the Penthouse area and the three floors just beneath for storage. The Giant was private, off-limits, except to those who ran the Market, and to the few special customers allowed to deal inside for highgrade goods. Such as R-11.

At the end of the corridor another guard stopped Logan. Same gray uniform. Same eyes. The hard look of the Sandman. Ex-DS, fitting their new roles as skin fits muscle.

"Pass," said the guard.

Logan produced the notched foilslip.

The guard pressed a section of wall. A door oiled back.

"Keep moving," said the guard.

Another corridor. Much shorter.

Logan faced a heavy flexcurtain, woven entirely from gold mesh. The curtain stirred, folded back.

"Come in, Logan 3."

A woman's voice. Sensual. Low-pitched.

Logan entered a chamber draped in silks and lit by firebirds. The small, feathered creatures, whose metallic bodies pulsed with inner light, swooped in glowing arcs around the large center room, settling, strutting, ruffling their multicolored plumage . . .

Logan hesitated, scanning the room. He saw no one. Only the birds, like moving fire jewels.

Then the woman appeared, rising from one corner of the chamber. She had been lying on a fall of snowpillows and, in standing, seemed to materialize from the room itself, seemed made of silks and smoked ivory.

Her body was perfection – a rich orchestration of scented peaks and soft valleys, tautly accented by the white flowgown she wore. A cat-emerald burned at her throat.

"I'm Lacy 14," she said.

"Since you know my name," said Logan. "I assume you also know what I came for."

A firebird fluttered to her shoulder and she stroked the glowing plumage, her large green-black eyes fixed on Logan.

"Why so abrupt?" she smiled. "I never conduct business without getting to know my buyers. Sit down, Logan."

Snowpillows. A soft peltrug of worked silver. No couch or chairs. Logan sat, adjusting one of the larger pillows at his back.

"Much better," said Lacy. "Drink?"

"No."

"I insist. I have a really excellent fruitwine from Spain which is impossible to duplicate," she told him.

Logan nodded. "Since you insist."

She brought him the wine, settled next to him. "Let us drink to the satisfactory conclusion of pleasure."

Logan was edgy, off-balance; he had expected a hard-faced Marketer who would waste no time, no words. He'd expected to deal quickly and be gone without ceremony. But, instead, here was Lacy . . .

Logan tasted the wine, allowing the smoked flavor to permeate his tongue. "You're right," he said. "This is excellent."

"I've heard about you, Logan."

"What have you heard?"

"That you sought out and destroyed the Borgias. Alone, at Steinbeck. One against twelve. Is it true?"

"It's true," said Logan. "But I'm not going to talk about it."

"That's not necessary," she smiled. "You're obviously a man of great passion. I've . . . been waiting for someone extraordinary."

Logan slipped a sack of Mooncoins from his belt.

"All I want here is what I came to get," he said. "A quantampac of R-11."

"That will be produced in due course. After you've earned it."

"I have these," he said, handing her the Mooncoins. "There's nothing like them on Earth."

She put the sack aside, unopened. "We'll deal with these later. *I* come first."

Logan was suddenly angry.

"Get a merchantman to penetrate you," he said. "Or one of your ex-DS. They all have fine bodies. They'll do a very satisfactory job."

She laughed, a throaty sound, deep and assured. "I don't want you – or any other male," she told him. "I never allow a man to touch me. Ever."

"Well, what *do* you want?"

"Follow me and find out." She stood, putting aside her wine.

Logan got up. "Can't we just – "

"This way," said Lacy. "If you want the pac, you do as I say."

Sighing, Logan followed her out of the chamber.

They moved together down a short hallway. Lacy opened a mirrored door, beckoned Logan forward.

The room he entered was a large bedchamber, draped in crimson and gold. Soft lights shone through the draperies, and at least half of the floor area was occupied by two deep, expansive flowbeds.

"Recline," said Lacy. "On the farther bed. I'll take this one."

Logan did as she asked. What did she have planned for him?

Lacy kept her eyes on Logan as she touched a magclasp at her neck; the gown fell away from her body in a soft spill of white. "Am I not beautiful?" she asked him.

"You are," he said.

Her breasts were coned and delicate, tapering to a waist which swelled to perfect hips and long, superbly-muscled legs. "Many men have desired me. Do you desire me, Logan?"

"At another time, in another place . . ."

She draped herself across the bed, facing his, cat-smiled at him. "I am not your concern here," she said. "You shall provide a show . . . for my stimulation."

"I don't understand."

She clapped her hands sharply.

The drapes parted at the rear of the chamber.

There were three of them. All nude. All beautiful. All black-skinned and full-figured and arousing. Perfect females, who would have been the pride of any glasshouse from Moscow to Paris.

"They're for you, Logan," said Lacy. "And you are for them."

"You expect me to – "

"Pleasure them. That's what you shall do if you want to please me. And if you do *not* please me, you will not get the thing you came for."

She turned to the girls. Her eyes were bright and hot. "Undress him," she said. "Caress him. Erect him."

They swayed toward Logan like dusky flowers.

So *this* is how she obtains her satisfaction? All right, Logan told himself, I'll do as she asks. I'll give her a show. And I'll enjoy what I'm doing. I'll steep myself in warm flesh . . . lose myself in sexuality.

140

Indeed, why not?

And Logan took them into his arms.

Logan followed Lacy 14 down the short hallway. As they entered her living quarters a firebird settled on Logan's shoulder, splashing his face with vivid colors. He shook the bird off, and the creature wing whispered away.

"I did what you asked," he said to Lacy.

"A splendid performance," she agreed. She was wearing the white gown once again, and it billowed as she turned.

"Do I get the pac now?"

"Let me see what you've brought." She picked up the sack of Mooncoins, spilled them into her hand. They were round, bright, stamped with Moon symbols.

"I brought them down from Darkside," said Logan. "You won't find any others. Anywhere."

"They're . . . attractive," she said. "I can use them. But they won't pay for a full dex. Not of R-11."

Logan flushed with anger. "I did what you asked with the females . . ."

"And enjoyed yourself handsomely in the process," she said.

"Wasn't that what you wanted – to watch me pleasuring them to pleasure yourself?" He tightened his jaw. "I've given you all I have. Everything."

"Not everything," she said.

"What's left?"

"Your paravane. It should fetch a good price. I'll take the coins, *and* your ship." She smiled. "You know, I'm really being generous about this. You're here alone, unarmed. Normally, I would just have my men *take* your ship and give you nothing in return. But . . . since you've . . . amused me, I'm willing to turn over the drug."

"I can't get back to camp without my ship," said Logan. "And I *need* Jonath. It's impossible to take R-11 without someone to – "

141

"Take it here," said Lacy. "I'll provide a liftroom for you, and see to your needs."

Logan considered it. There was nothing left for him in Old Washington. Why *not* stay here in the New York Complex? One city was no better or worse than another now, without Jess.

"I accept," said Logan.

"There's risk in a full dex," said Lacy. "It could kill you."

Logan said nothing.

"There's no body or mind control with such a high dosage," she said. "You're at the mercy of the drug."

"I want maximum lift," said Logan. "A *full* re-live. And only a dex will give me that."

"Your decision," shrugged Lacy. "Get whatever personal belongings you have in the ship, then come back here. I'll have the R-11."

He hated losing the paravane. It was a high price to pay. Still, Lacy could have simply taken it, as she said. In dealing with the Market there were no guarantees. You took what they gave you.

Logan had the Gun when the guard said, "You can't go back inside with that." His name was Stile, and he captained Lacy's men. Huge. Slab-bodied. Cruel-faced.

"Lacy made the deal," said Logan. "She gets the ship and I get my personal belongings. This is mine. It goes with me."

Stile looked sullen. "All right . . . I'll make an exception this time," he said. "But keep it holstered."

"Couple of Fusers in there you can have," said Logan. "They were never mine to begin with."

He fixed the Gun holster to his belt.

There was nothing else. The ship was theirs now.

As the R-11 would soon be his.

The small liftroom was stark and empty, dun-colored, without ornament or decoration. Four walls, a floor and a ceiling. No windows or vents.

"You'll need this," Lacy said, and gestured. A gray-clad

guard dumped a bodymat, quickly unrolled it. The mat covered the floor, wall to wall.

"What about oxygen?"

"Enough. The room's not sealed."

"I'll need water."

"At necessary intervals. Pelletgun . . . directly into your system."

"I don't want to be observed," said Logan.

"You won't be," said Lacy. "But if you convulse . . ."

"*No* observation. Just the injections . . . water when I require it. Agreed?"

"Agreed."

"The drug?" asked Logan.

From her belt, Lacy withdrew a small silver disc. She pressed its center and the disc released a single milky-white pearl. It rolled, catching the light, in the palm of her hand.

"Hard to believe that's a full dex," said Logan.

She smiled. "You've never used R-11?"

"No," he admitted.

"A normal dosage is almost microscopic," she told him. "This is a quantam, full-dex strength. Usually this much R-11 is broken into powder, administered in several stages. I've never seen anyone take a pearl."

"The Re-Live drawers died with the cities," said Logan. "This is the only way left to go back."

"Is going back *that* important?"

"Yes," said Logan. "It's that important."

She looked at him for a long moment, then handed him the pearl.

"Just place it in the middle of your tongue," she said. "Let it dissolve directly into the tissue. It's effective immediately after ingestion."

And she left him.

Logan brought up the pearl, holding it between the thumb and index finger of his right hand; he studied it in the subdued light of the room. Harmless looking. Beautiful in its simple perfection.

But potent. Very, very potent.

The surface-distortion drug he'd been given by the Scavengers was Candee next to R-11, which was designed to penetrate to the deepest levels of stored life-experience. Science had long since proven, beyond any doubt, that every experience, however trivial, is permanently retained: every sight, sound, odor, every sensory moment of touch, every spoken word . . . all there, all three-dimensionally alive in the depths of the human brain.

The Re-Live parlors were built on this principle. In their metal wombs it had been possible to re-experience, at choice, any hour, or day, or moment of one's past.

That was the key word: *choice*. The Re-Live drawers gave you selective control, provided you wished to exercise it. And there were built-in shutoffs if the emotional surge threatened body-health. A Re-Live drawer was safe.

Not so with R-11. At maximum dosage, there was no control; it prowled the vaults of memory at will, and all choice was removed. However, short of maximum, Logan was not certain he could reach his full experiences with Jaq and Jessica. Under a light dosage he might never find them again.

R-11 had one basic advantage over any other minddrug. It gave back *truth*, not fantasy; experiences, not hallucinations. It did not distort as Lysergic Foam did. What Logan re-lived would be *real* events from his past.

And, buried in that past, his wife and son waited for him.

Logan sat down on the mat which gave softly under his weight.

Now.

Pearl into mouth. On the tongue. Dissolving . . .

Logan was fighting for balance. The wind whipped at his tunic, fisting him with short, savage gusts. He wasn't sure he could maintain his footing – and a fall was death.

He was sixteen, and new to DS. A raw Sandman, just out of Deep Sleep Training, hunting his first female, nervous, and over-anxious to prove himself.

Logan's runner, Brandith 2, had glass-danced the Arcades before her flower blacked; she was extremely agile, with an incredible sense of body-control. She had lured her nervous pursuer onto a narrow outside repair-ramp, dipping and weaving her way along the thin ridge of metal ahead of him. Luring him forward.

You should have fired the homer; the homer would have finished her!

In his excitement, Logan had set the Gun at ripper, and to be effective a ripper must be fired at fairly close range. He could re-set for homer, but to do so would require taking both hands off the ledgerail, and that was impossible. He'd lose his balance for sure.

"What's the matter, Sandman?" her voice mocked him. "Can't you catch me?"

She had passed an angle-beam, and was no longer in direct sight. Logan moved faster along the ramp, reached the beam. She was waiting for him.

"You're dead, Sandman!" And, braced on the beam, Brandith 2 delivered a smashing blow to his chest with her left foot.

Logan swayed, pitched forward to his knees. The Gun slipped from his clawing fingers. He twisted, hooking his right arm into a strut-support, and slashed up with the heel of his left hand.

The surprise blow took Brandith 2 at throat level, and crushed her windpipe. She clutched at her neck, gasped blood, and fell over the edge in a long, screaming death drop.

Logan felt relief, and instant shame. He'd failed to homer her, and worse yet – much worse – he'd lost the Gun. A Sandman must *never* relinquish his weapon: the first rule of DS. And now he had allowed a female runner to disarm him, and almost kill him.

On the ramp, alone in the crying wind, Logan could not move. He was locked into his misery. "Failure!" he said aloud. "Failure!"

Would he *ever* deserve to wear the uniform of a Sandman?

Egypt was a bore.

Logan was eight, and had taken a robocamel to the Pyramids with his best friend, Evans 9. They'd been to Japan earlier that morning, and found Kyoto dull with its restored temples and fat, bronze deities. But, in Tokyo, a sumo wrestler had taught them how to immobilize an opponent by a theatrical display of aggression, without actual body contact. Fascinating.

But Egypt was all heat and endless sand and ugly-snouted robot camels. The Pyramids were a disappointment – smaller than Logan expected, and badly in need of repair. The surface was pitted and crumbling, with many large stones near the top missing entirely.

"They ought to fix them," said Logan. "Smooth them out."

"No, tear them down," said Evans. "Put up new ones, *better* ones. Old things aren't worth saving."

"Old things are ugly," said Logan.

And that night they took a mazecar to Uganda.

"I can leave here, go with you," she told him.

"No, that's not possible."

"Why isn't it?"

"Because it isn't."

"But you find me exciting? You enjoy my body?"

"Yes."

"Then we'll pair-bond. Until it goes bad. When it goes bad, I'll leave. What's wrong with that?"

"A lot," he said. "I live alone."

"Why?"

"Because of what I am."

This silenced her.

The lovelights of the glasshouse played over their bodies. Gold . . .

Silver . . .

Red . . .

Yellow . . .

Blue . . .

And still she did not speak.

When Logan left the glasshouse he was angry. Why *couldn't* he form an alliance? Why *must* he live alone, finding sexual satisfaction on this fragmented, impulse basis?

Because of what I am.

A DS man cannot function effectively if he is pair-bonded. All emotional ties must be severed. Commitments must not be made. Nothing must interfere with duty.

Duty.

Duty.

"Show me your hand, Logan," said the psyc doctor.

Logan obeyed.

"Do you know why you have this?" he said, tapping the palmflower with an index finger.

"To tell my age," Logan said.

"And how old are you?"

"I'm six."

"And what happens when you're seven?"

Logan looked down at his palm. "It goes to blue. And I . . . leave Nursery."

The doctor nodded. He had kind eyes. "And you are afraid?"

"Yes," said Logan.

"Why? Why are you afraid, Logan?"

The words spilled out in a rush: "Because I love my talk puppet and because I don't want to leave Nursery and because . . ."

"Go on, tell me."

"Because the world is so big and I'm so little."

"But every boy and girl feels that way, and *they're* not afraid."

"I'll bet *some* of them are," said Logan. "Or they wouldn't use a machine like you."

"I deal with many problems at Nursery," said the doctor. He whirred to a medcab, took out a packet of Candees.

"I don't want a Candee," said Logan.

"But they taste good and they make you feel good," said the doctor.

"They make me sleepy."

"Take a Candee, Logan."

"No."

"*Do as I say!* Take one."

"No."

Logan backed away, but the square machine whirred after him. The doctor's kind eyes were no longer kind. They glittered with determination.

"I'll report this to Autogoverness," he threatened. "You'll be punished."

"I don't care," said Logan defiantly.

"Very well," said the doctor. And he pushed a button on his desk. An Autogoverness rolled into the office.

"Logan 3 is to be punished. After punishment, he will be given a Candee."

"Yes, doctor," said the round, many-armed robot. She took Logan's hand in one of hers.

"You see, Logan," said the doctor as the boy was being led out. "You *can't* win."

"How long has he been under?" asked Lacy.

"Two days, six hours," said Stile.

"Convulsions?"

"Minor so far."

"Heartbeat?"

"Erratic, but holding."

"Skincount?"

"One over fifteen. The chemical balance is distorted, but not critical. Of course, he's going in deeper. It could get worse. No way of telling."

"If he dies, notify me immediately."

"Of course," said Stile.

The blow caught Logan at the upper part of the shoulder, a deltoid chop, delivered with force and precision. He felt his left arm go numb, angled his body sharply to keep Francis in the direct line of attack.

He lashed out with a reverse savate kick, catching Francis at rib-level, causing him to lurch back, gasping for breath.

"You're good, Logan," said the tall, mantis-thin man, slowly circling his opponent.

"You're better, damn you!" Logan said. "But I'm learning."

"More each day," agreed Francis. "Shall we end this?"

Logan nodded, rubbing his shoulder. "I've had enough."

They hit the needleshower, standing together silently in the cutting spray. Francis had paid for his reputation; his body, in contrast to Logan's unmarked one, bore the scars of a hundred near-death encounters with fanatic runners, cubs, gypsies . . . Of the crack DS men at Angeles Complex, Francis was the fastest, the most dangerous, the best. Logan was still his pupil, but soon he might be his equal – with natural talent, good fortune, supreme dedication.

Francis had all these.

They walked back into the combat room, got into fresh grays.

"There's a lift party tonight at Stanhope's," said Logan. "Why not unbend, take it in?"

Francis smiled thinly. The smile was bloodless. "I don't party," he said.

"But we're off-duty until – "

"A Sandman's never off-duty," said Francis coldly. "We could be called in for backup."

"That's never happened to me yet," declared Logan.

"It might," said Francis.

Logan looked at him. "What *do* you do with your free time?"

"Use it properly. I don't waste it on witless females and lift parties."

"I give up," sighed Logan. He grinned. "You know, Francis, I wouldn't be surprised to find little wires and cogs and springs under your skin . . . You're not *quite* human."

"I get my job done," said Francis stiffly.

"Sure. Sure you do," said Logan. "Forget what I said."

But, as he watched Francis walk out, Logan wondered: what the hell *does* he do with his free time?

"This one's dangerous," said Evans. "He's stolen a paravane and he's got a Fuser with him. I think we need backup."

Logan agreed. "Get on it, while I see if I can run him down."

"With a stick? Can you handle one?"

"I've ridden them before," said Logan. "They're much faster than a paravane."

"Take care," said Evans, sprinting for a callbox.

Logan checked his ammopac. Full load. He could use a nitro on the runner's ship if he had to. He kicked the hoverstick into life, soaring up at a dizzy angle. Too much thrust. He throttled down a bit, gained full control, gradually increasing his airspeed.

The runner's paravane had been tracked at dead center on the Kansas Missouri line – which meant if he cut through Greater KC, Logan should intercept near the Jefferson Complex.

The Missouri River rolled below him, brown and sluggish. A few speedtugs, a private sailjet or two, otherwise the river was undisturbed. It didn't worry about runners or callboxes or backups or devilsticks or Sleep. Old Man River . . . just keeps rolling along.

Logan had been correct in his calculations. He spotted the stolen paravane just past Jefferson. Moving at full bladepower.

The runner saw Logan bearing in, swung his ship to face the new threat.

He's bringing up the Fuser! Time to show him what you can do with a stick.

The runner fired.

And missed.

And fired again.

Logan was a sun-dazzled dragonfly – darting, dipping, swooping erratically. An impossible target.

He unholstered the Gun.

The paravane rushed at him.

Logan had the charge set at nitro. *Now!*

The runner and his ship erupted into gouting, blue-white flame. The stricken craft tipped over and down, diving into Missouri earth with a roar.

Logan brought the stick in, dismounted, checked the runner. Nothing left of him but his right arm and hand, jutting grotesquely out of the flame-charred control pod.

Centered in his palm: a black flower.

"Any change?" asked Lacy.

"He's worse," said Stile. "Into severe muscle convulsions. Skincount's up. And his heart is taking a beating."

"He can't go on, then?"

"He's a hard man," Stile said. "He might surprise you."

They were waiting at Darkside, where their rocket was being readied for the jump to Argos – and Logan held

Jessica close, telling her how much he loved her, telling her he'd never known that it was possible to experience such intense emotion, such care-bonding.

"We're free now," she told him. "We can live without fear, build a life together, raise children, be thirty, forty, fifty . . ."

He smiled, touched at her hair. God, but she was lovely!

"I want a son," he told her.

"We'll have him," she said squeezing Logan's hand.

"And he'll have children of *his* own . . . and we'll be . . . what did they call them?"

"Grandparents," she said. "Grandma and Grandpa."

Logan chuckled, shaking his head. "That's hard to believe, to accept. No dreams. No fantasies. A *real* life ahead of us on Argos."

"Ballard said it wouldn't be easy there," she reminded him. Her eyes clouded. "I wish – "

"What?"

"– that Ballard could have come with us. We *need* a man like that on Argos."

"He's needed more on Earth," said Logan. "To handle the Sanctuary Line. To help more runners."

"I know," she nodded. "We owe him our lives."

"Everybody here owes him the same debt," said Logan.

And, touching, they stared out beyond the port, at the chalked, lifeless horizon of the Moon.

When Jaq was five Logan and Jess gave him a special party. Only the spaceborn were invited – those who had been conceived on Argos and who, like Jaq, had never known their mother planet.

Logan told the children about Earthgames he'd played in Nursery, about vibroballs and teeter-swings and talk puppets. It seemed they could never hear enough about Earth.

"Were there really Sandmen who chased you?" asked a girl of six.

Logan nodded.

"And were the Sandmen really bad?" asked the little girl.

"Yes," said Logan. "But they were taught to be. Some of them changed . . . They didn't all stay bad."

"You were one, weren't you?" asked a ten-year-old, eyes alight.

"I was one," admitted Logan. ·

"And were you bad?"

"For a while."

"No!" screamed little Jaq, running across the chamber to his father, hugging him fiercely. "Logan was *never* bad!"

The boy was sobbing.

Jessica came to them, held them both. She kissed Logan's cheek.

In the sudden, strained silence a six-year-old tugged at Logan's wrist.

"Can we play now? *Can we?*"

"He's calmer," said Stile. "Relaxed. Almost tranquil. His mind seems to have found what it was looking for. He's in very deep."

Lacy looked pensive. "What do you think a Sandman's Gun would bring on the Market?"

"A great deal. But it would have to be de-fused, the pore-pattern detonation device neutralized."

"Can that be done?"

"It can be. It's a very delicate procedure."

She paced the room, thinking.

"He'll never trade or sell the Gun," said Stile.

"I know," she said. "It won't be possible to negotiate with him." She stopped, looked directly at Stile. "We'll have to kill him."

Sprawled face-down across the mat, deep in his mental dreamworld with Jessica and Jaq, Logan was not aware that the room had changed, that something was being *added* to the atmosphere. From a small opening under the door a colorless substance was being piped into the chamber.

Tetrahyde. Toxic and totally effective on human body-tissue. Once absorbed into the lungs, it destroyed them with deadly efficiency.

Logan breathed in . . . breathed out . . . breathed in . . .

He had exactly ten more minutes of life.

Logan, Logan, do you hear me?

I . . . hear you.

You are in great danger. You must come out!

No. Here with Jessica . . . with Jaq.

Listen to me, Logan. It's Dia.

How? How did you find me?

Jonath. When you didn't return to the camp he sent word to me. He knew no one else could reach you.

Where – are you now?

Close to you. Close to the Giant. I knew they'd never let me see you – so I'm sending my mind to you, my thoughts . . . You must come out to me!

No. Won't come out.

They're killing you, Logan.

Not true. They help me, give me water . . .

All that's over. The woman, Lacy, she has made up her mind to take the Gun. I know her thoughts . . . she wills you dead. Poison is in the air. You must come out, now! I'll help you . . . our two minds, together . . . Only minutes remain!

Logan willed his body to fight the drug – and Dia linked her mind to his; the images inside Logan's head began to mix, break up . . .

. . . and Jessica was . . .

the Loveroom, and "Mother loves you," said Ballard . . .

who was Francis, who was . . . Jaq, only five,

but already he . . .

kissed her deeply, knowing they were

154

never going to . . .

Harder! Try harder, Logan!
Trying. Can't. No use.
Fight! Break free!

. . . because Box was . . . in the cave . . .

falling . . .
      and love was . . .
               fa
                 l
                        ling . . .
everything w
             a
               s
                 fa
                 l
                   l
                     i
                        n
                          g
                          .
                            .
                              .

No. Too deep . . . too far in . . .
But you're doing it . . . we're doing it together . . . you're
almost . . .
. . . out!

Logan blinked stupidly; his head pounded – as if a thousand
hot needles had been driven into his skull.

Only a few seconds left! Use the Gun, Logan! Use it!

Logan fumbled dizzily at his belt holster, his nostrils filled with the acid odor of Tetrahyde . . . The gas was upon him. He held his breath, pulled the Gun free . . .

Fired.

The nitro charge exploded the door from its hingelocks, flooding the liftroom with fresh air.

Logan staggered to his feet, plowed across the mat toward the gaping exit.

Where are you, Dia?

Outside. On the street just below the Giant. You'll see me. I'll be there. Soon.

Stile was in the corridor, running toward Logan, a weapon in his hand.

Gun on ripper.

Logan fired, tearing him apart. He scooped up Stile's Fuser.

Lacy saw this, darted back into her chambers. The firebirds cawed and fluttered.

Gaining strength by the second, Logan swept past her, reached the outside door, raced for the roofport.

Behind him, Lacy was screaming: "Stop him! Stop him!"

Three guards tried to – without success. Logan chopped them aside with blows from Gun and body.

Lacy appeared in the roof door, Fuser in hand, firing as Logan reached his paravane. Her first beamblast sheared away a section of alum sheeting next to Logan's head.

He swung bitterly toward her, triggered the Gun, on tangler.

The swift whirl of steelmesh filament engulfed her – and she fell back, clawing at the choking, constricting coils of metal.

Dia was not alone when Logan reached her. The man from the Wilderness camp who had flown her to New York was there.

"How did you find another paravane?" Logan asked him.

"There are still a few around," the man told him. "Found this one in West Virginia. She needed a new gyrounit, but she's fine now."

"Tell Jonath how grateful I am," said Logan.

"He'll be glad to hear you're all right."

Thanks to you, Logan thought, looking at Dia.

And she smiled at him.

"Will you be going back?" the man asked Logan.

No. We're going west. Together.

"No," said Logan. "We'll be going west."

The two men shook hands.

Where now? asked Logan. *How far west?*

All the way to the Coast, she told him, sitting beside him in the humming paravane. The New York Territory unrolled below them, nightblack and massive.

I want to take you home, Logan. She smiled, her hands touching gently at the planes of his face. *West, to my home.*

As heat is felt on skin, Logan felt the passion radiating from her mind.

He owed her his life, but could he give her something more than gratitude? Was he capable, now, of a greater commitment to her?

Logan wasn't sure.

He would know when the time for knowing was at hand.

STAR TREK: THE MOTION PICTURE

> (Paramount, 1979)
> Starring: William Shatner, Leonard Nimoy
> & DeForest Kelley
> Directed by Robert Wise
> Television story "The Unreal McCoy" by James Blish

Ten years after it had been an NBC television series which lasted for just three seasons, *Star Trek* graduated to the cinema screen and there became a huge box office winner which has helped turn the adventures of the Starship *Enterprise* and her crew into an unparalleled phenomenon. Expansively directed by Robert Wise with impressive-looking hardware special effects by Douglas Trumbull (again), John Dykstra and Dave Stewart, the picture's success has led to five sequels (at the present count) and two further television series: all of which have made *Star Trek* into a world-wide cult and multi-million-dollar merchandising industry. This is all, though, a far cry from the original low-budget TV concept devised by Gene Roddenberry, a former Second World War bomber pilot, who had begun his career in television writing for shows such as *Dragnet* and *Highway Patrol*, before being asked by NBC for an idea for a series and coming up with *Star Trek* inspired, he claimed, by his admiration for C. S. Forester's historical maritime novels featuring Captain Horatio Hornblower! Gene's stories about Captain James Kirk, Science Officer Spock, Doctor McCoy and the other members of the Enterprise who "boldly go where no man has gone before" – to quote one of the series' well-known catch-phrases – not only took viewers into the far reaches of space, but also made some important statements about racial and sexual equality, humanity and optimism. These elements have continued in the subsequent movies as well as in the TV series, helping to enhance the legend still further . . .

Interestingly, the plot of *Star Trek: The Motion Picture* was not very different from one of the earliest episodes in the original TV series. In the movie, Kirk, Spock and McCoy found themselves in conflict with an alien who had taken on the form of one of the crew members. Earlier, in "The Unreal McCoy", the same trio faced a similar threat, but one more intent on enslaving the doctor. This adaptation of the television script is by James Blish (1921–1975), a Science Fiction fan who studied microbiology and zoology before becoming one of the leading writers of "intellectual" SF with books like *A Case of Conscience* (1959), one of the first serious attempts to deal with religion in SF. In complete contrast to these works, Jim wrote a number of the earliest novels to be based on *Star Trek* during the years its popularity was developing and first editions of these are now eagerly collected. Other writers have since followed James Blish in expanding the legend of *Star Trek*, but in the following pages he retells one of the stories of how it all began . . .

The crater campsite – or the Bierce campsite, as the records called it – on Regulus VIII was the crumbling remains of what might once have been a nested temple, surrounded now by archeological digs, several sheds, and a tumble of tools, tarpaulins, and battered artifacts. Outside the crater proper, the planet was largely barren except for patches of low, thorny vegetation, all the way in any direction to wherever the next crater might be – there were plenty of those, but there'd been no time to investigate them, beyond noting that they had all been inhabited once, unknown millennia ago. There was nothing uncommon about that, the galaxy was strewn with ruins about which nobody knew anything, there were a hundred such planets for every archeologist who could even dream of scratching such a surface. Bierce had just been lucky – fantastically lucky.

All the same, Regulus VIII made Kirk – Capt. James Kirk of the starship *Enterprise*, who had seen more planets than most men knew existed – feel faintly edgy. The *Enterprise* had landed here in conformity to the book; to be specific, to that part of the book which said that research personnel on alien planets must have their health certified by a starship's surgeon at one-year intervals. The *Enterprise* had been in Bierce's vicinity at the statutory time, and Ship's Surgeon McCoy had come down by transporter from the orbiting *Enterprise* to do the job. Utterly, completely routine, except for the fact that McCoy had mentioned that Bierce's wife Nancy had been a serious interest of McCoy's pre-Bierce, well over ten years ago. And after all, what could be more commonplace than that?

Then Nancy came out of the temple – if that is what it was – to meet them.

There were only three of them: McCoy and a crewman, Darnell, out of duty, and Kirk, out of curiosity. She came forward with outstretched hands, and after a moment's hesitation, McCoy took them. "Leonard!" she said. "Let me look at you."

"Nancy," McCoy said. "You . . . haven't aged a year."

Kirk restrained himself from smiling. Nancy Bierce was handsome, but nothing extraordinary: a strongly built woman of about forty, moderately graceful, her hair tinged with gray. It wasn't easy to believe that the hard-bitten medico could have been so smitten, even at thirty or less, as to be unable to see the signs of aging now. Still she did have a sweet smile.

"This is the Captain of the *Enterprise*, Jim Kirk," McCoy said. "And this is Crewman Darnell."

Nancy turned her smile on the Captain, and then on the crewman. Darnell's reaction was astonishing. His jaw swung open; he was frankly staring. Kirk would have kicked him had he been within reach.

"Come in, come in," she was saying. "We may have to wait a little for Bob; once he starts digging, he forgets time. We've made up some quarters in what seems to have been an old altar chamber – not luxurious, but lots of room. Come on in, Plum."

She ducked inside the low, crumbling stone door.

"Plum?" Kirk said.

"An old pet name," McCoy said, embarrassed. He followed her. Embarrassed himself at his own gaucherie, Kirk swung on the crewman.

"Just what are you goggling at, Mister?"

"Sorry, sir," Darnell said stiffly. "She reminds me of somebody is all. A girl I knew once on Wrigley's Planet. That is – "

"That's enough," Kirk said drily. "The next thought of that kind you have will probably be in solitary. Maybe you'd better wait outside."

"Yessir. Thanks." Darnell seemed genuinely grateful. "I'll explore a little, if that suits you, Captain."

"Do that. Just stay within call."

Commonplace; Darnell hadn't seen a strange woman since his last landfall. But most peculiar, too.

Bierce did not arrive, and after apologies, Nancy left again to look for him, leaving Kirk and McCoy to examine the stone room, trying not to speak to each other. Kirk could not decide whether he would rather be back on board the *Enterprise*, or just plain dead; his diplomacy had not failed him this badly in he could not think how many years.

Luckily, Bierce showed up before Kirk had to decide whether to run or suicide. He was an unusually tall man, all knuckles, knees, and cheekbones, wearing faded coveralls. Slightly taller than McCoy, his face was as craggy as his body; the glint in the eyes, Kirk thought, was somehow both intelligent and rather bitter. But then, Kirk had never pretended to understand the academic type.

"Dr. Briece," he said, "I'm Captain Kirk, and this is Ship's Surgeon – "

"I know who you are," Bierce broke in, in a voice with the blaring rasp of a busy signal. "We don't need you here. If you'll just refill us on aspirin, salt tablets, and the like, you needn't trouble yourselves further."

"Sorry, but the law requires an annual checkup," Kirk said. "If you'll co-operate, I'm sure Dr. McCoy will be as quick as possible." McCoy, in fact, already had his instruments out.

"McCoy?" Bierce said. "I've heard that name . . . Ah, yes, Nancy used to talk about you."

"Hands out from your sides, please, and breathe evenly . . . Yes, didn't she mention I'd arrived?"

After the slightest of pauses, Bierce said, "You've . . . seen Nancy?"

"She was here when we arrived," Kirk said. "She went to look for you."

"Oh. Quite so. I'm pleased, of course, that she can meet an old friend, have a chance of some company. I enjoy solitude, but it's difficult for a woman sometimes."

"I understand," Kirk said, but he was none too sure he did. The sudden attempt at cordiality rang false, somehow, after the preceding hostility. At least *that* had sounded genuine.

McCoy had finished his checkup with the tricorder and produced a tongue depressor with a small flourish. "She hasn't changed a bit," he said. "Open your mouth, please."

Reluctantly, Bierce complied. At the same instant, the air was split by a full-throated shriek of horror. For an insane moment Kirk had the impression that the sound had issued from Bierce's mouth. Then another scream ripped the silence, and Kirk realized that it was, of course, a female voice.

They all three bolted out of the door. In the open, Kirk and McCoy outdistanced Bierce quickly; for all his outdoor life, he was not a good runner. But they hadn't far to go. Just beyond the rim of the crater, Nancy, both fists to her mouth, was standing over the body of Darnell.

As they came pounding up she moved toward McCoy, but he ignored her and dropped beside the body. It was lying on its face. After checking the pulse, McCoy gently turned the head to one side, grunted, and then turned the body over completely.

It was clear even to Kirk that the crewman was dead. His face was covered with small ringlike red blotches slowly fading. "What hit him?" Kirk said tensely.

"Don't know. Petachiae a little like vacuum mottling, or maybe some sort of immunological – hullo, what's this?"

Bierce came panting up as McCoy slowly forced open one of Darnell's fists. In it was a twisted, scabrous-looking object of no particular color, like a mummified parsnip. It looked also as though part of it had been bitten away. Now *that* was incredible. Kirk swung on Nancy.

"What happened?" he asked tersely.

"Don't snap at my wife, Captain," Bierce said in his busy-signal voice. "Plainly it's not her fault!"

"One of my men is dead. I accuse nobody, but Mrs. Bierce is the only witness."

McCoy rose and said to Nancy, gently: "Just tell us what you saw, Nancy. Take your time."

"I was just . . ." she said, and then had to stop and swallow, as if fighting for control. "I couldn't find Bob, and I'd . . . I'd just started back when I saw your crewman. He had that borgia root in his hand and he was smelling it. I was just going to call out to him when – he bit into it. I had no idea he was going to – and then his face twisted and he fell – "

She broke off and buried her face in her hands. McCoy took her gently by one shoulder. Kirk, feeling no obligation to add one bedside more, said evenly: "How'd you know what the root was if you'd just come within calling distance?"

"This cross-examination – " Bierce grated.

"Bob, please. I didn't know, of course. Not until I saw it now. But it's dangerous to handle any plant on a new world."

Certainly true. Equally certainly, it would have been no news to Darnell. His face impassive, Kirk told McCoy: "Pack up, Bones. We can resume the physicals tomorrow."

"I'm sure that won't be necessary," Bierce said. "If you'll just disembark our supplies, Captain – "

"It's not going to be that easy, Dr. Bierce," Kirk said. He snapped open his communicator. "Kirk to Transporter Room. Lock and beam: two transportees and a corpse."

The autopsied body of Darnell lay on a table in the sick bay, unrecognizable now even by his mother, if so veteran a spaceman had ever had one. Kirk, standing near a communicator panel, watched with a faint physical uneasiness as McCoy lowered Darnell's brain into a shallow bowl and then turned and washed his hands until they were paper-white. Kirk had seen corpses in every conceivable state of distortion and age in one battle and another, but this clinical bloodiness was not within his experience.

"I can't rule poison out entirely," McCoy said, in a matter-of-fact voice. "Some of the best known act just as fast and leave just as little trace: botulinus, for example. But there's no trace of any woody substance in his stomach or even between his teeth. All I can say for sure is that he's got massive capillary damage – which could be due to almost anything, even shock – and those marks on his face."

McCoy covered the ruined body. "I'll be running some blood chemistry tests, but I'd like to know what I'm testing for. I'd also like to know what symptoms that 'borgia root' is *supposed* to produce. Until then, Jim, I'm really rather in the dark."

"Spock's running a library search on the plant," Kirk said. "It shouldn't take him long. But I must confess that what you've said thus far doesn't completely surprise me.

Darnell was too old a hand to bite into any old thing he happened to pick up."

"Then what's left? Nancy? Jim, I'm not quite trusting my own eyes lately, but Nancy didn't use to be capable of murder – certainly not of an utter stranger, to boot!"

"It's not only people who kill – hold it, here's the report. Go ahead, Mr. Spock."

"We have nothing on the borgia root but what the Bierces themselves reported in their project request six years ago," Spock's precise voice said. "There they call it an aconite resembling the *Lilium* family. Said to contain some twenty to fifty different alkaloids, none then identifiable specifically with the equipment to hand. The raw root is poisonous to mice. No mention of any human symptoms. Except . . ."

"Except what?" McCoy snapped.

"Well, Dr. McCoy, this isn't a symptom. The report adds that the root has a pleasant perfume, bland but edible-smelling, rather like tapioca. And that's all there is."

"Thanks." Kirk switched off. "Bones, I can't see Darnell having been driven irresistibly to bite into an unknown plant because it smelled like tapioca. He wouldn't have bitten into something that smelled like a brandied peach unless he'd known its pedigree. He was a seasoned hand."

McCoy spread his hands expressively. "You knew your man, Jim – but where does that leave us? The symptoms do vaguely resemble aconite poisoning. Beyond that, we're nowhere."

"Not quite," Kirk said. "We still have to check on the Bierces, I'm afraid, Bones. And for that I'm still going to need your help."

McCoy turned his back and resumed washing his hands. "You'll get it," he said; but his voice was very cold.

Kirk's method of checking on the Bierces was simple but drastic: he ordered them both on board the ship. Bierce raged.

"If you think you can beam down here, bully us, interfere with my work – considering the inescapable fact that you are a trespasser on my planet – "

"Your complaint is noted," Kirk said. "I apologize for the inconvenience. But it's also an inescapable fact that something we don't understand killed one of our men. It could very well be a danger to you, too."

"We've been here almost five years. If there was something hostile here we'd know about it by now, wouldn't we?"

"Not necessarily," Kirk said. "Two people can't know all the ins and outs of a whole planet, not even in five years – or a lifetime. In any event, one of the missions of the *Enterprise* is to protect human life in places like this. Under the circumstances, I'm going to have to be arbitrary and declare the argument closed."

It was shortly after they came aboard that McCoy forwarded his reports on the analyses of Darnell's body. "It was shock, all right," he told Kirk grimly by vid-screen. "But shock of a most peculiar sort. His blood electrolytes were completely deranged: massive salt depletion, hell – there isn't a microgram of salt in his whole body. Not in the blood, the tears, the organs, not anywhere. I can't even begin to guess how that could have happened at all, let alone all at once."

"What about the mottling on his face?"

"Broken capillaries. There are such marks all over the body. They're normal under the circumstances – except that I can't explain why they should be most marked on the face, or why the mottling should be ring-shaped. Clearly, though, he wasn't poisoned."

"Then the bitten plant," Kirk said equally grimly, "was a plant – in the criminal, not the botanical sense. A blind. That implies intelligence. I can't say I like that any better."

"Nor I," McCoy said. His eyes were averted.

"All right. That means we'll have to waste no time grilling the Bierces. I'll take it on. Bones, this has been a tremendous strain on you. I know, and you've been without sleep for two days. Better take a couple of tranquilizers and doss down."

"I'm all right."

"Orders," Kirk said. He turned off the screen and set off for the quarters he had assigned the Bierces.

But there was only one Bierce there. Nancy was missing.

"I expect she's gone below," Bierce said indifferently. "I'd go myself if I could get access to your Transporter for ten seconds. We didn't ask to be imprisoned up here."

"Darnell didn't ask to be killed, either. Your wife may be in serious danger. I must say, you seem singularly unworried."

"She's in no danger. This menace is all in your imagination."

"I suppose the body is imaginary, too?"

Bierce shrugged. "Nobody know what could have killed him. For all I know, you brought your own menace with you."

There was nothing further to be got out of him. Exasperated, Kirk went back to the bridge and ordered a general search. The results were all negative – including the report from the Transporter Room, which insisted that nobody had used its facilities since the party had returned to the ship from the camp.

But the search, though it did not find Nancy, found something else: Crewman Barnhart, dead on Deck Twelve. The marks on his body were the same as those on Darnell's.

Baffled and furious, Kirk called McCoy. "I'm sorry to bust in on your sleep, Bones, but this has gone far enough. I want Bierce checked out under pentathol."

"Um," McCoy said. His voice sounded fuzzy, as though he had still not quite recovered from his tranquilizer dose.

"Pentathol. Truth dope. Narcosynthesis. Um. Takes time. What about the patient's civil rights?"

"He can file a complaint if he wants. Go and get him ready."

An hour later, Bierce was lying on his bunk in half-trance. Kirk bent over him tensely; McCoy and Spock hovered in the background.

"Where's your wife?"

"Don't know . . . Poor Nancy, I loved her . . . The last of its kind . . ."

"Explain, please."

"The passenger pigeon . . . the buffalo . . ." Bierce groaned. "I feel strange."

Kirk beckoned to McCoy, who checked Bierce's pulse and looked under his eyelids. "He's all right," he said. "The transfer of questioner, from me to you, upset him. He's recovering."

"What about buffalo?" Kirk said, feeling absurd.

"Millions of them . . . prairies black with them. One single herd that covered three states. When they moved . . . like thunder. All gone now. Like the creatures here."

"Here? You mean down on the planet?"

"On the planet. Their temples . . . great poetry . . . Millions of them once, and now only one left. Nancy understood."

"Always the past tense," Spock's voice murmured.

"Where is Nancy? Where is she *now*?"

"Dead. Buried up on the hill. It killed her."

"Buried! But – how long ago was this, anyhow?"

"A year . . ." Bierce said. "Or was it two? I don't know. So confusing, Nancy and not Nancy. They needed salt, you see. When it ran out, they died . . . all but one."

The implication stunned Kirk. It was Spock who put the question.

"Is the creature masquerading as your wife?"

"Not a masquerade," Bierce droned. "It can *be* Nancy."

"Or anybody else?"

"Anybody. When it killed Nancy, I almost destroyed it. But I couldn't. It was the last."

The repetition was becoming more irritating every minute. Kirk said stonily: "Is that the only reason, Bierce? Tell me this: When it's with you, is it always Nancy?"

Bierce writhed. There was no answer. McCoy came forward again.

"I wouldn't press that one if I were you, Jim," he said. "You can get the answer if you need it, but not without endangering the patient."

"I don't need any better answer," Kirk said. "So we've intruded here into a little private heaven. This thing can be wife, lover, best friend, idol, slave, wise man, fool – anybody. A great life, having everyone in the universe at your beck and call – and you win all the arguments."

"A one-way road to paranoia," Spock said. Kirk swung back to the drugged man.

"Then you can recognize the creature – no matter what form it takes?"

"Will you help us?"

"No."

Kirk had expected no more. He gestured to McCoy. "I've got to go organize a search. Break down that resistance, Bones, I don't care how you do it or how much you endanger Bierce. In his present state of mind he's as big a danger to us as his 'wife'. Spock, back him up, and be ready to shoot if he should turn violent."

He stalked out. On the bridge, he called a General Quarters Three; that would put pairs of armed men in every corridor, on every deck. "Every man inspect his mate closely," he told the intercom. "There's one extra person aboard, masquerading as one of us. Lieutenant Uhura, make television rounds of all posts and stations. If you see any person twice in different places, sound the alarm. Got it?"

A sound behind him made him swing around. It was Spock. His clothes were torn, and he was breathing heavily.

"Spock! I thought I told you – what happened?"

"It was McCoy," Spock said shakily. "Or rather, it wasn't McCoy. You were barely out of the cabin when it grabbed me. I got away, but it's got my sidearm. No telling where it's off to now."

"McCoy! I *thought* he seemed a little reluctant about the pentathol. Reluctant, and sort of searching his memory, too. No wonder. Well, there's only one place it can have gone to now; right back where it came from."

"The planet? It can't."

"No. McCoy's cabin." He started to get up, but Spock lifted a hand sharply.

"Better look first, Captain. It may not have killed him yet, and if we alarm it – "

"You're right." Quickly, Kirk dialed in the intercom to McCoy's cabin, and after only a slight hesitation, punched the override button which would give him vision without sounding the buzzer on the other end.

McCoy was there. He was there twice: a sleeping McCoy on the bunk, and another one standing just inside the closed doorway, looking across the room. The standing form moved, passing in front of the hidden camera and momentarily blocking the view. Then it came back into the frame – but no longer as McCoy. It was Nancy.

She sat down on the bed and shook the sleeping doctor. He muttered, but refused to wake.

"Leonard," Nancy's voice said. "It's me. Nancy. Wake up. Please wake up. Help me."

Kirk had to admire the performance. What he was seeing was no doubt an alien creature, but its terror was completely convincing. Quite possibly it *was* in terror; in any event, the human form conveyed it as directly as a blow.

She shook McCoy again. He blinked his eyes groggily, and then sat up.

"Nancy! What's this? How long have I been sleeping?"

"Help me, Leonard."

"What's wrong? You're frightened."

"I am, I am," she said. "Please help me. They want to kill me!"

"Who?" McCoy said. "Easy. Nobody's going to hurt you."

"That's enough," Kirk said, unconsciously lowering his voice, though the couple on the screen could not hear him. "Luckily, the thing's trying to persuade him of something instead of killing him. Let's get down there fast, before it changes its mind."

Moments later, they burst into McCoy's cabin. The surgeon and the girl swung towards them. "Nancy" cried out.

"Get away from her, Bones," Kirk said, holding his gun rock steady.

"What? What's going on here, Jim?"

"That isn't Nancy, Bones."

"It isn't? Of course it is. Are you off your rocker?"

"It killed two crewmen."

"Bierce, too," Spock put in, his own gun leveled.

"*It?*"

"It," Kirk said. "Let me show you."

Kirk held out his free hand, unclenching it slowly. In the palm was a little heap of white crystals, diminishing at the edges from perspiration. "Look, Nancy," he said. "Salt. Free for the taking. Pure, concentrated salt."

Nancy took a hesitant step toward him, then stopped.

"Leonard," she said in a low voice. "Send him away. If you love me, make him go away."

"By all means," McCoy said harshly. "This is crazy behavior, Jim. You're frightening her."

"Not fright," Kirk said. "Hunger. Look at her!"

The creature, as if hypnotized, took another step forward. Then, without the slightest warning, there was a hurricane of motion. Kirk had a brief impression of a blocky body, man-sized but not the least like a man, and of suction-cup tentacles reaching for his face. Then there was a blast of sound and he fell.

It took a while for both Kirk and McCoy to recover – the captain from the nimbus of Spock's close-range phaser bolt, McCoy from emotional shock. By the time they were all back on the bridge, Bierce's planet was receding.

"The salt was an inspiration," Spock said. "Evidently the creature only hunted when it couldn't get the pure stuff; that's how Bierce kept it in control."

"I don't think the salt supply was the only reason why the race died out, though," Kirk said. "It wasn't really very intelligent – didn't use its advantages nearly as well as it might have."

"They could well have been residual," Spock suggested. "We still have teeth and nails, but we don't bite and claw much these days."

"That could well be. There's one thing I don't understand, though. How did it get into your cabin in the first place, Bones? Or don't you want to talk about it?"

"I don't mind," McCoy said. "Though I do feel like six kinds of a fool. It was simple. She came in just after I'd taken the tranquilizer and was feeling a little afloat. She said she didn't love her husband any more – wanted me to take her back to Earth. Well . . . it was a real thing I had with Nancy, long ago. I wasn't hard to tempt, especially with the drug already in my system. And later on, while I was asleep, she must have given me another dose – otherwise I couldn't have slept through all the excitement, the general quarters call and so on. It just goes to prove all over again – never mess with civilians."

"A good principle," Kirk agreed. "Unfortunately, an impossible one to live by."

"There's something *I* don't understand, though," McCoy

added. "The creature and Bierce had Spock all alone in Bierce's cabin – and from what I've found during the dissection, it was twice as strong as a man anyhow. How did you get out, Mr. Spock, without losing anything but your gun?"

Spock smiled. "Fortunately, my ancestors spawned in quite another ocean than yours, Dr. McCoy," he said. "My blood salts are quite different from yours. Evidently, I wasn't appetizing enough."

"Of course," McCoy said. He looked over at Kirk. "You still look a little pensive, Jim. Is there still something else wrong?"

"Mmm?" Kirk said. "Wrong? No, not exactly. I was just thinking about the buffalo."

TOTAL RECALL

(Tristar Pictures, 1990)
Starring: Arnold Schwarzenegger, Rachel Ticotin
& Sharon Stone
Directed by Paul Verhoeven
Based on "We Can Remember It For You Wholesale"
by Philip K. Dick

Total Recall is in my opinion the best of the recent spate of "megabuck" spectaculars in which hardcore SF has been combined with nightmarish fantasy to provided vehicles for the monosyllabic acting styles of Sylvester Stallone, Jean-Claude Van Damme and the former Mr Universe, Arnold Schwarzenegger. Directed by Paul Verhoeven and awash with blood, gore and violence, *Total Recall* is said to have cost $70 million – a very large proportion of which was spent on the special effects. Indeed, it is these truly amazing effects created by Thomas Fisher and Eric Revig which remain longest in the memory about the story of Doug Quail, a construction worker in the year 2084, who has nightmares of living on Mars and suspects that his mind may have been tampered with. But by whom? The truth finally begins to dawn on him when he visits a simulated holiday agency that uses artificial memory implanting to give its clients the sensation of travel and encounters an android killer, "Michael Ironsides". The mayhem which follows certainly contributed to making *Total Recall* a huge box office success and the forerunner of a whole series of similar violent, SF-orientated movies. The film originated from a short story by the American Philip K. Dick (1928–1982) who many regard as one of the greatest of contemporary SF writers. British novelist Fay Weldon has gone even further in an essay on Dick's wildly imaginative and often halucinatory writing by calling him, "California's own William Blake, a visionary and prophet". Certainly he was a man of contradictions and obsessions, and although largely self-educated, subsequently wrote a number of Science Fiction novels and short stories that are admired by fans and critics all over the world. Sadly, the adaptation of Philip Dick's work for the screen only began in the year of his death when Ridley Scott directed *Blade Runner*, starring Harrison Ford. This multi-layered story of a sinister Los Angeles of the future (circa 2019) was based on his novel, *Do Androids Dream of Electric Sheep?* (1968). *Total Recall*, in its turn, was derived from Dick's short story "We Can Remember It For You Wholesale" which had first appeared in the *Magazine of Fantasy & Science Fiction* in 1966. It was adapted for the screen by Ronald Shusett, Dan O'Bannon and Gary Goldman and provided another landmark in the history of Space Movies as well as bringing something of the genius of Philip K. Dick to an ever wider audience.

He awoke – and wanted Mars. The valleys, he thought. What would it be like to trudge among them? Great and greater yet: the dream grew as he became fully conscious, the dream and the yearning. He could almost feel the enveloping presence of the other world, which only Government agents and high officials had seen. A clerk like himself? Not likely.

"Are you getting up or not?" his wife Kirsten asked drowsily, with her usual hint of fierce crossness. "If you are, push the hot coffee button on the darn stove."

"Okay," Douglas Quail said, and made his way barefoot from the bedroom of their conapt to the kitchen. There, having dutifully pressed the hot coffee button, he seated himself at the kitchen table, brought out a yellow, small tin of fine Dean Swift snuff. He inhaled briskly, and the Beau Nash mixture stung his nose, burned the roof of his mouth. But still he inhaled; it woke him up and allowed his dreams, his nocturnal desires and random wishes, to condense into a semblance of rationality.

I will go, he said to himself. Before I die I'll see Mars.

It was, of course, impossible, and he knew this even as he dreamed. But the daylight, the mundane noise of his wife now brushing her hair before the bedroom mirror – everything conspired to remind him of what he was. A miserable little salaried employee, he said to himself with bitterness. Kirsten reminded him of this at least once a day and he did not blame her; it was a wife's job to bring her husband down to Earth. Down to Earth, he thought, and laughed. The figure of speech in this was literally apt.

"What are you sniggering about?" his wife asked as she swept into the kitchen, her long busy-pink robe wagging after her. "A dream, I bet. You're always full of them."

"Yes," he said, and gazed out the kitchen window at the hovercars and traffic runnels, and all the little energetic people hurrying to work. In a little while he would be among them. As always.

"I'll bet it has to do with some woman," Kirsten said witheringly.

"No," he said. "A god. The god of war. He has wonderful craters with every kind of plant-life growing deep down in them."

"Listen." Kirsten crouched down beside him and spoke earnestly, the harsh quality momentarily gone from her voice, "The bottom of the ocean – *our* ocean is much more, an infinity of times more beautiful. You know that; everyone knows that. Rent an artificial gill-outfit for both of us, take a week off from work, and we can descend and live down there at one of those year-round aquatic resorts. And in addition – " She broke off. "You're not listening. You should be. Here is something a lot better than that compulsion, that obsession you have about Mars, and you don't even listen!" Her voice rose piercingly. "God in heaven, you're doomed, Doug! What's going to become of you?"

"I'm going to work," he said, rising to his feet, his breakfast forgotten. "That's what's going to become of me."

She eyed him. "You're getting worse. More fanatical every day. Where's it going to lead?"

"To Mars," he said, and opened the door to the closet to get down a fresh shirt to wear to work.

Having descended from the taxi Douglas Quail slowly walked across three densely-populated foot runnels and to the modern, attractively inviting doorway. There he halted, impeding mid-morning traffic, and with caution read the shifting-color neon sign. He had, in the past, scrutinized this sign before . . . but never had he come so close. This was very different; what he did now was something else. Something which eventually had to happen.

REKAL, INCORPORATED

Was this the answer? After all, an illusion, no matter how convincing, remained nothing more than an illusion. At least objectively. But subjectively – quite the opposite entirely.

And anyhow he had an appointment. Within the next five minutes.

Taking a deep breath of mildly smog-infested Chicago air, he walked through the dazzling polychromatic shimmer of the doorway and up to the receptionist's counter.

The nicely-articulated blonde at the counter, bare-bosomed and tidy, said pleasantly, "Good morning, Mr Quail."

"Yes," he said. "I'm here to see about a Rekal course. As I guess you know."

"Not 'rekal' but recall," the receptionist corrected him. She picked up the receiver of the vidphone by her smooth elbow and said into it, "Mr Douglas Quail is here, Mr McClane. May he come inside, now? Or is it too soon?"

"Giz wetwa wum-wum wamp," the phone mumbled.

"Yes, Mr Quail," she said. "You may go on in; Mr McClane is expecting you." As he started off uncertainly she called after him, "Room D, Mr Quail. To your right."

After a frustrating but brief moment of being lost he found the proper room. The door hung open and inside, at a big genuine walnut desk, sat a genial-looking man, middle-aged, wearing the latest Martian frog-pelt gray suit; his attire alone would have told Quail that he had come to the right person.

"Sit down, Douglas," McClane said, waving his plump hand toward a chair which faced the desk. "So you want to have gone to Mars. Very good."

Quail seated himself, feeling tense. "I'm not so sure this is worth the fee," he said. "It costs a lot and as far as I can see I really get nothing." Costs almost as much as going, he thought.

"You get tangible proof of your trip," McClane disagreed emphatically. "All the proof you'll need. Here; I'll show you." He dug within a drawer of his impressive desk. "Ticket stub." Reaching into a manila folder he produced a small square of embossed cardboard. "It proves you went – and returned. Postcards." He laid out four franked picture 3-D full-color postcards in a neatly-arranged row on the desk for Quail to see. "Film. Shots you took of local sights on Mars with a rented movie camera." To Quail he displayed those, too. "Plus the names of people you met, two hundred poscreds worth of souvenirs, which will arrive – from Mars – within the following month. And passport, certificates listing the shots you received. And more." He glanced up keenly at Quail. "You'll know you went, all right," he said. "You won't remember us, won't remember me or ever having been here. It'll be a real trip in your mind; we guarantee that. A full two weeks of recall; every last piddling detail. Remember this: if at any time you doubt that you really took an extensive trip to Mars you can return here and get a full refund. You see?"

"But I didn't go," Quail said. "I won't have gone, no matter what proofs you provide me with." He took a deep, unsteady breath. "And I never was a secret agent with Interplan." It seemed impossible to him that Rekal, Incorporated's extra-factual memory implant would do its job – despite what he had heard people say.

"Mr Quail," McClane said patiently. "As you explained in your letter to us, you have no chance, no possibility in the slightest, of ever actually getting to Mars; you can't afford it, and what is much more important, you could never qualify as an undercover agent for Interplan or anybody else. This is the only way you can achieve your, ahem, life-long dream; am I not correct, sir? You can't be this; you can't actually do this." He chuckled. "But you can *have been* and *have done*. We see to that. And our fee is reasonable; no hidden charges." He smiled encouragingly.

"Is an extra-factual memory that convincing?" Quail asked.

"More than the real thing, sir. Had you really gone to Mars as an Interplan agent, you would by now have forgotten a great deal; our analysis of truemem systems – authentic recollections of major events in a person's life – shows that a variety of details are very quickly lost to the person. Forever. Part of the package we offer you is such deep implantation of recall that nothing is forgotten. The packet which is fed to you while you're comatose is the creation of trained experts, men who have spent years on Mars; in every case we verify details down to the last iota. And you've picked a rather easy extra-factual system; had you picked Pluto or wanted to be Emperor of the Inner Planet Alliance we'd have much more difficulty . . . and the charges would be considerably greater."

Reaching into his coat for his wallet, Quail said, "Okay. It's been my life-long ambition and I can see I'll never really do it. So I guess I'll have to settle for this."

"Don't think of it that way," McClane said severely. "You're not accepting second-best. The actual memory, with all its vagueness, omissions and ellipses, not to say distortions – that's second-best." He accepted the money and pressed a button on his desk. "All right, Mr Quail," he said, as the door of his office opened and two burly men swiftly entered. "You're on your way to Mars as a secret agent." He rose, came over to shake Quail's nervous, moist hand. "Or rather, you have been on your way. This afternoon at four-thirty you will, um, arrive back here on Terra; a cab will leave you off at your conapt and as I say you will never remember seeing me or coming here; you won't, in fact, even remember having heard of our existence."

His mouth dry with nervousness, Quail followed the two technicians from the office; what happened next depended on them.

Will I actually believe I've been on Mars? he wondered. That I managed to fulfill my lifetime ambition? He had a strange, lingering intuition that something would go wrong. But just what – he did not know.

He would have to wait to find out.

The intercom on McClane's desk, which connected him with the work-area of the firm, buzzed and a voice said, "Mr Quail is under sedation now, sir. Do you want to supervise this one, or shall we go ahead?"

"It's routine," McClane observed. "You may go ahead, Lowe; I don't think you'll run into any trouble." Programming an artificial memory of a trip to another planet – with or without the added fillip of being a secret agent – showed up on the firm's work-schedule with monotonous regularity. In one month, he calculated wryly, we must do twenty of these . . . ersatz interplanetary travel has become our bread and butter.

"Whatever you say, Mr McClane," Lowe's voice came, and thereupon the intercom shut off.

We Can Remember It For You Wholesale

Going to the vault section in the chamber behind his office, McClane searched about for a Three packet – trip to Mars – and a Sixty-two packet: secret Interplan spy. Finding the two packets, he returned with them to his desk, seated himself comfortably, poured out the contents – merchandise which would be planted in Quail's conapt while the lab technicians busied themselves installing the false memory.

A one-poscred sneaky-pete side arm, McClane reflected; that's the largest item. Sets us back financially the most. Then a pellet-sized transmitter, which could be swallowed if the agent were caught. Code book that astonishingly resembled the real thing . . . the firm's models were highly accurate: based, whenever possible, on actual U.S. military issue. Odd bits which made no intrinsic sense but which would be woven into the warp and woof of Quail's imaginary trip, would coincide with his memory: half an ancient silver fifty cent piece, several quotations from John Donne's sermons written incorrectly, each on a separate piece of transparent tissue-thin paper, several match folders from bars on Mars, a stainless steel spoon engraved PROPERTY OF DOME-MARKS NATIONAL KIBBUZIM, a wire tapping coil which –

The intercom buzzed. "Mr McClane, I'm sorry to bother you but something rather ominous has come up. Maybe it would be better if you were in here after all. Quail is already under sedation; he reacted well to the narkidrine; he's completely unconscious and receptive. But – "

"I'll be in." Sensing trouble, McClane left his office; a moment later he emerged in the work area.

On a hygienic bed lay Douglas Quail, breathing slowly and regularly, his eyes virtually shut; he seemed dimly – but only dimly – aware of the two technicians and now McClane himself.

"There's no space to insert false memory-patterns?" McClane felt irritation. "Merely drop out two work weeks; he's employed as a clerk at the West Coast Emigration Bureau, which is a government agency, so he undoubtedly has or had two weeks vacation within the last year. That ought to do it." Petty details annoyed him. And always would.

"Our problem," Lowe said sharply, "is something quite different." He bent over the bed, said to Quail, "Tell Mr McClane what you told us." To McClane he said, "Listen closely."

The gray-green eyes of the man lying in the bed focused on McClane's face. The eyes, he observed uneasily, had become hard; they had a polished, inorganic quality, like semi-precious tumbled stones. He was not sure that he liked what he saw; the brilliance was too cold. "What do you want now?" Quail said harshly. "You've broken my cover. Get out of here before I take you all apart." He studied McClane, "Especially you, you're in charge of this counter-operation."

Lowe said, "How long were you on Mars?"

"One month," Quail said gratingly.

"And your purpose there?" Lowe demanded.

The meager lips twisted; Quail eyed him and did not speak. At last, drawling the words out so that they dripped with hostility, he said, "Agent for Interplan. As I already told you. Don't you record everything that's said? Play your vid-aud tape back for your boss and leave me alone." He shut his eyes, then; the hard brilliance ceased. McClane felt, instantly, a rushing splurge of relief.

Lowe said quietly, "This is a tough man, Mr McClane."

"He won't be," McClane said. "After we arrange for him to lose his memory-chain again. He'll be as meek as before." To Quail he said, "So *this* is why you wanted to go to Mars so terribly badly."

Without opening his eyes Quail said, "I never wanted to go to Mars. I was assigned it – they handed it to me and there I was: stuck. Oh yeah, I admit I was curious about it;

who wouldn't be?" Again he opened his eyes and surveyed the three of them, McClane in particular. "Quite a truth drug you've got here; it brought up things I had absolutely no memory of." He pondered. "I wonder about Kirsten," he said, half to himself. "Could she be in on it? An Interplan contact keeping an eye on me . . . to be certain I didn't regain my memory? No wonder she's been so derisive about my wanting to go there." Faintly, he smiled; the smile – one of understanding – disappeared almost at once.

McClane said, "Please believe me, Mr Quail; we stumbled onto this entirely by accident. In the work we do – "

"I believe you," Quail said. He seemed tired, now; the drug was continuing to pull him under, deeper and deeper. "Where did I say I'd been?" he murmured. "Mars? Hard to remember – I know I'd like to see it; so would everybody else. But me – " His voice trailed off. "Just a clerk, a nothing clerk."

Straightening up, Lowe said to his superior. "He wants a false memory implanted that corresponds to a trip he actually took. And a false reason which is the real reason. He's telling the truth; he's a long way down in the narkidrine. The trip is very vivid in his mind – at least under sedation. But apparently he doesn't recall it otherwise. Someone, probably at a government military-sciences lab, erased his conscious memories; all he knew was that going to Mars meant something special to him, and so did being a secret agent. They couldn't erase that; it's not a memory but a desire, undoubtedly the same one that motivated him to volunteer for the assignment in the first place."

The other technician, Keeler, said to McClane, "What do we do? Graft a false memory-pattern over the real memory? There's no telling what the results would be; he might remember some of the genuine trip, and the confusion might bring on a psychotic interlude. He'd have to hold two opposite premises in his mind simultaneously: that he went to Mars and that he didn't. That he's a genuine agent for Interplan and he's not, that it's spurious. I think we ought to revive him without any false memory implantation and send him out of here; this is hot."

"Agreed," McClane said. A thought came to him. "Can you predict what he'll remember when he comes out of sedation?"

"Impossible to tell," Lowe said. "He probably will have some dim, diffuse memory of his actual trip, now. And he'd probably be in grave doubt as to its validity; he'd probably decide our programming slipped a gear-tooth. And he'd remember coming here – unless you want it erased."

"The less we mess with this man," McClane said, "the better I like it. This is nothing for us to fool around with; we've been foolish enough to – or unlucky enough to – uncover a genuine Interplan spy who has a cover so perfect that up to now even he didn't know what he was – or rather is." The sooner they washed their hands of the man calling himself Douglas Quail the better.

"Are you going to plant packets Three and Sixty-two in his conapt?" Lowe said.

"No," McClane said. "And we're going to return half his fee."

"Half! Why half?"

McClane said lamely, "It seems to be a good compromise."

As the cab carried him back to his conapt at the residential end of Chicago, Douglas Quail said to himself, It's sure good to be back on Terra.

Already the month-long period on Mars had begun to waver in his memory; he had only an image of profound gaping craters, an ever present ancient erosion of hills, of vitality, of motion itself. A world of dust where little happened, where a good part of the day was spent checking and rechecking one's portable oxygen source. And then the life forms, the unassuming and modest gray-brown cacti and maw-worms.

As a matter of fact he had brought back several moribund examples of Martian fauna; he had smuggled them through customs. After all, they posed no menace; they couldn't survive in Earth's heavy atmosphere.

Reaching into his coat pocket he rummaged for the container of Martian maw-worms –

And found an envelope instead.

Lifting it out, he discovered, to his perplexity, that it contained five hundred and seventy poscreds, in cred bills of low denomination. Where'd I get this? he asked himself. Didn't I spend every 'cred I had on my trip?

With the money came a slip of paper marked: *one-half fee ret'd. By McClane.* And then the date. Today's date.

"Recall," he said aloud.

"Recall what, sir or madam?" the robot driver of the cab inquired respectfully.

"Do you have a phone book?" Quail demanded.

"Certainly, sir or madam." A slot opened: from it slid a microtape phone book for Cook County.

"It's spelled oddly," Quail said as he leafed through the pages of the yellow section. He felt fear, then; abiding fear. "Here it is," he said. "Take me there, to Rekal, Incorporated. I've changed my mind; I don't want to go home."

"Yes, sir, or madam, as the case may be," the driver said. A moment later the cab was zipping back in the opposite direction.

"May I make use of your phone?" he asked.

"Be my guest," the robot driver said. And presented a shiny new emperor 3-D color phone to him.

He dialed his own conapt. And after a pause found himself confronted by a miniature but chillingly realistic image of Kirsten on the small screen. "I've been to Mars," he said to her.

"You're drunk." Her lips writhed scornfully. "Or worse."

"'S god's truth."

"When?" she demanded.

"I don't know." He felt confused. "A simulated trip, I think. By means of one of those artificial or extra-factual or whatever it is memory places. It didn't take."

Kirsten said witheringly, "You *are* drunk." And broke the connection at her end. He hung up, then, feeling his face flush. Always the same tone, he said hotly to himself. Always the retort, as if she knows everything and I know nothing. What a marriage. Keerist, he thought dismally.

A moment later the cab stopped at the curb before a modern, very attractive little pink building, over which a shifting, poly-chromatic neon sign read: REKAL, INCORPORATED.

The receptionist, chic and bare from the waist up, stared in surprise, then gained masterful control of herself. "Oh hello Mr Quail," she said nervously. "H-how are you? Did you forget something?"

"The rest of my fee back," he said.

More composed now, the receptionist said, "Fee? I think you are mistaken, Mr Quail. You were here discussing the feasibility of an extrafactual trip for you, but – " She shrugged her smooth pale shoulders. "As I understand it, no trip was taken."

Quail said, "I remember everything, miss. My letter to Rekal, Incorporated, which started this whole business off. I remember my arrival here, my visit with Mr McClane. Then the two lab technicians taking me in tow and administering a drug to put me out." No wonder the firm had returned half his fee. The false memory of his "trip to Mars" hadn't taken – at least not entirely, not as he had been assured.

"Mr Quail," the girl said, "although you are a minor clerk you are a good-looking man and it spoils your features to become angry. If it would make you feel any better, I might, ahem, let you take me out . . ."

He felt furious, then. "I remember you," he said savagely. "For instance the fact that your breasts are sprayed blue; that stuck in my mind. And I remember Mr McClane's promise that if I remembered my visit to Rekal, Incorporated I'd receive my money back in full. Where is Mr McClane?"

After a delay – probably as long as they could manage – he found himself once more seated facing the imposing walnut desk, exactly as he had been an hour or so earlier in the day.

"Some technique you have," Quail said sardonically. His disappointment – and resentment – were enormous, by now. "My so-called 'memory' of a trip to Mars as an undercover agent for Interplan is hazy and vague and shot full of contradictions. And I clearly remember my dealings here with you people. I ought to take this to the Better Business Bureau." He was burning angry, at this point; his sense of being cheated had overwhelmed him, had destroyed his customary aversion to participating in a public squabble.

Looking morose, as well as cautious, McClane said, "We capitulate, Quail. We'll refund the balance of your fee. I fully concede the fact that we did absolutely nothing for you." His tone was resigned.

Quail said accusingly, "You didn't even provide me with the various artifacts that you claimed would 'prove' to me I had been on Mars. All that song-and-dance you went into – it hasn't materialized into a damn thing. Not even a ticket stub. Nor postcards. Nor passport. Nor proof of immunization shots. Nor – "

"Listen, Quail," McClane said. "Suppose I told you – " He broke off. "Let it go." He pressed a button on his intercom. "Shirley, will you disburse five hundred and seventy more creds in the form of a cashier's check made out to Douglas Quail? Thank you." He released the button, then glared at Quail.

Presently the check appeared; the receptionist placed it before McClane and once more vanished out of sight, leaving the two men alone, still facing each other across the desk.

"Let me give you a word of advice," McClane said as he signed the check and passed it over. "Don't discuss your, ahem, recent trip to Mars with anyone."

"What trip?"

"Well, that's the thing." Doggedly, McClane said, "The trip you partially remember. Act as if you don't remember; pretend it never took place. Don't ask me why; just take my advice: it'll be better for all of us." He had begun to perspire. Freely. "Now, Mr Quail, I have other business, other clients to see." He rose, showed Quail to the door.

Quail said, as he opened the door, "A firm that turns out such bad work shouldn't have any clients at all." He shut the door behind him.

On the way home in the cab Quail pondered the wording of his letter of complaint to the Better Business Bureau, Terra Division. As soon as he could get to his typewriter he'd get started; it was clearly his duty to warn other people away from Rekal, Incorporated.

When he got back to his conapt he seated himself before his Hermes Rocket portable, opened the drawers and rummaged for carbon paper – and noticed a small, familiar box. A box which he had carefully filled on Mars with Martian fauna and later smuggled through customs.

Opening the box, he saw, to his disbelief, six dead maw-worms and several varieties of the unicellular life on which the Martian worms fed. The protozoa were dried-up, dusty, but he recognized them; it had taken him an entire day picking among the vast dark alien boulders to find them. A wonderful, illuminated journey of discovery.

But I didn't go to Mars, he realized.

Yet on the other hand –

Kirsten appeared at the doorway to the room, an arm-load of pale brown groceries gripped. "Why are you home in the middle of the day?" Her voice, in an eternity of sameness, was accusing.

"*Did I go to Mars?*" he asked her. "You would know."

"No, of course you didn't go to Mars; *you* would know that, I would think. Aren't you always bleating about going?"

He said, "By God, I think I went." After a pause he added, "And simultaneously I think I didn't go."

"Make up your mind."

"How can I?" He gestured. "I have both memory-tracks grafted inside my head; one is real and one isn't but I can't tell which is which. Why can't I rely on you? They haven't tinkered with you." She could do this much for him at least – even if she never did anything else.

Kirsten said in a level, controlled voice, "Doug, if you don't pull yourself together, we're through. I'm going to leave you."

"I'm in trouble." His voice came out husky and coarse. And shaking. "Probably I'm heading into a psychotic episode; I hope not, but – maybe that's it. It would explain everything, anyhow."

Setting down the bag of groceries, Kirsten stalked to the closet. "I was not kidding," she said to him quietly. She brought out a coat, got it on, walked back to the door of the conapt. "I'll phone you one of these days soon," she said tonelessly. "This is goodbye, Doug. I hope you pull out of this eventually; I really pray you do. For your sake."

"Wait," he said desperately. "Just tell me and make it absolute; I did go or I didn't – tell me which one." But they may have altered your memory-track also, he realized.

The door closed. His wife had left. Finally!

A voice behind him said, "Well, that's that. Now put up your hands, Quail. And also please turn around and face this way."

He turned, instinctively, without raising his hands.

The man who faced him wore the plum uniform of the Interplan Police Agency, and his gun appeared to be UN issue. And, for some odd reason, he seemed familiar to Quail; familiar in a blurred, distorted fashion which he could not pin down. So, jerkily, he raised his hands.

"You remember," the policeman said, "your trip to Mars. We know all your actions today and all your thoughts – in particular your very important thoughts on the trip home from Rekal, Incorporated." He explained, "We have a teletransmitter wired within your skull; it keeps us constantly informed."

A telepathic transmitter; use of a living plasma that had been discovered on Luna. He shuddered with self-aversion. The thing lived inside him, within his own brain, feeding, listening, feeding. But the Interplan police used them; that had come out even in the homeopapers. So this was probably true, dismal as it was.

"Why me?" Quail said huskily. What had he done – or thought? And what did this have to do with Rekal, Incorporated?

"Fundamentally," the Interplan cop said, "this has nothing to do with Rekal; it's between you and us." He tapped his right ear. "I'm still picking up your mentational processes by way of your cephalic transmitter." In the man's ear Quail saw a small white-plastic plug. "So I have to warn you: anything you think may be held against you." He smiled. "Not that it matters now; you've already thought and spoken yourself into oblivion. What's annoying is the fact that under narkidrine at Rekal, Incorporated you told them, their technicians and the owner, Mr McClane, about your trip; where you went, for whom, some of what you did. They're very frightened. They wish they had never laid eyes on you." He added reflectively, "They're right."

Quail said, "I never made any trip. It's a false memory-chain improperly planted in me by McClane's technicians."

But then he thought of the box, in his desk drawer, containing the Martian life forms. And the trouble and hardship he had had gathering them. The memory seemed real. And the box of life forms; that certainly was real. Unless McClane had planted it. Perhaps this was one of the "proofs" which McClane had talked glibly about.

The memory of my trip to Mars, he thought, doesn't convince me – but unfortunately it has convinced the Interplan Police Agency. They think I really went to Mars and they think I at least partially realize it.

"We not only know you went to Mars," the Interplan cop agreed, in answer to his thoughts, "but we know that you now remember enough to be difficult for us. And there's no use expunging your conscious memory of all this, because if we do you'll simply show up at Rekal, Incorporated again and start all over. And we can't do anything about McClane and his operation because we have no jurisdiction over anyone except our own people. Anyhow, McClane hasn't committed any crime." He eyed Quail. "Nor, technically, have you. You didn't go to Rekal, Incorporated with the idea of regaining your memory; you went, as we realize, for the usual reason people go there – a love by plain, dull people for adventure." He added, "Unfortunately you're not plain, not dull, and you've already had too much excitement; the last thing in the universe you needed was a course from Rekal, Incorporated. Nothing could have been more lethal for you or for us. And, for that matter, for McClane."

Quail said, "Why is it 'difficult' for you if I remember my trip – my alleged trip – and what I did there?"

"Because," the Interplan harness bull said, "what you did is not in accord with our great white all-protecting father public image. You did, for us, what we never do. As you'll presently remember – thanks to narkidrine. That box of dead worms and algae has been sitting in your desk drawer for six months, ever since you got back. And at no time have you shown the slightest curiosity about it. We didn't even know you had it until you remembered it on your way home from Rekal; then we came here on the double to look for it." He added, unnecessarily, "Without any luck; there wasn't enough time."

A second Interplan cop joined the first one; the two briefly conferred. Meanwhile, Quail thought rapidly. He did remember more, now; the cop had been right about narkidrine. They – Interplan – probably used it themselves. Probably? He knew darn well they did; he had seen them putting a prisoner on it. Where would *that* be? Somewhere on Terra? More likely Luna, he decided, viewing the image rising from his highly defective – but rapidly less so – memory.

And he remembered something else. Their reason for sending him to Mars; the job he had done.

No wonder they had expunged his memory.

"Oh God," the first of the two Interplan cops said, breaking off his conversation with his companion. Obviously, he had picked up Quail's thoughts. "Well, this is a far worse problem, now; as bad as it can get." He walked toward Quail, again covering him with his gun. "We've got to kill you," he said. "And right away."

Nervously, his fellow officer said, "Why right away? Can't we simply cart him off to Interplan New York and let them – "

"*He* knows why it has to be right away," the first cop said; he too looked nervous, now, but Quail realized that it was for an entirely different reason. His memory had been brought back almost entirely, now. And he fully understood the officer's tension.

"On Mars," Quail said hoarsely, "I killed a man. After getting past fifteen bodyguards. Some armed with sneakypete guns, the way you are." He had been trained, by Interplan, over a five year period to be an assassin. A professional killer. He knew ways to take out armed adversaries . . . such as these two officers; and the one with the earreceiver knew it, too.

If he moved swiftly enough –

The gun fired. But he had already moved to one side, and at the same time he chopped down the gun-carrying officer. In an instant he had possession of the gun and was covering the other, confused, officer.

"Picked my thoughts up," Quail said, panting for breath. "He knew what I was going to do, but I did it anyhow."

Half sitting up, the injured officer grated, "He won't use that gun on you, Sam; I pick that up, too. He knows he's finished, and he knows we know it, too. Come on, Quail." Laboriously, grunting with pain, he got shakily to his feet. He held out his hand. "The gun," he said to Quail. "You can't use it, and if you turn it over to me I'll guarantee not to kill you; you'll be given a hearing, and someone higher up in Interplan will decide, not me. Maybe they can erase your memory once more; I don't know. But you know the thing I was going to kill you for; I couldn't keep you from remembering it. So my reason for wanting to kill you is in a sense past."

Quail, clutching the gun, bolted from the conapt, sprinted for the elevator. If you follow me, he thought, I'll kill you. So don't. He jabbed at the elevator button and, a moment later, the doors slid back.

The police hadn't followed him. Obviously they had picked up his terse, tense thoughts and had decided not to take the chance.

With him inside the elevator descended. He had gotten away – for a time. But what next? Where could he go?

The elevator reached the ground floor, a moment later Quail had joined the mob of peds hurrying along the runnels. His head ached and he felt sick. But at least he had evaded death; they had come very close to shooting him on the spot, back in his own conapt.

And they probably will again, he decided. When they find me. And with this transmitter inside me, that won't take too long.

Ironically, he had gotten exactly what he had asked Rekal, Incorporated for. Adventure, peril, Interplan police at work, a secret and dangerous trip to Mars in which his life was at stake – everything he had wanted as a false memory.

The advantages of it being a memory – and nothing more – could now be appreciated.

On a park bench, alone, he sat dully watching a flock of perts: a semibird imported from Mars' two moons, capable of soaring flight, even against Earth's huge gravity.

Maybe I can find my way back to Mars, he pondered. But then what? It would be worse on Mars; the political organization whose leader he had assassinated would spot him the moment he stepped from the ship; he would have Interplan and *them* after him, there.

Can you hear me thinking? he wondered. Easy avenue to paranoia; sitting here along he felt them tuning in on him, monitoring, recording, discussing . . . he shivered, rose to his feet, walked aimlessly, his hands deep in his pockets. No matter where I go, he realized. You'll always be with me. As long as I have this device inside my head.

I'll make a deal with you, he thought to himself – and to them. Can't you imprint a false-memory template on me again, as you did before, that I lived an average, routine life, never went to Mars? Never saw an Interplan uniform up close and never handled a gun?

A voice inside his brain answered, "As has been carefully explained to you: that would not be enough."

Astonished, he halted.

"We formerly communicated with you in this manner," the voice continued. "When you were operating in the field, on Mars. It's been months since we've done it; we assumed, in fact, that we'd never have to do so again. Where are you?"

"Walking," Quail said, "to my death." By your officers' guns, he added as an afterthought. "How can you be sure it wouldn't be enough?" he demanded. "Don't the Rekal techniques work?"

"As we said. If you're given a set of standard, average memories you get – restless. You'd inevitably seek out Rekal or one of its competitors again. We can't go through this a second time."

"Suppose," Quail said, "once my authentic memories have been cancelled, something more vital than standard memories are implanted. Something which would act to satisfy my craving," he said. "That's been proved; that's probably why you initially hired me. But you ought to be able to come up with something else – something equal. I was the richest man on Terra but I finally gave all my money to educational foundations. Or I was a famous deep-space explorer. Anything of that sort; wouldn't one of those do?"

Silence.

"Try it," he said desperately. "Get some of your top-notch military psychiatrists; explore my mind. Find out what my most expansive daydream is." He tried to think. "Women," he said. "Thousands of them, like Don Juan had. An interplanetary playboy – a mistress in every city on Earth, Luna and Mars. Only I gave that up, out of exhaustion. Please," he begged. "Try it."

"You'd voluntarily surrender, then?" the voice inside his head asked. "If we agreed to arrange such a solution? *If* it's possible?"

After an interval of hesitation he said, "Yes." I'll take the risk, he said to himself. That you don't simply kill me.

"You make the first move," the voice said presently. "Turn yourself over to us. And we'll investigate that line of possibility. If we can't do it, however, if your authentic memories begin to crop up again as they've done at this time, then – " There was silence and then the voice finished, "We'll have to destroy you. As you must understand. Well, Quail, you still want to try?"

"Yes," he said. Because the alternative was death row – and for certain. At least this way he had a chance, slim as it was.

"You present yourself at our main barracks in New York," the voice of the Interplan cop resumed. "At 580 Fifth Avenue, floor twelve. Once you've surrendered yourself we'll have our psychiatrists begin on you; we'll have personality-profile tests made. We'll attempt to determine your absolute, ultimate fantasy wish – and then we'll bring you back to Rekal, Incorporated, here; get them in on it, fulfilling that wish in vicarious surrogate retrospection. And – good luck. We do owe you something; you acted as a capable instrument for us." The voice lacked malice; if anything, they – the organization – felt sympathy toward him.

"Thanks," Quail said. And began searching for a robot cab.

"Mr Quail," the stern-faced, elderly Interplan psychiatrist said, "you possess a most interesting wish-fulfillment dream fantasy. Probably nothing such as you consciously entertain or suppose. This is commonly the way; I hope it won't upset you too much to hear about it."

The senior ranking Interplan officer present said briskly, "He better not be too much upset to hear about it, not if he expects not to get shot."

"Unlike the fantasy of wanting to be an Interplan under-cover agent," the psychiatrist continued, "which, being rela-tively speaking a product of maturity, had a certain plausibility to it, this production is a grotesque dream of your childhood; it is no wonder you fail to recall it. Your fantasy is this: you are nine years old, walking alone down a rustic lane. An un-familiar variety of space vessel from another star system lands directly in front of you. No one on Earth but you, Mr Quail, sees it. The creatures within are very small and helpless, somewhat on the order of field mice, although they are attempting to invade Earth; ships will soon be on their way, when this advance party gives the go-ahead signal."

"And I suppose I stop them," Quail said, experiencing a mixture of amusement and disgust. "Single-handed I wipe them out. Probably by stepping on them with my foot."

"No," the psychiatrist said patiently. "You halt the invasion, but not by destroying them. Instead, you show them kindness and mercy, even though by telepathy – their mode of communication – you know why they have come. They have never seen such humane traits exhibited by any sentient organism, and to show their appreciation they make a covenant with you."

Quail said, "They won't invade Earth as long as I'm alive."

"Exactly." To the Interplan officer the psychiatrist said, "You can see it does fit his personality, despite his feigned scorn."

"So by merely existing," Quail said, feeling a growing pleasure, "by simply being alive, I keep Earth safe from alien rule. I'm in effect, then, the most important person on Terra. Without lifting a finger."

"Yes indeed, sir," the psychiatrist said. "And this is bedrock in your psyche; this is a life-long childhood fantasy. Which, without depth and drug therapy, you never would have recalled. But it has always existed in you; it went underneath, but never ceased."

To McClane, who sat intently listening, the senior police official said, "Can you implant an extrafactual memory pattern that extreme in him?"

"We get handed every possible type of wish-fantasy there is," McClane said. "Frankly, I've heard a lot worse than this. Certainly we can handle it. Twenty-four hours from now he won't just *wish* he'd saved Earth; he'll devoutly believe it really happened."

The senior police official said, "You can start the job, then. In preparation we've already once again erased the memory in him of his trip to Mars."

Quail said, "What trip to Mars?"

No one answered him, so, reluctantly, he shelved the question. And anyhow a police vehicle had now put in its appearance; he, McClane and the senior police officer crowded into it, and presently they were on their way to Chicago and Rekal, Incorporated.

"You had better make no errors this time," the police officer said to heavy-set, nervous-looking McClane.

"I can't see what could go wrong," McClane mumbled, perspiring. "This has nothing to do with Mars or Interplan. Single-handedly stopping an invasion of Earth from another star-system." He shook his head at that. "Wow, what a kid dreams up. And by pious virtue, too; not by force. It's sort of quaint." He dabbed at his forehead with a large linen pocket handkerchief.

Nobody said anything.

"In fact," McClane said, "it's touching."

"But arrogant," the police officer said starkly. "Inasmuch as when he dies the invasion will resume. No wonder he doesn't recall it; it's the most grandiose fantasy I ever ran across." He eyed Quail with disapproval. "And to think we put this man on our payroll."

When they reached Rekal, Incorporated, the receptionist, Shirley, met them breathlessly in the outer office. "Welcome back, Mr Quail," she fluttered, her melon-shaped breasts – today painted an incandescent orange – bobbing with agitation. "I'm sorry everything worked out so badly before; I'm sure this time it'll go better."

Still repeatedly dabbling at his shiny forehead with his neatly-folded Irish linen handkerchief, McClane said, "It better." Moving with rapidity he rounded up Lowe and Keeler, escorted them and Douglas Quail to the work area, and then, with Shirley and the senior police officer, returned to his familiar office. To wait.

"Do we have a packet made up for this, Mr McClane?" Shirley asked, bumping against him in her agitation, then coloring modestly.

"I think we do." He tried to recall; then gave up and consulted the formal chart. "A combination," he decided aloud, "of packages Eighty-one, Twenty, and Six." From the vault section of the chamber behind his desk he fished out the appropriate packets, carried them to his desk for inspection. "From Eighty-one," he explained, "a magic healing rod given him – the client in question, this time Mr Quail – by the race of beings from another system. A token of their gratitude."

"Does it work?" the police officer asked curiously.

"It did once," McClane explained. "But he, ahem, you see, used it up years ago, healing right and left. Now it's only a memento. But he remembers it working spectacularly." He chuckled, then opened packet Twenty. "Document from the UN Secretary General thanking him for saving Earth; this isn't precisely appropriate, because part of Quail's fantasy is that no one knows of the invasion except himself, but for the sake of verisimilitude we'll throw it in." He inspected packet Six, then. What came from this? He couldn't recall; frowning, he dug into the plastic bag as Shirley and the Interplan police officer watched intently.

"Writing," Shirley said. "In a funny language."

"This tells who they were," McClane said, "and where they came from. Including a detailed star map logging their flight here and the system of origin. Of course it's in *their* script, so he can't read it. But he remembers them reading it to him in his own tongue." He placed the three artifacts in the center of the desk. "These should be taken to Quail's conapt," he said to the police officer. "So that when he gets home he'll find them. And it'll confirm his fantasy. SOP – standard operating procedure." He chuckled apprehensively, wondering how matters were going with Lowe and Keeler.

The intercom buzzed. "Mr McClane, I'm sorry to bother you." It was Lowe's voice; he froze as he recognized it, froze and became mute. "But something's come up. Maybe it would be better if you came in here and supervised. Like before, Quail reacted well to the narkidrine; he's unconscious, relaxed and receptive. But – "

McClane sprinted for the work area.

On a hygienic bed Douglas Quail lay breathing slowly and regularly, eyes half-shut, dimly conscious of those around him.

"We started interrogating him," Lower said, white-faced. "To find out exactly when to place the fantasy memory of him single-handedly having saved Earth. And strangely enough – "

"They told me not to tell," Douglas Quail mumbled in a dull drug-saturated voice. "That was the agreement. I wasn't even supposed to remember. But how could I forget an event like that?"

I guess it would be hard, McClane reflected. But you did – until now.

"They even gave me a scroll," Quail mumbled. "of gratitude. I have it hidden in my conapt; I'll show it to you."

To the Interplan officer who had followed after him, McClane said, "Well, I offer the suggestion that you better not kill him. If you do they'll return."

"They also gave me a magic invisible destroying rod," Quail mumbled, eyes totally shut, now. "That's how I killed that man on Mars you sent me to take out. It's in my drawer along with the box of Martian maw-worms and dried-up plant life."

Wordlessly, the Interplan officer turned and stalked from the work area.

I might as well put those packets of proof-artifacts away, McClane said to himself resignedly. He walked, step by step, back to his office. Including the citation from the UN Secretary General. After all –

The real one probably would not be long in coming.

THE LAWNMOWER MAN

(Allied Vision, 1992)
Starring: Pierce Brosnan, Jeff Fahey & Jeremy Slate
Directed by Brett Leonard
Based on "The Lawnmower Man" by Stephen King

Special effects were not just a feature of *The Lawnmower Man*, but the subject of the movie itself. Indeed, its makers claimed when it was released that the picture "pioneered the concept of Virtual Reality in the cinema" – although there have been some dissenting voices to this claim, arguing that *The Lawnmower Man* is actually derivative of Ralph Nelson's *Charly* made in 1968 and Steven Lisberger's *Tron* (1982). But there can still be no denying that the movie represents another important landmark in the continuing story of Space Movies. Virtual Reality is, in fact, a set of 3-D environments, created by computors, which the person experiencing can touch, feel and even smell. In the movie, however, the world of Virtual Reality which is created in the confines of a laboratory is allowed to spread and soon threatens to transform reality itself. It tells the story of Dr Lawrence Angelo, played by Pierce Brosnan (the new James Bond), who is intent upon turning a dimwitted "lawnmower man" Jobe Smith (Jeff Fahey) into a genius. But when his work is tampered with at Cybertech, a top-secret science complex which experiments on chimpanzees, the unfortunate gardener turns aggressive and power hungry, wants to control everyone and everything, and then wreaks a terrible revenge on all those who have made him suffer in the past. The brilliant computer animation for the film was created by the specialist technicians at Angel Studios in Hollywood – a group who had previously worked with NASA and the U.S. Air Force. Yet despite all the praise heaped on the movie for these special effects and its popu-

larity with cinemagoers, author Stephen King (1946–), the world's leading writer of horror and fantasy fiction, complained that the film had strayed a long way from his original tale – in particular turning his obese, middle-aged villain into a handsome young man. Notwithstanding this, *The Lawnmower Man* is certainly one of the most visually exciting versions of King's stories to have been brought to the screen – a list which includes adaptations of *Carrie* by Brian DePalma (1976); Stanley Kubrick's *The Shining* (1980); *Christine* directed by John Carpenter (1983); and *Pet Sematary* which Stephen King himself scripted in 1989. King's short story originally appeared in *Cavalier* magazine in August 1974, and it was the idea of producer Milton Subotsky, one of the veterans of the British horror film industry who ran Amicus Films for many years, to add the element of Virtual Reality and create what one critic has described as "a futuristic Frankensteinian tale with brilliant computer animation".

In previous years, Harold Parkette had always taken pride in his lawn. He had owned a large silver Lawnboy and paid the boy down the block five dollars per cutting to push it. In those days Harold Parkette had followed the Boston Red Sox on the radio with a beer in his hand and the knowledge that God was in his heaven and all was right with the world, including his lawn. But last year, in mid-October, fate had played Harold Parkette a nasty trick. While the boy was mowing the grass for the last time of the season, the Castonmeyers' dog had chased the Smiths' cat under the mower.

Harold's daughter had thrown up half a quart of cherry Kool-Aid into the lap of her new jumper, and his wife had nightmares for a week afterward. Although she had arrived after the fact, she *had* arrived in time to see Harold and the green-faced boy cleaning the blades. Their daughter and Mrs Smith stood over them, weeping, although Alicia had taken time enough to change her jumper for a pair of blue jeans and one of those disgusting skimpy sweaters. She had a crush on the boy who mowed the lawn.

After a week of listening to his wife moan and gobble in the next bed, Harold decided to get rid of the mower. He didn't really *need* a mower anyway, he supposed. He had hired a boy this year; next year he would just hire a boy *and* a mower. And maybe Carla would stop moaning in her sleep. He might even get laid again.

So he took the silver Lawnboy down to Phil's Sunoco, and he and Phil dickered over it. Harold came away with a brand-new Kelly blackwall tire and a tankful of hi-test, and Phil put the silver Lawnboy out on one of the pump islands with a hand-lettered FOR SALE sign on it.

And this year, Harold just kept putting off the necessary hiring. When he finally got around to calling last year's boy, his mother told him Frank had gone to the state university. Harold shook his head in wonder and went to the refrigerator to get a beer. Time certainly flew, didn't it? My God, yes.

He put off hiring a new boy as first May and then June slipped past him and the Red Sox continued to wallow in fourth place. He sat on the back porch on the weekends and watched glumly as a never ending progression of young boys he had never seen before popped out to mutter a quick hello before taking his buxom daughter off to the local passion pit. And the grass thrived and grew in a marvelous way. It was a good summer for grass; three days of shine followed by one of gentle rain, almost like clockwork.

By mid-July, the lawn looked more like a meadow than a suburbanite's backyard, and Jack Castonmeyer had begun to make all sorts of extremely unfunny jokes, most of which concerned the price of hay and alfalfa. And Don Smith's four-year-old daughter Jenny had taken to hiding in it when there was oatmeal for breakfast or spinach for supper.

One day in late July, Harold went out on the patio during the seventh-inning stretch and saw a woodchuck sitting perkily on the overgrown back walk. The time had come, he decided. He flicked off the radio, picked up the paper, and turned to the classifieds. And half way down the Part Time column, he found this: *Lawns mowed. Reasonable. 776–2390.*

Harold called the number, expecting a vacuuming housewife who would yell outside for her son. Instead, a briskly professional voice said, "Pastoral Greenery and Outdoor Services . . . how may we help you?"

Cautiously, Harold told the voice how Pastoral Greenery could help him. Had it come to this, then? Were lawncutters starting their own businesses and hiring office help? He asked the voice about rates, and the voice quoted him a reasonable figure.

Harold hung up with a lingering feeling of unease and went back to the porch. He sat down, turned on the radio, and stared out over his glandular lawn at the Saturday clouds moving slowly across the Saturday sky. Carla and Alicia were at his mother-in-law's and the house was his. It would be a pleasant surprise for them if the boy who was coming to cut the lawn finished before they came back.

He cracked a beer and sighed as Dick Drago was touched for a double and then hit a batter. A little breeze shuffled across the screened-in porch. Crickets hummed softly in the long grass. Harold grunted something unkind about Dick Drago and then dozed off.

He was jarred awake a half hour later by the doorbell. He knocked over his beer getting up to answer it.

A man in grass-stained denim overalls stood on the front stoop, chewing a toothpick. He was fat. The curve of his belly pushed his faded blue overall out to a point where Harold half suspected he had swallowed a basketball.

"Yes?" Harold Parkette asked, still half asleep.

The man grinned, rolled his toothpick from one corner of his mouth to the other, tugged at the seat of his overalls, and then pushed his green baseball cap up a notch on his forehead. There was a smear of fresh engine oil on the bill of his cap. And there he was, smelling of grass, earth, and oil, grinning at Harold Parkett.

"Pastoral sent me, buddy," he said jovially, scratching his crotch. "You called, right? Right, buddy?" He grinned on endlessly.

"Oh. The lawn. You?" Harold stared stupidly.

"Yep, me." The lawnmower man bellowed fresh laughter into Harold's sleep-puffy face.

Harold stood helplessly aside and the lawnmower man tromped ahead of him down the hall, through the living room and kitchen, and onto the back porch. Now Harold had placed the man and everything was all right. He had seen the type before, working for the sanitation department and the highway repair crews out on the turnpike. Always with a spare minute to lean on their shovels and smoke Lucky Strikes or Camels, looking at you as if they were the salt of the earth, able to hit you for five or sleep with your wife anytime they wanted to. Harold had always been slightly afraid of men like this; they were always tanned dark brown, there were always nets of wrinkles around their eyes, and they always knew what to do.

"The back lawn's the real chore," he told the man, unconsciously deepening his voice. "It's square and there are no obstructions, but it's pretty well grown up." His voice faltered back into its normal register and he found himself apologizing: "I'm afraid I've let it go."

"No sweat, buddy. No strain. Great-great-great." The lawnmower man grinned at him with a thousand traveling-salesman jokes in his eyes. "The taller, the better. Healthy soil, that's what you got there, by Circe. That's what I always say."

By Circe?

The lawnmower man cocked his head at the radio. Yastrzemski had just struck out. "Red Sox fan? I'm a Yankees man, myself." He clumped back into the house and down the front hall. Harold watched him bitterly.

He sat back down and looked accusingly for a moment at the puddle of beer under the table with the overturned Coors can in the middle of it. He thought of getting the mop from the kitchen and decided it would keep.

No sweat. No strain.

He opened his paper to the financial section and cast a judicious eye at the closing stock quotations. As a good Republican, he considered the Wall Street executives behind the columned type to be at least minor demigods –

(By Circe??)

– and he had wished many times that he could better understand the Word, as handed down from the mount not on stone tablets but in such enigmatic abbreviations as pct. and Kdk and 3.28 up 23. He had once bought a judicious three shares in a company called Midwest Bisonburgers, Inc., that had gone broke in 1968. He had lost his entire seventy-five-dollar investment. Now, he understood, bison-burgers were quite the coming thing. The wave of the future. He had discussed this often with Sonny, the bartender down at the Goldfish Bowl. Sonny told Harold his trouble was that he was five years ahead of his time, and he should . . .

A sudden racketing roar startled him out of the new doze he had just been slipping into.

Harold jumped to his feet, knocking his chair over and staring around wildly.

"That's a lawnmower?" Harold Parkette asked the kitchen. "My God, *that's* a lawnmower?"

He rushed through the house and stared out the front door. There was nothing out there but a battered green van with the words PASTORAL GREENERY, INC. painted on the side. The roaring sound was in back now. Harold rushed through his house again, burst onto the back proch, and stood frozen.

It was obscene.

It was a travesty.

The aged red power mower the fat man had brought in his van was running on its own. No one was pushing it; in fact, no one was within five feet of it. It was running at a fever pitch, tearing through the unfortunate grass of Harold Parkette's back lawn like an avenging red devil straight from hell. It screamed and bellowed and farted oily blue smoke in a crazed kind of mechanical madness that made Harold feel ill with terror. The overripe smell of cut grass hung in the air like sour wine.

But the lawnmower man was the true obscenity.

The lawnmower man had removed his clothes – every stitch. They were folded neatly in the empty birdbath that was at the center of the back lawn. Naked and grass-stained, he was crawling along about five feet behind the mower, eating the cut grass. Green juice ran down his chin and dripped onto his pendulous belly. And every time the lawnmower whirled around a corner, he rose and did an odd, skipping jump before prostrating himself again.

"*Stop!*" Harold Parkette screamed. "*Stop that!*"

But the lawnmower man took no notice, and his screaming scarlet familiar never slowed. If anything, it seemed to speed up. Its nicked steel grill seemed to grin sweatily at Harold as it raved by.

Then Harold saw the mole. It must have been hiding in stunned terror just ahead of the mower, in the swath of grass about to be slaughtered. It bolted across the cut band of lawn toward safety under the porch, a panicky brown streak.

The lawnmower swerved.

Blatting and howling, it roared over the mole and spat it out in a string of fur and entrails that reminded Harold of the Smiths' cat. The mole destroyed, the lawnmower rushed back to the main job.

The lawnmower man crawled rapidly by, eating grass. Harold stood paralyzed with horror, stocks, bonds, and bisonburgers completely forgotten. He could actually see that huge, pendulous belly expanding. *The lawnmower man swerved and ate the mole.*

That was when Harold Parkette leaned out the screen door and vomited into the zinnias. The world went gray, and suddenly he realized he was fainting, *had* fainted. He collapsed backward onto the porch and closed his eyes . . .

Someone was shaking him. Carla was shaking him. He hadn't done the dishes or emptied the garbage and Carla was going to be very angry but that was all right. As long as she was waking him up, taking him out of the horrible dream he had been having, back into the normal world, nice normal Carla with her Playtex Living Girdle and her buck teeth –

Buck teeth, yes. But not Carla's buck teeth. Carla had weak-looking chipmunk buck teeth. But these teeth were –

Hairy.

Green hair was growing on these buck teeth. It almost looked like –

Grass?

"Oh my God," Harold said.

"You fainted, buddy, right, huh?" The lawnmower man was bending over him, grinning with his hairy teeth. His lips and chin were hairy, too. Everything was hairy. And green. The yard stank of grass and gas and too sudden silence.

Harold bolted up to a sitting position and stared at the dead mower. All the grass had been neatly cut. And there would be no need to rake this job, Harold observed sickly. If the lawnmower man had missed a single cut blade, he couldn't see it. He squinted obliquely at the lawnmower man and winced. He was still naked, still fat, still terrifying. Green trickles ran from the corners of his mouth.

"What is this?" Harold begged.

The man waved an arm benignly at the lawn. "This? Well, it's a new thing the boss has been trying. It works out real good. Real good, buddy. We're killing two birds with one stone. We keep getting along toward the final stage, and we're making money to support our other operations to boot. See what I mean? Of course every now and then we run into a customer who doesn't understand – some people got no respect for efficiency, right? – but the boss is always agreeable to a sacrifice. Sort of keeps the wheels greased, if you catch me."

Harold said nothing. One word knelled over and over in his mind, and that word was "sacrifice". In his mind's eye he saw the mole spewing out from under the battered red mower.

He got up slowly, like a palsied old man. "Of course," he said, and could only come up with a line from one of Alicia's folk-rock records. "God bless the grass."

The lawnmower man slapped one summer-apple-colored thigh. "That's pretty good, buddy. In fact, that's damned good. I can see you got the right spirit. Okay if I write that down when I get back to the office? Might mean a promotion."

"Certainly," Harold said, retreating toward the back door and striving to keep his melting smile in place. "You go right ahead and finish. I think I'll take a little nap – "

"Sure, buddy," the lawnmower man said, getting ponderously to his feet. Harold noticed the unusually deep split between the first and second toes, almost as if the feet were . . . well, cloven.

"It hits everybody kinda hard at first," the lawnmower man said. "You'll get used to it." He eyed Harold's portly figure shrewdly. "In fact, you might even want to give it a whirl yourself. The boss has always got an eye out for new talent."

"The boss," Harold repeated faintly.

The lawnmower man paused at the bottom of the steps and gazed tolerantly up at Harold Parkette. "Well, say, buddy. I figured you must have guessed . . . God bless the grass and all."

Harold shook his head carefully and the lawnmower man laughed.

"Pan. Pan's the boss." And he did a half hop, half shuffle in the newly cut grass and the lawnmower screamed into life and began to trundle around the house.

"The neighbors – " Harold began, but the lawnmower man only waved cheerily and disappeared.

Out front the lawnmower blatted and howled. Harold Parkette refused to look, as if by refusing he could deny the grotesque spectacle that the Castonmeyers and Smiths – wretched Democrats both – were probably drinking in with horrified but no doubt righteously I-told-you-so eyes.

Instead of looking, Harold went to the telephone, snatched it up, and dialed police headquarters from the emergency decal pasted on the phone's handset.

"Sergeant Hall," the voice at the other end said.

Harold stuck a finger in his free ear and said, "My name is Harold Parkette. My address is 1421 East Endicott Street. I'd like to report . . ." What? What would he like to report? A man is in the process of raping and murdering my lawn and he works for a fellow named Pan and has cloven feet?

"Yes, Mr Parkette?"

Inspiration struck. "I'd like to report a case of indecent exposure."

"Indecent exposure," Sergeant Hall repeated.

"Yes. There's a man mowing my lawn. He's in the, uh, altogether."

"You mean he's naked?" Sergeant Hall asked, politely incredulous.

"Naked!" Harold agreed, holding tightly to the frayed ends of his sanity. "Nude. Unclothed. Bare-assed. On my front lawn. Now will you get somebody the hell over here?"

"That address was 1421 West Endicott?" Sergeant Hall asked bemusedly.

"East!" Harold yelled. "For God's sake – "

"And you say he's definitely naked? You are able to observe his, uh, genitals and so on?"

Harold tried to speak and could only gargle. The sound of the insane lawnmower seemed to be growing louder and louder, drowning out everything in the universe. He felt his gorge rise.

"Can you speak up?" Sergeant Hall buzzed. "There's an awfully noisy connection there at your end – "

The front door crashed open.

Harold looked around and saw the lawnmower man's mechanized familiar advancing through the door. Behind it came the lawnmower man himself, still quite naked. With something approaching true insanity, Harold saw the man's pubic hair was a rich fertile green. He was twirling his basball cap on one finger.

"That was a mistake, buddy," the lawnmower man said reproachfully. "You shoulda stuck with God bless the grass."

"Hello? Hello, Mr Parkette – "

The telephone dropped from Harold's nerveless fingers as the lawnmower began to advance on him, cutting through the nap of Carla's new Mohawk rug and spitting out brown hunks of fiber as it came.

Harold stared at it with a kind of bird-and-snake fascination until it reached the coffee table. When the mower shunted it aside, shearing one leg into sawdust and splinters as it did so, he climbed over the back of his chair and began to retreat toward the kitchen, dragging the chair in front of him.

"That won't do any good, buddy," the lawnmower man said kindly. "Apt to be messy, too. Now if you was just to show me where you keep your sharpest butcher knife, we could get this sacrifice business out of the way real painless . . . I think the bird-bath would do . . . and then – "

Harold shoved the chair at the lawnmower, which had been craftily flanking him while the naked man drew his attention, and bolted through the doorway. The lawnmower roared around the chair, jetting out exhaust, and as Harold smashed open the porch screen door and leaped down the steps, he heard it – smelled it, felt it – right at his heels.

The lawnmower roared off the top step like a skier going off a jump. Harold sprinted across his newly cut back lawn, but there had been too many beers, too many afternoon naps. He could sense it nearing him, then on his heels, and then he looked over his shoulder and tripped over his own feet.

The last thing Harold Parkette saw was the grinning grill of the charging lawnmower, rocking back to reveal its flashing, greenstained blades, and above it the fat face of the lawnmower man, shaking his head in good-natured reproof.

"Hell of a thing," Lieutenant Goodwin said as the last of the photographs were taken. He nodded to the two men in white, and they trundled their basket across the lawn. "He reported some naked guy on his lawn not two hours ago."

"Is that so?" Patrolman Cooley asked.

"Yeah. One of the neighbors called in, too. Guy named Castonmeyer. He thought it was Parkette himself. Maybe it was, Cooley. Maybe it was."

"Sir?"

"Crazy with the heat," Lieutenant Goodwin said gravely, and tapped his temple. "Schizo-fucking-phrenia."

"Yes sir," Cooley said respectfully.

"Where's the rest of him?" one of the white-coats asked.

"The birdbath," Goodwin said. He looked profoundly up at the sky.

"Did you say the birdbath?" the white-coat asked.

"Indeed I did," Lieutenant Goodwin agreed. Patrolman Cooley looked at the birdbath and suddenly lost most of his tan.

"Sex maniac," Lieutenant Goodwin said. "Must have been."

"Prints?" Cooley asked thickly.

"You might as well ask for footprints," Goodwin said. He gestured at the the newly cut grass.

Patrolman Cooley made a strangled noise in his throat.

Lieutenant Goodwin stuffed his hands into his pockets and rocked back on his heels. "The world," he said gravely, "is full of nuts. Never forget that, Cooley. Schizos. Lab boys say somebody chased Parkette through his own living room with a lawnmower. Can you imagine that?"

"No sir," Cooley said.

Goodwin looked out over Harold Parkette's neatly manicured lawn. "Well, like the man said when he saw the black-haired Swede, it surely is a Norse of a different color."

Goodwin strolled around the house and Cooley followed him. Behind them, the scent of newly mown grass hung pleasantly in the air.

CANDYMAN

(Tristar Pictures, 1993)
Starring: Virginia Madsen, Tony Todd
& Xander Berkeley
Directed by Bernard Rose
Based on "The Forbidden" by Clive Barker

Few of today's film makers are more fascinated by special
effects and working harder to extend the boundaries of what is
possible on the screen than the English writer-turned-director
Clive Barker (1952–). Barker's books have put him in the
same category as Stephen King and he admits to being a great
admirer of Hollywood's leading exponents of movie wizardry,
George Lucas and Steven Spielberg. Like King, too, a
number of Clive's stories have been filmed with varying
degrees of success – in particular the Hellraiser series with
their grotesque and terrifying character Pinhead (played by
Doug Bradley). The first of these Barker directed himself at a
cost of $1million and the picture has subsequently taken over
$30 million at the box office and inspired two sequels – all of
which are notable for their spellbinding special effects. The
same is also true of the most recent of Barker's stories to be
filmed, *Candyman*, the success of which has already generated a follow-up and shows every sign of becoming a series,
too. It takes for its theme an "urban myth" – one of those
stories of supernatural creatures or contact with aliens which
have been around for some years in magazines and books but
now seem destined to become one of the latest developments in
the SF genre. This particular tale concerns a folklorist
(Virginia Madsen) who is researching a legend about the
Candyman (Tony Todd), a hook-handed, supernatural black
killer accompanied by a swarm of deadly bees, who she
quickly discovers is no myth and by merely speaking his

214

name five times finds herself plunged into a living hell. The special effects for the movie were created by Jane Stewart, one of the hottest new talents in Hollywood, who came to attention in 1991 for masterminding the ingenious wizardry in *Beetlejuice* starring Michael Keaton. Although *Candyman* was filmed amidst the run-down project buildings of Chicago, the original story was actually located in Clive Barker's native Liverpool – but other than that, Bernard Rose's screenplay remained faithful to Barker's short tale "The Forbidden". The story had originally been written for the fifth volume of Clive's ambitious *Books of Blood* series, launched in 1984, which has subsequently captured the reading public's imagination and led him to Hollywood where he now lives and plays a leading role in the making of fantasy movies. It has been a remarkable achievement for a young man who started out writing plays such as *The History of the Devil* and *Frankenstein in Love* for small theatre productions in London, and can now command millions of dollars for his scripts or directorial assignments. When *Candyman* was released in March 1993, *Time Out* magazine hailed it as "setting the standard for the 90's". There seems little doubt that Clive Barker is destined to become one of the film makers who will ensure the SF picture continues to flourish into the Twenty-First Century. And that the special effects which have been such an integral part of the genre since its inception at the start of this century will also reach even greater heights.

Like a flawless tragedy, the elegance of which structure is lost upon those suffering in it, the perfect geometry of the Spector Street Estate was only visible from the air. Walking in its drear canyons, passing through its grimy corridors from one grey concrete rectangle to the next, there was little to seduce the eye or stimulate the imagination. What few saplings had been planted in the quadrangles had long since been mutilated or uprooted; the grass, though tall, resolutely refused a healthy green.

No doubt the estate and its two companion developments had once been an architect's dream. No doubt the city-planners had wept with pleasure at a design which housed three and thirty-six persons per hectare, and still boasted space for a children's playground. Doubtless fortunes and reputations had been built upon Spector Street, and at its opening fine words had been spoken of it being a yardstick by which all future developments would be measured. But the planners – tears wept, words spoken – had left the estate to its own devices; the architects occupied restored Georgian houses at the other end of the city, and probably never set foot here.

They would not have been shamed by the deterioration of the estate even if they had. Their brain-child (they would doubtless argue) was as brilliant as ever: Its geometries as precise, its ratios as calculated; it was *people* who had spoiled Spector Street. Nor would they have been wrong in such an accusation. Helen had seldom seen an inner city environment so comprehensively vandalized. Lamps had been shattered and back-yard fences overthrown; cars, whose wheels and engines had been removed and chassis then burned, blocked garage facilities. In one courtyard three or four ground-floor maisonettes had been entirely gutted by fire, their windows and doors boarded up with planks and corrugated iron.

More startling still was the graffiti. That was what she had come here to see, encouraged by Archie's talk of the place, and she was not disappointed. It was difficult to believe, staring at the multiple layers of designs, names, obscenities, and dogmas that were scrawled and sprayed on every available brick, that Spector Street was barely three and a half years old. The walls, so recently virgin, were now so profoundly defaced that the Council Cleaning Department could never hope to return them to their former condition. A layer of whitewash to cancel this visual cacophony would only offer the scribes a fresh and yet more tempting surface on which to make their mark.

Helen was in seventh heaven. Every corner she turned offered some fresh material for her thesis: "*Graffiti: the semiotics of urban despair*". It was a subject which married her two favourite disciplines – sociology and aesthetics – and as she wandered around the estate she began to wonder if there wasn't a book, in addition to her thesis, in the subject. She walked from courtyard to courtyard, copying down a large number of the more interesting scrawlings, and noting their location. Then she went back to the car to collect her camera and tripod and returned to the most fertile of the areas, to make a thorough visual record of the walls.

It was a chilly business. She was not an expert photographer, and the late October sky was in full flight, shifting the light on the bricks from one moment to the next. As she adjusted and readjusted the exposure to compensate for the light changes her fingers steadily became clumsier, her temper correspondingly thinner. But she struggled on, the idle curiosity of passers-by notwithstanding. There were so many designs to document. She reminded herself that her present discomfort would be amply repaid when she showed the slides to Trevor, whose doubt of the project's validity had been perfectly apparent from the beginning.

"The writing on the wall?" he'd said, half smiling in that irritating fashion of his. "It's been done a hundred times."

This was true, of course; and yet not. There certainly were learned works on graffiti, chock-full of sociological jargon: *cultural disenfranchisement; urban alienation*. But she flattered herself that *she* might find something amongst this litter of scrawlings that previous analysts had not: Some unifying convention perhaps, that she could use as the lynchpin of her thesis. Only a vigorous cataloguing and cross-referencing of the phrases and images before her would reveal such a correspondence; hence the importance of the photographic study. So many hands had worked here; so many minds left their mark, however casually: If she could find some pattern, some predominant motive, or *motif*, the thesis would be guaranteed some serious attention, and so, in turn, would she.

"What are you doing?" a voice from behind her asked.

She turned from her calculations to see a young woman with a pushchair on the pavement behind her. She looked weary, Helen thought, and pinched by the cold. The child in the pushchair was mewling, his grimy fingers clutching an orange lollipop and the wrapping from a chocolate bar. The bulk of the chocolate, and the remains of previous jujubes, was displayed down the front of his coat.

Helen offered a thin smile to the woman; she looked in need of it.

"I'm photographing the walls," she said in answer to the initial enquiry, though surely this was perfectly apparent.

The woman – Helen judged she could barely be twenty – said: "You mean the filth?"

"The writing and the pictures," Helen said. Then: "Yes. The filth."

"You from the Council?"

"No, the University."

"It's bloody disgusting," the woman said. "The way they do that. It's not just kids, either."

"No?"

"Grown men. Grown men, too. They don't give a damn. Do it in broad daylight. You see 'em . . . broad daylight." She glanced down at the child, who was sharpening his lollipop on the ground. "Kerry!" she snapped, but the boy took no notice. "Are they going to wipe it off?" she asked Helen.

"I don't know," Helen said, and reiterated: "I'm from the University."

"Oh," the woman replied, as if this was new information, "so you're nothing to do with the Council?"

"No."

"Some of it's obscene, isn't it? Really dirty. Makes me embarrassed to see some of the things they draw."

Helen nodded, casting an eye at the boy in the pushchair. Kerry had decided to put his sweet in his ear for safe-keeping.

"Don't do that!" his mother told him, and leaned over to slap the child's hand. The blow, which was negligible, began the child bawling. Helen took the opportunity to return to her camera. But the woman still desired to talk. "It's not just on the outside, neither," she commented.

"I beg your pardon?" Helen said.

"They break into the flats when they go empty. The Council tried to board them up, but it does no good. They break in anyway. Use them as toilets, and write more filth on the walls. They light fires too. Then nobody can move back in."

The description piqued Helen's curiosity. Would the graffiti on the *inside* walls be substantially different from the public displays? It was certainly worth an investigation.

"Are there any places you know of around here like that?"

"Empty flats, you mean?"

"With graffiti."

"Just by us, there's one or two," the woman volunteered. "I'm in Butts' Court."

"Maybe you could show me?" Helen asked.

The woman shrugged.

"By the way, my name's Helen Buchanan."

"Anne-Marie," the mother replied.

"I'd be very grateful if you could point me to one of those empty flats."

Anne-Marie was baffled by Helen's enthusiasm, and made no attempt to disguise it, but she shrugged again and said: "There's nothing much to see. Only more of the same stuff."

Helen gathered up her equipment and they walked side by side through the intersecting corridors between one square and the next. Though the estate was lowrise, each court only five storeys high, the effect of each quadrangle was horribly claustrophobic. The walkways and staircases were a thief's dream, rife with blind corners and ill-lit tunnels. The rubbish-dumping facilities – chutes from the upper floors down which bags of refuse could be pitched – had long since been sealed up, thanks to their efficiency as fire-traps. Now plastic bags of refuse were piled high in the corridors, many torn open by roaming dogs, their contents strewn across the ground. The smell, even in the cold weather, was unpleasant. In high summer it must have been overpowering.

"I'm over the other side," Anne-Marie said, pointing across the quadrangle. "The one with the yellow door." She then pointed along the opposite side of the court. "Five or six maisonettes from the far end," she said. "There's two of them been emptied out. Few weeks now. One of the family's moved into Ruskin Court; the other did a bunk in the middle of the night."

With that, she turned her back on Helen and wheeled Kerry, who had taken to trailing spittle from the side of his pushchair, around the side of the square.

"Thank you," Helen called after her. Anne-Marie glanced over her shoulder briefly, but did not reply. Appetite whetted, Helen made her way along the row of ground floor maisonettes, many of which, though inhabited, showed little sign of being so. Their curtains were closely drawn; there were no milk-bottles on the doorsteps, nor children's toys left where they had been played with. Nothing, in fact, *of life* here. There *was* more graffiti however, sprayed, shockingly, on the doors of occupied houses. She granted the scrawlings only a casual perusal, in part because she feared one of the doors opening as she examined a choice obscenity sprayed upon it, but more because she was eager to see what revelations the empty flats ahead might offer.

The malign scent of urine, both fresh and stale, welcomed her at the threshold of number 14, and beneath that the smell of burnt paint and plastic. She hesitated for fully ten seconds, wondering if stepping into the maisonette was a wise move. The territory of the estate behind her was indisputably foreign, sealed off in its own misery, but the rooms in front of her were more intimidating still: A dark maze which her eyes could barely penetrate. But when her courage faltered she thought of Trevor, and how badly she wanted to silence his condescension. So thinking, she advanced into the place, deliberately kicking a piece of charred timber aside as she did so, in the hope that she would alert any tenant into showing himself.

There was no sound of occupancy however. Gaining confidence, she began to explore the front room of the maisonette which had been – to judge by the remains of a disembowelled sofa in one corner and the sodden carpet underfoot – a living room. The pale-green walls were, as Anne-Marie had promised, extensively defaced, both by minor scribblers – content to work in pen, or even more crudely in sofa charcoal – and by those with aspirations to public works, who had sprayed the walls in half a dozen colours.

Some of the comments were of interest, though many she had already seen on the walls outside. Familiar names and couplings repeated themselves. Though she had never set eyes on these individuals she knew how badly Fabian J. (A.OK.) wanted to deflower Michelle; and that Michelle, in her turn, had the hots for somebody called Mr Sheen. Here, as elsewhere, a man called White Rat boasted of his endowment, and the return of the Syllabub Brothers was promised in red paint. One or two of the pictures accompanying, or at least adjacent to these phrases were of particular interest. An almost emblematic simplicity informed them. Beside the word *Christos* was a stick man with his hair radiating from his head like spines, and other heads impaled on each spine. Close by was an image of intercourse so brutally reduced that at first Helen took it to illustrate a knife plunging into a sightless eye. But fascinating as the images were, the room was too gloomy for her film, and she had neglected to bring a flash. If she wanted a reliable record of these discoveries she would have to come again, and for now be content with a simple exploration of the premises.

The maisonette wasn't that large, but the windows had been boarded up throughout, and as she moved further from the front door the dubious light petered out altogether. The smell of urine, which had been strong at the door, intensified too, until by the time she reached the back living room and stepped along a short corridor into another room beyond, it was as cloying as incense. This room, being furthest from the front door, was also the darkest, and she had to wait a few moments in the cluttered gloom to allow her eyes to become useful. This, she guessed, had been the bedroom. What little furniture the residents had left behind them had been smashed to smithereens. Only the mattress had been left relatively untouched, dumped in the corner of the room amongst a wretched litter of blankets, newspapers, and pieces of crockery.

Outside, the sun found its way between the clouds, and two or three shafts of sunlight slipped between the boards nailed across the bedroom window and pierced the room like annunciations, scoring the opposite wall with bright lines. Here, the graffitists had been busy once more: The usual clamour of love-letters and threats. She scanned the wall quickly, and as she did so her eye was led by the beams of light across the room to the wall which contained the door she had stepped through.

Here, the artists had also been at work, but had produced an image the like of which she had not seen anywhere else.

Using the door, which was centrally placed in the wall, as a mouth, the artists had sprayed a single, vast head on to the stripped plaster. The painting was more adroit than most she had seen, rife with detail that lent the image an unsettling veracity. The cheekbones jutting through skin the colour of buttermilk; the teeth – sharpened to irregular points – all converging on the door. The sitter's eyes were, owing to the room's low ceiling, set mere inches above the upper lip, but this physical adjustment only lent force to the image, giving the impression that he had thrown his head back. Knotted strands of his hair snaked from his scalp across the ceiling.

Was it a portrait? There was something naggingly *specific* in the details of the brows and the lines around the wide mouth; in the careful picturing of those vicious teeth. A nightmare certainly: A facsimile, perhaps, of something from a heroin fugue. Whatever its origins, it was potent. Even the illusion of door-as-mouth worked. The short passageway between living room and bedroom offered a passable throat, with a tattered lamp in lieu of tonsils. Beyond the gullet, the day burned white in the nightmare's belly. The whole effect brought to mind a ghost train painting. The same heroic deformity, the same unashamed intention to scare. And it worked. She stood in the bedroom almost stupified by the picture, its red-rimmed eyes fixing her mercilessly. Tomorrow, she determined, she would come here again, this time with high-speed film and a flash to illuminate the masterwork.

As she prepared to leave the sun went in, and the bands of light faded. She glanced over her shoulder at the boarded windows, and saw for the first time that one four-word slogan had been sprayed on the wall beneath them.

"*Sweets to the sweet*" it read. She was familiar with the quote, but not with its source. Was it a profession of love? If so, it was an odd location for such an avowal. Despite the mattress in the corner, and the relative privacy of this room, she could not imagine the intended reader of such words ever stepping in here to receive her bouquet. No adolescent lovers, however heated, would lie down here to play at mothers and fathers; not under the gaze of the terror on the wall. She crossed to examine the writing. The paint looked to be the same shade of pink as had been used to colour the gums of the screaming man; perhaps the same hand?

Behind her, a noise. She turned so quickly she almost tripped over the blanket-strewn mattress.

"Who –?"

At the other end of the gullet, in the living room, was a scab-kneed boy of six or seven. He stared at Helen, eyes glittering in the half-light, as if waiting for a cue.

"Yes?" she said.

"Anne-Marie says do you want a cup of tea?" he declared without pause or intonation.

Her conversation with the woman seemed hours past. She was grateful for the invitation however. The damp maisonette had chilled her.

"Yes . . ." she said to the boy. "Yes please."

The child didn't move, but simply stared on at her.

"Are you going to lead the way?" she asked him.

"If you want," he replied, unable to raise a trace of enthusiasm.

"I'd like that."

"You taking photographs?" he asked.

"Yes. Yes, I am. But not in here."

"Why not?"

"It's too dark," she told him.

"Don't it work in the dark?" he wanted to know.

"No."

The boy nodded at this, as if the information somehow fitted well into his scheme of things, and about-turned without another word, clearly expecting Helen to follow.

If she had been taciturn in the street, Anne-Marie was

anything but in the privacy of her own kitchen. Gone was the guarded curiosity, to be replaced by a stream of lively chatter and a constant scurrying between half-a-dozen minor domestic tasks, like a juggler keeping several plates spinning simultaneously. Helen watched this balancing act with some admiration; her own domestic skills were negligible. At last, the meandering conversation turned back to the subject that had brought Helen here.

"Them photographs," Anne-Marie said, "why'd you want to take them?"

"I'm writing about graffiti. The photos will illustrate my thesis."

"It's not very pretty."

"No, you're right, it isn't. But I find it interesting."

Anne-Marie shook her head. "I hate the whole estate," she said. "It's not safe here. People getting robbed on their own doorsteps. Kids setting fire to the rubbish day in, day out. Last summer we had the fire brigade here two, three times a day, 'til they sealed them chutes off. Now people just dump the bags in the passageways, and that attracts rats."

"Do you live here alone?"

"Yes," she said, "since Davey walked out."

"That your husband?"

"He was Kerry's father, but we weren't never married. We lived together two years, you know. We had some good times. Then he just upped and went off one day when I was at me Mam's with Kerry." She peered into her tea-cup. "I'm better off without him," she said. "But you get scared sometimes. Want some more tea?"

"I don't think I've got time."

"Just a cup," Anne-Marie said, already up and unplugging the electric kettle to take it across for a re-fill. As she was about to turn on the tap she saw something on the draining board, and drove her thumb down, grinding it out. "Got you, you bugger," she said, then turned to Helen: "We got these bloody ants."

"Ants?"

"Whole estate's infected. From Egypt, they are: Pharoah ants, they're called. Little brown sods. They breed in the central heating ducts, you see; that way they get into all the flats. Place is plagued with them."

This unlikely exoticism (ants from Egypt?) struck Helen as comical, but she said nothing. Anne-Marie was staring out of the kitchen window and into the backyard.

"You should tell them – " she said, though Helen wasn't certain whom she was being instructed to tell, "tell them that ordinary people can't even walk the sreets any longer – "

"Is it really so bad?" Helen said, frankly tiring of this catalogue of misfortunes.

Anne-Marie turned from the sink and looked at her hard.

"We've had murders here," she said.

"Really?"

"We had one in the summer. An old man he was, from Ruskin. That's just next door. I didn't know him, but he was a friend of the sister of the woman next door. I forget his name."

"And he was murdered?"

"Cut to ribbons in his own front room. They didn't find him for almost a week."

"What about his neighbours? Didn't they notice his absence?"

Anne-Marie shrugged, as if the most important pieces of information – the murder and the man's isolation – had been exchanged, and any further enquiries into the problem were irrelevant. But Helen pressed the point.

"Seems strange to me," she said.

Anne-Marie plugged in the filled kettle. "Well, it happened," she replied, unmoved.

"I'm not saying it didn't, I just – "

"His eyes had been taken out," she said, before Helen could voice any further doubts.

Helen winced. "No," she said, under her breath.

"That's the truth," Anne-Marie said. "And that wasn't all'd been done to him." She paused, for effect, then went on: "You wonder what kind of person's capable of doing things like that, don't you? You wonder." Helen nodded. She was thinking precisely the same thing.

"Did they ever find the man responsible?"

Anne-Marie snorted her disparagement. "Police don't give a damn what happens here. They keep off the estate as much as possible. When they do patrol all they do is pick up kids for getting drunk and that. They're afraid, you see. That's why they keep clear."

"Of this killer?"

"Maybe," Anne-Marie replied. Then: "He had a hook."

"A hook?"

"The man what done it. He had a hook, like Jack the Ripper."

Helen was no expert on murder, but she felt certain that the Ripper hadn't boasted a hook. It seemed churlish to question the truth of Anne-Marie's story however; though she silently wondered how much of this – the eyes taken out, the body rotting in the flat, the hook – was elaboration. The most scrupulous of reporters was surely tempted to embellish a story once in a while.

Anne-Marie had poured herself another cup of tea, and was about to do the same for her guest.

"No thank you," Helen said, "I really should go."

"You married?" Anne-Marie asked, out of the blue.

"Yes. To a lecturer from the University."

"What's his name?"

"Trevor."

Anne-Marie put two heaped spoonfuls of sugar into her cup of tea. "Will you be coming back?" she asked.

"Yes, I hope to. Later in the week. I want to take some photographs of the pictures in the maisonette across the court."

"Well, call in."

"I shall. And thank you for your help."

"That's all right," Anne-Marie replied. "You've got to tell somebody, haven't you?"

"The man apparently had a hook instead of a hand."

Trevor looked up from his plate of *tagliatelle con prosciutto*.

"Beg your pardon?"

Helen had been at pains to keep her recounting of this story as uncoloured by her own response as she could. She was interested to know what Trevor would make of it, and she knew that if she once signalled her own stance he would instinctively take an opposing view out of plain bloody-mindedness.

"He had a hook," she repeated, without inflexion.

Trevor put down his fork, and plucked at his nose, sniffing. "I didn't read anything about this," he said.

"You don't look at the local press," Helen returned. "Neither of us do. Maybe it never made any of the nationals."

"'Geriatric Murdered By Hook-Handed Maniac'"?' Trevor said, savouring the hyperbole. "I would have thought it very newsworthy. "When was all of this supposed to have happened?"

"Sometime last summer. Maybe we were in Ireland."

"Maybe," said Trevor, taking up his fork again. Bending to his food, the polished lens of his spectacles reflected only the plate of pasta and chopped ham in front of him, not his eyes.

"Why do you say *maybe*?" Helen prodded.

"It doesn't sound quite right," he said. "In fact it sounds bloody preposterous."

"You don't believe it?" Helen said.

Trevor looked up from his food, tongue rescuing a speck of *tagliatelle* from the corner of his mouth. His face had relaxed into that non-committal expression of his – the same face he wore, no doubt, when listening to his students.

"Do *you* believe it?" he asked Helen. It was a favourite time-gaining device of his, another seminar trick, to question the questioner.

"I'm not certain," Helen replied, too concerned to find some solid ground in this sea of doubts to waste energy scoring points.

"All right, forget the tale – " Trevor said, deserting his food for another glass of red wine. "– What about the teller? Did *you* trust her?"

Helen pictured Anne-Marie's earnest expression as she told the story of the old man's murder. "Yes," she said. "Yes; I think I would have known if she'd been lying to me."

"So why's it so important, anyhow? I mean, whether she's lying or not, what the fuck does it matter?"

It was a reasonable question, if irritatingly put. Why *did* it matter? Was it that she wanted to have her worst feelings about Spector Street proved false? That such an estate be filthy, be hopeless, be a dump where the undesirable and the disadvantaged were tucked out of public view – all that was a liberal commonplace, and she accepted it as an unpalatable social reality. But the story of the old man's murder and mutilation was something other. An image of violent death that, once with her, refused to part from her company.

She realized, to her chagrin, that this confusion was plain on her face, and that Trevor, watching her across the table, was not a little entertained by it.

"If it bothers you so much," he said, "why don't you go back there and ask around, instead of playing believe-in-it-or-not over dinner?"

She couldn't help but rise to his remark. "I thought you liked guessing games," she said.

He threw her a sullen look.

"Wrong again."

The suggestion that she investigate was not a bad one, though doubtless he had ulterior motives for offering it. She viewed Trevor less charitably day by day. What she had once thought in him a fierce commitment to debate she now recognized as mere power-play. He argued, not for the thrill of dialectic, but because he was pathologically competitive. She had seen him, time and again, take up attitudes she knew he did not espouse, simply to spill blood. Nor, more's the pity, was he alone in this sport. Academe was one of the last strongholds of the professional time-waster. On occasion their circle seemed entirely dominated by educated fools, lost in a wasteland of stale rhetoric and hollow commitment.

From one wasteland to another. She returned to Spector Street the following day, armed with a flashgun in addition to her tripod and high-sensitive film. The wind was up today, and it was Arctic, more furious still for being trapped in the maze of passageways and courts. She made her way to number 14, and spent the next hour in its befouled confines, meticulously photographing both the bedroom and living-room walls. She had half expected the impact of the head in the bedroom to be dulled by re-acquaintance; it was not. Though she struggled to capture its scale and detail as best she could, she knew the photographs would be at best a dim echo of its perpetual howl.

Much of its power lay in its context, of course. That such an image might be stumbled upon in surroundings so drab, so conspicuously lacking in mystery, was akin to finding an icon on a rubbish-heap: A gleaming symbol of transcendence from a world of toil and decay into some darker but more tremendous realm. She was painfully aware that the intensity of her response probably defied her articulation. Her vocabulary was analytic, replete with buzz-words and academic terminology, but woefully impoverished when it came to evocation. The photographs, pale as they would be, would, she hoped, at least hint at the potency of this picture, even if they couldn't conjure the way it froze the bowels.

When she emerged from the maisonette the wind was as uncharitable as ever, but the boy was waiting outside – the same child as had attended upon her yesterday – dressed as if for spring weather. He grimaced in his effort to keep the shudders at bay.

"Hello," Helen said.

"I waited," the child announced.

"Waited?"

"Anne-Marie said you'd come back.

"I wasn't planning to come until later in the week," Helen said. "You might have waited a long time."

The boy's grimace relaxed a notch. "It's all right," he said, "I've got nothing to do."

"What about school?"

"Don't like it," the boy replied, as if unobliged to be educated if it wasn't to his taste.

"I see," said Helen, and began to walk down the side of the quadrangle. The boy followed. On the patch of grass at the centre of the quadrangle several chairs and two or three dead saplings had been piled.

"What's this?" she said, half to herself.

"Bonfire Night," the boy informed her. "Next week."

"Of course."

"You going to see Anne-Marie?" he asked.

"Yes."

"She's not in."

"Oh. Are you sure?"

"Yeah."

"Well, perhaps *you* can help me . . ." She stopped and turned to face the child; smooth sacs of fatigue hung beneath his eyes. "I heard about an old man who was murdered near here," she said to him. "In the summer. Do you know anything about that?"

"No."

"Nothing at all? You don't remember anybody getting killed?"

"No," the boy said again, with impressive finality. "I don't remember."

"Well; thank you anyway."

This time, when she retraced her steps back to the car, the boy didn't follow. But as she turned the corner out of the quadrangle she glanced back to see him standing on the spot where she'd left him, staring after her as if she were a madwoman.

By the time she had reached the car and packed the photographic equipment into the boot there were specks of rain in the wind, and she was sorely tempted to forget she'd ever heard Anne-Marie's story and make her way home, where the coffee would be warm even if the welcome wasn't. But she needed an answer to the question Trevor had put the previous night. Do *you* believe it?, he'd asked when she'd told him the story. She hadn't known how to answer then, and she still didn't. Perhaps (why did she sense this?) the terminology of verifiable truth was redundant here; perhaps the final answer to his question was not an answer at all, only another question. If so; so. She had to find out.

Ruskin Court was as forlorn as its fellows, if not more so. It didn't even boast a bonfire. On the third floor balcony a woman was taking washing in before the rain broke; on the grass in the centre of the quadrangle two dogs were absent-mindedly rutting, the fuckee staring up at the blank sky. As she walked along the empty pavement she set her face determinedly; a purposeful look, Bernadette had once said, deterred attack. When she caught sight of the two women talking at the far end of the court she crossed over to them hurriedly, grateful for their presence.

"Excuse me?"

The women, both in middle-age, ceased their animated exchange and looked her over.

"I wonder if you can help me?"

She could feel their appraisal, and their distrust; they

went undisguised. One of the pair, her face florid, said plainly: "What do you want?"

Helen suddenly felt bereft of the least power to charm. What was she to say to these two that wouldn't make her motives appear ghoulish? "I was told . . ." she began, and then stumbled, aware that she would get no assistance from either woman. ". . . I was told there'd been a murder near here. Is that right?"

The florid woman raised eyebrows so plucked they were barely visible. "Murder?" she said.

"Are you from the press?" the other woman enquired. The years had soured her features beyond sweetening. Her small mouth was deeply lined; her hair, which had been dyed brunette, showed a half-inch of grey at the roots.

"No, I'm not from the press," Helen said, "I'm a friend of Anne-Marie's in Butts' Court." This claim of *friend* stretched the truth, but it seemed to mellow the women somewhat.

"Visiting are you?" the florid woman asked.

"In a manner of speaking – "

"You missed the warm spell – "

"Anne-Marie was telling me about somebody who'd been murdered here, during the summer. I was curious about it."

"Is that right?"

"– do you know anything about it?"

"Lots of things go on around here," said the second woman. "You don't know the half of it."

"So it's true," Helen said.

"They had to close the toilets," the first woman put in.

"That's right. They did," the other said.

"The toilets?" Helen said. What had this to do with the old man's death?

"It was terrible," the first said. "Was it your Frank, Josie, who told you about it?"

"No, not Frank," Josie replied. "Frank was still at sea. It was Mrs Tyzack."

The witness established, Josie relinquished the story to her companion, and turned her gaze back upon Helen. The suspicion had not yet died from her eyes.

"This was only the month before last," Josie said. "Just about the end of August. It was August, wasn't it?" She looked to the other woman for verification. "You've got the head for dates, Maureen."

Maureen looked uncomfortable. "I forget, she said, clearly unwilling to offer testimony.

"I'd like to know," Helen said. Josie, despite her companion's reluctance, was eager to oblige.

"There's some lavatories," she said, "outside the shops – you know, public lavatories. I'm not quite sure how it all happened exactly, but there used to be a boy . . . well, he wasn't a boy really, I mean he was a man of twenty or more, but he was . . ." she fished for the words, ". . . mentally subnormal, I suppose you'd say. His mother used to have to take him around like he was a four-year-old. Anyhow, she let him go into the lavatories while she went to that little supermarket, what's it called?" she turned to Maureen for a prompt, but the other woman just looked back, her disapproval plain. Josie was ungovernable, however. "Broad daylight, this was," she said to Helen. "Middle of the day. Anyhow, the boy went to the toilet, and the mother was in the shop. And after a while, you know how you do, she's busy shopping, she forgets about him, and then she thinks he's been gone a long time . . ."

At this juncture Maureen couldn't prevent herself from butting in: The accuracy of the story apparently took precedence over her wariness.

"– She got into an argument," she corrected Josie, "with the manager. About some bad bacon she'd had from him. That was why she was such a time . . ."

"I see," said Helen.

"– anyway," said Josie, picking up the tale, "she finished her shopping and when she came out he still wasn't there – "

"So she asked someone from the supermarket – " Maureen began, but Josie wasn't about to have her narrative snatched back at this vital juncture.

"She asked one of the men from the supermarket – " she repeated over Maureen's interjection, "to go down into the lavatory and find him."

"It was terrible," said Maureen, clearly picturing the atrocity in her mind's eye.

"He was lying on the floor, in a pool of blood."

"Murdered?"

Josie shook her head. "He'd have been better off dead. He'd been attacked with a razor – " she let this piece of information sink in before delivering the *coup de grâce*, "– and they'd cut off his private parts. Just cut them off and flushed them down a toilet. No reason on earth to do it."

"Oh my God."

"Better off dead," Josie repeated. "I mean, they can't mend something like that, can they?"

The appalling tale was rendered worse still by the *sang-froid* of the teller, and by the casual repetition of "Better off dead".

"The boy," Helen said, "Was he able to describe his attackers?"

"No," said Josie, "he's pratically an imbecile. He can't string more than two words together."

"And nobody saw anyone go into the lavatory? Or leaving it?"

"People come and go all the time – " Maureen said. This, though it sounded like an adequate explanation, had not been Helen's experience. There was not a great bustle in the quadrangle and passageways; far from it. Perhaps the shopping mall was busier, she reasoned, and might offer adequate cover for such a crime.

"So they haven't found the culprit," she said.

"No," Josie replied, her eyes losing their fervour. The crime and its immediate consequences were the nub of this story; she had little or no interest in either the culprit or his capture.

"We're not safe in our own beds," Maureen observed. "You ask anyone."

"Anne-Marie said the same," Helen replied. "That's how she came to tell me about the old man. Said he was murdered during the summer, here in Ruskin Court."

"I do remember something," Josie said. "There *was* some talk I heard. An old man, and his dog. He was battered to death, and the dog ended up . . . I don't know. It certainly wasn't here. It must have been one of the other estates.

"Are you sure?"

The woman looked offended by this slur on her memory. "Oh yes," she said, "I mean if it had been here, we'd have known the story, wouldn't we?"

Helen thanked the pair for their help and decided to take a stroll around the quadrangle anyway, just to see how many more maisonettes were out of operation here. As in Butts' Court, many of the curtains were drawn and all the doors locked. But then if Spector Street *was* under siege from a maniac capable of the murder and mutilation such as she'd heard described, she was not surprised that the residents took to their homes and stayed there. There was nothing much to see around the court. All the unoccupied maisonettes and flats had been recently sealed, to judge by a litter of nails left on a doorstep by the council workmen. One sight *did* catch her attention, however. Scrawled on the paving stones she was walking over – and all but erased by rain and the passage of feet – the same phrase she'd seen in the bedroom of number 14: *Sweets to the sweet.* The words were so benign; why did she seem to sense menace in them? Was it in their excess, perhaps, in the sheer overabundance of sugar upon sugar, honey upon honey?

She walked on, though the rain persisted, and her walk-about gradually led her away from the quadrangles and into a concrete no-man's-land through which she had not previously passed. This was – or had been – the site of the estate's amenities. Here was the children's playground, its metal-framed rides overturned, its sandpit fouled by dogs, its paddling pool empty. And here too were shops. Several had been boarded up now; those that hadn't were dingy and unattractive, their windows protected by heavy wire-mesh.

She walked along the row, and rounded a corner, and there in front of her was a squat brick building. The public lavatory, she guessed, though the signs designating it as such had gone. The iron gates were closed and padlocked. Standing in front of the charmless building, the wind gusting around her legs, she couldn't help but think of what had happened here. Of the man-child, bleeding on the floor, helpless to cry out. It made her queasy even to contemplate it. She turned her thoughts instead to the felon. What would he look like, she wondered, a man capable of such depravities? She tried to make an image of him, but no detail she could conjure carried sufficient force. But then monsters were seldom very terrible once hauled into the plain light of day. As long as this man was known only by his deeds he held untold power over the imagination; but the human truth beneath the terrors would, she knew, be bitterly disappointing. No monster he; just a whey-faced apology for a man more needful of pity than awe.

The next gust of wind brought the rain on more heavily. It was time, she decided, to be done with adventures for the day. Turning her back on the public lavatories she hurried back through the quadrangles to the refuge of the car, the icy rain needling her face to numbness.

The dinner guests looked gratifyingly appalled at the story, and Trevor, to judge by the expression on his face, was furious. It was done now, however; there was no taking it back. Nor could she deny the satisfaction she took in having silenced the interdepartmental babble about the table. It was Bernadette, Trevor's assistant in the History Department, who broke the agonizing hush.

"When was this?"

"During the summer," Helen told her.

"I don't recall reading about it," said Archie, much the better for two hours of drinking; it mellowed a tongue which was otherwise fulsome in its self-corruscation.

"Perhaps the police are suppressing it," Daniel commented.

"Conspiracy?" said Trevor, plainly cynical.

"It's happening all the time," Daniel shot back.

"Why should they suppress something like this?" Helen said. "It doesn't make sense."

"Since when has police procedure made sense?" Daniel replied.

Bernadette cut in before Helen could answer. "We don't even bother to read about these things any longer," she said.

"Speak for yourself," somebody piped up, but she ignored them and went on:

"We're punch-drunk with violence. We don't see it any longer, even when it's in front of our noses."

"On the screen every night," Archie put in, "Death and disaster in full colour."

"There's nothing very modern about that," Trevor said. "An Elizabethan would have seen death all the time. Public executions were a very popular form of entertainment."

The table broke up into a cacophony of opinions. After two hours of polite gossip the dinner-party had suddenly caught fire. Listening to the debate rage Helen was sorry she hadn't had time to have the photographs processed and printed; the graffiti would have added further fuel to this exhilarating row. It was Purcell, as usual, who was the last to weigh in with his point of view; and – again, as usual – it was devastating.

"Of course, Helen, my sweet – " he began, that affected weariness in his voice edged with the anticipation of controversy "– your witnesses could all be lying, couldn't they?"

The talking around the table dwindled, and all heads turned in Purcell's direction. Perversely, he ignored the attention he'd garnered, and turned to whisper in the ear of the boy he'd brought – a new passion who would, on past form, be discarded in a matter of weeks for another pretty urchin.

"Lying?" Helen said. She could feel herself bristling at the observation already, and Purcell had only spoken a dozen words.

"Why not?" the other replied, lifting his glass of wine to his lips. "Perhaps they're all weaving some elaborate fiction or other. The story of the spastic's mutilation in the public toilet. The murder of the old man. Even that hook. All quite familiar elements. You must be aware that there's something *traditional* about these atrocity stories. One used to exchange them all the time; there was a certain *frisson* in them. Something competitive maybe, in attempting to find a new detail to add to the collective fiction; a fresh twist that would render the tale that little bit more appalling when you passed it on."

"It may be familiar to you – " said Helen defensively. Purcell was always so *poised*; it irritated her. Even if there were validity in his argument – which she doubted – she was damned if she'd concede it. "– *I've* never heard this kind of story before."

"Have you not?" said Purcell, as though she were admitting to illiteracy. "What about the lovers and the escaped lunatic, have you heard that one?"

"I've heard that . . ." Daniel said.

"The lover is disembowelled – usually by a hook-handed man – and the body left on the top of the car, while the fiancée cowers inside. It's a cautionary tale, warning of the evils of rampant heterosexuality." The joke won a round of laughter from everyone but Helen. "These stories are very common."

"So you're saying that they're telling me lies – " she protested.

"Not lies, exactly – "

"You said *lies*."

"I was being provocative," Purcell returned, his placatory tone more enraging than ever. "I don't mean to imply there's any serious mischief in it. But you *must* concede that so far you haven't met a single *witness*. All these events have happened at some unspecified date to some unspecified person. They are reported at several removes. They occurred at best to the brothers of friends of distant relations. Please consider the possibility that perhaps these events do not exist in the real world at all, but are merely titillation for bored housewives – "

Helen didn't make an argument in return, for the simple reason that she lacked one. Purcell's point about the conspicuous absence of witnesses was perfectly sound; she herself had wondered about it. It was strange, too, the way the women in Ruskin Court had speedily consigned the old man's murder to another estate, as though these atrocities always occurred just out of sight – round the next corner, down the next passageway – but never *here*.

"So why?" said Bernadette.

"Why what?" Archie puzzled.

"The stories. Why tell these horrible stories if they're not true?"

"Yes," said Helen, throwing the controversy back into Purcell's ample lap. "*Why*?"

Purcell preened himself, aware that his entry into the debate had changed the basic assumption at a stroke. "I don't know," he said, happy to be done with the game now that he'd shown his arm. "You really mustn't take me too seriously, Helen. *I* try not to." The boy at Purcell's side tittered.

"Maybe it's simply taboo material," Archie said.

"Suppressed – " Daniel prompted.

"Not the way you mean it," Archie retorted. "The whole world isn't politics, Daniel."

"Such naiveté."

"What's so *taboo* about death?" Trevor said. "Bernadette already pointed out: It's in front of us all the time. Television; newspapers."

"Maybe that's not close enough," Bernadette suggested.

"Does anyone mind if I smoke?" Purcell broke in. "Only dessert seems to have been indefinitely postponed – "

Helen ignored the remark, and asked Bernadette what she meant by "not close enough"?

Bernadette shrugged. "I don't know precisely," she confessed, "maybe just that death has to be *near*; we have to *know* it's just round the corner. The television's not intimate enough – "

Helen frowned. The observation made some sense to her, but in the clutter of the moment she couldn't root out its significance.

"Do you think they're stories too?" she asked.

"Andrew has a point – " Bernadette replied.

"Most kind," said Purcell. "Has somebody got a match? The boy's pawned my lighter."

"– about the absence of witnesses."

"All that proves is that I haven't met anybody who's actually *seen* anything," Helen countered, "not that witnesses don't exist."

"All right," said Purcell. "Find me one. If you can prove to me that your atrocity-monger actually lives and breathes, I'll stand everyone dinner at *Appollinaires*. How's that? Am I generous to a fault, or do I just know when I can't lose?" He laughed, knocking on the table with his knuckles by way of applause.

"Sounds good to me," said Trevor. "What do you say, Helen?"

She didn't go back to Spector Street until the following Monday, but all weekend she was there in thought: Standing outside the locked toilet, with the wind bringing rain or in the bedroom, the portrait looming. Thoughts of the estate claimed all her concern. When, late on Saturday afternoon, Trevor found some petty reason for an argument, she let the insults pass, watching him perform the familiar ritual of self-martyrdom without being touched by it in the least. Her indifference only enraged him further. He stormed out in high dudgeon, to visit whichever of his women was in favour this month. She was glad to see the back of him. When he failed to return that night she didn't even think of weeping about it. He was foolish and vacuous. She despaired of ever seeing a haunted look in his dull eyes; and what worth was a man who could not be haunted?

He did not return Sunday night either, and it crossed her mind the following morning, as she parked the car in the heart of the estate, that nobody even knew she had come, and that she might lose herself for days here and nobody be any the wiser. Like the old man Anne-Marie had told her about: Lying forgotten in his favourite armchair with his eyes hooked out, while the flies feasted and the butter went rancid on the table.

It was almost Bonfire Night, and over the weekend the small heap of combustibles in Butts' Court had grown to a substantial size. The construction looked unsound, but that didn't prevent a number of boys and young adolescents clambering over it and into it. Much of its bulk was made up of furniture, filched, no doubt, from boarded-up properties. She doubted if it could burn for any time: If it did, it would go chokingly. Four times, on her way across to Anne-Marie's house, she was waylaid by children begging for money to buy fireworks.

"Penny for the guy," they'd say, though none had a guy to display. She had emptied her pockets of change by the time she reached the front door.

Anne-Marie was in today, though there was no welcoming smile. She simply stared at her visitor as if mesmerised.

"I hope you don't mind me calling . . ."

Anne-Marie made no reply.

". . . I just wanted a word."

"I'm busy," the woman finally announced. There was no invitation inside, no offer of tea.

"Oh. Well . . . it won't take more than a moment."

The back door was open and the draught blew through the house. Papers were flying about in the back yard. Helen could see them lifting into the air like vast white moths.

"What do you want?" Anne-Marie asked.

"Just to ask you about the old man."

The woman frowned minutely. She looked as if she was sickening, Helen thought: Her face had the colour and texture of stale dough, her hair was lank and greasy.

"What old man?"

"Last time I was here, you told me about an old man who'd been murdered, do you remember?"

"No."

"You said he lived in the next court."

"I don't remember," Anne-Marie said.

"But you *distinctly* told me – "

Something fell to the floor in the kitchen, and smashed. Anne-Marie flinched, but did not move from the doorstep, her arm barring Helen's way into the house. The hallway was littered with the child's toys, gnawed and battered.

"Are you all right?"

Anne-Marie nodded. "I've got work to do," she said.

"And you don't remember telling me about the old man?"

"You must have misunderstood," Anne-Marie replied, and then, her voice hushed: "You shouldn't have come. Everybody *knows*."

"Knows what?"

The girl had begun to tremble. "You don't understand, do you? You think people aren't watching?"

"What does it matter? All I asked was – "

"I don't know *anything*," Anne-Marie reiterated. "Whatever I said to you, I lied about it."

"Well, thank you anyway," Helen said, too perplexed by the confusion of signals from Anne-Marie to press the point any further. Almost as soon as she had turned from the door she heard the lock snap closed behind her.

That conversation was only one of several disappointments that morning brought. She went back to the row of shops, and visited the supermarket that Josie had spoken of. There she inquired about the lavatories, and their recent history. The supermarket had only changed hands in the last month, and the new owner, a taciturn Pakistani, insisted that he knew nothing of when or why the lavatories had been closed. She was aware, as she made her enquiries, of being scrutinized by the other customers in the shop; she felt like a pariah. That feeling deepened when, after leaving the supermarket, she saw Josie emerging from the launderette, and called after her only to have the woman pick up her pace and duck away into the maze of corridors. Helen followed, but rapidly lost both her quarry and her way.

Frustrated to the verge of tears, she stood amongst the overturned rubbish bags, and felt a surge of contempt for her foolishness. She didn't belong here, did she? How many times had she criticized others for their presumption in claiming to understand societies they had merely viewed from afar? And here was she, committing the same crime, coming here with her camera and her questions, using the lives (and deaths) of these people as fodder for party conversation. She didn't blame Anne-Marie for turning her back; had she deserved better?

Tired and chilled, she decided it was time to concede Purcell's point. It *was* all fiction she had been told. They had played with her – sensing her desire to be fed some horrors – and she, the perfect fool, had fallen for every ridiculous word. It was time to pack up her credulity and go home.

One call demanded to be made before she returned to the car however: She wanted to look a final time at the painted head. Not as an anthropologist amongst an alien tribe, but as a confessed ghost train rider: For the thrill of it. Arriving at number 14, however, she faced the last and most crushing disappointment. The maisonette had been sealed up by conscientious council workman. The door was locked; the front window boarded over.

She was determined not to be so easily defeated however. She made her way around the back of Butt's Court and located the yard of number 14 by simple mathematics. The gate was wedged closed from the inside, but she pushed hard upon it, and, with effort on both parts, it opened. A heap of rubbish – rotted carpets, a box of rain-sodden magazines, a denuded Christmas tree – had blocked it.

She crossed the yard to the boarded-up windows, and peered through the slats of wood. It wasn't bright outside, but it was darker still within; it was difficult to catch more than the vaguest hint of the painting on the bedroom wall. She pressed her face close to the wood, eager for a final glimpse.

A shadow moved across the room, momentarily blocking her view. She stepped back from the window, startled, not certain of what she'd seen. Perhaps merely her own shadow, cast through the window? But then *she* hadn't moved; it had.

She approached the window again, more cautiously. The air vibrated; she could hear a muted whine from somewhere, though she couldn't be certain whether it came from inside or out. Again, she put her face to the rough boards, and suddenly, something leapt at the window. This time she let out a cry. There was a scrabbling sound from within, as nails raked the wood.

A dog! – And a big one to have jumped so high.

"Stupid," she told herself aloud. A sudden sweat bathed her.

The scrabbling had stopped almost as soon as it had started, but she couldn't bring herself to go back to the window. Clearly the workmen who had sealed up the maisonette had failed to check it properly, and incarcerated the animal by mistake. It was ravenous, to judge by the slavering she'd heard; she was grateful she hadn't attempted to break in. The dog – hungry, maybe half-mad in the stinking darkness – could have taken out her throat.

She stared at the boarded-up window. The slits between the boards were barely a half-inch wide, but she sensed that the animal was up on its hind legs on the other side, watching her through the gap. She could hear its panting now that her own breath was regularizing; she could hear its claws raking the sill.

"Bloody thing . . ." she said. "Damn well stay in there."

She backed off towards the gate. Hosts of wood-lice and spiders, disturbed from their nests by moving the carpets behind the gate, were scurrying underfoot, looking for a fresh darkness to call home.

She closed the gate behind her, and was making her way around the front of the block when she heard the sirens; two ugly spirals of sound that made the hair on the back of her neck tingle. They were approaching. She picked up her speed, and came round into Butts' Court in time to see several policemen crossing the grass behind the bonfire and an ambulance mounting the pavement and driving around to the other side of the quadrangle. People had emerged from their flats and were standing on their balconies, staring down. Others were walking around the court, nakedly curious, to join a gathering congregation. Helen's stomach seemed to drop to her bowels when she realized *where* the hub of interest lay: At Anne-Marie's doorstep. The police were clearing a path through the throng for the ambulance men. A second police-car had followed the route of the ambulance onto the pavement; two plain-clothes officers were getting out.

She walked to the periphery of the crowd. What little talk there was amongst the on-lookers was conducted in low voices; one or two of the older women were crying. Though she peered over the heads of the spectators she could see nothing. Turning to a bearded man, whose child was perched on his shoulders, she asked what was going on. He didn't know. Somebody dead, he'd heard, but he wasn't certain.

"Anne-Marie?" she asked.

A woman in front of her turned and said: "You know her?" almost awed, as if speaking of a loved one.

"A little," Helen replied hesitantly. "Can you tell me what's happened?"

The woman involuntarily put her hand to her mouth, as if to stop the words before they came. But here they were nevertheless: "The child – " she said.

"Kerry?"

"Somebody got into the house around the back. Slit his throat."

Helen felt the sweat come again. In her mind's eye the newspapers rose and fell in Anne-Marie's yard.

"No," she said.

"Just like that."

She looked at the tragedian who was trying to sell her this obscenity, and said, "No," again. It defied belief; yet her denials could not silence the horrid comprehension she felt.

She turned her back on the woman and paddled her way out of the crowd. There would be nothing to see, she knew, and even if there had been, she had no desire to look. These people – still emerging from their homes as the story spread – were exhibiting an appetite she was disgusted by. She was not of them; would never *be* of them. She wanted to slap every eager face into sense; wanted to say: "It's pain and

247

grief you're going to spy on. Why? Why?" But she had no courage left. Revulsion had drained her of all but the energy to wander away, leaving the crowd to its sport.

Trevor had come home. He did not attempt an explanation of his absence, but waited for her to cross-question him. When she failed to do so he sank into an easy *bonhomie* that was worse than his expectant silence. She was dimly aware that her disinterest was probably more unsettling for him than the histrionics he had been anticipating. She couldn't have cared less.

She tuned the radio to the local station, and listened for news. It came surely enough, confirming what the woman in the crowd had told her. Kerry Latimer was dead. Person or persons unknown had gained access to the house via the back yard and murdered the child while he played on the kitchen floor. A police spokesman mouthed the usual platitudes, describing Kerry's death as an "unspeakable crime", and the miscreant as "a dangerous and deeply disturbed individual". For once, the rhetoric seemed justified, and the man's voice shook discernibly when he spoke of the scene that had confronted the officers in the kitchen of Anne-Marie's house.

"Why the radio?" Trevor casually inquired, when Helen had listened for news through three consecutive bulletins. She saw no point in withholding her experience at Spector Street from him; he would find out sooner or later. Coolly, she gave him a bald outline of what had happened at Butts' Court.

"This Anne-Marie is the woman you first met when you went to the estate; am I right?"

She nodded, hoping he wouldn't ask her too many questions. Tears were close, and she had no intention of breaking down in front of him.

"So you were right," he said.

"Right?"

"About the place having a maniac."

"No," she said. "No."

"But the kid – "

She got up and stood at the window, looking down two storeys into the darkened street below. Why did she feel the need to reject the conspiracy theory so urgently? Why was she now praying that Purcell had been right, and that all she'd been told had been lies? She went back and back to the way Anne-Marie had been when she'd visited her that morning: Pale, jittery; *expectant*. She had been like a woman anticipating some arrival, hadn't she? – eager to shoo unwanted visitors away so that she could turn back to the business of waiting. But waiting for what, or *whom*? Was it possible that Anne-Marie actually knew the murderer? Had perhaps invited him into the house?

"I hope they find the bastard," she said still watching the street."

"They will," Trevor replied. "A baby-murderer, for Christ's sake. They'll make it a high priority."

A man appeared at the corner of the street, turned, and whistled. A large Alsatian came to heel, and the two set off down towards the Cathedral.

"The dog," Helen murmured.

"What?"

She had forgotten the dog in all that had followed. Now the shock she'd felt as it had leapt at the window shook her again.

"What dog?" Trevor pressed.

"I went back to the flat today – where I took the pictures of the graffiti. There was a dog in there. Locked in."

"So?"

"It'll starve. Nobody knows it's there."

"How do you know it wasn't locked in to kennel it?"

"It was making such a noise – " she said.

"Dogs bark," Trevor replied. "That's all they're good for."

"No . . ." she said very quietly, remembering the noises through the boarded window. "It didn't bark . . ."

"Forget the dog," Trevor said. "And the child. There's nothing you can do about it. You were just passing through."

His words only echoed her own thoughts of earlier in the day, but somehow – for reasons that she could find no words to convey – that conviction had decayed in the last hours. She was not just passing through. Nobody ever just *passed through*; experience always left its mark. Sometimes it merely scratched; on occasion it took off limbs. She did not know the extent of her present wounding, but she knew it more profound than she yet understood, and it made her afraid.

"We're out of booze," she said, emptying the last dribble of whisky into her tumbler.

Trevor seemed pleased to have a reason to be accommodating. "I'll go out, shall I?" he said. "Get a bottle or two?"

"Sure," she replied. "If you like."

He was gone only half an hour; she would have liked him to have been longer. She didn't want to talk, only to sit and think through the unease in her belly. Though Trevor had dismissed her concern for the dog – and perhaps justifiably so – she couldn't help but go back to the locked maisonette in her mind's eye: To picture again the raging face on the bedroom wall, and hear the animal's muffled growl as it pawed the boards over the window. Whatever Trevor had said, she didn't believe the place was being used as a makeshift kennel. No, the dog was *imprisoned* in there, no doubt of it, running round and round, driven, in its desperation, to eat its own faeces, growing more insane with every hour that passed. She became afraid that somebody – kids maybe, looking for more tinder for their bonfire – would break into the place, ignorant of what it contained. It wasn't that she feared for the intruders' safety, but that the dog, once liberated, would come for her. It would know where she was (so her drunken head construed) and come sniffing her out.

Trevor returned with the whisky, and they drank together until the early hours, when her stomach revolted. She took refuge in the toilet – Trevor outside asking her if she needed anything, her telling him weakly to leave her alone. When, an hour later, she emerged, he had gone to bed. She did not join him, but lay down on the sofa and dozed through until dawn.

The murder was news. The next morning it made all the tabloids as a front page splash, and found prominent positions in the heavy-weights too. There were photographs of the stricken mother being led from the house, and others, blurred but potent, taken over the back yard wall and through the open kitchen door. Was that blood on the floor, or shadow?

Helen did not bother to read the articles – her aching head rebelled at the thought – but Trevor, who had bought the newspapers in, was eager to talk. She couldn't work out if this was further peace-making on his part, or a genuine interest in the issue.

"The woman's in custody," he said, poring over the *Daily Telegraph*. It was a paper he was politically averse to, but its coverage of violent crime was notoriously detailed.

The observation demanded Helen's attention, unwilling or not. "Custody?" she said. "Anne-Marie?"

"Yes."

"Let me see."

He relinquished the paper, and she glanced over the page.

"Third column," Trevor prompted.

She found the place, and there it was in black and white. Anne-Marie had been taken into custody for questioning to justify the time-lapse between the estimated hour of the child's death, and the time that it had been reported. Helen read the relevant sentences over again, to be certain that she'd understood properly. Yes, she had. The police pathologist estimated Kerry to have died between six and six-thirty that morning; the murder had not been reported until twelve.

She read the report over a third and fourth time, but repetition did not change the horrid facts. The child had been murdered before dawn. When she had gone to the house that morning Kerry had already been dead four hours. The body had been in the kitchen, a few yards down the hallway from where she had stood, and Anne-Marie had said *nothing*. That air of expectancy she had had about her – what had it signified? That she awaited some cue to lift the receiver and call the police?

"My Christ . . ." Helen said, and let the paper drop.

"What?"

"I have to go to the police."

"Why?"

"To tell them I went to the house," she replied. Trevor looked mystified. "The baby was dead, Trevor. When I saw Anne-Marie yesterday morning, Kerry was already dead."

She rang the number in the paper for any persons offering information, and half an hour later a police car came to pick her up. There was much that startled her in the two hours of interrogation that followed, not least the fact that nobody had reported her presence on the estate to the police, though she had surely been noticed.

"They don't want to know – " the detective told her. "You'd think a place like that would be swarming with witnesses. If it is, they're not coming forward. A crime like this . . ."

"Is it the first?" she said.

He looked at her across a chaotic desk. "First?"

"I was told some stories about the estate. Murders. This summer."

The detective shook his head. "Not to my knowledge.

There's been a spate of muggings; one woman was put in hospital for a week or so. But no; no murders."

She liked the detective. His eyes flattered her with their lingering, and his face with their frankness. Past caring whether she sounded foolish or not, she said: "Why do they tell lies like that? About people having their eyes cut out. Terrible things."

The detective scratched his long nose. "We get it too," he said. "People come in here, they confess to all kinds of crap. Talk all night, some of them, about things they've done, or *think* they've done. Give you it all in the minutest detail. And when you make a few calls, it's all invented. Out of their minds."

"Maybe if they didn't tell you those stories . . . they'd actually go out and do it."

The detective nodded. "Yes," he said. "God help us. You might be right at that."

And the stories *she'd* been told, were they confessions of uncommitted crimes? Accounts of the worst-imaginable, imagined to keep fiction from becoming fact? The thought chased its own tail: These terrible stories still needed a *first cause*, a well-spring from which they leapt. As she walked home through the busy streets she wondered how many of her fellow citizens knew such stories. Were these inventions common currency, as Purcell had claimed? Was there a place, however small, reserved in every heart for the monstrous?

"Purcell rang," Trevor told her when she got home. "To invite us out to dinner."

The invitation wasn't welcome, and she made a face.

"Appollinaires, remember?" he reminded her. "He said he'd take us all to dinner, if you proved him wrong."

The thought of getting a dinner out of the death of Anne-Marie's infant was grotesque, and she said so.

"He'll be offended if you turn him down."

"I don't give a damn. I don't want dinner with Purcell."

"Please," he said softly. "He can get difficult; and I want to keep him smiling just at the moment."

She glanced across at him. The look he'd put on made him resemble a drenched spaniel. Manipulative bastard, she thought; but said: "All right, I'll go. But don't expect any dancing on the tables."

"We'll leave that to Archie," he said. "I told Purcell we were free tomorrow night. Is that all right with you?"

"Whenever."

"He's booking a table for eight o'clock."

The evening papers had relegated The Tragedy of Baby Kerry to a few column inches on an inside page. In lieu of much fresh news they simply described the house-to-house enquiries that were now going on at Spector Street. Some of the later editions mentioned that Anne-Marie had been released from custody after an extended period of questioning, and was now residing with friends. They also mentioned, in passing, that the funeral was to be the following day.

Helen had not entertained any thoughts of going back to Spector Street for the funeral when she went to bed that night, but sleep seemed to change her mind, and she woke with the decision made for her.

Death had brought the estate to life. Walking through to Ruskin Court from the street she had never seen such numbers out and about. Many were already lining the kerb to watch the funeral cortège pass, and looked to have claimed their niche early, despite the wind and the ever-present threat of rain. Some were wearing items of black clothing – a coat, a scarf – but the overall impression, despite the lowered voices and the studied frowns, was one of celebration. Children running around, untouched by reverence; occasional laughter escaping from between gossiping adults – Helen could feel an air of anticipation which made her spirits, despite the occasion, almost buoyant.

Nor was it simply the presence of so many people that reassured her; she was, she conceded to herself, happy to be back here in Spector Street. The quadrangles, with their stunted saplings and their grey grass, were more real to her than the carpeted corridors she was used to walking; the anonymous faces on the balconies and streets meant more than her colleagues at the University. In a word, she felt *home*.

Finally, the cars appeared, moving at a snail's pace through the narrow streets. As the hearse came into view – its tiny white casket decked with flowers – a number of women in the crowd gave quiet voice to their grief. One on-looker fainted; a knot of anxious people gathered around her. Even the children were stilled now.

Helen watched, dry-eyed. Tears did not come very easily to her, especially in company. As the second car, containing Anne-Marie and two other women, drew level with her, Helen saw that the bereaved mother was also eschewing any public display of grief. She seemed, indeed, to be almost elevated by the proceedings, sitting upright in the back of the car, her pallid features the source of much admiration. It was a sour thought, but Helen felt as though she was seeing Anne-Marie's finest hour; the one day in an other-wise anonymous life in which she was the centre of atten-tion. Slowly, the cortège passed by and disappeared from view.

The crowd around Helen was already dispersing. She detached herself from the few mourners who still lingered at the kerb and wandered through from the street into Butts' Court. It was her intention to go back to the locked maisonette, to see if the dog was still there. If it was, she would put her mind at rest by finding one of the estate caretakers and informing him of the fact.

The quadrangle was, unlike the other courts, practically empty. Perhaps the residents, being neighbours of Anne-Marie's, had gone on to the Crematorium for the service.

Whatever the reason, the place was eerily deserted. Only children remained, playing around the pyramid bonfire, their voices echoing across the empty expanse of the square.

She reached the maisonette and was surprised to find the door open again, as it had been the first time she'd come here. The sight of the interior made her lightheaded. How often in the past several days had she imagined standing here, gazing into that darkness. There was no sound from inside. The dog had surely run off; either that, or died. There could be no harm, could there? in stepping into the place one final time, just to look at the face on the wall, and its attendant slogan.

Sweets to the sweet. She had never looked up the origins of that phrase. No matter, she thought. Whatever it had stood for once, it was transformed here, as everything was; herself included. She stood in the front room for a few moments, to allow herself time to savour the confrontation ahead. Far away behind her the children were screeching like mad birds.

She stepped over a clutter of furniture and towards the short corridor that joined living-room to bedroom, still delaying the moment. Her heart was quick in her: A smile played on her lips.

And there! At last! The portrait loomed, compelling as ever. She stepped back in the murky room to admire it more fully and her heel caught on the mattress that still lay in the corner. She glanced down. The squalid bedding had been turned over, to present its untorn face. Some blankets and and a rag-wrapped pillow had been tossed over it. Something glistened amongst the folds of the uppermost blanket. She bent down to look more closely and found there a handful of sweets – chocolate and caramels – wrapped in bright paper. And littered amongst them, neither so attractive nor so sweet, a dozen razor-blades. There was blood on several. She stood up again and backed away from the mattress, and as she did so a buzzing sound reached her ears from the next room. She turned, and the light in the bedroom diminished as a figure stepped into the gullet between her and the outside world. Silhouetted against the light, she could scarcely see the man in the doorway, but she smelt him He smelt like candy-floss; and the buzzing was with him or in him.

"I just came to look – " she said, "– at the picture."

The buzzing went on: The sound of a sleepy afternoon, far from here. The man in the doorway did not move.

"Well . . ." she said, "I've seen what I wanted to see." She hoped against hope that her words would prompt him to stand aside and let her pass, but he didn't move, and she couldn't find the courage to challenge him by stepping towards the door

"I have to go," she said, knowing that despite her best efforts fear seeped between every syllable. "I'm expected . . ."

That was not entirely untrue. Tonight they were all invited to Appollinaires for dinner. But that wasn't until eight, which was four hours away. She would not be missed for a long while yet.

"If you'll excuse me," she said.

The buzzing had quietened a little, and in the hush the man in the doorway spoke. His unaccented voice was almost as sweet as his scent.

"No need to leave yet," he breathed.

"I'm due . . . due . . ."

Though she couldn't see his eyes, she felt them on her, and they made her feel drowsy, like that summer that sang in her head.

"I came for you," he said.

She repeated the four words in her head. *I came for you.* If they were meant as a threat, they certainly weren't spoken as one.

"I don't . . . know you," she said.

"No," the man murmured. "But you doubted me."

"Doubted?"

"You weren't content with the stories, with what they wrote on the walls. So I was obliged to come."

The drowsiness slowed her mind to a crawl, but she grasped the essentials of what the man was saying. That he was legend, and she, in disbelieving him, had obliged him to show his hand. She looked, now, down at those hands. One of them was missing. In its place, a hook.

"There will be some blame," he told her. "They will say your doubts shed innocent blood. But I say – what's blood for, if not for shedding? And in time the scrutiny will pass. The police will leave, the cameras will be pointed at some fresh horror, and they will be left alone, to tell stories of the Candyman again."

"Candyman?" she said. Her tongue could barely shape that blameless word.

"I came for you," he murmured so softly that seduction might have been in the air. And so saying, he moved through the passageway and into the light.

She knew him, without doubt. She had known him all along, in that place kept for terrors. It was the man on the wall. His portrait painter had not been a fantasist: The picture that howled over her was matched in each extraordinary particular by the man she now set eyes upon. He was bright to the point of gaudiness: His flesh a waxy yellow, his thin lips pale blue, his wild eyes glittering as if their irises were set with rubies. His jacket was a patchwork, his trousers the same. He looked, she thought, almost ridiculous, with his blood-stained motley, and the hint of rouge on his jaundiced cheeks. But people were facile. They needed these shows and shams to keep their interest. Miracles; murders; demons driven out and stones rolled from tombs. The cheap glamour did not taint the sense beneath. It was only, in the natural history of the mind, the bright feathers that drew the species to mate with its secret self.

And she was almost enchanted. By his voice, by his colours, by the buzz from his body. She fought to resist the rapture, though. There was a *monster* here, beneath this fetching display; its nest of razors was at her feet, still drenched in blood. Would it hesitate to slit her own throat if it once laid hands on her?

As the Candyman reached for her she dropped down and snatched the blanket up, flinging it at him. A rain of razors and sweetmeats fell around his shoulders. The blanket followed, blinding him. But before she could snatch the moment to slip past him, the pillow which had lain on the blanket rolled in front of her.

It was not a pillow at all. Whatever the forlorn white casket she had seen in the hearse had contained, it was not the body of Baby Kerry. That was *here*, at her feet, its blood-drained face turned up to her. He was naked. His body showed everywhere signs of the fiend's attentions.

In the two heartbeats she took to register this last horror, the Candyman threw off the blanket. In his struggle to escape from its folds, his jacket had come unbuttoned, and she saw – though her senses protested – that the contents of his torso had rotted away, and the hollow was now occupied by a nest of bees. They swarmed in the vault of his chest, and encrusted in a seething mass the remnants of flesh that hung there. He smiled at her plain repugnance.

"Sweets to the sweet," he murmured, and stretched his hooked hand towards her face. She could no longer see light from the outside world, nor hear the children playing in Butts' Court. There was no escape into a saner world than this. The Candyman filled her sight; her drained limbs had no strength to hold him at bay.

"Don't kill me," she breathed.

"Do you believe in me?" he said.

She nodded minutely. "How can I not?" she said.

"Then why do you want to live?"

She didn't understand, and was afraid her ignorance would prove fatal, so she said nothing.

"If you would learn," the fiend said, "just a *little* from me . . . you would not beg to live." His voice had dropped to a whisper. "I am rumour," he sang in her ear. "It's a blessed condition, believe me. To live in people's dreams; to be whispered at street-corners; but not have to *be*. Do you understand?"

Her weary body understood. Her nerves, tired of jangling, understood. The sweetness he offered was life without living: Was to be dead, but remembered everywhere; immortal in gossip and graffiti.

"Be my victim," he said.

"No . . ." she murmured.

"I won't force it upon you," he replied, the perfect gentleman. "I won't oblige you to die. But think; *think*. If I kill you here – if I unhook you . . ." he traced the path of the promised wound with his hook. It ran from groin to neck. "Think how they would mark this place with their talk . . . point it out as they passed by and say: '*She* died there; the woman with the green eyes'. Your death would be a parable to frighten children with. Lovers would use it as an excuse to cling closer together . . ."

She had been right: This *was* a seduction.

"Was fame ever so easy?" he asked.

She shook her head. "I'd prefer to be forgotten," she replied, "than be remembered like that."

He made a tiny shrug. "What do they know?" he said. "Except what the bad teach them by their excesses?" He raised his hooked hand. "I said I would not oblige you to die and I'm true to my word. Allow me, though, a kiss at least . . ."

He moved towards her. She murmured some nonsensical threat, which he ignored. The buzzing in his body had risen in volume. The thought of touching his body, of the proximity of the insects, was horrid. She forced her lead-heavy arms up to keep him at bay.

His lurid face eclipsed the portrait on the wall. She couldn't bring herself to touch him, and instead stepped back. The sound of the bees rose; some, in their excitement, had crawled up his throat and were flying from his mouth. They climbed about his lips; in his hair.

She begged him over and over to leave her alone, but he would not be placated. At last she had nowhere left to retreat to, the wall was at her back. Steeling herself against the stings, she put her hands on his crawling chest and pushed. As she did so his hand shot out and around the back of her neck, the hook nicking the flushed skin of her throat. She felt blood come; felt certain he would open her jugular in one terrible slash. But he had given his word: And he was true to it.

Aroused by this sudden activity, the bees were everywhere. She felt them moving on her, searching for morsels of wax in her ears, and sugar at her lips. She made no attempt to swat them away. The hook was at her neck. If she so much as moved it would wound her. She was trapped, as in her childhood nightmares, with every chance of escape stymied. When sleep had brought her to such hopelessness – the demons on every side, waiting to tear her limb from limb – one trick remained. To let go; to give up all ambition to life, and leave her body to the dark. Now, as the Candyman's face pressed to hers, and the sound of bees blotted out even her own breath, she played that hidden hand. And, as surely as in dreams, the room and the fiend were painted out and gone.

She woke from brightness into dark. There were several panicked moments when she couldn't think of where she was, then several more when she remembered. But there was no pain about her body. She put her hand to her neck; it was, barring the nick of the hook, untouched. She was lying on the mattress she realized. Had she been assaulted as she lay in a faint? Gingerly, she investigated her body. She was not bleeding; her clothes were not disturbed. The Candyman had, it seemed, simply claimed his kiss.

She sat up. There was precious little light through the boarded window – and none from the front door. Perhaps it was closed, she reasoned. But no; even now she heard somebody whispering on the threshold. A woman's voice.

She didn't move. They were crazy, these people. They had known all along what her presence in Butts' Court had summoned, and they had *protected* him – this honeyed psychopath; given him a bed and an offering of bonbons, hidden him away from prying eyes, and kept their silence when he brought blood to their doorsteps. Even Anne-Marie, dry-eyed in the hallway of her house, knowing that her child was dead a few yards away.

The child! That was the evidence she needed. Somehow they had conspired to get the body from the casket (what had they substituted; a dead dog?) and brought it here – to the Candyman's tabernacle – as a toy, or a lover. She would take Baby Kerry with her – to the police – and tell the whole story. Whatever they believed of it – and that would probably be very little – the fact of the child's body was incontestable. That way at least some of the crazies would suffer for their conspiracy. Suffer for *her* suffering.

The whispering at the door had stopped. Now somebody was moving towards the bedroom. They didn't bring a light with them. Helen made herself small, hoping she might escape attention.

A figure appeared in the doorway. The gloom was too impenetrable for her to make out more than a slim figure, who bent down and picked up a bundle on the floor. A fall of blonde hair identified the newcomer as Anne-Marie: The bundle she was picking up was undoubtedly Kerry's corpse. Without looking in Helen's direction, the mother about-turned and made her way out of the bedroom.

Helen listened as the footsteps receded across the living room. Swiftly, she got to her feet, and crossed to the passage-way. From there she could vaguely see Anne-Marie's outline in the doorway of the maisonette. No lights burned in the quadrangle beyond. The woman disappeared and Helen followed as speedily as she could, eyes fixed on the door ahead. She stumbled once, and once again, but reached the door in time to see Anne-Marie's vague form in the night ahead.

She stepped out of the maisonette and into the open air. It was chilly; there were no stars. All the lights on the balconies and corridors were out, nor did any burn in the flats; not even the glow of a television. Butts' Court was deserted.

She hesitated before going in pursuit of the girl. Why didn't she slip away now, cowardice coaxed her, and find her way back to the car? But if she did that the conspirators would have time to conceal the child's body. When she got back here with the police there would be sealed lips and shrugs, and she would be told she had imagined the corpse and the Candyman. All the terrors she had tasted would recede into rumour again. Into words on a wall. And every day she lived from now on she would loathe herself for not going in pursuit of sanity.

She followed. Anne-Marie was not making her way around the quadrangle, but moving towards the centre of the lawn in the middle of the court. To the bonfire! Yes; to the bonfire! It loomed in front of Helen now, blacker than the night-sky. She could just make out Anne-Marie's figure, moving to the edge of the piled timbers and furniture, and ducking to climb into its heart. *This* was how they planned to remove the evidence. To bury the child was not certain enough; but to cremate it, and pound the bones – who would ever know?

She stood a dozen yards from the pyramid and watched as Anne-Marie climbed out again and moved away, folding her figure into the darkness.

Quickly, Helen moved through the long grass and located the narrow space in amongst the piled timbers into which

Anne-Marie had put the body. She thought she could see the pale form; it had been laid in a hollow. She couldn't reach it however. Thanking God that she was as slim as the mother, she squeezed through the narrow aperture. Her dress snagged on a nail as she did so. She turned round to disengage it, fingers trembling. When she turned back she had lost sight of the corpse.

She fumbled blindly ahead of her, her hands finding wood and rags and what felt like the back of an old armchair, but not the cold skin of the child. She had hardened herself against contact with the body: She had endured worse in the last hours than picking up a dead baby. Determined not to be defeated, she advanced a little further, her shins scraped and her fingers spiked with splinters. Flashes of light were appearing at the corners of her aching eyes; her blood whined in her ears. But there! *there!* the body was no more a yard and a half ahead of her. She ducked down to reach beneath a beam of wood, but her fingers missed the forlorn bundle by millimetres. She stretched further, the whine in her head increasing, but still she could not reach the child. All she could do was bend double and squeeze into the hidey-hole the children had left in the centre of the bonfire.

It was difficult to get through. The space was so small she could barely crawl on hands and knees; but she made it. The child lay face down. She fought back the remnants of squeamishness and went to pick it up. As she did so, something landed on her arm. The shock startled her. She almost cried out, but swallowed the urge, and brushed the irritation away. It buzzed as it rose from her skin. The whine she had heard in her ears was not her blood, but the hive.

"I knew you'd come," the voice behind her said, and a wide hand covered her face. She fell backwards and the Candyman embraced her.

"We have to go," he said in her ear, as flickering light spilled between the stacked timbers. "Be on our way, you and I."

She fought to be free of him, to cry out for them not to light the bonfire, but he held her lovingly close. The light grew: Warmth came with it; and through the kindling and the first flames she could see figures approaching the pyre out of the darkness of Butts' Court. They had been there all along: Waiting, the lights turned out in their homes, and broken all along the corridors. Their final conspiracy.

The bonfire caught with a will, but by some trick of its construction the flames did not invade her hiding-place quickly; nor did the smoke creep through the furniture to choke her. She was able to watch how the children's faces gleamed; how the parents called them from going too close, and how they disobeyed; how the old women, their blood thin, warmed their hands and smiled into the flames. Presently the roar and the crackle became deafening, and the Candyman let her scream herself hoarse in the certain knowledge that nobody could hear her, and even if they had, would not have moved to claim her from the fire.

The bees vacated the fiend's belly as the air became hotter, and mazed the air with their panicked flight. Some, attempting escape, caught fire, and fell like tiny meteors to the ground. The body of Baby Kerry, which lay close to the creeping flames, began to cook. Its downy hair smoked, it back blistered.

Soon the heat crept down Helen's throat, and scorched her pleas away. She sank back, exhausted, into the Candyman's arms, resigned to his triumph. In moments they would be on their way, as he had promised, and there was no help for it.

Perhaps they would remember her, as he had said they might, finding her cracked skull in tomorrow's ashes. Perhaps she might become, in time, a story with which to frighten children. She had lied, saying she preferred death to such questionable fame; she did not. As to her seducer, he laughed as the conflagration sniffed them out. There was no permanence for him in this night's death. His deeds were on a hundred walls and ten thousand lips, and should he be doubted again his congregation could summon him with sweetness. He had reason to laugh. So, as the flames crept upon them, did she, as through the fire she caught sight of a familiar face moving between the on-lookers. It was Trevor. He had forsaken his meal at Appollinaires and come looking for her.

She watched him questioning this fire-watcher and that, but they shook their heads, all the while staring at the pyre with smiles buried in their eyes. Poor dupe, she thought, following his antics. She willed him to look past the flames in the hope he might see her burning. Not so that he could save her from death – she was long past hope of that – but because she pitied him in his bewilderment and wanted to give him, though he would not have thanked her for it, something to be haunted. That, and a story to tell.

PART II

PROLOGUE

'Worlds of Space in the Living Room'

Orson Welles' notorious radio broadcast of H.G. Wells' *War of the Worlds* which was transmitted on the night of Hallowe'en in 1938 and convinced thousands of American listeners that Martians were landing in New Jersey and even panicked hundreds into fleeing from their homes, has a parallel occurrence in the annals of British television. This was a programme called *Alternative 3* which Anglia Television networked on May 13, 1977.

A former newscaster, Tim Brinton, played a similar role to that of Orson Welles as the straight-faced front man who informed viewers that a number of high IQ citizens had gone missing in recent months and there were various theories as to *why* they had disappeared. One of these theories was the subject of *Alternative 3*, Brinton announced earnestly, and would prove that the missing people had actually being 'recruited' to form the nucleus of a standby civilization on Mars against the possibility of the end of the World resulting from a nuclear disaster.

The documentary-style programme, which had been written by David Ambrose and directed with breathless pace by Chris Miles, cleverly utilized NASA footage of the surface of Mars along with photographs of the 'missing' people to baffle and enthral its nine million viewers. Although unquestionably a clever spoof intended to satirize some of the fashionable conspiracy theories of the time – just as Orson Welles' radio play had done forty years earlier – there were still a number of viewers who believed that it was all *true*. Even assurances from Anglia that *Alternative 3* was pure fiction and had originally been scheduled for screening on April 1 could do nothing to shake the conviction of these people – and as a result the programme has now joined *War of the Worlds* and a handful of other similar SF hoax broadcasts in becoming a legend.

That any viewers would accept the premise of *Alternative 3* as possible let alone probable says much for the power of television. Indeed, although Science Fiction stories have been around almost as long as the medium itself and have had to make use of the most rudimentary special effects until recent years, the genre has thrown up a number of classic productions whose very titles are instantly recognizable: *Superman, Quatermass, The Twilight Zone, Doctor Who* and *High-Hiker's Guide to the Galaxy*, to name just five. All the evidence points to the conclusion that SF is every bit as popular on TV as it is in the cinema, and over the years virtually all space movies made for the big screen have sooner or later turned up on television.

Archive records show that the first SF programme was *Captain Video* (1949–1953) a 'live' American series for youngsters about an intrepid spaceman (played by Richard Coogan) who battled various threats from outer space aided by his Video Rangers. Despite all the shortcomings of being confined to a small New York studio – although the early scriptwriters included such important names as Damon Knight, C.M. Kornbluth and Robert Sheckley – the five nights a week serial enjoyed great popularity and it was not long before other superheroes of space were joining the Captain including *Buck Rogers* (starring Ken Dibbs, 1950), *Tom Corbett, Space Cadet* (with Frankie Thomas, 1950), *Space Patrol* (with Ed Kermer, Lynn Osborn and Ken Mayer, 1954), *Commando Cody – Sky Marshal of the Universe* (starring Judd Holdren, 1955) and, most famous of all, *Superman* with George Reeves (1953), of which more later.

Prologue

Despite the often wooden acting and crude attempts at portraying space flight and the terrains of distant planets, the success of these programmes lead to the still highly-regarded 'anthology' shows such as *Tales of Tomorrow* (1952), *Out Of This World* (1952) and *Science Fiction Theatre* (1955) which drew the material for their weekly, half-hour episodes from the short stories of a number of leading SF authors.

It was in the Fifties with *The Quatermass Experiment* in Britain and *The Twilight Zone* in America that Science Fiction really came of age on television. And once the TV programme makers on both sides of the Atlantic had realized that the genre was not just fantasy fare for children but had much to say to adult audiences about the probabilites of space travel and the possibilites of life on other worlds – as well as entertaining and exciting them – it has never looked back as the selections in this collection which span the past half century will make very evident. For herein are representative stories from some of the best Science Fiction television shows written by some of the genre's most famous writers.

Space may well be a thousand miles away in reality, but thanks to television and space movies it is only the distance to the other side of the living room . . .

PETER HAINING

SUPERMAN

(ABC TV, 1953–)
Starring: George Reeves, Phyllis Coates &
John Hamilton
Directed by Thomas Carr
Adapted from the screenplay by George Lowther

Superman is undoubtedly the most enduring television series hero of all, having first made his small screen debut in the days of black and white TV in 1953, and today, forty years later, is the star of a multi-million dollar production which benefits from all the advances in special effects and film-making technology. Now the famous 'Man of Steel' really does seem to fly on the screen! Superman actually made his debut as a strip cartoon character in 1938 in *Action Comics*, and two years later had his own animated cartoon series directed by Dave Fleischer for Paramount. In 1948 a serial for cinema audiences was made with Kirk Alyn (1948), and then in 1953 he finally reached the television screen with George Reeve in the title role. The original concept of this man who, as a child, had escaped from a cataclysm which overwhelmed his home planet of Krypton and come to live on Earth in the dual role of self-effacing newspaperman, Clark Kent, and indestructable caped crime fighter, had been jointly devised by writer Jerome Siegel and artist Joseph Shuster. Within a matter of years of their first strip cartoons, Superman had become the most influential Science Fiction comic hero as well as an icon in contemporary culture. Such indeed is the character's fame that a copy of the issue of *Action*

Comics in which he made his debut sold recently at auction for over £14,000!

The original ABC TV series was produced for much of its five-year run by the versatile Whitney Ellsworth who part-scripted the opening episode, 'Superman on Earth' with Robert Maxwell. The impact on viewers of the early 25-minute episodes was instantaneous, and even Thol Thomson's special effects – crude by today's standards – still held audiences spellbound when George Reeves appeared to leap over skyscrapers and halt speeding trains with his bare hands. Reeves, who had actually made his screen debut in *Gone With The Wind*, unfortunately became hopelessly typecast in the role and when the series ended in 1957 he was unable to find other work and tragically committed suicide in 1959, aged just 45. Nothing, however, could diminish the appeal of Superman: and comic books, radio series and the constant use of his image in advertising and promotion ensured world-wide popularity. In 1978 he returned to the cinema again in a blockbuster movie starring Christopher Reeve and Marlon Brando; and then in 1984 he was back on TV once more in 'The New Adventures of Superman', played by former American football player, Dean Cain, with Teri Hatcher as Lois Lane. This latest version has, in fact, made the 'Man of Steel' a rather more 'realistic' figure, while the stories themselves contain cynical remarks about his prowess and moments of irony that would never have been possible in the original. Nonetheless, it has proved a ratings winner with audiences on both sides of the Atlantic. The following adaptation by American television writer George Lowther (1914–) is based on the original script by Ellsworth and Maxwell and relates how the legend of the unique crime-fighter began half a century ago. As a result of the success of Superman, the era of Science Fiction on TV had effectively begun . . .

1

The Great Hall of Krypton's magnificent Temple of Wisdom was a blaze of light. Countless chandeliers of purest crystal reflected the myriad lights into a dome of glass where they were shattered into a million fragments and fell dazzling over the Great Hall.

Below the brilliant dome the Council of One Hundred waited. Attired in togas of scarlet and blue, they looked impatiently for the arrival of Jor-el, Krypton's celebrated scientist. They had been summoned from the length and breadth of the planet to hear a message Jor-el would deliver. What the message was they did not know. They knew only that when Jor-el spoke all men listened.

Now they waited, curious as to the nature of Jor-el's message. Rarely did the brilliant young scientist leave the mysterious regions of his laboratory. Whatever he had to say tonight they knew would be of great importance to Krypton and its people.

There was a sudden movement and a murmuring wave of voices rose and fell, echoing in the Great Hall.

Jor-el had arrived at last.

All eyes centered on the tall, thin figure that moved forward on the raised platform and took the hand of white-bearded Ro-zan, supreme leader of the Council. There were those who noticed at once that the handsome face of Jor-el was drawn and haggard. Something, they knew, was wrong. The Council of One Hundred waited in hushed suspense.

Wearily, the young scientist turned to the gathering. Standing tall in the yellow and purple robes of his calling, he drew a deep breath. There was a moment's pause and then his voice filled the vast Hall.

"Krypton is doomed!"

Had a thunderbolt crashed through the crystal dome of the Temple at that moment it could not have produced a more startling effect!

Ro-zan rapped heavily for order, and in time the tumult aroused by Jor-el's startling words died down. Silence reigned as the two men, one the aged supreme leader of the Council, the other Krypton's foremost scientist, faced each other. Ro-zan's kindly face was grim as he strove to keep his voice steady.

"Say on, Jor-el."

Jor-el nodded and again faced his audience. He spoke slowly now, carefully, choosing his words.

"Members of the Council, I repeat – Krypton is doomed!"

A gathering wave of protest began, but Jor-el stilled it with a lifted hand. The wide yellow sleeve of the gown he wore fell away from his upraised arm and showed the gauntness of it, accentuating the thin boniness of his fingers. Whether the Councilmen believed him or not, they could see that long hard weeks of toil had aged this man. They listened respectfully as he went on.

"Would that I could bring you good news, but I cannot. Week upon week, pausing for little sleep and less food, I have worked in my laboratory, striving to understand the signs which have come to us from outer space. You, my friends, for months past have seen the sudden showers of stars that have fallen upon our planet. Comets of great magnitude have appeared from nowhere, whirling dangerously close to Krypton. Not many weeks ago a monstrous tidal wave rose from the sea and roared toward our city. Good fortune was with us, for the wave died before it reached our shores. It was then I first realized there might be something wrong and I set myself to discover the meaning of these phenomena. I have found out. Krypton is doomed to destruction."

Again a murmur of protest rose among the Councilmen and again Ro-zan was forced to rap for order. When quiet had been restored, he said, "Jor-el, how explain you this?"

The young scientist shook his head.

"Would that I might answer you, Ro-zan, but even the

learned men of science who work under me cannot fully comprehend my equations and formulae. I will be as clear as I can. The Planet Krypton may be likened to a volcano – a volcano that for years has slumbered peacefully. Now it begins to come awake. Soon it will erupt! Whether that eruption will be slow or sudden, I cannot tell. *But it will come!* And when it does, the mightly Planet Krypton will burst into a million molten fragments!"

The glowing eyes set deep in the haggard face of the young scientist held everyone in the Chamber spellbound as he added, "Time is short! I bid you prepare!"

The spell, however, lasted only for a moment. Then, with a mighty surge, a roar of anger and protest burst forth. Jor-el had lost his mind, some cried; others that he had made a mistake in his calculations. He was overwearied with too much work and needed rest. In brief, they could not and would not believe him.

His arms half raised, the scientist turned beseechingly toward Ro-zan, a tragic, almost helpless figure.

"Make them understand," he pleaded. "You, Ro-zan, can make them believe!"

Ro-zan's smile was filled with pity. He spoke in a kindly voice.

"Come, Jor-el," he said softly, "surely you have made a mistake. Surely—'

"I have made no mistake! Ro-zan, you must believe—'

Ro-zan's upraised hand commanded silence.

"I understand well what faith you must have in your deductions, Jor-el. But certainly it is difficult to believe the thing you tell us. Krypton doomed? Krypton fated to destruction? Impossible! You yourself must realize that, Jor-el, in your – er – saner moments."

The scientist stiffened, as if Ro-zan had struck him across the face. He waited a moment to master himself before replying. "You think me out of my mind?"

Ro-zan shook his head slowly, smiling patiently as he did so.

"No, Jor-el. I think that not at all. A mind as lordly

as yours knows not destruction. But certain it is, friend, that you are weary. You have toiled long and well in the service of the people of Krypton, and you need rest."

"I tell you—" Jor-el began, but again Ro-zan stayed him with an upraised hand. There was now a slight trace of annoyance in the older man's voice.

"Please, Jor-el, this is unlike you! What if your strange deductions are correct? What if your scientific equations and astronomical formulae are true? What can we do about it? Where can we go?"

With desperate eagerness Jor-el seized the opportunity to answer Ro-zan's question.

"I have not come here with this tragic news," he said hastily, "without bringing with me a solution for it. You ask me where we can go? My answer is – to the Planet Earth!"

There was a pause before the Councilmen realized what Jor-el had said. Then the Great Hall racked with laughter.

"Listen to me! Listen to me!" Jor-el cried over and over again. But his voice was drowned in the thunderous laughter. Even Ro-zan did not rap for order this time, but turned away to hide the sudden smile that came to his lips. Only when the laughter had worn itself out did he again address Jor-el.

"Dear friend," he said, "you see how right we are? You see how badly you do need rest? No – please – speak not till I have finished. You say if Krypton is destroyed we can escape to the Planet Earth. How could we live there, Jor-el? You yourself – you who have studied the Earth for years through the great telescope – have told us how inferior to ourselves are the Earth People. They are thousands of years behind us in everything, mental and physical. Their cities are as nothing compared to the cities that have existed here on Krypton for centuries. Their minds are so far beneath the capacity of our own that actually, in comparison, they have no intellect at all! As for their bodies, you yourself have said that they are weaklings. It takes a hundred Earth People together to do what one man on Krypton can do alone! They have not the power to fly, but must walk at snail's pace on the Earth's surface! They cannot breathe beneath the sea!"

Ro-zan shook his head slowly from side to side.

"Would you send us to live among such a people, Jor-el? Nay, I think not! Death is preferable to life in a world of such inferior people."

"I have studied the problem with the utmost care, Ro-zan," Jor-el persisted. "The atmosphere that surrounds the Earth is the only one that can sustain us. There is no other planet to which we can go, no other—"

"Stop! Don't say another word!"

Ro-zan's voice was harsh and his face had become stern.

"I would not be angry with you, Jor-el, but you drive me beyond patience. The Council of One Hundred and I have heard enough. What you tell us is sheer nonsense. Krypton is not doomed, nor will it ever be! You are weary and need rest – I hope it is no more than that. Now, until you have recovered your senses, please come to us no more."

Again Jor-el stiffened, for again it was as if Ro-zan had struck him. After a moment's pause he turned to go, then stopped and faced the Council.

"I will go," he said, bitterly, "but before I do, I would have you know one thing." He paused, letting his eyes rove over the assembly. "I am right. I know this. You must learn it. When you do learn it, I trust it will not be too late. I am at work on a model of a Space Ship—" A titter ran through the audience, but Jor-el did not stop. "– a Space Ship that I had hoped would carry us all to the Earth! I shall continue with my work, for only in that way may I still save you from yourselves when this tragedy comes upon us. And now – I leave you."

Not a word was spoken as Jor-el turned and moved slowly out of sight through the high arched doorway – a tragic, beaten figure.

2

A long Silver rocket – the model of Jor-el's Space Ship – gleamed under the powerful lights of the scientist's laboratory, amidst a clutter of scientific instruments. Jor-el, the sleeves of his robe rolled back, worked over the model with feverish haste. So deep was his concentration that he did not hear a panel in one of the walls slide back, and did not see his wife, Lara, as she entered with their child in her arms. She waited until Jor-el looked up and noticed her.

"I heard you at work," she said. "I knew you had returned. What did the Council say?"

Jor-el shook his head sadly. "As you warned me, Lara, they refused to believe me."

"But you intend to continue your work on the Space Ship?"

Jor-el fitted a valve into place before he answered. "Of course! Whatever they think, Lara, I am right – I know it! And if there is still time, I will save them!" He gave the valve a final twist. "I shall start constructing the Space Ship itself as soon as this model is finished."

Lara nodded, understanding. The child in her arms whimpered and she began to rock it back and forth. "Little Kal-el has been strangely restless these past few days," she said. "He has scarcely slept at all. Jor-el, do you think he feels the approach of this thing you have foretold?"

"It may be," said Jor-el. "He has always been sensitive to the elements."

The scientist continued his work, his thin hands moving swiftly and surely over the intricate mechanism of the model Space Ship. Lara sat and watched, rocking the child in her arms. Finally she gave voice to the question that troubled her. "Is there much time, Jor-el?"

"No," he answered, "there is little time. That is why I

hasten to finish the model. It is almost ready. I have only to install the Atomic Pressure Valve and—"

Whatever he was about to say froze in his throat as an ear-shattering crash burst over Krypton! He clutched the model Space Ship to steady himself, for the entire room was rocking. Things were falling and splintering all about. A tall cabinet filled with tubes and measuring glasses fell with a mighty crash. Gaping cracks appeared in the walls and the cement floor surged underfoot like an awakening monster. The high arched window broke into a thousand fragments. And through the yawning hole where the window had stood, Jor-el saw a seething fan of flame spread upward and envelop the sky.

"It has come, Lara!" he cried. "It has come!"

And come it had! In seconds, night was turned into flaming day. Across the sky, countless comets whirled screaming through brilliant space. The stars began to fall, showering upon Krypton a rain of liquid fire. Asteroids of every color careened across the heavens. Lights of every size and hue, dazzling and eye-searing, scattered over Krypton.

The elements, as Jor-el had predicted, had gone mad!

Jor-el, a man of science, remained calm in the face of this sudden cataclysm. As the sky fell, as the ground seethed, his mind teemed with the possibilities of the moment. The Space Ship was not ready. It was too late to save the people of Krypton. Too late to save Lara and himself. But the child—

"Lara!" his voice commanded. "We can do naught for ourselves or the others. But there is hope for Kal-el!"

"Jor-el— ?"

He answered her question before she asked it.

"The model of the Space Ship!" he cried. "I have only to install the Atomic Pressure Valve. A few moments will do it! And then, Lara, if it works—"

Even as he spoke he was collecting the tools he would need. And as he worked, Lara stood with the child in her arms, gazing out at a crumbling world.

Flames of every color roared from great fissures in the land. Against the frightful glow could be seen the majestic spires of Krypton shattering into dust. And under all this was a strange rumbling, as if some mighty force were stirring fitfully and gathering its strength for one great and final upheaval. Lara knew that when that upheaval came it would be the end.

"It is ready!"

She turned at Jor-el's words to see him standing beside the gleaming silver model.

"Give me the child," he said, "and pray the model works! For in it we shall send him to the Earth and to safety!"

Lara said not a word but placed the tiny form of Kal-el in his father's arms. She watched silently as Jor-el placed it, whimpering, into the model of the Space Ship and closed the steel door. When he was certain the door was sealed securely, he quickly threw a lever.

Together they waited. And, waiting, they heard the strange rumble gathering under them for the final up-heaving surge that would spell the end of Krypton. As the rumbling increased, the flaming sky grew brighter, the comets whirled faster, the stars fell in greater showers!

They heard but saw none of this, for their eyes were fixed on the needle of the gauge that marked the atomic pressure of the model. Something seemed to be wrong. The needle had not moved. The pressure necessary to send the steel bullet hurtling into space was not increasing. But the ominous rumble beneath *was* increasing, building toward that final cataclysm that would burst the Planet Krypton!

Jor-el clutched at the lever, working it back and forth. He stared at Lara with wild eyes, and beads of sweat stood out on his forehead. Seconds, literally, stood between the infant Kalel and safety. The moment of Doom had come! A monstrous crash in the distance marked the end of Krypton! The fissures in the ground opened into yawning chasms. The laboratory began to fall about them! And the atomic pressure of the tiny, futile Space Ship—

The needle moved. There was a hissing, as of some tremendous skyrocket. Jor-el had only time to let go the lever as the model strained and trembled and, rending loose, shrieked into flaming space, bearing toward Earth its tiny passenger.

3

Eben Kent reined his horse to a stop, leaned on the worn handle of his plow, and looked off across the rolling land he had just tilled, to the point where hill met sky. There was something strange about that sky. He knew the weather, as well as any farmer born to the soil, and off-hand he would have said a storm was brewing. Yet he was not quite sure. It seemed to him there was the feeling of something more than just a storm in the air. He had seen that same slate sky before, had felt the same heaviness in the air, had seen the thunderheads rising in the west. And yet—

Eben reflected for a moment, shook his head in a puzzled way, clucked to the horse, and set about finishing the South Forty before night closed in.

He heard thunder rumble in the distance, and thought vaguely that there was something peculiar even about that. Unlike the thunder he had ever heard before, it did not die away but was continuous, increasing in volume. He clucked again to the horse, for the animal had stopped in its tracks with the first rumbling sound, its ears flattened against its head.

As Eben continued his plowing, the sun broke through the heavy slate sky. At least he thought it was the sun, for there was a sudden blaze of light in the heavens, a light that grew larger as he watched it. In the next instant he became alive to the fact that it was not the sun!

The plow was wrenched from his strong hands as the

horse reared, screamed in fright, and bolted across the fields, dragging the plow after it. As Eben stood in mute amazement at the animal's singular behavior, he heard a strange whine in the air, and then a distant roar that changed to a series of thunderous explosions. Dizziness overcame the old farmer as the whining filled his ears. He almost cried out for help as, reaching out with his hands, he sought to steady himself. It was then, as he stood tottering and afraid, that the growing blaze he had thought to be the sun struck the earth not far from him. Blinded and afraid, he threw himself to the ground, burying his face in the new-turned loam, his fingers clutching the good brown earth for safety. Then, trying feebly to crawl away on his hands and knees, he fainted.

The crackling of flames was the first sound he heard as consciousness returned to him. The air was unbearably hot, but not so hot that he could not stand it. The thunderous explosions had stopped and the strange whine in the air had died away. Eben raised his head and looked about him.

Not a hundred yards away was a strange, bullet-shaped object, almost completely enveloped in flames. Hesitating only a moment, Eben ran toward it, a conviction growing within him that someone might be inside that flaming silver shell.

Peering through the flames, he saw a child lying helpless behind the thick glass window of the door that sealed the rocket. Already Eben had come as close as the wall of heat would let him. He realized instantly that unless he broke through that searing wall the child would die.

He made up his mind quickly, took a deep breath, and plunged through to the rocket. When he emerged again from the flame and smoke, agony stood in his eyes, for he had been severely burned. But in his blackened arms he held the child!

Eben Kent and his wife, Sarah, never knew where the

child had come from, never pierced the mystery that surrounded his strange appearance on earth. Destiny perhaps played a part in directing the rocket to the Kent farm, for the Kents were childless and desired a child above anything else on earth. And here, like a gift from Heaven, was the infant Kal-el. The old couple took him into their home and raised him as their own.

They called him Clark, because that was Sarah Kent's family name. The circumstances surrounding his peculiar arrival were almost forgotten as year ran into year and the infant grew to be a strong and handsome boy, helping Eben with the chores about the farm, listening to stories at Sarah's knee in the long winter evenings. He seemed no different from other boys of his age. He attended the little country school, played games, went fishing in the hot summer afternoons, and worked and studied as all boys do.

It was not until his thirteenth year that the incident occurred that was to set him apart from ordinary humans, and was to give him his first glimpse of the powers he possessed, beyond those of the earth people who were his companions.

It happened on the last day of school. The pupils of the eighth grade, young Clark's class, waited with great expectations for the arrival of Mr Jellicoe, the principal. It was Mr Jellicoe's custom to award personally any prizes that had been won by the pupils during the year – prizes for excellence in composition, mathematics, spelling and so on.

Miss Lang, Clark's teacher, had taken the prizes from the drawer of her desk and placed them on a small table, where the children's eyes could feast on them while waiting for Mr Jellicoe. There were books of all descriptions, medals, and ribbons. Hearts beat faster as each child wondered which of these he would receive.

At last Mr Jellicoe arrived, a short, bald, and immensely stout man who was much given to laughter. There was great excitement as he began to award the prizes – a book for one, a medal for another, a blue or gold ribbon for a third. Young Clark himself was awarded a copy of Shakespeare's plays. He had shown remarkable talent in composition and had the highest marks in English Literature. He had even begun to have thoughts of making his living later on as a writer – a novelist, perhaps, or a playwright, or what was even more exciting, a reporter.

As he returned to his desk, carrying the book Mr Jellicoe had just given him, he heard Miss Lang say, "That's strange, Mr Jellicoe. I'm sure it was here."

"I don't see it," Mr Jellicoe said.

"Then it must still be in the desk," Miss Lang answered. "I'll get it."

She opened the drawer of her desk and began searching for something. Mr Jellicoe went on handing out the awards, occasionally casting an anxious glance in Miss Lang's direction.

It was at this moment that the strange thing happened.

Clark watched the teacher as she poked about in the desk drawer, and as he did so he became slowly aware that he was also looking at the inside of the desk, that his eyes had pierced the wood, and that the interior of the desk was quite plain to him. Caught behind the top drawer where Miss Lang could not see it was a blue ribbon.

"Are you looking for a blue ribbon?" Clark asked.

Miss Lang looked up in surprise. "Yes, Clark," she said.

"It's a ribbon for General Excellence," said Mr Jellicoe. "It's for Lucy Russell. But it doesn't appear to be on the table here. Do you know where it is, Clark?"

"Why, yes," Clark answered. "It's caught behind the top drawer of Miss Lang's desk. If you'll pull the drawer out, you'll – you'll—" He paused and began to falter. The eyes of everyone were upon him, eyes filled with a growing amazement. He realized suddenly that what had seemed to him a natural and ordinary thing was actually most remarkable.

Miss Lang lost no time in pulling out the top drawer of

her desk. A moment later she was holding the blue ribbon in her hand. She looked at Mr Jellicoe, then at Clark, and then back to Mr Jellicoe again.

The silence that filled the classroom was almost more than Clark could bear, and he was relieved when Miss Lang said, finally, "How did you know the ribbon was at the back of that drawer, Clark?"

Clark tried to answer but the words would not come. He was as startled as anyone else at what had happened. The simple truth was that he *had looked through the desk* as though the wood were transparent. He was about to say as much when he realized that he would not be believed.

"I – I just knew," he said at last. "I had a – a feeling that – that was the only place the ribbon *could* be."

There were another few moments of silence in which everyone looked at him queerly. Then Mr Jellicoe frowned and cleared his throat.

"Very strange," he said. "*Very* strange."

The cold, unfriendly tone of Mr Jellicoe's voice could mean only one thing. Clark looked at Miss Lang. Her mouth was set in a hard, thin line. Even his classmates seemed to shrink away from him. All at once he realized what they were thinking – that he had rummaged through Miss Lang's desk – that he had done a dishonest thing. And there was no way of clearing himself.

When he arrived home puzzled and confused he found a surprise waiting for him. Greeting Eben and Sarah as he came in, he showed them the book he had won.

Eben rose from his chair and put an arm around the boy.

"Son," said old Eben, "ye've done a fine job – a mighty fine job. That book – that book of plays – why, shucks, boy, that's one o' the finest things that's ever happened to yer ma and me. We're proud o' ye!"

Clark looked up at them and felt everything going soft inside him. He loved these two, loved them as nothing else on earth.

Old Eben cleared his throat.

"Yer ma's got a – well, a kinda present fer ye, son. Ye know the masquerade thet's bein' given up to Judge Marlow's place tonight—"

"Yes, I know," said young Clark. "But we decided I couldn't go."

"'Course ye kin!" cried Eben, slapping him on the back. "It's bein' given in honor of all them young students that won prizes! Ye got t' go!"

"But we talked this all over, Dad!" said Clark. "You said we couldn't afford to rent a costume from the city—"

"That's right, son," Sarah Kent said. "We couldn't afford to rent a costume, but there was nothin' stoppin' me from makin' one – now was there?"

"Get the costume, ma, and let him see it," Eben said.

When Sarah Kent returned with the costume and draped it over Clark's arm, he felt he had never seen anything quite so exciting. There was a tight-fitting suit of blue, a wide belt of leather, knee-length boots, and – most thrilling of all – a scarlet cape. He could hardly wait till he reached his room to try it on.

It took him but a few moments to slip out of his clothes and into the costume. Arrayed in the blue suit, with the scarlet cape draped from his shoulders, he stood before the mirror and surveyed himself. It was a wonderful costume! And to think that he had not expected to go to the party at all—! He whooped suddenly with delight and leaped into the air, spreading the cape for effect.

The shock of what happened next was almost more than he could bear. He had merely started to jump up and down in his boyish happiness over the costume. When his feet touched the floor again, he was standing *at the other end of the room!*

He stood motionless, staring about him in utter amazement. He could not believe that he had actually flown across the room, and yet—. He decided to try it again.

He bent his knees and pushed upward. And then – he was in the air, flying about the room!

He was frightened at first and his heart beat like a triphammer. Just as his eyes could pierce the wood of Miss Lang's desk, so he could fly. What was the answer? How could he do these things when other boys, he knew, could not? Was he different from other boys? He had never thought so before and he didn't want to think so now. He had a feeling that to be different would set him apart, and he saw himself as a queer and lonely figure, shunned by all.

He tried in the months that followed to forget the strange powers he had discovered in himself. Yet as time wore on he would begin to wonder whether he still possessed them, and the temptation would be too great. At such times he would look at whatever was nearest and, using his remarkable vision, see straight through it. At others, when he was sure no one could see him, he would leap lightly into the air and fly about. And after a time, when his fear of these odd things wore off, he came to like them and found joy in practicing them.

As months became years, a superhuman strength was growing in him as well, but he was not aware of it. It was not until he was seventeen that he had his first knowledge of it. It came about in an unexpected way.

The Kent farm had never been successful. Old Eben was a good farmer and a hard worker, but as far back as Clark could remember, bad luck always struck at the very moment when it seemed the Kents were about to find some small measure of success. About the time Clark reached his seventeenth birthday old Eben found himself heavily in debt. He told the boy about it on the eve of the State Fair.

They were standing in the field together. Eben had finished haying for the day and was unhitching the old horse in the light of the setting sun. Clark, having completed his chores about the house, had come to help him put the horse in the barn.

"Looks like a mighty fine day for the Fair tomorrow," Eben said, gazing off across the fields to where the sun was dropping behind the hills.

"Yes, Dad, it does," Clark said.

Eben seemed thoughtful and moody, and Clark knew he had something on his mind. He would speak of it in his own good time. He did. He said, finally, "Son, what would ye say if I was t' tell ye I was thinkin' o' enterin' the Anvil Contest tomorrow?"

Clark straightened up and looked at Eben in surprise. He could not believe the old man meant it.

"I know it sounds silly to ye, lad," Eben went on, "but we need the money bad! I won the contest once. 'Twas many a year ago when I was a younger man. Still mebbe I might have a chance. If I can win the prize—"

But how could he hope to win it? Only young men – yes, and only those noted for their strength in the county – ever thought of entering the Anvil Contest. To compete, a man had to grasp an anvil in his arms and lift it from the ground; whoever lifted it highest won $500. The prize had been won the year before by a farmer who, because of his tremendous strength, was locally known as 'The Bull'. A close second had been Fred Hornbach, whose powerful muscles had made him the champion wrestler of the state. Both were young men, and both would undoubtedly enter the Anvil Contest this year, yet here was Eben Kent, an aging man, proposing to pit himself against two such adversaries. The need for money must be desperate indeed.

It was, as Clark now learned. For the first time, Eben unburdened himself to the boy, told him of the unsuccessful struggles of the past years, and of the inability to make both ends meet. As the two walked toward the barn, Clark listened and found growing within him an overwhelming desire to help Eben Kent.

How he was to do it only time could tell.

4

The day of the State Fair dawned bright and clear, but there was little happiness in Clark Kent's heart. He had slept poorly during the night, his active mind trying vainly to invent some method, to find some way, of helping the aging farmer. He found none, and as dawn broke he sat at his window, looking out across the misty fields, vaguely troubled at thoughts of what the day might bring.

After a hearty breakfast, old Eben and Clark started for the Fair Grounds. Sarah Kent remained at home. The misfortunes of the past years had been harder on her than on her husband, and she had aged, it seemed, much more than he. Fair-going days were over for her, and she preferred now to sit at home.

The Fair Grounds presented a lively sight. Hordes of farmers and their wives and children milled about the various exhibits, and as the sun rose higher and hotter in the heavens the scene became even more hectic. There were competitions of all sorts, prizes given for the finest cows, the best hogs, the sturdiest bulls, the plumpest chickens. There were horse-shoe contests, potato-sack races, all sorts of tests of skill and strength. People filled themselves with hotdogs and ice-cream and pickles and a hundred other good things to eat. And everywhere there were laughter and gleeful shouts and the happy din of people who have come to celebrate.

Somehow young Clark and Eben bore the suspense of waiting through the day, for the Anvil Contest was not held until late in the afternoon. At last, as the shadows lengthened across the Fair Grounds, the crowd began to move toward the platform on which stood the mighty anvil.

The platform itself was decked out gaily with red-white-and-blue bunting. Toward the rear was a bench reserved for the three judges, and to the side another bench where the contestants were to sit. The anvil, newly polished, stood in the very center for all to see.

Clark's eyes roved over the crowd, sought and found what he most feared – the faces of 'The Bull' and Fred Hornbach. Throughout the day he had hoped they would not be there, that something might happen to keep them away. He was not disappointed when he saw them, however, for he had felt from the outset that his hopes would be in vain.

Old Eben looked at his son. Clark did not like what he saw in the farmer's face, for one glance was enough to convince him that Eben regretted having come. The old man realized, perhaps for the first time, the impossibility of his winning against such heavy odds. It was too late for him to back down now, however, for his name had been entered on the list, and already one of the judges was beckoning to him to come up on the platform.

"Well, son," he said, "wish me luck!"

"Good luck, Dad!" Clark said, and as he said it he felt empty inside. If only he could help, if only *he* could mount that platform in Eben's place. But how futile that would be! Even now, Fred Hornbach and 'The Bull' were taking their places on the side bench, and there was no mistaking the power of their muscles, the strength of their broad backs. Instinctively he felt the muscles of his own arms. Yes, they were strong arms, but they could hardly compare with those of the other two. His heart sank as old Eben mounted the steps.

A ripple of laughter went through the crowd as it caught sight of Eben. Beside the other two he looked indeed a futile, piteous figure. The crowd could not know the desperation that had brought the aged farmer here, could not know the dire need for money that had spurred him to take his chances against impossible odds. It knew only that he looked ridiculous in comparison with the other two.

Clark looked about at the laughing faces and felt a rage smoldering within him. Jeers and cat-calls were heard as the old man's name was called, and he took his place beside Hornbach and 'The Bull'. Clark, watching Eben, saw his face flush.

"There's no fool like an old fool," a voice said close to Clark. The owner of the voice was a middle-aged man with graying hair and a face as sour as a lemon. He wore rimless glasses and squinted through them as if he found difficulty in seeing anything even with their aid. He was well dressed, and it needed but a glance to tell that he was from the city.

Clark glared at the man, who returned the unfriendly stare. He was about to say something, when one of the judges was heard announcing that the contest was about to begin.

The first name called was that of a man who had mounted the platform after Eben. He was not a young man but his strength was apparent. He walked to the anvil and stood over it a moment. Then, amidst encouraging shouts from his friends, he took the anvil in his arms and tried to lift it. Strain and struggle as he might, the anvil would not budge, and he was forced at length to give up.

Fred Hornbach's name was called next. Standing beside the anvil, he spat upon his hands, tightened his broad leather belt about his waist, and waited for the crowd to quiet down. Then he braced himself, his arms about the anvil, and lifted. His face grew dark with the effort it cost him, and the muscles bulged on his arms and neck and shoulders. A roar of approval burst from the crowd as the anvil left the floor. Hornbach held it as the judges quickly measured the distance. One inch. The relief on Hornbach's face was evident as he sat the anvil back in its place.

Now came 'The Bull' – huge in body, with sturdy legs and a broad muscular back. He was stripped to the waist, and as he approached the anvil the crowd, noting his deep chest, his powerful stomach muscles, the strength of his mighty arms, cheered their champion.

This was 'The Bull's' moment, and he did not intend

to let it pass quickly. He clasped his hands above his head in the manner of a prize fighter and turned to all corners of the platform, acknowledging the plaudits of his admirers. As his gaze moved over the crowd it fell upon young Clark. Their eyes met, and the boy disliked the man instantly. There was a smugness in 'The Bull's' smile, an arrogance in the curve of his lips, that brought a flush to Clark's face and stirred his heart to anger.

Having given his followers time to admire him, 'The Bull' now prepared to lift the anvil. His legs spread wide, his feet firmly planted, he put his arms around the anvil and lifted it from the floor. He seemed to accomplish the feat almost without effort, holding the anvil a good three inches above the boards. He waited till the judges had accurately marked the distance, and then slowly lowered the anvil. Strutting a bit, he returned to his seat amid deafening applause.

Now the name of Eben Kent was called and again a ripple of laughter was heard. Jeers and derisive shouts filled the air as Eben moved toward the anvil in the center of the platform.

"Ye ain't got a chance now, Bull!" somebody called, and the crowd rocked with mirth.

Eben Kent was not a man to be stopped by the unfriendliness of others. He braced himself, gripped the anvil and, gathering all his strength, heaved mightily. Slowly the laughter died and the cat-calls ceased, for Eben Kent had succeeded in lifting the anvil off the floor and was now straining to win the contest! One inch – two inches – Clark, watching the old man's face, saw it slowly redden, saw the veins standing out like whipcords on his neck. He felt like screaming, "Put it down, Dad! You'll never make it! You'll kill yourself!" But he could do nothing except stand in the crowd and watch, as Eben Kent refused to own himself beaten and strained in vain to raise the anvil more than three inches from the floor!

A spasm of agonizing pain suddenly shattered the old man's face. He gasped and dropped the anvil. He staggered for a moment – but only for a moment. In the next instant he had straightened up and was smiling gallantly but painfully at the crowd.

Many laughed, for now that Eben had failed he again became for them a ridiculous figure. He was something to laugh at, and the crowd wanted to be amused. Again jeers and cat-calls and derisive remarks were thrown his way. As Eben sat down on the contestants' bench, 'The Bull' made a dumb show of being afraid of him, throwing up his arms in mock fear. This was what the crowd wanted and they encouraged 'The Bull' to continue. This he obligingly did, to their great delight.

Clark could stand it no longer. Blinded by hot, unreasoning anger he fought his way through the crowd and onto the platform. He stood before 'The Bull' with tears of rage streaming down his cheeks.

"Let my father alone!" he shouted. "Let him alone – you hear?"

'The Bull' looked at him in mild astonishment and amusement. He reached out a powerful arm to push Clark away.

"Go 'way, kid, or I'll—"

He never finished what he started to say. As his hand reached out for Clark, the boy stepped aside and swung his fist against the other's jaw. 'The Bull' shuddered and sank limply to the floor.

Hardly realizing what he had done, white-hot anger still seething within him, Clark turned toward the anvil, his eyes blazing. Laugh at his father, would they? He'd show them! He reached down, gripped the anvil in both hands, and lifted. He was almost thrown off balance at the ease with which he raised it and held it aloft, high above his head!

Not a sound, not a breath, came from the astounded onlookers. Clark stood there, looking into the amazed faces of a silent, gaping crowd. And then slowly the wonderment of what he had done came over him. He raised his eyes to the anvil, held aloft in his hands. He shifted it a little to feel its weight. There was no weight. The anvil was like a feather.

He looked toward the other end of the platform. Three of the four contestants, Eben amongst them, were staring at him dumbly. The fourth, 'The Bull', lay stretched full-length on the floor. He turned his head still further to where the judges sat. Three pairs of startled eyes were looking at him.

He lowered the anvil to the floor.

And then the crowd went wild!

Shouting and cheering, they surged toward the platform and onto it, milling about the boy. Hands clapped him on the shoulders approvingly and fingers reached out to feel the muscles of his arms.

Questions came from all sides. How had he managed to do it? Had he practiced a long time? What was the secret of such amazing strength?

A middle-aged man with graying hair pushed his way through the crowd to where Clark stood. It was the man with rimless spectacles and the city clothes who had stood beside him not so long ago and called Eben an old fool. He took hold of Clark's arm.

"Young man," he said, "you're what I've been looking for! You're a scoop! I represent the *Daily Planet* in Metropolis. I want the full story of how you developed your amazing strength!"

Clark gulped and seemed unable to find his voice.

"Out with it!" snapped the reporter. "No false modesty now! Give me the story — all of it!"

Clark tried to speak but the words would not come.

"All right, all right, have it your way!" the man barked. "I'll write the story *my* way! But I'm in your debt, anyway, young man. You've given me the beat I've been looking for all day. If you ever need anything, look me up at the *Daily Planet!*"

He shook the boy's hand and started off through the crowd.

"I don't know your name," Clark called after him.

"Eh?" He paused, squinting back at the boy. "Oh yes. Couldn't very well find me without knowing my name, could you? Well, son, if you ever come to the *Daily Planet* just ask for Perry White. That's all. Just Perry White!"

A moment later he was gone in the crowd.

5

Clark Kent never forgot that day, nor the night that followed. When the wonder of what he had done abated somewhat and the crowd began to move off and leave him, he found his way to Eben who still sat on the contestants' bench. In his hand Clark held five new one hundred dollar bills, which the judges had awarded him, and he was anxious to give these to the old farmer, happy that a kind, though rather strange, fortune had given him the chance to help.

Eben Kent looked up at the boy and tried to smile, but his face was ashen with pain.

"I – I've done somethin' – inside – here," he faltered, pressing his hand against his chest. "We'd – we'd best be gettin' on for home."

Supporting the tired old man, Clark broke a way through the crowd. Five miles or more lay between them and home. They had walked the distance that morning, but Clark knew Eben would never be able to walk it now. How right he was he did not know until they reached the narrow wagonroad that led to the Kent farm. Here Eben suddenly went limp in the boy's arms, and Clark knew he had collapsed.

Clark looked about him. There was no one in sight. Speed was vital. He must get to the farm quickly and call a doctor. There was no time to waste. And so now he did what he had never attempted before. He lifted Eben Kent in his arms as easily as if he were a child and, like a bird, left the ground.

Sweeping through the air, with the old man cradled

in his arms, the full realization of his powers dawned on him. Up to now this curious ability of his to fly, to see through things – this wondrous strength discovered only that afternoon – all these had seemed like strange playthings, not to be taken seriously. But now, as he sped through the air, he knew suddenly that he was a man apart, that he was not like ordinary men, that he was a super-being. He understood more than this. He understood that these miraculous powers could be harnessed and put to use. If a man could fly, if his eyes were gifted with X-ray vision, if he possessed the strength of countless men – what could he not do? He turned these things over in his mind as he flew toward home.

Once arrived at the farm, he quickly summoned the local doctor. Clark and Sarah Kent waited anxiously while the doctor completed his examination of Eben. At last he finished and joined them in the parlor.

"Well?" Clark questioned anxiously. "What is it, doctor?"

The gray-haired physician placed his instrument bag on the table.

"It isn't easy to tell you this, Sarah, or you, son, but lifting that anvil, I'm afraid, was too much for Eben's heart – more than it could stand. I could put it into scientific language for you, but – well – the simplest way to say it is that he used up all his strength. I – well, frankly – I don't expect him to last the night."

When the doctor had left, Sarah Kent went into the room where Eben lay. She was with him a long time. When she came out, Clark saw that she had been crying, even though now her eyes were dry.

"He wants to see you," she said.

Clark nodded and entered the room.

Eben lay propped up in bed. Against the white pillows his face was haggard and drawn with pain. He smiled wanly as Clark entered the room. He motioned the boy to a chair near the window through which a setting sun was sending its last, weak rays.

"Dad—" Clark began, but the old man raised a restraining hand.

"There's not much time, lad," he said, "so I'll do the talkin'."

He leaned back against the pillows and regarded Clark with a sad smile. For some moments he lay thus without saying a word. Then he began to talk. As he talked the shadows deepened in the room as the sun sank lower behind the hills. The western sky became a blazing flood of color. Then the colors began to fade, melting into each other, blending at last into a somber gray. And the old man talked on, telling the boy the story of how he had been found and adopted, of his early years, of the mystery that surrounded his life before the arrival of the miniature Space Ship on earth.

"And now ye know," he said at length. "Lad, ye have within ye powers there's no explainin'. Ye're a – a modern miracle, that's what ye be. 'Tis not for you nor me to question the ways of God." He raised himself against the pillows. "But these powers ye have, lad, and it rests with you whether ye'll put them to good use or to bad!"

Clark said nothing. He sat looking out at the western hills, tears burning his eyes. Old Eben went on.

"Let me guide ye, son, as I have these seventeen years. There's great work t' be done in this world, and you can do it. Ye must use these powers of yours to help all mankind. There are men in this world who prey on decent folk – theives, murderers, criminals of every sort. Fight such men, son! Pit your miraculous powers against them! With you on the side of law and order, crime and oppression and in justice must perish in the end!"

Clark sat and said nothing and the shadows deepened in the room.

"One thing more—" Old Eben's voice came feebly out of the growing darkness.

"One thing more. Men are strange. They believe the wrong things, say the wrong things, do the wrong things. 'Tisn't that they want to, but, somehow, they do. They'd not understand ye, lad. 'Tis not given me t'say how they'd act toward ye, but I know it would not be in the right way."

He took a deep breath before going on.

"So ye must hide your true self from them. They must never know that you're a – a superman. Aye, ye must hide yerself from 'em—"

His voice trailed off oddly.

"Ye must hide yerself – from – 'em—"

Clark leaped from the chair to the bedside, and his arms were around the old man in an instant.

"Dad—" he choked.

"Listen to me, son." Clark could barely hear the words and bent his ear close to old Eben's mouth. "It strikes me now. I called ye a – a superman, and that's what ye be. Remember that. You're *Superman!*"

Once again, for the second time that day, Eben Kent went limp in Clark's arms. But this time was the last. No need for words now. Clark left the room. Sarah Kent was waiting outside. Their eyes met. Without a word she stepped into the room and closed the door behind her.

Clark walked to the front door, opened it, and went out into the cool, night air. Stars were twinkling now in the blue vault of the heavens. He started across the fresh-turned fields, the smell of the earth in his nostrils, the damp air against his cheeks. He never knew how long or how far he walked. He only knew that when finally he sat down on the brow of a lonely hill, with nothing about him but the quiet moonlit land, he had decided definitely what he must do, what course his life must take.

TALES OF TOMORROW

(ABC TV, 1952–3)
Starring: Leslie Nielsen, William Redfield &
Robert Keith, Jr
Directed by Don Medford
Story 'What Price Venus?' by S.A. Lombino
(Evan Hunter)

Tales of Tomorrow **has the distinction of being the first Science Fiction anthology series to be shown on television. Planned from as early as 1951 by ABC TV in co-operation with the The Science Fiction League of America, the show not only adapted several of the classic SF writers like Jules Verne and H.G.Wells, but also introduced a number of new magazine writers including Julian C. May, Robert Lewine and Frank De Felitta. The show was the brainchild of producer George Foley and Richard H. Gordon, a rising young TV executive who would later make several successful horror movies such as** *Grip of the Strangler* **and** *Corridors of Blood.* **Anxious to portray SF as accurately as possible, the pair recruited the expertise of the Science Fiction League of America. Founded in 1934 in the pages of** *Wonder Stories* **by the editor Hugo Gernsback and his friend, Charles D.Hornig, the League's purpose was to bring together all those with an interest in the genre. The success of the group lead to the formation of local 'chapters' in England and countries as far away as Australia and New Zealand. It was, therefore, very appropriate that the League – the first professional sponsored SF organization in the world – should have been** instrumental in the making of television's first SF anthology series.

Surviving kinescope copies of the episodes of *Tales of Tomorrow* make it plain that Foley and Gordon had ambitious plans for the series, but like so many productions of the time it had to be screened live with all the technical problems inherent in such broadcasts. The first two half-hour episodes were an adaptation of Jules Verne's *Twenty Thousand Leagues Under The Sea*, starring Thomas Mitchell, and with the TV cameras apparently positioned behind water tanks to simulate underwater scenes! This was followed by a version of H.G.Well's story, 'The Crytal Egg' with Thomas Mitchell once again the star. Richard Gordon's penchant for horror was obvious in at least two of the episodes, 'Momento' and 'Past Tense' both of which starred Boris Karloff; while his ability to spot stars of the future can be judged by his casting of the young Rod Steiger and even younger Paul Newman in leading roles. The titles of the most popular stories indicate the variety of themes and locations used in the ground-breaking series: 'The Dune Roller', 'The Lost Planet', 'Ice From Space' and 'Appointment on Mars'. This last story is perhaps the most interesting of all because it was written by one Salvatore A. Lombino (1926–) a New York teacher and SF fan who would soon afterwards write a novel around his experiences in a violent local school, change his name, and alter the entire course of his life. The book was *The Blackboard Jungle* (1954) and the author's name appeared as Evan Hunter. Lombino had actually begun writing SF as early as 1951, with a series of magazine stories and two pseudonymous novels, *Rocket to Luna* (as by Richard Marsten) and *Tomorrow and Tomorrow* (as Hunt Collins). Today, of course, he is best known of all as the thriller writer, Ed McBain. Hunter's contribution to *Tales of Tomorrow* was inspired by 'What Price Venus?' a story he had written for

Fantastic Universe **magazine and it was brought to the small screen with the same characters but a change of planet – Mars being considered more familiar to the show's viewers. Starring in 'Appointment on Mars' was the ubiquitous Leslie Nielsen, and even in 1953 some of the wry humour and off-beat acting skills which he has employed in making himself a major star after a lifetime in secondary roles was evident as he stomped around a curious alien landscape which had been recreated in one of ABC's tiny New York studios . . .**

1

Tod Bellew balanced on the tip of the diving board. His was a tall figure against the blue of the sky. His body was muscular, compact and lithe. His hair was blond and close cropped, his eyes narrow and pale blue.

He leaped suddenly into space, down into the shimmering pool below. His world became a cloudy blue, swirling before his eyes. He thought, *It's good to be away from people.*

Silence, dead silence, except for the pounding of blood in his veins. A blue silence that shifted and shimmered. No people. No fools.

His blond head popped up above the surface. The sunlight blinded him momentarily. He shook his head and swam toward the side of the pool with bold easy strokes.

He clambered out, shook himself, walked to a drying chamber. Methodically he adjusted the dials and waited patiently while the warm gusts of air covered his body. In two minutes, fully dried, he stepped out into the sunlight again.

A short man in a tight tunic, much too tight for the stomach that preceded him, smiled at Tod. "Mr Bellew?" he asked.

"Yes," Tod replied, thinking, *What can this fool want? Why can't they all leave me alone?*

"A message for you, sir." The man handed him an official-looking blue envelope. Tod glanced at it briefly. The man waited.

"Well?" Tod asked.

The man grinned sheepishly and said, "Nothing, sir. I . . ."

"Nothing is exactly right," Tod said drily. "I don't carry credits in my swimming trunks."

The balding man looked embarrassed. He bowed obsequiously and turned away.

Tod dropped into a foam chair by the side of the pool. The palm trees whispered softly in the mild breeze. A few clouds, gauzy and white, tiptoed aimlessly across the Neopolitan blue of the sky

It was all very pleasant – easily one of the nicest areas on Earth, Tod thought. He wondered idly if it could be bought. It would be nice to get rid of the tourists. The Earth, Tod thought, would be a wonderful place if it weren't for people. Perhaps a few – carefully chosen and skillfully disposed of as soon as they began to show signs of wearing around the edges. They would have to be perfect specimens of . . .

The letter.

Tod glanced idly at the blue envelope. Behind the cellophane window were his name and the address of the hotel. In the upper left hand corner, in bold black letters, were the words OFFICE OF THE MILITARY. Below that was the seal of Earth Seven.

Earth Seven – the entire area extending through what had been Canada, the United States, Mexico, South America, the Atlantic Ocean and England.

Tod tore open the flap of the envelope and unfolded the letter that had been inside.

'*Mr Tod Bellew*
Hotel Crestshore
Miami Beach, Florida
 You are requested to report immediately to the Office of the Military, New York, New York. ETA 2100 Tuesday, March 29, 1989.
(signed)
Leonard Altz

Commander, Earth Seven.'

Tod looked at the brief message again. Estimated time of arrival was 2100 Tuesday, March . . . Why, that was today! His eyes swept rapidly to the large clock in the face of the bath-house wall. He had exactly four hours to dress, pack, eat and get to New York. True, he could probably make it in less than an hour by fast ship, but it was still damned inconsiderate.

Just what did the military want of him? He considered ignoring the message, then thought better of it. *A sad commentary on society*, he thought wryly, *when a citizen can be ordered to be someplace he doesn't want to be*. The worst part of it was that the order had to be obeyed.

Fred Trupa, tall, gangling, his thick brown hair matted on his skull, glanced briefly at the scattered garbage cans in front of the building. He hitched up his pants and started up the steps.

A tall girl, redheaded, with a nose too long for the small oval of her face, glanced up from a magazine she was reading. "Hi, Trooper."

"Hi," Trooper said.

The girl wore a tight tunic, molded firmly to the curves of her body, ending abruptly above her knees.

What was her name? Trooper wondered. What difference did it make? All the same, every last one of them. Pigs stuffed together in a filthy hot concrete coffin.

"What's your hurry?" the redhead asked.

"Why don't you read your book?" Trooper said rudely.

"Pretty damned stuck-up, ain't you?" the girl said.

"Look . . ." Trooper began. He considered the futility of arguing with her, added, "The hell with you."

He started into the building, a black uninviting maw. For an instant, he turned to look at the street again. Dull gray tenements reaching concrete fingers toward a gray sky.

Doesn't the sun ever shine here? He wondered. Stinking city. Stinking dirty city pressing against a guy. All day and all night, reaching for him, ready to snatch him up and turn him into a machine like all the rest.

He took a last disgusted look at the street and walked into the gloomy hallway. The redhead stared at him curiously. He stopped before the row of mailboxes, peered into the one marked *Joseph Trupa*. The lock had been broken long ago. He lifted the flap of the box and reached inside for a blue official-looking envelope.

His name was visible in the cellophane window on the front of the envelope. In the upper left hand corner, in bold black letters, were the words OFFICE OF THE MILITARY. Below that was the crest of Earth Seven.

He stuffed the envelope into the back pocket of his breeches and started up the steps in the dim hallway. She'd be waiting, probably drunk again, fat and sloppy. *Mother!*

He passed another tenant in the hallway, quickly looked away. *Everyone with a gimmick*, he thought. *Everyone trying to slit everyone else's throat. A nice big cheerful rat race in a concrete-and-steel maze. I don't trust any of them. And I'll never trust them.*

He stopped before the door of his apartment and listened. Inside a woman was singing in an offkey voice, loud and raucous. Drunk, as usual, no doubt.

He opened the door and stepped into the ancient living room. Mrs Trupa came from the kitchen. She was a short squat woman with black hair clinging wetly to the back of her neck. Her sloppy house tunic bore the filth of kitchen drippings. She walked flatfooted, like a big duck in oversized slippers.

"About time you're home," she complained in her usual whine.

"Lay off," Trooper replied. "Lay off, will you?"

"Ingrate, that's all you are. An ingrate. Ain't done a stitch of work since you served your Compulsory. Think all I got to do is slave all day for—"

"Oh, cut it out, for God's sake."

"Sure, sure. Your father can break his back for you, though, can't he? Out every morning early just to—"

"I said cut it out! A guy comes home and gets a lecture. Always lectures. Why don't you get yourself a soap-box?"

"Don't talk to *me* like that, you little . . ."

Trooper whipped the blue envelope out of his pocket and walked over to the window, where it was lighter. He tore open the flap and read the brief message. His eyes narrowed and then a strange smile spread over his face.

"What is it?" Mrs Trupa asked.

"I'm leaving," Trooper said. "I have to report to the Military in two hours."

Maybe they'll call me again, he thought. *Maybe it's goodbye again, you lousy fat slob!*

2

They stood before the desk of Commander Altz – Tod Bellew and Fred Trupa. Tod wore an expensive tunic, carefully molded to fit his body. Trooper wore dark ill-fitting breeches and a shirt with a tear in the left sleeve.

They stood and waited for the commander to speak, two men with two things in common – their youth and a deep aversion toward all of mankind.

The commander wore the bright yellow uniform of the Military with the Earth Seven insignia on his collar. His hair was snow-white, clipped short. His eyes were brown. He was tapping a pencil on the desk, looking at the two young men standing before him.

306

Tod shifted uneasily. Trooper clenched and unclenched his hands in anticipation. Commander Altz cleared his throat.

"You're both wondering why you're here, I imagine," he said.

"Yes," Tod replied with a trace of arrogance.

The commander lifted black eyebrows. "There's a seed on Venus," he said abruptly. "Earth Seven wants it, must have it."

He looked at the two men, appraising their reactions to his blunt statement.

"And?" Tod asked.

"You two are going after it," Altz went on.

Tod and Trooper looked at each other, then back to the commander. "Why us?" Tod asked. "Why not somebody else?"

Altz lifted his eyebrows again. "Oh, various reasons – progress reports during both your Compulsories – physical condition – Height, stature, general bone structure, facial proportions – things like that."

"What's that got to do with it?" Trooper wanted to know. He was anxious to leave New York but the idea of Venus didn't exactly appeal.

Altz smiled. "A great deal – a great deal."

"I wish you'd get to the point," Tod said, forgetting for a moment that Altz, in this particular situation, commanded more authority than he did himself.

"All right, I'll get to the point. Earth Seven is strong. We've got more weapons and machinery than practically all the other Earth Sectors put together. There's only one thing we lack – people. Men to man the weapons and the machines – fighting men. The entire population of Earth Seven is hardly equal to one third that of the other Sectors combined."

Tod sighed. "And for this we have to go to Venus?"

"Earth Seven is ready for a merger," Altz continued. "I don't have to tell you, of course, that this is top-secret stuff. The balance here is a stagnant one. We're ready to expand – west to Earth Eight and Nine, east to Earth Six, Five, and Four."

"Expand?" Trooper asked.

"A consolidated Earth," Altz explained, "with a central command here in Earth Seven."

Trooper nodded.

"We're ready to go, as soon as we get what we need. I'll describe the seed you're to bring back from Venus."

"I still don't understand why we were chosen for this particular job." Tod frowned. "What's our physical appearance got to do with this job? Why *us?*"

"We've tried to get the seed before. We've failed each time. This time we can't afford to fail. We either get it now or drop our plan entirely. The men we've already sent to Venus never returned."

"Why?" This was Trooper.

"The Venerians are somewhat reluctant about giving up this seed. It's fairly important to their culture."

"And how will we succeed where the others have failed?" Tod asked.

"That's where your physical appearance comes in. You'll go to Venus as Venerians. Tall, blue and big-boned."

"There must be a million men in Earth Seven who are tall and big-boned," Trooper protested.

"Yes, but a certain mental attitude is necessary for the job too. Your records seemed to indicate you were the right men."

"What kind of mental attitude?" Tod asked.

"That's not important. We've made the choice and you're the men we want."

"This is fantastic," Tod said. "Of what possible use can a Venerian seed be? I'm afraid I don't approve of this at—"

"I feel I should tell you both that from here on in it's no longer a matter of choice. You are both under martial law."

"We've already served our Compulsory," Tod reminded the commander.

"I'm well aware of that, Bellew." Altz' voice hardened.

A deep silence shouldered its way into the room. Altz began tapping the pencil on the desk again.

"You'll leave in a week. The necessary adjustments in appearance will be made before then. You'll be instructed in language, culture, topography – everything you'll need to know to pass as Venerians."

"And the seed?"

"It's small, no more than a quarter of an inch in diameter. It's a pale blue in color, with a thin network of fibre under the translucent covering. You'll see pictures of it and you'll study models before you leave. Everything will be taken care of."

"How many of these seeds will you want?" Trooper asked.

"Two will be sufficient. You'll be given specific orders before you leave."

"And this seed is so very important?" Tod asked.

"Very important."

"How?"

"I've already told you. It can mean the difference between a stagnant *status quo* – or a vibrant new change."

"How?" Tod asked again.

"You'll report to surgery first," Altz said, completely ignoring Tod's question.

Bellew and Trupa turned to go. Altz rapped on the desk with the end of his pencil.

"You're forgetting something, aren't you?"

Trooper was the first to turn. Tod moved more slowly.

"I told you that you're both under military orders now, didn't I?"

Instantly Trooper brought up his hand in salute. Tod eyed the commander for a hostile instant. Slowly he brought his hand in salute.

"Dismissed," Altz snapped.

The room was long and white and antiseptic. The doctor hovered over Trooper's body, carefully making measurements.

"Wrist to elbow, thirteen," he called.

An assistant in a white gown wrote the figures down.

"Elbow to shoulder, thirteen and one quarter."

Again the pencil moved over the pad.

"Ankle to knee, eighteen and one half."

On and on, measurements, measurements, measurements. Trooper lay stretched out on the long table, waiting for it to end.

"Hair, brown," the doctor said. "Eyes . . ." he looked at Trooper's face, ". . . brown."

"Will I live?" Trooper cracked.

"I think so." The doctor smiled. "We'll have to add a few inches to your elbows but that'll be fairly simple. And your legs are a little short but they can be fixed too, of course."

Trooper frowned as the doctor went on.

"Your eyes, of course, are all wrong. Blue lenses should take care of that nicely. Your hair will have to be dyed blue. And your skin, of course . . ."

"Is all this permanent?" Trooper asked.

"Worried about your good looks, eh?" The doctor chuckled. "No, it's not permanent. We can undo anything we do and the skin coloring will wear off in a year or so of its own accord."

Trooper sighed loudly and deeply.

"We'll start whenever you're ready," the doctor said.

"I'm ready right now," Trooper answered, somewhat resigned to his fate. If it wasn't one damned rat race it was another. Always being pushed, always being pushed, always . . .

The anesthetic cup covered his nose and mouth and he drifted off into a peaceful blackness in which tiny rodents scurried back and forth noiselessly.

*   *   *

What Price Venus?

They sat together in the Hypnobooth, earphones clapped tightly to their ears. Before them the Tridim flashed brilliant scenes of Venus as the words droned on and on and on in their ears.

They saw its position in the galaxy, were told its diameter, its density, its atmospheric conditions, its allotment of heat and light.

Now a picture of a large plant flashed onto the screen. It was a pale pink, with enormous petals that flapped like the ears of a cocker spaniel.

"Among the varied plants found on Venus is the Pink Eucador, startling for its enormous size and sensitivity to sunlight. The Eucador family includes the Striped Eucador, the Violet Eucador, and the Pink Eucador."

In rapid succession, pictures of these plants were flashed onto the three-dimensional screen.

"The Striped Eucador" – here the striped flower, pink, and pale violet, flashed onto the screen – "is smallest of the group. There are five petals on each bloom. The stem is short and the plant grows close to the ground. Its smell may be compared, to a mixture between Earth's muskmelon and magnolia."

At this point there was a slight hissing in the Hypnobooth. The odor slithered from holes in the walls and into the nostrils of Trooper and Tod.

There were more plants, so many plants that the mind reeled. Slowly the voice went through each variety, from the simplest to the infinitely complex.

"Most startling in the development of plant life on Venus, however," the voice said, "is the . . ."

Came a scratching sound and a garbled medley of noises. Undoubtedly a defective tape, Trooper thought. The screen flashed through a series of blinding colors, then focused on the tall blue figure of a Venerian native.

" . . . closely resembling the human being," the voice began abruptly. "Notice the long limbs, tapering toward the wrists and ankles. The skull covering is much like human hair, deep blue in color, as are the eyes. The skin, if we may call it such, is blue."

The screen presented a closeup of the hands, showing long sensitive-looking blue fingers.

"The hands are probably the most important part of the entire structure. It is with these that nourishment . . ."

Again, the annoying scratching garbled the tape as the screen continued to display the picture of the hand. Scraps of meaning penetrated the uproar in disjointed phrases.

". . . after the free-moving stage has been achieved . . . pedal extremities no longer . . . Venerian soil is . . . and blossoming . . ."

The scratching stopped abruptly and the screen went blank. A man in white snapped on the lights. He removed the headphones from Tod's head and snapped his fingers. Tod blinked and stared around him. The attendant repeated the process with Trooper.

"That's all for today, boys," he said cheerfully.

"Better get a new tape," Trooper said. "That one's pretty muddled."

"Nothing really important," the attendant said. "You're getting enough to keep you going up there, never fear."

"I hope so," Tod said. He looked at Trupa who was now almost a carbon copy of himself. They were both tall and blue – their bones lengthened, their skins dyed, their hair blue.

It was remarkable how much they resembled the natives they'd seen on the screen, Tod thought. For an instant, his mind flashed back to Miami and the whole foolish mission washed over him despairingly. Venus! Of all the idiotic places to . . .

"You coming along?" Trooper asked.

Tod turned appraising eyes on Trooper. *A gutter rat*, he thought. *Straight from the slums. Give him a new skin and a few lengthened bones and he thinks he's my equal.*

"No, thanks," Tod answered. "I've got a few things to do."

Trooper nodded curtly. *Just like all the rest*, he thought.

What Price Venus?

A rich bastard with his own particular gimmick. This was going to be some picnic. Some damned picnic!

The language lessons had already begun. At night it droned into their ears via Somnophone. During the day, they spoke it to instructors, catching the inflection, the subtle undertones of the speech.

And in the meantime they were constantly exposed to the Hynobooth, with its three-dimensional screen and its tape recordings. There were pictures of the seed and it was almost as Altz had described it.

Actually it appeared to be a tiny celluloid pellet, pale blue and translucent. Beneath the outside covering a network of blue lines could be seen criss-crossing wildly. These terminated, it appeared, just below the surface of the seed, probably ready to burst forth as roots, once the seed was nourished.

There were models too. Trooper held one in his fingers, turning it over slowly. "All the way to Venus for this," he said to Tod.

Tod didn't answer.

Trooper turned and held up the seed. "All the way to——" he repeated.

"I heard you," Tod snapped angrily.

Trooper's eyes narrowed behind their blue contact lenses. "I don't like this any better than you do, friend," he said.

"Don't 'friend' me," said Tod.

"That would suit me just fine," Trooper said.

"It had better, because that's the way it's going to be."

"Let's get one thing straight," Trooper said. "I'm here because the job was assigned to me. I don't like blue skin, blue hair *or* blue eyes. And while I hadn't given much thought to it before, I don't think I like you a hell of a lot either."

"The feelings are mutual, I assure you," Tod said.

"Just so we understand each other. This isn't a fraternity

reunion. We're going after that goddamned seed. Once we get it and bring it back, that's that."

"Precisely," Tod said. "And now, if you'll excuse me."

He turned on his heel, a tall blue figure striding regally down the wide corridor.

Trooper stared after him. He had the feeling, as he'd had many times before, that he was standing on a fast-moving treadmill.

3

The long silver ship streaked through space. The stars blinked around it in mute disapproval. Commander Altz stood before the two men in space-suits. They were tall men with blue skins and the suits had been constructed especially for them. Altz wore his yellow uniform with a maroon cape slung over his shoulder. A smart officer's cap perched on his white hair. He seemed to be in a cheerful mood.

"A few minutes," he said. "Just a few minutes and you'll be on Venus — on your own."

Tod nodded. It had been a grueling business but he felt he knew as much about Venus as there was to know. Now, if everything went well, they'd get the seed, make the necessary radar contact with Earth and be picked up as soon as a rocket could be dispatched. That, of course, was still in the future. Once they left the security of the ship they would indeed be on their own.

"You understand, of course, that you're to contact us as soon as you've found the seed," said Altz.

"We understand," Trooper said.

"Then, you'll stay in the exact spot from which you sent the signal. A ship will pick you up in five days."

"We've gone over this at least a dozen times," Tod snapped. "Do we look like first-grade morons?"

"What was that, Bellew?" Altz asked, anger in his voice.

"Do we look like first grade morons, *sir?*" Tod asked, emphasizing the last word in mock respect for Altz' rank.

"That's better," Altz said, appearently satisfied. "I just wanted to make sure everything was understood. We can't afford to bungle this again."

A uniformed cadet poked his head into the cabin. "Three minutes to peak, sir," he said.

"Ah, good," Altz said. He turned to the two blue men. "We're almost at the peak of our orbit. You understand, of course, that we're not landing. Our orbit is plotted to overshoot the planet. When we reach the turning point we'll decellerate slightly. You'll leave us then."

"We've gone over this before too," Tod said.

"I'm not sure I like your attitude, Bellew," Altz warned.

"Why, Commander," Tod said in surprise, "you said it was my attitude that was partly responsible for this lovely assignment."

A warning buzzer sounded in the cabin, a red light flashed on the bulkhead. "Get your helmets on," Altz said.

Trooper and Tod slipped plasteel bubbles over their heads. Rapidly they tightened the bolts on each other's helmets, as they had practiced so many times on Earth.

Tod cut in his oxygen, hearing a slight hiss in his helmet as he adjusted the flow. He pressed the button set in the chest of his suit and tested his radio. "Can you hear me?" he asked Trooper.

Trooper's hand went to his chest and a moment later his voice sounded in Tod's helmet. "I can hear you."

A cadet opened the airlock as a green light flashed on the bulkhead. Ponderously the two men stepped into the lock. Altz saluted. He was the last being they saw before the door clanged shut at their backs.

Tod turned the big wheel on the outer hatch, held

it for a moment as he waited for the light in the bulkhead to blink.

"There it is," Trooper's voice said.

The blue light over their heads blinked rapidly, on and off, on and off. Tod threw his shoulder against the hatch as the big ship seemed to hang in space for a moment, preparing to reverse its course. He pushed outward into the blackness, fell free for a few seconds to give Trooper time to clear the wash of his jets, then turned them on full.

A yellow-red trail of dust seared backward from the shoulder jets and he streaked through the blackness, feeling terribly alone for the first time in his life, alone in a pinpointed blackness that seemed to stretch away forever.

He glanced backward, saw Trooper clear the ship and turn on his jets. Trooper pulled alongside as the big ship dipped around, shuddered with a new burst of power and vanished into the blackness.

"That's that," Tod said.

"That's that," Trooper said.

Below them, covered with pale shifting clouds, was Venus. They hung in space, two bloated grotesque figures against a glistening backdrop of stars, watching the wash of the big ship smoulder and die.

Like a startled rabbit then Tod whirled, jets flashing, and dived for the shrouded planet.

They dropped silently into the jungle, lay flat on their stomachs for several moments, waiting, waiting. When they were sure they had landed unseen Tod Bellew pressed the speaker button on his chest.

"You think we should take off our helmets?"

"They *said* the atmosphere was breathable," Trooper answered.

Tod peered through the bubble and looked at Trooper suspiciously. "Come on," Trooper said, "I'll unhitch you."

"No," Tod said sharply. "I'll help you with *your* helmet first."

Trooper shrugged and stood before Tod as he un-screwed the bolts that held the helmet to the breast-plate. Trooper reached for Tod's helmet and Tod backed away.

"We've got to get that seed," he told Trooper. "One of us has to get back with it. No sense in both of us taking off our helmets until we're sure about the atmosphere."

Trooper smiled grimly and said, "What makes you think I'm volunteering? What makes you think I trust Altz any more than you do?"

"This is ridiculous," Tod said, pressing the button on his chest. "We can't just stand here all day, waiting to take off our helmets."

"Then why don't you take *yours* off," Trooper asked.

Tod's eyes suddenly widened in fear. "Look out," he called, "behind you!"

Trooper whirled, reaching for the blaster that hung on the trouser leg of the space-suit. At the same instant, Tod lurched forward, putting the strength of his shoulders and back against Trooper's turning body. Caught off balance, Trooper toppled to the ground.

Tod leaped onto his body, straddling Trooper's chest with his knees. With a deft movement he snapped the helmet from Trooper's head and tossed it into the tall grass. He held Trooper pinned to the ground as he waited, his eyes glued to Trooper's angry face.

After a long while, Trooper smiled and said something. Tod watched his lips, unable to hear inside the plastic bubble. Trooper nodded and formed the letters O and K with his lips.

It was then that Tod let him up and unscrewed the bolts he could reach on his helmet. Trooper unloosened the rest of the bolts and Tod lifted the plastic bubble from his head.

He took a deep breath and turned to Trooper. "Looks as if Altz was telling the truth after all," he said.

Trooper's eyes narrowed. "Lucky, aren't we?"

Tod glanced sharply at Trooper, startled by the tone of his voice. "We'd better get out of these suits," he said softly.

They shrugged out of the suits, standing blue and tall in the Venerian jungle. They wore loin cloths, nothing else. Quickly, they extracted folding shovels from the pockets of the suits and began to spade the soft earth.

Trooper stopped digging once to examine the portable radar unit encased in the breastplate of the suit.

"Come on," Tod said. "Come on."

Trooper joined in the digging again, beginning to sweat freely. "I wonder if this stuff runs," he said, dead-panned.

"Very funny," Tod said drily. He began stuffing his suit into the hole he had dug. "We'd better speak Venerian from here on in," he suggested.

Trooper considered this as he began burying his suit. "You go for this cloak-and-dagger stuff, don't you?" he asked.

Tod glanced up. "Sure, I adore it. Nothing I like better than sweating in a stinking jungle with a—"

He cut himself short and finished covering his suit. "Can't you hurry?" he asked.

"I'm doing my best," Trooper replied. "What's the rush anyway? Have you got any idea where we're going to find this damn seed? It might be in any one of these plants."

"The sooner we get started the sooner we get back. That's all I'm interested in."

Trooper dumped his shovel on top of the space-suit and covered the rest with his hands. He tore up some weeds and scattered them over the fresh mound of earth.

"Okay," he said, "let's go."

4

They struck out through the jungle, speaking only Venerian now, stopping at each plant to examine the petals, to prod deep within the flower, searching for a translucent blue-veined seed.

"A botanist," Trooper said, frowning. "A goddamn botanist."

They pushed on, the sun searing down through the magnifying layers of clouds that covered the planet. Trooper was hot – he was hotter than he ever remembered being. Somehow, he was sure that if his skin weren't blue he'd be cooler. He began to curse the color of his skin, began to curse the plants that stretched in endless monotony around them, began to curse the planet itself.

A seed – a lousy seed! All the way to Venus for a seed. Like looking for a needle in a haystack. Why hadn't they told them just what plant the seed belonged to? Why all the hush-hush?

He trudged along behind Tod, stopping at a tall flowering plant, tearing open an elongated pod near the top. Six brown seeds tumbled to the ground and Trooper scrambled after them, cutting his hand on the jagged weeds in the undergrowth. He picked up the seeds and stared at them.

"Brown," he muttered. *"Brown!"*

"Any luck?" Tod asked.

"No," Trooper said sullenly. "No luck."

"Let's get moving."

They began to move again, pushing their way through the jungle, scrutinizing each plant, each shrub, each bush, each weed, with inquisitive eyes and probing fingers. Trooper was sweating more freely now, the moisture oozing from every pore in his body.

"Let's go," Tod said.

Let's go, Trooper thought. *Let's go. Let's go. Let's go.*

And all at once, quite unreasonably, all the heat, all the plants, all the treacherous undergrowth, the reaching thorns, the pulling weeds, all of these seemed to center themselves in the plodding figure of Tod Bellew. A surging hatred boiled up in Trooper's being. For a blind moment he thought of killing the blue figure that trudged along before him, of killing him, of sending the radar signal back, of sitting down to wait for the pickup ship.

It would be nice to sit somewhere in the shade – somewhere out of this heat that . . .

"Wake up, damn you." It was Tod's voice. "There's something up ahead."

"What?" Trooper said wearily.

"I think it's a village. You remember the pictures they showed us."

"Glory be," Trooper said, "a village! Goody goody gum drop."

"The next time you speak Terran . . ." Tod warned.

"Shove it," Trooper said. Then, in Venerian, "Do you see any natives?"

"No. Let me do the talking until we're on safe ground."

"Who nominated you for leader of this little party?" Trooper asked, sarcasm thick in his voice.

"I just nominated myself."

"And who seconded the nomination, may I ask?"

They were close to the village now. A cluster of huts, conical in shape, thatched, laid out in a neat circle, the center of which seemed to be a high mound of soft earth.

Quite suddenly a tall Venerian crossed the clearing in the center of the huts. He saw Tod and Trooper and waved his arm in a gesture of friendly greeting.

"I'll handle this," Tod whispered.

Trooper was about to answer, thought better of it.

The Venerian grinned and approached the two Terrans. It was amazing what a job the surgeons and magic men on Earth had done, Trooper mused. If he hadn't known better he would have sworn he was watching himself cross the clearing.

The Venerian stopped before the two men and raised his arm, folding the other across his chest.

Trooper automatically made the greeting sign they'd practiced on Earth.

"Welcome," the Venerian said. "Our village is honored twice."

"And we," Tod repeated the customary acknowledgement of welcome, "are honored to be welcome – doubly honored because we are two."

"I am called Ragoo," the Venerian said, "son of Tandor."

"Toda do they call me," Tod answered, "son of Palla, and here with my brother Troo."

"Welcome, Toda and Troo."

"We have traveled far," Tod said, "and would know the name of your village that we may honor it when we return home again."

"Crescent Eight," the Venerian replied, "and to which village do we owe the honor of your presence?"

Trooper watched Tod carefully. He knew he was probably making a few fast mental calculations, picturing Crescent Eight on the projected diagram they'd seen back on Earth.

Crescent Eight – that would be pretty close to Crescent Eleven, Nine and Ten being far distant to the South. A good safe bet would . . .

"Crescent Five," Tod said, just as Trooper completed the same mental calculation.

"Welcome," the Venerian Ragoo said again. Trooper wondered how many times he was going to repeat *welcome* before he invited them in and gave them something to eat or a place to sleep.

They started into the village and natives appeared magically, swarming over the clearing, shouting their welcomes loudly. The men were dressed exactly like Tod and Trooper, naked except for loin-cloths.

They looked amazingly human, except for their peculiar proportions. Long and thin they were, with a subtle hint of strength rippling beneath their bright blue skins.

Trooper stared in interest as he noticed some women

321

come into the clearing for the first time. The women too were naked, except for a waist cloth that reached almost to their knees. Their breasts were bare, full, blooming like the flowers of a rare tropical plant.

And where the peculiar length gave the men an elongated somewhat-stretched appearance, it added a willowy sensuous beauty to the women of the village.

Their skin too seemed to shimmer and glow in the intense glare of the filtered sunlight. Their hair, long and blue, hung like vibrant seaweed about their shoulders. Their eyes tilted slightly, giving them an Oriental slant. But Trooper saw nothing exotic in the eyes themselves. They were open and frank and honest.

About the necks of each of the women, glistening brightly in the sunlight, were strands of jewels – delicate beautifully-rounded spheres that glowed in incandescent beauty.

As the women came closer Trooper noticed that the older ones among them wore no jewelry at all. And the youngest of the group wore tiny spheres, lacking in lustre – dull rounded pebbles. It was the middle group, those who were neither girls nor matrons, those who were women in the full bloom of maturity, that wore the brightest largest spheres.

Trooper stared at these until he felt his close scrutiny was becoming too obvious. He realized they were being led to one of the thatched huts. Ragoo chattered incessantly to Tod as they walked slowly across the clearing.

"You will stay," Ragoo was saying, "for at least a little while. The Planting is not far off, you know."

Trooper watched Tod as the cloud of confusion spread over his face. "The Planting?" Tod asked.

Trooper searched in his mind for some record, some mention of the Planting. He could remember nothing about a planting.

Ragoo smiled and put an arm around each of the men. His arm felt cool to the touch, almost like the arm of a dead man.

"Then you have not sown," Ragoo said, still smiling. "It is an even greater honor that you visit our village at this time."

Trooper smiled wearily as Tod went through the *mutual honor* business once more.

"You must be weary," Ragoo said. "You will rest here and feed whenever you are ready."

"Thank you," Tod said.

"Thank you," Trooper said.

Ragoo left them alone in the cool interior of the hut.

"*Well!*" Trooper said in English.

"If I have to tell you again!" Tod warned. "Venerian! Speak Venerian, do you understand?"

"Keep your shirt on," Trooper said. "I'm as anxious to get out of here with my blue skin on as you are."

Tod glanced out at the clearing, then lowered the flap of the opening. The hut grew darker instantly. "What did you think of them?" he asked Trooper.

Trooper shrugged. "No different from anyone else. They're all the same – Earth, Venus." He shrugged again.

"They seem like a simple lot," Tod said.

"Yeah," Trooper said. He wiped a hand across his sweating brow. "You know, I can't figure out how Ragmop, or whatever his name is, stays so cool."

"Did you notice that too?"

For the length of a heartbeat the two men's eyes met. They had noticed something together, had shared an instant of mutual recognition, however small.

And then, like a fist smothering a dim candle, distrust closed tightly about them, bringing with it the old wariness.

"Sure, I noticed it," Trooper snapped. "I wouldn't have mentioned it if I hadn't."

Tod's brow wrinkled in a frown. He turned to the flap and threw it backward. "Simple dolts," he said vehemently.

"I'm getting hungry," Trooper said.

He lifted his loin-cloth. Strapped about his waist was a

323

leather belt inset with a series of pockets. He unsnapped two, removed blue tablets from one, white tablets from the other.

These he threw into his mouth, swallowing quickly. "Some meal," he said.

"They warned us against trying any Venerian food," Tod said. "They're not sure whether it's edible or not."

"I'm not sure whether these pills are edible or not, either."

"They're not supposed to be tasty," Tod said. "They're supposed to supply all of our daily calory requirements."

"I wonder what I should have for dessert," Trooper said. He reached into one of the pockets and extracted a pink pill which he popped into his mouth. "Lemon meringue pie," he said sarcastically.

"I hope we find that seed soon."

Trooper burped. "I should have tried the chocolate pudding," he said morosely.

5

The next day they started out into the jungle long before the natives were up. It was hot – just as hot as it had been the day before.

Tod thought of Miami Beach, thought of the luxurious hotel and the swimming pool. And then his mind reverted to the present situation. He rubbed a hand across his forehead, breathing deeply. There was a rank smell to the jungle, a smell of ancient crowded growth, a smell of plants growing in wild profusion.

He pushed a vine aside, ducked under it, stared around him. There were so many plants, too many plants. Altz had been crazy to send two men on this ridiculous hunt. What he needed was an army of botanists, equipped to stay on Venus for thirty years, searching for a seed as elusive as truth.

The simile pleased him somehow. *As elusive as truth.* As elusive as truth in a world of thieves and liars, he should have added. Again he thought of Earth and he compared it to Venus.

There wasn't very much difference, he realized. Venus was a jungle of plants, Earth a jungle of animals. Here in this primitive sprawling jungle the plants fought for supremacy, putting tendril against tendril, vine against vine, root against root. Arguing for the right to a stretch of soil or a ray of sunshine. The weaker plant succumbed, smothered by the stronger, and was left to rot on the fetid floor of the jungle.

On Earth it was the same. He was lucky. He was one of the stronger plants. He was capable of buying and selling a hundred stinking crawling Earth humans – the animal counterparts of the weaker Venerian plants.

He had no sympathy for the sniveling creatures of Earth, no more sympathy than he had for a strangled bush here in the vicious jungle. But he was a paradox in that he had no sympathy for the stronger plants either, the men who controlled the Earth, the men like Altz who were ready to grab more and more, smothering, strangling like the powerful denizens of this jungle.

With an honesty he had previously fancied himself incapable of, he realized that he too was one of these men, that he too would as soon squelch a trembling beggar as look at him.

A product of my society, he mused. *A product of the society I hate.*

He sighed deeply and stopped, turning to face Trooper behind him. "Let's take a break," he said. "I'm tired."

Trooper nodded and dropped to the jungle floor, stretching out languorously. Tod dropped down beside him, mopping his brow again.

After awhile, Trooper sat up and stood staring into the jungle. "There's a new one," he said.

"A new *what?*"

"Plant. Haven't seen that one before."

325

"Mmm," Tod murmured lazily.

"Might as well take a look," Trooper said. He struggled to his feet. "Might be the one we're after."

Tod closed his eyes as Trooper made his way toward the bright yellow plant ahead. The plant had a long thick stem. Branches, stout and green, jutted out from the stem and tendrils dropped from these to trail limply on the ground. An enormous yellow bloom topped the stem, exuding a peculiarly sweet smell.

Trooper stepped up to the plant, close to the stem, and started to part the closed petals of the yellow bloom.

"*Holy . . . !*"

The cry tore through the jungle like the abortive scream of a wounded animal. Tod leaped to his feet, his eyes widening in terror. He stood glued to the spot, incapable of moving. Sweat broke out on his brow, streamed down his neck, cascaded off his chest in little rivulets. He shivered, tried to summon up the muscle-power he no longer possessed.

Not more than seven feet away Trooper clawed at his throat, trying to loosen the tendril that was wrapped tightly about it. The plant had suddenly come to life, limp tendrils snapping like bull-whips, lashing about his body, curling tightly about his arms and legs, pulling him closer to the yellow bloom.

"*Tod!*" Trooper screamed. "For *God's* sake . . . !"

He kicked out at the stem and a tendril dropped from his arm. He coughed, pried at the steely vine that was tightening about his throat. Another tendril lashed out, wrapped itself around his wrist, pulled it away from Trooper's throat.

"*Tod!*"

Silence – a silence as heavy as the clouds that smothered the planet, as intense as the sun that beat down firecely through the treetops. Silence – except for the thrashing of plant and a human.

Tod stood motionless, watching the struggle like a spectator in a box seat. Trooper loosened the tendril from his throat, tried to step back. Another tendril slapped out across his face and he blinked his eyes in pain. The tendril curled about his throat again, slowly, like a boa-constrictor tightening its death grip. Trooper thrashed about wildly as the plant seemed to exert itself in a supreme effort to lift him off his feet.

He kicked again as he was raised from the ground. And at the same instant, the yellow blossom parted, petals opening wide to reveal a fuzzy opening.

Tod sprang forward and wrapped his arms about Trooper's legs. A probing tendril reached out for him and he slapped it aside. He held onto Trooper, fighting the tremendous lifting power of the plant. A tendril loosened from Trooper's waist and curled around Tod's arm. Tod sank his teeth into it and a bitter taste flooded over his tongue. He spit and bit again as the tendril loosened.

Trooper hung limply in the grip of the plant while Tod tore at it, ripping, scratching, biting. He kicked at the stem, dodged the swinging vines, pulled at the petals of the yellow bloom. Trooper dropped to the ground, one tendril wrapped tightly about his ankle.

Tod descended on this with a fanatic fury, stamping it with his feet, kicking. He fell to the ground and pounded it with his fists, sinking his teeth into it at last. The tendril withdrew slowly, slithering across the jungle floor.

Tod seized Trooper's wrists and pulled him away from the plant – far away.

When at last he stopped, he looked back at a peaceful-looking yellow flower blooming in the distance. He sat down, panting his lungs out. Trooper lay at his feet, his eyes closed.

When Tod had caught his breath he reached over and slapped Trooper across the face. Trooper's eyes blinked. Tod slapped him again.

This time the eyes fluttered open. Trooper stared blankly at Tod Bellew for several minutes, then his face cracked into a weak smile. "Thanks," he said.

Every instinct in Tod's body shouted for him to snap

at Trooper. Every facet of his training, every ounce of experience, every previous human relationship, urged him to say, "I'd do the same for any dog."

But he didn't say it. He was sweating with the struggle and his hands trembled a little but he didn't say it. Instead he looked off to the side, avoiding Trooper's eyes and murmured, "You had a close call, Trupa."

Trooper nodded, still smiling weakly. "Goddamn seed," he said. This time Tod smiled with him in spite of himself.

When they told Ragoo about the encounter with the plant he nodded sagely and said, "There are good and bad in everything."

They didn't understand what he meant at the time but they learned a little more fully later.

Every since they'd come to the village they had been living on the calory pills from their belts. They hadn't had a real chance to observe the eating habits of the Venerians and it hadn't really interested them anyway. But after the experience with the plant, they spent more and more time in the village and were puzzled to note that the Venerians seemed to have no regular eating habits. In fact they never saw one of them eating.

"It's impossible," Tod said. "Everyone has to eat."

"Have *you* ever seen them eat?"

"No, but . . ." Tod stopped, shrugging his shoulders. "We'll just have to watch more closely."

They began to watch more closely.

The Venerians were a simple race. They rose early, escaping the rays of the sun in the conical huts for long rest periods. They seemed to do little work during the day. Their time was spent in playing games, singing, dancing. The only work they really did was of a seemingly religious nature. Or so Trooper and Tod thought.

In the center of the village was the large mound of earth. The huts were clustered about it, the mound was easily accessible to all of them. Parties of men would go off into the jungle and return with fresh soil daily. This they would pile onto the mound.

Tod and Trooper were confused until they hit on their hosts' religious theory. The theory seemed to be substantiated by the peculiar rites the Venerians performed.

At irregular intervals one or another of them would go to the mound and thrust his hands deep into the soft soil. He would leave them there for several minutes and then withdraw them.

"It's a ritual," Tod said. "It can't be anything else."

But they continued watching.

They were surprised that they saw no Venerians they could classify as children. There were the old, the middle-aged, the mature and the adolescent. But no children.

"I can't understand a society without children," Tod said, still confused.

"Maybe they eat their young," Trooper suggested.

Tod frowned. "I doubt it. I've never seen an easier-going people."

"They *do* kind of grow on you," Trooper admitted. "They're just what you said they were in the beginning – a simple people."

It was about then that a new activity began in the village. The mound in the center was replenished daily but in addition to that a new area of soil was being laid down. The area was a large rectangle, also within the ring of huts. But in contrast to the mount it was flat.

Trooper stopped Ragoo and asked him what it was all about.

Ragoo smiled. "You are joking."

"No – no, really," Trooper said.

Ragoo chuckled out loud this time. "Be patient, my friend. We are preparing for the Planting."

"Oh," Trooper said.

"You will sow," Ragoo promised.

When the rectangle had reached a size approximately sixty by a hundred feet the Venerians stopped carrying soil from the jungle.

After this a new sort of game began to be played. The young girls of the village, their translucent jewelry gleaming at their throats, began to circulate among the young men. They danced for them and sang for them, displayed their breasts and their hair, followed them about the village.

Trooper was surprised to find a doe-eyed Venerian parked outside his hut after his sleep one morning. He blinked at her, his eyes still not accustomed to the glare of the sun.

"Hello," she said. "You are the one they call Troo."

"I am he," Trooper said, "son of Palla, here with my brother Toda."

The girl smiled, her teeth glistening like the baubles around her throat. Trooper noticed that they were set in a single line, curving gracefully about her neck, gleaming brilliantly in the sunlight.

"Are you not sorry to be away from your village at the time of the Planting?" she asked.

Trooper hesitated.

"Or do you find our village a worthy one in which to sow?"

Trooper nodded. "Indeed," he faltered, "it is a worthy one."

The girl smiled again and looked shyly at the ground. "I am happy," she said. "I am called Donya and this is my first Season of the Planting."

"It is my first too," Trooper said.

The girl looked up with wonder in her eyes. "Really?" she asked. "Is it really?"

"Why, yes."

"And have you already made arrangements?"

"No. No, I – er – haven't."

The girl lowered her eyes again. "You will consider me bold."

"Why, no, not at all. I think you're very sweet."

She smiled up at him. "I will come to you," she said, then she fled in my embarrassment.

When Trooper told Tod what had happened Tod nodded knowingly. "Me, too," he said. "Perhaps there's a sort of festival at the Planting. Perhaps the girls are asking us to escort them or something."

"Sure," Trooper said, snapping his fingers. "I should have realized."

"After all," Tod said, "we are eligible Venerian males, you know."

"Oh, you kid," Trooper said.

6

The time of the Planting came the following week. Trooper and Tod stood in the opening of their hut as the men watched the young women dance before them in the circle formed by the huts.

Donya came to Trooper, a secret smile on her face. She knelt before him and lowered her head.

"I come, as I promised."

Trooper nodded.

She rose then and took Trooper's hand in hers. Her hand was cool to the touch. She led him into the darkness of the hut and lowered the flap. She turned then and huddled into his arms. Trooper caressed her cautiously, unfamiliarly.

"You hesitate," she said shyly. "We will learn together."

The afternoon was one of whispered words and fond caresses. Slowly, tenderly, Donya guided Trooper's hands to the glowing spheres at her throat. He didn't know what to do. She closed his fingers on the first sphere, then gently pulled his hand away. The sphere clung to her skin for an instant and then shook loose. Donya gripped him tightly.

They waited and again she guided his fingers to the spheres. One by one they fell loose into his hands.

And then, when all the spheres had been plucked, Donya whispered, "I will wait while you sow."

He lifted the flap and stepped out into the sunshine. Tod met him there and they stared in bewilderment at each other.

They followed the other young men to the new rectangular plot of earth. They watched silently.

The young men gripped the translucent spheres in the palms of their hands, closed their eyes and thrust their fists deeply into the soft soil. When they withdrew their hands the spheres were gone.

Tod turned a glistening, translucent sphere in his fingers. "Trooper," he whispered, "I think we have finally found the seed!"

"What?" His mouth fell open.

"The seed, Trooper. This is *it!*"

Trooper stared at the glistening ball for a long time. "No," he said. "You're wrong. The other seed had blue veins beneath the surface."

Tod nodded his head. "The other seeds were fertilized, Trooper."

"Fertilized? What are you saying, Tod? You're talking as if these people were . . ." The word caught in his throat as they approached the rectangular plot. *"Plants."*

They went through the motions, thrusting their hands into the soil, releasing the seeds. Over and over again they repeated the process until all the seeds were in the ground.

Trooper went back to the hut then and Donya was waiting. "And have you sown?" she asked. She touched him with cold fingers.

"Yes," he said, "I have sown."

"Thank you," she murmured, "thank you, thank you!"

Tod and Trooper watched the development of the seeds. After a week, they plucked one from the earth and studied it. A blue network of lines had begun to form beneath the surface of the sphere.

"That bastard," Trooper said. "He wants us to bring back people. *Seeds!* Seeds that grow people!"

"We're not sure," Tod cautioned. "We'll wait and see."

They waited. The weeks dragged into months and the seeds began to sprout. A tall stem at first, then four secondary branches. A large bulb formed slowly at the top of the stem and by the fourth month this bulb had assumed the half-shaped contours of a face. The branches had grown longer, bright blue in color.

Trooper thought back to the sessions in the Hypno-booth, to the garbled sentences the tape had tried to reveal through the scratches.

. . . after the free-moving stage has been achieved . . .

This was after the eighth month. The plants seemed to shake themselves free of the soil, emerged as perfect figures.

. . . pedal extremities no longer . . .

No longer *what*, Trooper wondered. Why, no longer provide nourishment to the plant, he realized in amazement. The hands became a substitute. And he knew then that the mound in the village was the Venerian method of feeding.

. . . Venerian soil is . . .

Venerian soil was the staff of Venerian life – because all Venerian life was plant life.

. . . and blossoming . . .

And blossoming around the throat of the female of the species, he filled in, *is the precious seed that guarantees preservation of the species.*

And Altz would have them bring these seeds back. So that he could plant them, and use them as robots in his expansion plans.

People – men to man the weapons and the machines . . .

And Altz would have them bring back the seed of a slave race, a race to fight the wars. What was it he had said? *. . . a certain mental attitude is necessary for the job.*

And he and Tod had that mental attitude. Their records showed it.

333

Bellew and Trupa pondered this together for long hours, the rich boy and the poor boy – the two Altz had thought specially fitted for the job of securing a slave race.

It was difficult at first to break down the walls each had built through the years – difficult to override the pull of inbred instinct – difficult to pour out their emotions to each other, to break the wall of hate and loneliness.

But they turned the problem over, comparing the simple, happy existence these people now led to the one awaiting them on Earth.

They made the only decision possible.

They said their goodbyes the next morning. The young girls, the new crop that was now free-moving, were already beginning to develop tiny translucent spheres around their necks.

The space-suits were where they'd left them. Bellew and Turba dug them up, two men who knew exactly what they were ready to do. The radar units were intact and they sent the signal back to Earth.

The ship came promptly five days later, hovering over the planet like a silver needle in the sky. They adjusted their bubbles, took blasters in hand and turned on the power in their shoulder jets.

The men on the ship were jubilant. "The Commander will blow his top," they shouted. "You'll get medals, both of you."

The two were strangely silent throughout the entire trip. Their skins were beginning to fade back to normal colors. They talked little, answered questions tersely.

When the ship landed on Earth five days later they had subdued the small crew. They dropped them off on the outskirts of New York, bound and gagged, then headed for the Office of the Military.

Commander Altz greeted Bellew and Turba with a broad grin. They wore the clothes the crew had provided for them and their holstered blasters hung at their sides.

334

"Well," Altz cried. "You made it!"

"We made it," Tod repeated.

"And the seeds – did you get the seeds?"

Trooper's blaster flicked into his hand.

"Wha –?" Altz began.

"Here's the only seed you'll ever know," Trooper said. His finger tightened on the trigger and a searing yellow beam knifed across the room. Tod's blaster echoed Trooper's as Altz dropped to the floor.

They ran to the ship, slammed the hatches, pointed the nose toward the sky.

It streaked out into space, a slim promise, trailing the sparks of a dead civilization. The stars in infinite numbers blinked curiously.

"There must be other worlds," Tod said.

"Better worlds," Trooper said.

They aimed the nose of the ship at one of the curious stars and smiled in the darkness of the cabin.

THE QUATERMASS EXPERIMENT

> (BBC TV 1953–1979)
> Starring: Reginald Tate, Isabel Dean &
> Duncan Lamont
> Directed by Rudolph Cartier
> Story 'Enderby and the Sleeping Beauty' by
> Nigel Kneale

Saturday nights on British television were never to be the same after 8.15 p.m. on 18 July, 1953 when the first 30-minute episode of *The Quatermass Experiment* entitled 'Contact Has Been Established' was transmitted live after an afternoon of sport, children's TV and news. Those who might have been in any doubt about what they were about to see were warned by an unseen announcer, "This programme may be unsuitable for children or persons of a nervous disposition." At a stroke Science Fiction was introduced to the nation's viewers and a legend was born that has endured to this day. The bold decision to feature an SF story on TV was taken by the BBC's new Head of Drama, Michael Barry, who gave the go-ahead to staff writer Nigel Kneale to dramatize his idea about a space mission which inadvertently brings back an alien virus to Earth. What made the series so remarkable was that it anticipated the Apollo moonshot by 16 years as well as many of the fears about manned space-flight which were later to be proved uncannily accurate. To those like myself who can remember the series with its rudimentary special effects – still no mean achievement by Richard R. Greenhough and Stewart Marshall on a total budget of just £3,500

– and the show's frequent tendency to overrun its alloted time span, it was nevertheless a landmark production that Rudolph Cartier's direction made believable and somehow far beyond the confines of the studios in which it was acted. Unknown to us at the time, the spectacular finale in which the apparently 100-foot high vegetable-like 'monster' wrecked havoc in Westminster Abbey was actually the author Nigel Kneale using his gloved hands covered with vegetation inside a blown-up photograph of the famous cathedral!

Nigel Kneale (1922-) had trained to be a lawyer before becoming a playwright and even undertook a little acting prior to joining the BBC. The success of Quatermass lead to three sequels: *Quatermass II* (1955), *Quatermass and the Pit* (1958) and *Quatermass* (1979) which was comissioned by the BBC but when the production was cancelled on cost grounds, Thames TV took up the option and transmitted it in four episodes with Sir John Mills as Professor Bernard Quatermass – a name, incidentally, that Kneale had plucked from the London telephone directory! Since then he has continued to enhance his reputation with a number of TV dramas, contributions to several series and the creation of two more of his own: *Beasts* (1976), a horror series about human attitudes towards animals, and the much underrated *Kinvig* (1987). This series had grown out of Nigel's fascination then with stories of contacts with aliens. Profoundly cynical at the claims of numbers of people to have seen flying saucers and by others to have actually flown in them, he devised the story of an everyday little repair man, Kinvig (Tony Haygarth) who unexpectedly encounters a beutiful alien from Mercury (Pruncella Gee) who takes him on board her spaceship. Overnight the statuesque Miss Gee in her revealing costumes – mostly variations on swimsuits and bikinis – became unmissable to a lot of the adult male population, while

Nigel Kneale's brillaintly comic scripts put meetings with aliens into a whole new context. *Kinvig* remains a series that deserves a reshowing – and here as a reminder is an earlier story by Kneale written in 1949 which explores the same theme of an ordinary man suddenly coming face to face with an otherworld beauty . . .

A double-size chin. With a wide, pleasant mouth to say the thoughts from the long, tipped-back cranium above. These thoughts were just so many, docile and wholesome, like a well-ordered flock. Most concerned the laws and functions of machines, for Fred Enderby had been a mechanic since he began to screw strips of painted tin together in his mother's back-yard in Warrington.

L.A.C. Enderby, Frederick, is the only man, I believe, to know the factual core of a legend that every child can tell when it has reached half a dozen years. How a princess pricked her finger on a magic needle and slept for a hundred years, with the whole palace, courtiers, scullions, dogs, in a trance where they fell. Round the palace grew a hedge of thorns so that no one could get in, or, once in, out. Until at the end of the appointed time, a handsome prince broke through and kissed the princess back to life, while every creature in the court stirred and moved again. That is the legend. Here are the facts:

In 1942, Enderby was in North Africa on maintenance duty with an R.A.F. survey truck. They were far to the south of the battle area when the great retreat to El Alamein reached its height. Helpless in the radio silence, knowing only from the rumbling, and the glow by night, that the enemy was closing on Egypt.

Several times the party spotted planes, slow, sightless specks. To avoid the chance of capture they turned to the south-east, deeper into the desert. Flat barrenness gave place gradually to the wallowing Sahara.

They were deep in that wilderness when the kamsin storm came upon them.

The wind was of unnatural violence, Enderby said. Sand shifted in whole dunes. The party were totally unprepared. To go on was impossible. To leave the truck seemed suicidal. The sides of the thing trembled and drummed. Cans of petrol and a spare wheel tumbled away into the whirling dust.

The truck itself became unstable. Twice they felt the three offside wheels lift and settle again. Then, even while they shifted gear to balance it, the vehicle went over.

The officer in charge had his head crushed by falling equipment. Another man was trapped. A third smelt petrol, forced his way out, and was choked to death a few yards from the truck he could no longer see.

Enderby was in the cab, unconscious.

He woke at last from his own coughing. There was sand in his mouth. He lay upside down across the body of the driver.

Enderby levered himself up and examined his mate. The man was dead, his face buried in a soft, suffocating layer that covered the inside of the splintered window.

Enderby forced up the other door. Sand poured from it. The simoon had become a gritty breeze across the reshaped land. He slid out, coughing.

The truck was half-buried. The rear door, once opened, had been held wide by the blast that poured inside. Nothing lived in there now. The man from Warrington rested a while, still half-stunned, among the smothered shapes.

When Enderby set off alone the sun was still fierce. He had water in a full bottle: some fresh, some from the truck's tank: and sufficient emergency rations to reach safety, if he could trust the sun and himself. He felt weakly bitter that the radio had smashed itself.

At the top of each rise he stopped and turned about, shading his eyes: blinked and went on. He walked slowly, to conserve his strength. The glare beat up against his body.

It was perhaps an hour after starting, Enderby says, that he first saw the thing.

As he came to the sliding, coarse top of a shallow dune, its brighter colour struck his eye. A few hundred yards away. There was something man-made about that pale stone that he could just barely see.

Enderby shouted once and began to run, slithering among the brown ripples.

It was a building. Sand was heaped about it on every side. Only a part jutted from the desert, like a half-buried box. The roof and corners were formless, the pale walls deeply corroded.

Enderby's heart sank. He walked haltingly along the bare side of the place, turned a corner into the black, cool shadow. Just where the desert rose up under his feet and hid the building, he found a door.

It was recessed between two of the flat, shallow buttresses that ran up the walls at intervals. Surprisingly, the lock was on the outside of the thin stone. (As Enderby said later, "An ordinary lock mechanism with no cover. It was all made of stone bars and big – it must 'ave spread over 'alf the door.")

He was able to open it. His dread of the desert forced and fought the lock until it submitted. The door ground and scraped until there was a gap wide enough for a man to enter. On the other side was complete blackness. "'Allo, in there!" Enderby shouted. "Ey!"

The answer was a long, clapping echo.

He found matches, stepped into the cool darkness and struck one. He was in a small, bricked antechamber. As the second match flared up he saw a heap of faggots. ("Sort of compressed fibre, they were made of," Enderby said. "They lit easily. Queer. Made you feel you were kind of expected.")

With the slow-burning, smoky torch held high, and two cold spares stuffed inside his shirt, he entered a passage. The air was dry and dead and sweet.

Then he dived to the wall, crouching, quivering.

Nothing stirred.

"Who's that?" said Enderby. "If it's anybody, come 'ere!" Then, remembering, he threw the torch.

("I saw a statue," he said afterwards. "I felt – well, a sort of daft relief. Like a false alarm in a U certificate thriller.")

The figure stood man-high against the wall. Stone drapes exposed one polished shoulder and its arms were crossed. Round the head was a wide beaded band of blue stones. And the face—

("That's what'd given me the start," said Enderby. "The eyes, long, bulging black ovals – no pupils – they were the worst. And the mouth and that – as if 'e'd sucked every dirty thing in the world into 'is mind, and was damn 'appy about it.")

When he picked up the torch he began to see others. They stood in two facing rows, lining the walls of the high tunnel.

He walked in the middle. The black eyes flickered in the light. His feet were like a cat's in the deep, black dust.

The figures were of both men and women. Some were painted, in dull colours: blue and green stones sparkled in their dress: more than once Enderby saw gold in the carved folds of a woman's hair. And every face repelled him.

They were amazingly expressive, he said. Each seemed to have a double meaning. A twisting of the brows and a wrinkling round the empty eyes, and madness showed through the face's laugh. Were they heavy and stupid, there was vicious cunning also. In eagerness was slavering depravity: in innocence treachery. Gentleness meant cruelty. ("It was like people in a bad dream. They wanted to make y' see through them. Indecent.") He was puzzled by small holes drilled in the centre of each forehead and throat, and in the robes below.

On the walls between them, depressed in the brick, were tablets of writing. Symbols were nicked out like tiny tooth-prints, row upon row. ("Like something a tike's chewed.")

The tunnel curved gradually. Enderby reckoned himself fifty yards along when he could no longer see the entrance. He began to whistle without a tune because hope had dropped to vague curiosity. The walls echoed against him. He walked in silence.

Then he saw that the figures ended just ahead. He passed the last leering face into an open darkness that must have been far under the desert. The air was thick.

Enderby crept like a glow-worm in his circle of light. His eyes went left and right.

He watched the guiding walls so intently that his knee struck what he did not see. It was a high-mounted slab. The top was carved to such a likeness of soft cushioning. ("Like petrified silk. It'd 'ave made y' sleepy to look at it. Like the mattress adverts.")

Enderby strongly disclaims any knowledge of art. Sculpture bores him and his only visit to a gallery was to the engineering section.

But what he saw on the stone couch, he says, was not sculpture.

He forgot the darkness, the unnatural figures, the choking air. He forgot the truck disaster and that he was lost in the desert.

("She wasn't just wonderful in the ordinary way. I can't tell you 'ow. Look 'ere, if y' take the most smashing film stars – Betty 'Utton, Garson – as many as y' like – and all they've got between 'em, and multiply it by ten, and then . . . oh, I dunno! She was different to them anyway – Eastern, of course – but so different in other ways. What I said, I just can't begin to describe her . . .")

But she was made of stone.

Enderby stood worshipping until the torch hand sank and the figure was shadowed.

He went to the magnificent head. The stone, he says, was tinted to life, but no paint showed itself.

Light from one raised hand smoked down across the

Lancashire man's wide eyes and long chin and tunic: and over the pale-sallow nestling stone creature with the sleeping eyes. At last Enderby leaned forward.

Very gently he kissed the sculpture on the mouth.

("She was – I've told you. Oh, I suppose it was, well – perverted. A statue, I mean. Her lips were cold.")

Then fear replaced all he felt.

For the figure moved.

Enderby started back. The delicate face had turned away. Now it came back again, very slowly. Coy. Away, back. Away, back. Rhythmically, swivelling on the carved throat, the beautiful lady shook her head.

"'Inge," said Enderby's whisper, because he was very much afraid. "'Inge, that."

The movement grew stronger, pendulum-regular. And now the eyes opened, black, horribly void. His throat seemed to wither.

Points of light moved. In the tunnel. From side to side they went, slowly. Jet eyes in metronome faces. ("Like the Chinese ornaments that keep rocking their 'eads when y've started them. Only slowly. Terribly slowly. And these shook them.")

Enderby sweated. He pulled the other faggots from his shirt. A moment later the whole chamber flared into light.

From it led not one passage, he saw, but five. And in each were figures that leered in perfect time. Somewhere there was a heavy murmuring rumble.

Enderby collected himself. He touched the icy stone body of the beauty. From a pocket of his shirt he fumbled a stump of blue copying pencil.

Across the perfect waist he printed, thick and almost steadily: 'F. ENDERBY, WARRINGTON, R.A.F. 1942.'

He stuffed the defiling pencil away. "And now," he said, much too loudly, "I will go and get started again."

It was when he turned towards the tunnels that he saw the spikes.

They were coming out very slowly. About the pace of

a common slug in a Warrington allotment, and with no more noise.

One from the forehead, one from the throat and one from the folded hands; others from the studded robes. From each figure, and above to the ceiling, the points shone and grew, sprouting across the passages. Closing them.

"Christ!" Enderby said.

He sprang into the centre tunnel, opposite the slab, ran with the waving treble torch. It cast stubby points in a forest of pikes upon the ceiling. Nightmarishly, the dust muffled his boots.

Twice he kicked up yellow-white human fragments. He tripped on a carpeted cage of ribs and slashed his hand on a lengthening spike.

He saw no daylight.

Instead, a wall of arrow-lettered brick faced him at the end. He tore and kicked, trying to open it, before he realised he could be in the wrong passage.

Then he was flying back between the sprouting pikes. They covered half the space with a mass of jagged bars. Even the spaces between them would be death cages. Back across the bones.

The chamber itself, when he reached it, sprouted iron from each wall. A deep throb shook everything. The whole building was thrusting at him.

Enderby panted by the slab without a glance. Down the left-hand tunnel.

At each nod from the jet-eyed lines, the points sprang a little farther across.

If he had not seen the light of the entrance, Enderby swears he would have been insane before the points took him.

As it was, he dragged himself through the last twenty feet when they were little more than a foot apart. Another second and the spike which ripped open his water-bottle would have held him by the rib bones.

But he was outside. He stood in the shadowed sand with

blood and water trickling together down his body ("In the nick of time. Like a film 'ero.") One of the last things he remembers is heaving the door shut and stumbling away from the ponderous booming that hung in the still heat.

Four days later Enderby was spotted by a reconnaissance car. He was walking in small circles.

When they brought him in, three of the deep lacerations in his side and arms were infected. He was totally collapsed. During his travels he had written two half-legible letters in his pay-book. One to his fiancée, a feverishly confused apology for something unspecified. The second was addressed to the Warrington Town Council, complaining of floods. He had almost died of thirst.

As he recovered, Enderby was eager at first to tell his story. Coupled with his letters, it made them prescribe further sleep.

"Do y' think it could 'ave been only that?" he asked me later. "Sometimes it makes y' wonder." Then he indicated the parallel scars. "Truck accident I don't think!"

He told me the story while he carved a piece of perspex into a Spitfire badge to send his fiancée. "Y' know," said Enderby, as I had not laughed, "if I 'ad a lot more leave and that, I wouldn't mind 'aving a look back there some time. Bet it's covered up again, though.

"Y' see, I 'ardly touched 'er face more than a feather, like. And it started all that. Stone weights and pendulums, I suppose.

"Now, listen! Where did the acceleration come from? Tell me that!" He put down the transparent Spitfire and prodded me and paused to impress.

"There's a machine in that place, boy! Damn near perpetual motion, that's what. They'd be worth something, I tell y', them plans—"

First and last a mechanic, Enderby.

But also a prince. Who left his claim in writing.

THE TWILIGHT ZONE

(CBS TV, 1959–64)
Starring: Claude Atkins, Jack Weston &
Mary Gregory
Directed by Ron Winston
Story 'The Monsters Are Due on Maple Street'
by Rod Serling

Like *The Quatermass Experiment, The Twilight Zone* now enjoys a celebrity that has transcended the passage of time and changes in TV fashions. Such was the programme's sheer originality and bredth of imagination that it has been frequently rerun since the Sixties as well as inspiring a sequel in the Eighties and a big-budget film, *Twilight Zone – The Movie*, made by Steven Speilberg, a fan who used all the special effects wizardry of Hollywood to pay his own tribute to the landmark programme. The series had originally been the brainchild of Rod Serling (1924–1975), a highly respected television scritpwriter whose plays *Patterns* (1955), *Requiem for a Heavyweight* (1956) and *The Comedian* (1957) all won Emmy awards. He turned his back on television drama after growing increasingly frustrated at the way his more outspoken scripts were censored by network executives anxious not to offend sponsors. The format of *The Twilight Zone* enabled him to mix fantasy and science fiction and give free reign to his boundless imagination. The result was a programme that was memorable from the opening lines of each half hour episode which Serling himself spoke in a measured and matter-of-fact voice: "There is a fifth dimension beyond that which is known to

346

man. It is a dimension as vast as space and as timeless as infinity. It is the middle ground between science and superstition; between the pit of man's fears and the summit of his knowledge. It is an area we call . . . *The Twilight Zone*."

During its critically acclaimed run on American TV, a total of 156 episodes of the *Zone* were screened, many written by Serling and the rest by two popular SF writers, Charles Beaumont and Richard Matheson. The series also featured a number of actors who would later become famous including Robert Redford, Charles Bronson, Lee Marvin and Burt Reynolds; as well as a duo destined to be the mainstays of another legendary TV series, *Star Trek*: William Shatner and Leonard Nimoy. Apart from occasionally poking fun at the mentality of the TV executives who had so enraged him – in stories like 'The Bard' in which Jack Weston played a hack writer who summoned up William Shakespeare to help him finish a script – Serling also tackled a number of controversial themes including Fascism (in 'He Lives') and mass hysteria in 'The Monsters Are Due on Maple Street', the episode included here. It is a salutory tale of how hysteria can turn neighbour against neighbour when confronted with inexplicable events that are actually the work of aliens. Serling introduced a typical wry joke for those able to spot the fact by filming the scenes of hysteria on a set normally used by M.G.M. for their comic Andy Hardy series. He also clothed the two visitors from space in outfits that had been used in the movie *Forbidden Planet*, and cleverly utilized a clip from the same picture for his own UFO. What he did was to take some footage of the alien craft flying through space and run it upside down and going backwards! Jack West from 'The Bard' returned to the series as one of the people accused of being an alien. Curiously, just before the episode was transmitted Serling once more found himself at the centre of controversy

when several newspapers accused him of writing a story *about* prejudice – the complete opposite of his intention!

It was Saturday afternoon on Maple Street and the late sun retained some of the warmth of a persistent Indian summer. People along the street marveled at winter's delay and took advantage of it. Lawns were being mowed, cars polished, kids played hopscotch on the sidewalks. Old Mr. Van Horn, the patriarch of the street, who lived alone, had moved his power saw out on his lawn and was fashioning new pickets for his fence. A Good Humor man bicycled in around the corner and was inundated by children and by shouts of "Wait a minute!" from small boys hurrying to con nickels from their parents. It was 4:40 P.M. A football game blared from a portable radio on a front porch, blending with the other sounds of a Saturday afternoon in October. Maple Street. 4:40 P.M. Maple Street in its last calm and reflective moments – before the monsters came.

Steve Brand, fortyish, a big man in an old ex-Marine set of dungarees, was washing his car when the lights flashed across the sky. Everyone on the street looked up at the sound of the whoosh and the brilliant flash that dwarfed the sun.

"What was that?" Steve called across at his neighbor, Don Martin, who was fixing a bent spoke on his son's bicycle.

Martin, like everyone else, was cupping his hands over his eyes, to stare up at the sky. He called back to Steve, "Looked like a meteor, didn't it? I didn't hear any crash though, did you?"

Steve shook his head. "Nope. Nothing except that roar."

Steve's wife came out on the front porch. "Steve?" she called. "What was that?"

Steve shut off the water hose. "Guess it was a meteor, honey. Came awful close, didn't it?"

"Much too close for my money," his wife answered. "Much too close."

She went back into the house, and became suddenly conscious of something. All along Maple Street people paused and looked at one another as a gradual awareness took hold. All the sounds had stopped. All of them. There was a silence now. No portable radio. No lawn mowers. No clickety-click of sprinklers that went round and round on front lawns. There was a silence.

Mrs Sharp, fifty-five years of age, was talking on the telephone, giving a cake recipe to her cousin at the other end of town. Her cousin was asking Mrs Sharp to repeat the number of eggs when her voice clicked off in the middle of the sentence. Mrs Sharp, who was not the most patient of women, banged furiously on the telephone hook, screaming for an operator.

Pete Van Horn was right in the middle of sawing a 1 × 4 piece of pine when the power saw went off. He checked the plug, the outlet on the side of the house and then the fuse box in his basement. There was just no power coming in.

Steve Brand's wife, Agnes, came back out on the porch to announce that the oven had stopped working. There was no current or something. Would Steve look at it? Steve couldn't look at it at that moment because he was preoccupied with a hose that suddenly refused to give any more water.

Across the street Charlie Farnsworth, fat and dumpy, in a loud Hawaiian sport shirt that featured hula girls with pineapple baskets on their heads, barged angrily out toward the road, damning any radio outfit that manufactured a portable with the discourtesy to shut off in the middle of a third-quarter forward pass.

Voices built on top of voices until suddenly there was no more silence. There was a conglomeration of questions and protests; of plaintive references to half-cooked dinners, half-watered lawns, half-washed cars, half-finished phone conversations. Did it have anything to do with the meteor? That was the main question – the one most asked. Pete Van Horn disgustedly threw aside the electric cord of his power mower and announced to the group of people who were collected around Steve Brand's station wagon that he was going on over to Bennett Avenue to check and see if the power had gone off there, too. He disappeared into his back yard and was last seen heading into the back yard of the house behind his.

Steve Brand, his face wrinkled with perplexity, leaned against his car door and looked around at the neighbors who had collected. "It just doesn't make sense," he said. "Why should the power go off all of a sudden *and* the phone line?"

Don Martin wiped bicycle grease off his fingers. "Maybe some kind of an electrical storm or something."

Dumpy Charlie's voice was always unpleasantly high. "That just don't seem likely," he squealed. "Sky's just as blue as anything. Not a cloud. No lightning. No thunder. No nothin'. How could it be a storm?"

Mrs Sharp's face was lined with years, but more deeply by the frustrations of early widowhood. "Well, it's a terrible thing when a phone company can't keep its line open," she complained. "Just a terrible thing."

"What about my portable radio," Charlie demanded. "Ohio State's got the ball on Southern Methodist's eighteen-yard line. They throw a pass and the damn thing goes off just then."

There was a murmur in the group as people looked at one another and heads were shaken.

Charlie picked his teeth with a dirty thumbnail. "Steve," he said in his high, little voice, "why don't you go downtown and check with the police?"

"They'll probably think we're crazy or something," Don Martin said. "A little power failure and right away we get all flustered and everything."

"It isn't just the power failure," Steve answered. "If if was, we'd still be able to get a broadcast on the portable."

There was a murmur of reaction to this and heads nodded.

Steve opened the door to his station wagon. "I'll run downtown. We'll get this all straightened out."

He inched his big frame onto the front seat behind the wheel, turned on the ignition and pushed the starter button. There was no sound. The engine didn't even turn over. He tried it a couple of times more, and still there was no response. The others stared silently at him. He scratched his jaw.

"Doesn't that beat all? It was working fine before."

"Out of gas?" Don offered.

Steve shook his head. "I just had it filled up."

"What's it mean?" Mrs Sharp asked.

Charlie Farnsworth's piggish little eyes flapped open and shut. "It's just as if – just as if everything had stopped. You better *walk* downtown, Steve."

"I'll go with you," Don said.

Steve got out of the car, shut the door and turned to Don. "Couldn't be a meteor," he said. "A meteor couldn't do *this*." He looked off in thought for a moment, then nodded. "Come on, let's go."

They started to walk away from the group, when they heard the boy's voice. Tommy Bishop, aged twelve, had stepped out in front of the others and was calling out to them.

"Mr Brand! Mr Martin. You better not leave!"

Steve took a step back toward him.

"Why not?" he asked.

"They don't want you to," Tommy said.

Steve and Don exchanged a look.

"*Who* doesn't want us to?" Steve asked him.

Tommy looked up toward the sky. "Them," he said.

"Them?" Steve asked.

"Who are 'them'?" Charlie squealed.

"Whoever was in that thing that came by overhead," Tommy said intently.

Steve walked slowly back toward the boy and stopped close to him. "What, Tommy?" he asked.

"Whoever was in that thing that came over," Tommy repeated. "I don't think they want us to leave here."

Steve knelt down in front of the boy "What do you mean, Tommy? What are you talking about?"

"They don't want us to leave, that's why they shut everything off."

"What makes you say that?" Irritation crept into Steve's voice. "Whatever gave you *that* idea?"

Mrs Sharp pushed her way through to the front of the crowd. "That's the craziest thing I ever heard," she announced in a public-address-system voice. "Just about the craziest thing I ever did hear!"

Tommy could feel the unwillingness to believe him. "It's always that way," he said defensively, "in every story I've ever read about a space ship landing from outer space!"

Charlie Farnsworth whinnied out his derision.

Mrs Sharp waggled a bony finger in front of Tommy's mother. "If you ask me, Sally Bishop," she said, "you'd better get that boy of yours up to bed. He's been reading too many comic books or seeing too many movies or something."

Sally Bishop's face reddened. She gripped Tommy's shoulders tightly. "Tommy," she said softly. "Stop that kind of talk, honey."

Steve's eyes never left the boy's face. "That's all right, Tom. We'll be right back. You'll see. That wasn't a ship or anything like it. That was just a – a meteor or something, likely as not—" He turned to the group, trying to weight his words with an optimism he didn't quite feel. "No doubt it did have something to do with all this power failure and the rest of it. Meteors can do crazy things. Like sun spots."

"That's right," Don said, as if picking up a cue. "Like

sun spots. That kind of thing. They can raise cain with radio reception all over the world. And this thing being so close – why there's no telling what sort of stuff it can do." He wet his lips nervously. "Come on, Steve. We'll go into town and see if that isn't what's causing it all."

Once again the two men started away.

"Mr Brand!" Tommy's voice was defiant and frightened at the same time. He pulled away from his mother and ran after them. "Please, Mr Brand, please don't leave here."

There was a stir, a rustle, a movement among the people. There was something about the boy. Something about the intense little face. Something about the words that carried such emphasis, such belief, such fear. They listened to these words and rejected them because intellect and logic had no room for spaceships and green-headed things. But the irritation that showed in the eyes, the murmuring and the compressed lips had nothing to do with intellect. A little boy was bringing up fears that shouldn't be brought up; and the people on Maple Street this Saturday afternoon were no different from any other set of human beings. Order, reason, logic were slipping, pushed by the wild conjectures of a twelve-year-old boy.

"Somebody ought to spank that kid," an angry voice muttered.

Tommy Bishop's voice continued defiant. It pierced the murmurings and rose above them. "You might not even be able to get to town," he said. "It was that way in the story. *Nobody* could leave. Nobody except—"

"Except who?" Steve asked.

"Except the people they'd sent down ahead of them. They looked just like humans. It wasn't until the ship landed that—"

His mother grabbed him by the arm and pulled him back. "Tommy," she said in a low voice. "Please, honey . . . don't talk that way."

"Damn right he shouldn't talk that way," came the

voice of the man in the rear again. "And we shouldn't stand here listening to him. Why this is the craziest thing I ever heard. The kid tells us a comic-book plot and here we stand listening—"

His voice died away as Steve stood up and faced the crowd. Fear can throw people into a panic, but it can also make them receptive to a leader and Steve Brand at this moment was such a leader. The big man in the ex-Marine dungarees had an authority about him.

"Go ahead, Tommy," he said to the boy. "What kind of story was this? What about the people that they sent out ahead?"

"That was the way they prepared things for the landing, Mr Brand," Tommy said. "They sent four people. A mother and a father and two kids who looked just like humans. But they weren't."

There was a murmur – a stir of uneasy laughter. People looked at one another again and a couple of them smiled.

"Well," Steve said, lightly but carefully, "I guess we'd better run a check on the neighborhood, and see which ones of us are really human."

His words were a release. Laughter broke out openly. But soon it died away. Only Charlie Farnsworth's horse whinny persisted over the growing silence and then he too lapsed into a grim quietness, until all fifteen people were looking at one another through changed eyes. A twelve-year-old boy had planted a seed. And something was growing out of the street with invisible branches that began to wrap themselves around the men and women and pull them apart. Distrust lay heavy in the air.

Suddenly there was the sound of a car engine and all heads turned as one. Across the street Ned Rosen was sitting in his convertible trying to start it, and nothing was happening beyond the labored sound of a sick engine getting deeper and hoarser, and finally giving up altogether. Ned Rosen, a thin, serious-faced man in his thirties, got out of his car and closed the door. He stood there staring at it for a moment, shook his head, looked across the street at his neighbors and started toward them.

"Can't get her started, Ned?" Don Martin called out to him.

"No dice," Ned answered. "Funny, she was working fine this morning."

Without warning, all by itself, the car started up and idled smoothly, smoke briefly coming out of the exhaust. Ned Rosen whirled around to stare at it, his eyes wide. Then, just as suddenly as it started, the engine sputtered and stopped.

"Started all by itself!" Charlie Farnsworth squealed excitedly.

"How did it do that?" Mrs Sharp asked. "How could it just start all by itself?"

Sally Bishop let loose her son's arm and just stood there, shaking her head. "How in the world—" she began.

Then there were no more questions. They stood silently staring at Ned Rosen who looked from them to his car and then back again. He went to the car and looked at it. Then he scratched his head again.

"Somebody explain it to me," he said. "I sure never saw anything like that happen before!"

"He never did come out to look at that thing that flew overhead. He wasn't even interested," Don Martin said heavily.

"What do you say we ask him some questions," Charlie Farnsworth proposed importantly. "I'd like to know what's going on here!"

There was a chorus of assent and the fifteen people started across the street toward Ned Rosen's driveway. Unity was restored, they had a purpose, a feeling of activity and direction. They were *doing* something. They weren't sure what, but Ned Rosen was flesh and blood – askable, reachable and seeable. He watched with growing apprehension as his neighbors marched toward him. They stopped on the sidewalk close to the driveway and surveyed him.

Ned Rosen pointed to his car. "I just don't understand it, any more than you do! I tried to start it and it *wouldn't* start. You saw me. All of you saw me."

His neighbors seemed massed against him, solidly, alarmingly.

"I don't understand it!" he cried. "I swear – I don't understand. What's happening?"

Charlie Farnsworth stood out in front of the others. "Maybe you better tell us," he demanded. "Nothing's working on this street. Nothing. No lights, no power, no radio. Nothing except one car – *yours*!"

There were mutterings from the crowd. Steve Brand stood back by himself and said nothing. He didn't like what was going on. Something was building up that threatened to grow beyond control.

"Come on, Rosen," Charlie Farnsworth commanded shrilly, "let's hear what goes on! Let's hear how you explain your car startin' like that!"

Ned Rosen wasn't a coward. He was a quiet man who didn't like violence and had never been a physical fighter. But he didn't like being bullied. Ned Rosen got mad.

"Hold it!" he shouted. "Just hold it. You keep your distance. All of you. All right, I've got a car that starts by itself. Well, that's a freak thing – I admit it! But does that make me some sort of a criminal or something? I don't know why the car works – it just does!"

The crowd were neither sobered nor reassured by Rosen's words, but they were not too frightened to listen. They huddled together, mumbling, and Ned Rosen's eyes went from face to face till they stopped on Steve Brand's. Ned knew Steve Brand. Of all the men on the street, this seemed the guy with the most substance. The most intelligent. The most essentially decent.

"What's it all about, Steve?" he asked.

"We're all on a monster kick, Ned," he answered quietly. "Seems that the general impression holds that maybe one family isn't what we think they are. Monsters from outer space or something. Different from us. Fifth columnists from the vast beyond." He couldn't keep the sarcasm out of his voice. "Do you know anybody around here who might fit that description?"

Rosen's eyes narrowed. "What is this, a gag?" He looked around the group again. "This a practical joke or something?" And without apparent reason, without logic, without explanation, his car started again, idled for a moment, sending smoke out of the exhaust, and stopped.

A woman began to cry, and the bank of eyes facing Ned Rosen looked cold and accusing. he walked to his porch steps and stood on them, facing his neighbors.

"Is that supposed to incriminate me?" he asked. "The car engine goes on and off and that really does it, huh?" He looked down into their faces. "I don't understand it. Not any more than you do."

He could tell that they were unmoved. This couldn't really be happening, Ned thought to himself.

"Look," he said in a different tone. "You all know me. We've lived here four years. Right in this house. We're no different from any of the rest of you!" He held out his hands toward them. The people he was looking at hardly resembled the people he'd lived alongside of for the past four years. They looked as if someone had taken a brush and altered every character with a few strokes. "Really," he continued, "this whole thing is just . . . just weird—"

"Well, if that's the case, Ned Rosen," Mrs Sharp's voice suddenly erupted from the crowd – "maybe you'd better explain why—" She stopped abruptly and clamped her mouth shut, but looked wise and pleased with herself.

"Explain what?" Rosen asked her softly.

Steve Brand sensed a special danger now. "Look," he said, "let's forget this right now—"

Charlie Farnsworth cut him off. "Go ahead. Let her talk. What about it? Explain what?"

Mrs Sharp, with an air of great reluctance, said, "Well, sometimes I go to bed late at night. A couple of times – a couple of times I've come out on the porch, and I've seen Ned Rosen here, in the wee hours of the morning, standing out in front of his house looking up at the sky." She looked around the circle of faces. "That's right, looking up at the sky as if – as if he was waiting for something." She paused for emphasis, for dramatic effect. "As if he was looking for something!" she repeated.

The nail on the coffin, Steve Brand thought. One, dumb, ordinary, simple idiosyncrasy of a human being – and that probably was all it would take. He heard the murmuring of the crowd rise and saw Ned Rosen's face turn white. Rosen's wife, Ann, came out on the porch. She took a look at the crowd and then at her husband's face.

"What's going on, Ned?" she asked.

"I don't know what's going on," Ned answered. "I just don't know, Ann. But I'll tell you this. I don't like these people. I don't like what they're doing. I don't like them standing in my yard like this. And if any one of them takes another step and gets close to my porch – I'll break his jaw. I swear to God, that's just what I'll do. I'll break his jaw. Now go on, get out of here, all of you!" he shouted at them. "Get the hell out of here."

"Ned," Ann's voice was shocked.

"You heard me," Ned repeated. "All of you get out of here."

None of them eager to start an action, the people began to back away. But they had an obscure sense of gratification. At least there was an opponent now. Someone who wasn't one of them. And this gave them a kind of secure feeling. The enemy was no longer formless and vague. The enemy had a front porch and a front yard and a car. And he had shouted threats at them.

They started slowly back across the street forgetting for the moment what had started it all. Forgetting that there was no power, and no telephones. Forgetting even that there had been a meteor overhead not twenty minutes earlier. It wasn't until much later, as a matter of fact, that anyone posed a certain question.

Old man Van Horn had walked through his back yard over to Bennett Avenue. He'd never come back. Where was he? It was not one of the questions that passed through the minds of any of the thirty or forty people on Maple Street who sat on their front porches and watched the night come and felt the now menacing darkness close in on them.

There were lanterns lit all along Maple Street by ten o'clock. Candles shone through living-room windows and cast flickering, unsteady shadows all along the street. Groups of people huddled on front lawns around their lanterns and a soft murmur of voices was carried over the Indian-summer night air. All eyes eventually were drawn to Ned Rosen's front porch.

He sat there on the railing, observing the little points of light spotted around in the darkness. He knew he was surrounded. He was the animal at bay.

His wife came out on the porch and brought him a glass of lemonade. Her face was white and strained. Like her husband, Ann Rosen was a gentle person, unarmored by temper or any proclivity for outrage. She stood close to her husband now on the darkened porch feeling the suspicion that flowed from the people around lanterns, thinking to herself that these were people she had entertained in her house. These were women she talked to over clotheslines in the back yard; people who had been friends and neighbors only that morning. Oh dear God, could all this have happened in those few hours? It must be a nightmare, she thought. It had to be a nightmare that she could wake up from. It couldn't be anything else.

Across the street Mabel Farnsworth, Charlie's wife, shook her head and clucked at her husband who was drinking a can of beer. "It just doesn't seem right though, Charlie, keeping watch on them. Why he was right when he said he was one of our neighbors. I've known Ann Rosen ever since they moved in. We've been good friends."

Charlie Farnsworth turned to her disgustedly. "That don't prove a thing," he said. "Any guy who'd spend his time lookin' up at the sky early in the morning – well there's something wrong with that kind of person. There's something that ain't legitimate. Maybe under normal circumstances we could let it go by. But these aren't normal circumstances." He turned and pointed toward the street. "Look at that," he said. "Nothin' but candles and lanterns. Why it's like goin' back into the Dark Ages or something!"

He was right. Maple Street had changed with the night. The flickering lights had done something to its character. It looked odd and menacing and very different. Up and down the street, people noticed it. The change in Maple Street. It was the feeling one got after being away from home for many, many years and then returning. There was a vague familiarity about it, but it wasn't the same. It was different.

Ned Rosen and his wife heard footsteps coming toward their house. Ned got up from the railing and shouted out into the darkness.

"Whoever it is, just stay right where you are. I don't want any trouble, but if anybody sets foot on my porch, that's what they're going to get – trouble!" He saw that it was Steve Brand and his features relaxed.

"Ned—" Steve began.

Ned Rosen cut him off. "I've already explained to you people, I don't sleep very well at night sometimes. I get up and I take a walk and I look up at the sky. I look at the stars."

Ann Rosen's voice shook as she stood alongside of him. "That's exactly what he does. Why this whole thing, it's – it's some kind of a madness or something."

Steve Brand stood on the sidewalk and nodded grimly. "That's exactly what it is – some kind of madness."

Charlie Farnsworth's voice from the adjoining yard was

spiteful. "You'd best watch who you're seen with, Steve. Until we get this all straightened out, you ain't exactly above suspicion yourself."

Steve whirled around to the outline of the fat figure that stood behind the lantern in the other yard. "Or you either, Charlie," he shouted. "Or any of the rest of us!"

Mrs Sharp's voice came from the darkness across the street. "What I'd like to know is – what are we going to do? Just stand around here all night?"

"There's nothin' else we can do," Charlie Farnsworth said. He looked wisely over toward Ned Rosen's house. "One of 'em'll tip their hand. They *got* to."

It was Charlie's voice that did it for Steve Brand at this moment. The shrieking, pig squeal that came from the layers of fat and the idiotic sport shirt and the dull, dumb, blind prejudice of the man. "There's something *you* can do, Charlie," Steve called out to him. "You can go inside your house and keep your mouth shut!"

"You sound real anxious to have that happen, Steve," Charlie's voice answered him back from the little spot of light in the next yard. "I think we'd better keep our eye on you, too!"

Don Martin came up to Steve Brand, carrying a lantern. There was something hesitant in his manner, as if he were about to take a bit in his teeth, but wondered whether it would hurt. "I think everything might as well come out now," Don said. "I really do. I think everything should come out."

People came off porches, from front yards, to stand around in a group near Don who now turned directly toward Steve.

"Your wife's done plenty of talking, Steve, about how odd you are," he said.

Charlie Farnsworth trotted over. "Go ahead. Tell us what she said," he demanded excitedly.

Steve Brand knew this was the way it would happen. He was not really surprised but he still felt a hot anger rise up inside of him. "Go ahead," he said. "What's my wife said? Let's get it *all* out." He peered around at the shadowy figures of the neighbors. "Let's pick out every Goddamned peculiarity of every single man, woman and child on this street! Don't stop with me and Ned. How about a firing squad at dawn, so we can get rid of all the suspects! Make it easier for you!"

Don Martin's voice retreated fretfully. "There's no need getting so upset, Steve—"

"Go to hell, Don," Steve said to him in a cold and dispassionate fury.

Needled, Don went on the offensive again but his tone held something plaintive and petulant. "It just so happens that, well, Agnes has talked about how there's plenty of nights you've spent hours in your basement working on some kind of a radio or something. Well none of us have ever *seen* that radio—"

"Go ahead, Steve," Charlie Farnsworth yelled at him. "What kind of a 'radio set' you workin' on? I never seen it. Neither has anyone else. Who do you talk to on that radio set? And who talks to you?"

Steve's eyes slowly traveled in an arc over the hidden faces and the shrouded forms of neighbors who were now accusers. "I'm surprised at you, Charlie," he said quietly. "I really am. How come you're so God-damned dense all of a sudden? Who do I talk to? I talk to monsters from outer space. I talk to three-headed green men who fly over here in what look like meteors!"

Agnes Brand walked across the street to stand at her husband's elbow. She pulled at his arm with frightened intensity. "Steve! Steve, please," she said. "It's just a ham radio set," she tried to explain. "That's all. I bought him a book on it myself. It's just a ham radio set. A lot of people have them. I can show it to you. It's right down in the basement."

Steve pulled her hand off his arm. "You show them nothing," he said to her. "If they want to look inside our house, let them get a search warrant!"

Charlie's voice whined at him. "Look, buddy, you can't afford to—"

"Charlie," Steve shouted at him. "Don't tell me what I can afford. And stop telling me who's dangerous and who isn't. And who's safe and who's a menace!" He walked over to the edge of the road and saw that people backed away from him. "And you're with him — all of you," Steve bellowed at them. "You're standing there all set to crucify — to find a scapegoat — desperate to point some kind of a finger at a neighbor!" There was intensity in his tone and on his face, accentuated by the flickering light of the lanterns and the candles. "Well look, friends, the only thing that's going to happen is that we'll eat each other up alive. Understand? *We are going to eat each other up alive!*"

Charlie Farnsworth suddenly ran over to him and grabbed his arm. "That's not the *only* thing that can happen to us," he said in a frightened, hushed voice. "Look!"

"Oh, my God," Don Martin said.

Mrs Sharp screamed. All eyes turned to look down the street where a figure had suddenly materialized in the darkness and the sound of measured footsteps on concrete grew louder and louder as it walked toward them. Sally Bishop let out a stifled cry and grabbed Tommy's shoulder.

The child's voice screamed out, "It's the monster! It's the monster!"

There was a frightened wail from another woman, and the residents of Maple Street stood transfixed with terror as something unknown came slowly down the street. Don Martin disappeared and came back out of his house a moment later carrying a shotgun. He pointed it toward the approaching form. Steve pulled it out of his hands.

"For God's sake, will somebody think a thought around here? Will you people wise up? What good would a shotgun do against—"

A quaking, frightened Charlie Farnsworth grabbed the

gun from Steve's hand. "No more talk, Steve," he said. "You're going to talk us into a grave! You'd let whoever's out there walk right over us, wouldn't yuh? Well, some of us won't!"

He swung the gun up and pulled the trigger. The noise was a shocking, shattering intrusion and it echoed and reechoed through the night. A hundred yards away the figure collapsed like a piece of clothing blown off a line by the wind. From front porches and lawns people raced toward it.

Steve was the first to reach him. He knelt down, turned him over and looked at his face. Then he looked up toward the semi-circle of silent faces surveying him.

"All right, friends," he said quietly. "It happened. We got our first victim – Pete Van Horn!"

"Oh, my God," Don Martin said in a hushed voice. "He was just going over to the next block to see if the power was on—"

Mrs Sharp's voice was that of injured justice. "You killed him, Charlie! You shot him dead!"

Charlie Farnsworth's face looked like a piece of uncooked dough, quivering and shaking in the light of the lantern he held.

"I didn't know who he was," he said. "I certainly didn't know who he was." Tears rolled down his fat cheeks. "He comes walking out of the dark – how am I supposed to know who he was?" He looked wildly around and then grabbed Steve's arm. Steve could explain things to people. "Steve," he screamed, "you know why I shot. How was I supposed to know he wasn't a monster or something?"

Steve looked at him and didn't say anything. Charlie grabbed Don.

"We're all scared of the same thing," he blubbered. "The very same thing. I was just tryin' to protect my home, that's all. Look, all of you, that's all I was tryin' to do!" He tried to shut out the sight of Pete Van Horn who stared up at him with dead eyes and a shattered chest. "Please, please, please," Charlie Farnsworth sobbed, "I didn't know it was somebody we knew. I swear to God I didn't know—"

The lights went on in Charlie Farnsworth's house and shone brightly on the people of Maple Street. They looked suddenly naked. They blinked foolishly at the lights and their mouths gaped like fishes'.

"Charlie," Mrs Sharp said, like a judge pronouncing sentence, "how come you're the only one with lights on now?"

Ned Rosen nodded in agreement. "That's what I'd like to know," he said. Something inside tried to check him, but his anger made him go on. "How come, Charlie? You're quiet all of a sudden. You've got nothing to say out of that big, fat mouth of yours. Well, let's hear it, Charlie? Let's hear why you've got lights!"

Again the chorus of voices that punctuated the request and gave it legitimacy and a vote of support. "Why, Charlie?" the voices asked him. "How come you're the only one with lights?" The questions came out of the night to land against his fat wet cheeks. "You were so quick to kill," Ned Rosen continued, "and you were so quick to tell us who we had to be careful of. Well maybe you *had* to kill, Charlie. Maybe Pete Van Horn, God rest his soul, was trying to tell us something. Maybe he'd found out something and had come back to tell us who there was among us we should watch out for."

Charlie's eyes were little pits of growing fear as he backed away from the people and found himself up against a bush in front of his house. "No," he said. "No, please." His chubby hands tried to speak for him. They waved around, pleading. The palms outstretched, begging for forgiveness and understanding. "Please – please, I swear to you – it isn't me! It really isn't me."

A stone hit him on the side of the face and drew blood. He screamed and clutched at his face as the people began to converge on him.

"No," he screamed. "No."

Like a hippopotamus in a circus, he scrambled over the

bush, tearing his clothes and scratching his face and arms. His wife tried to run toward him, somebody stuck a foot out and she tripped, sprawling head first on the sidewalk. Another stone whistled through the air and hit Charlie on the back of the head as he raced across his front yard toward his porch. A rock smashed at the porch light and sent glass cascading down on his head.

"It isn't me," he screamed back at them as they came toward him across the front lawn. "It isn't me, but I know who it is," he said suddenly, without thought. Even as he said it, he realized it was the only possible thing to say.

People stopped, motionless as statues, and a voice called out from the darkness. "All right, Charlie, who is it?"

He was a grotesque, fat figure of a man who smiled now through the tears and the blood that cascaded down his face. "Well, I'm going to tell you," he said. "I am now going to tell you, because I know who it is. I really know who it is. It's . . ."

"Go ahead, Charlie," a voice commanded him. "Who's the monster?"

Don Martin pushed his way to the front of the crowd. "All right, Charlie, now! Let's hear it!"

Charlie tried to think. He tried to come up with a name. A nightmare engulfed him. Fear whipped at the back of his brain. "It's the kid," he screamed. "That's who it is. It's the kid!"

Sally Bishop screamed and grabbed at Tommy, burying his face against her. "That's crazy," she said to the people who now stared at her. "That's crazy. He's a little boy."

"But he knew," said Mrs Sharp. "He was the only one who knew. He told us all about it. Well how did he know? How *could* he have known?"

Voices supported her. "How could he know?" "Who told him?" "Make the kid answer." A fever had taken hold now, a hot, burning virus that twisted faces and forced out words and solidified the terror inside of each person on Maple Street.

Tommy broke away from his mother and started to run. A man dove at him in a flying tackle and missed. Another man threw a stone wildly toward the darkness. They began to run after him down the street. Voices shouted through the night, women screamed. A small child's voice protested – a playmate of Tommy's one tiny voice of sanity in the middle of a madness as men and women ran down the street, the sidewalks, the curbs, looking blindly for a twelve-year-old boy.

And then suddenly the lights went on in another house – a two-story, gray stucco house that belonged to Bob Weaver. A man screamed, "It isn't the kid. It's Bob Weaver's house!"

A porch light went on at Mrs Sharp's house and Sally Bishop screamed, "It isn't Bob Weaver's house. It's Mrs Sharp's place."

"I tell you it's the kid," Charlie screamed.

The lights went on and off, on and off down the street. A power mower suddenly began to move all by itself lurching crazily across a front yard, cutting an irregular path of grass until it smashed against the side of the house.

"It's Charlie," Don Martin screamed. "He's the one." And then he saw his own lights go on and off.

They ran this way and that way, over to one house and then back across the street to another. A rock flew through the air and then another. A pane of glass smashed and there was the cry of a woman in pain. Lights on and off, on and off. Charlie Farnsworth went down on his knees as a piece of brick plowed a two-inch hole in the back of his skull. Mrs Sharp lay on her back screaming, and felt the tearing jab of a woman's high heel in her mouth as someone stepped on her, racing across the street.

From a quarter of a mile away, on a hilltop, Maple Street looked like this, a long tree-lined avenue full of lights going on and off and screaming people racing back and forth. Maple Street was a bedlam. It was an outdoor asylum for the insane. Windows were broken, street lights sent clusters of broken glass down on the heads of women and children. Power mowers started up and car engines and radios. Blaring music mixed with the screams and shouts and the anger.

Up on top of the hill two men, screened by the darkness, stood near the entrance to a space ship and looked down on Maple Street.

"Understand the procedure now?" the first figure said. "Just stop a few of their machines and radios and telephones and lawn mowers. Throw them into darkness for a few hours and then watch the pattern unfold."

"And this pattern is always the same?" the second figure asked.

"With few variations," came the answer. "They pick the most dangerous enemy they can find and it's themselves. All we need do is sit back – and watch."

"Then I take it," figure two said, "this place, this Maple Street, is not unique?"

Figure one shook his head and laughed. "By no means. Their world is full of Maple Streets and we'll go from one to the other and let them destroy themselves." He started up the incline toward the entrance of the space ship. "One to the other," he said as the other figure followed him. "One to the other." There was just the echo of his voice as the two figures disappeared and a panel slid softly across the entrance. "One to the other," the echo said.

When the sun came up on the following morning Maple Street was silent. Most of the houses had been burned. There were a few bodies lying on sidewalks and draped over porch railings. But the silence was total. There simply was no more life. At four o'clock that afternoon there was no more world, or at least not the kind of world that had greeted the morning. And by Wednesday afternoon of the following week, a new set of residents had moved into Maple Street. They were a handsome race of people. Their faces showed great character. Great character indeed. Great character and excellently shaped heads. Excellently shaped heads – two to each new resident!

From Rod Serling's closing narration, 'The Monsters Are Due on Maple Street,' The Twilight Zone, January 1, 1960, CBS Television Network.

Now the CAMERA PANS UP for a shot of the starry sky and over this we hear the Narrator's Voice.

NARRATOR'S VOICE
The tools of conquest do not necessarily come
with bombs and explosions and fall-out. There
are weapons that are simply thoughts, attitudes,
prejudices – to be found only in the minds of men.
For the record, prejudices can kill and suspicion
can destroy and a thoughtless, frightened search
for a scapegoat has a fall-out all of its own for the
children . . . and the children yet unborn.
   (a pause)
   And the pity of it is, that these things cannot be
confined to . . . The Twilight Zone!

FADE TO BLACK

OUT OF THIS WORLD

(ABC TV, 1962)
Starring: William Lucas, Hilda Schroder &
Ray Barrett
Directed by Charles Jarrott
Story: 'Dumb Martian' by John Wyndham

In 1962, Boris Karloff who had starred in the first American Science Fiction TV series, *Tales of Tomorrow*, returned to his native England to host Britain's first SF anthology show, *Out Of This World*. This pioneer show which ran to 13, one hour long episodes through the summer of 1962 saw SF finally come of age on the small screen in the UK through a combination of excellent stories by leading genre writers and fine acting by accomplished players obviously enjoying working in a completely different entertainment medium. The success of the ambitious, black and white series was also very much due to the dedicated work of its producer Leonard White and story editor Irene Shubik, who had earlier launched the very popular *Armchair Theatre*. The Science Fiction stories adapted for the screen varied from tense dramas to black comedies and included the work of such distinguished names as Isaac Asimov, Clifford Simak, Philip K. Dick and Britain's own John Wyndham. Among the scriptwriters who worked on the series were Leon Griffiths, Clive Exton and Terry Nation whose place in the pantheon of SF TV writers was assured the day he created the infamous Daleks for *Dr Who*. The cast lists of many of the episodes also looked like a Who's Who of the best contemporary television actors and actress including – among others – Dinsdale Landen, Peter Wyngarde, Maurice Denham, Charles Gray, Geraldine McEwan and Jane Asher.

'Dumb Martian' by John Wyndham (1903–1969), one of Britain's leading Twentieth Century SF writers and forever remembered for *The Day of the Triffids* (1951) which has also been filmed and adapted for TV, was chosen as the story to launch the series and was transmitted on June 24, 1962. Following the closing credits, Karloff materialized onto the nation's screens to urge viewers to watch the impending series. In Wyndham's tale an uncouth space pilot, Duncan Weaver (Lucas) buys a Martian girl Lellie (Schroder) to act as his wife and housekeeper, but when he begins treating her badly soon finds he has underestimated her intelligence as well as provoking an unexpected rival to his domestic harmony. The episode offered a form of entertainment that few viewers had seen before, but *Out Of This World* quickly caught on in the following weeks. It would not be long, in fact, before the BBC would latch onto the popularity of the anthology format and put out their own rival show.

When Duncan Weaver bought Lellie for – no, there could be trouble putting it that way – when Duncan Weaver paid Lellie's parents one thousand pounds in compensation for the loss of her services, he had a figure of six, or, if absolutely necessary, seven hundred in mind.

Everybody in Port Clarke that he had asked about it assured him that that would be a fair price. But when he got up country it hadn't turned out quite as simple as the Port Clarkers seemed to think. The first three Martian families he had tackled hadn't shown any disposition to sell their daughters at all; the next wanted £1,500, and wouldn't budge; Lellie's parents had started at £1,500, too, but they came down to £1,000 when he'd made it plain that he wasn't going to stand for extortion. And when, on the way back to Port Clarke with her, he came to work it out, he found himself not so badly pleased with the deal after all. Over the five-year term of his appointment it could only cost him £200 a year at the worst – that is to say if he were not able to sell her for £400, maybe £500 when he got back. Looked at that way, it wasn't really at all unreasonable.

In town once more, he went to explain the situation and get things all set with the Company's Agent.

"Look," he said, "you know the way I'm fixed with this five-year contract as Way-load Station Superintendent on Jupiter IV/II? Well, the ship that takes me there will be travelling light to pick up cargo. So how about a second passage on her?" He had already taken the precautionary step of finding out that the Company was accustomed to grant an extra passage in such circumstances, though not of right.

The Company's Agent was not surprised. After consulting some lists, he said that he saw no objection to an extra passenger. He explained that the Company was also prepared in such cases to supply the extra ration of food for one person at the nominal charge of £200 per annum, payable by deduction from salary.

"What! A thousand pounds!" Duncan exclaimed.

"Well worth it," said the Agent. "It *is* nominal for the rations, because it's worth the Company's while to lay out the rest for something that helps to keep an employee from going nuts. That's pretty easy to do when you're fixed alone on a way-load station, they tell me – and I believe them. A thousand's not high if it helps you to avoid a crack-up."

Duncan argued it a bit, on principle, but the Agent had the thing cut and dried. It meant that Lellie's price went up to £2,000 – £400 a year. Still, with his own salary at £5,000 a year, tax free, unspendable during his term on Jupiter IV/II, and piling up nicely, it wouldn't come to such a big slice. So he agreed.

"Fine," said the Agent. "I'll fix it, then. All you'll

need is an embarkation permit for her, and they'll grant that automatically on production of your marriage certificate."

Duncan stared.

"Marriage certificate! What, me! Me marry a Mart!"

The Agent shook his head reprovingly.

"No embarkation permit without it. Anti-slavery regulation. They'd likely think you meant to sell her — might even think you'd bought her."

"What, me!" Duncan said again, indignantly.

"Even you," said the Agent. "A marriage licence will only cost you another ten pounds — unless you've got a wife back home, in which case it'll likely cost you a bit more later on."

Duncan shook his head.

"I've no wife," he assured him.

"Uh-huh," said the Agent, neither believing, nor disbelieving. "Then what's the difference?"

Duncan came back a couple of days later, with the certificate and the permit. The Agent looked them over.

"That's okay," he agreed. "I'll confirm the booking. My fee will be one hundred pounds."

"Your fee! What the— ?"

"Call it safeguarding your investment," said the Agent.

The man who had issued the embarkation permit had required one hundred pounds, too. Duncan did not mention that now, but he said, with bitterness:

"One dumb Mart's costing me plenty."

"Dumb?" said the Agent, looking at him.

"Speechless plus. These hick Marts don't know they're born."

"H'm," said the Agent. "Never lived here, have you?"

"No," Duncan admitted. "But I've laid-over here a few times."

The Agent nodded.

"They act dumb, and the way their faces are makes them look dumb," he said, "but they were a mighty clever people, once."

"Once, could be a long time ago."

"Long before we got here they'd given up bothering to think a lot. Their planet was dying, and they were kind of content to die with it."

"Well, I call that dumb. Aren't all planets dying, anyway?"

"Ever seen an old man just sitting in the sun, taking it easy? It doesn't have to mean he's senile. It may do, but very likely he can snap out of it and put his mind to work again if it gets really necessary. But mostly he finds it not worth the bother. Less trouble just to let things happen."

"Well, this one's only about twenty – say ten and a half of your Martian years – and she certainly lets 'em happen. And I'd say it's a kind of acid test for dumbness when a girl doesn't know what goes on at her own wedding ceremony."

And then, on top of that, it turned out to be necessary to lay out yet another hundred pounds on clothing and other things for her, bringing the whole investment up to £2,310. It was a sum which might possibly have been justified on a really *smart* girl, but Lellie . . . But there it was. Once you made the first payment, you either lost on it, or were stuck for the rest. And, anyway, on a lonely way-load station even she would be company – of a sort . . .

The First Officer called Duncan into the navigating room to take a look at his future home.

"There it is," he said, waving his hand at a watch-screen.

Duncan looked at the jagged-surfaced crescent. There was no scale to it: it could have been the size of Luna, or of a basket-ball. Either size, it was still just a lump of rock, turning slowly over.

"How big?" he asked.

"Around forty miles mean diameter."

"What'd that be in gravity?"

"Haven't worked it out. Call it slight, and reckon there isn't any, and you'll be near enough."

"Uh-huh," said Duncan.

On the way back to the mess-room he paused to put his head into the cabin. Lellie was lying on her bunk, with the spring-cover fastened over her to give some illusion of weight. At the sight of him she raised herself on one elbow.

She was small – not much over five feet. Her face and hands were delicate; they had a fragility which was not simply a matter of poor bone-structure. To an Earthman her eyes looked unnaturally round, seeming to give her permanently an expression of innocence surprised. The lobes of her ears hung unusually low out of a mass of brown hair that glinted with red among its waves. The paleness of her skin was emphasized by the colour on her cheeks and the vivid red on her lips.

"Hey," said Duncan. "You can start to get busy packing up the stuff now."

"Packing up?" she repeated doubtfully, in a curiously resonant voice.

"Sure. Pack," Duncan told her. He demonstrated by opening a box, cramming some clothes into it, and waving a hand to include the rest. Her expression did not change, but the idea got across.

"We are come?" she asked.

"We are nearly come. So get busy on this lot," he informed her.

"Yith – okay," she said, and began to unhook the cover.

Duncan shut the door, and gave a shove which sent him floating down the passage leading to the general mess and living-room.

Inside the cabin, Lellie pushed away the cover. She reached down cautiously for a pair of metallic soles, and attached them to her slippers by their clips. Still cautiously holding on to the bunk, she swung her feet over the side and lowered them until the magnetic soles clicked into contact with the floor. She stood up, more confidently. The brown overall suit she wore revealed proportions that might be admired among Martians, but by Earth standards they were not classic – it is said to be the consequence of the thinner air of Mars that has in the course of time produced a greater lung capacity, with consequent modification. Still ill at ease with her condition of weightlessness, she slid her feet to keep contact as she crossed the room. For some moments she paused in front of a wall mirror, contemplating her reflection. Then she turned away and set about the packing.

"– one hell of a place to take a woman to," Wishart, the ship's cook, was saying as Duncan came in.

Duncan did not care a lot for Wishart – chiefly on account of the fact that when it had occurred to him that it was highly desirable for Lellie to have some lessons in weightless cooking, Wishart had refused to give the tuition for less than £50, and thus increased the investment cost to £2,360. Nevertheless, it was not his way to pretend to have misheard.

"One hell of a place to be given a job," he said, grimly.

No one replied to that. They knew how men came to be offered way-load jobs.

It was not necessary, as the Company frequently pointed out, for superannuation at the age of forty to come as a hardship to anyone: salaries were good, and they could cite plenty of cases where men had founded brilliant subsequent careers on the savings of their space-service days. That was all right for the men who had saved, and had not been obsessively interested in the fact that one four-legged animal can run faster than another. But this was not even an enterprising way to have lost one's money, so when it came to Duncan's time to leave crew work they made him no more than the routine offer.

He had never been to Jupiter IV/II, but he knew just what it would be like – something that was second moon to Callisto; itself fourth moon, in order of discovery, to Jupiter; would inevitably be one of the grimmer kinds of cosmic pebble. They offered no alternative, so he signed up at the usual terms: £5,000 a year for five years, all found, plus five months waiting time on half-pay before he could get there, plus six months afterwards, also on half-pay, during 'readjustment to gravity'.

Well – it meant the next six years taken care of; five of them without expenses, and a nice little sum at the end.

The splinter in the mouthful was: could you get through five years of isolation without cracking up? Even when the psychologist had okayed you, you couldn't be sure. Some could: others went to pieces in a few months, and had to be taken off, gibbering. If you got through two years, they said, you'd be okay for five. But the only way to find out about the two was to try . . .

"What about my putting in the waiting time on Mars? I could live cheaper there," Duncan suggested.

They had consulted planetary tables and sailing schedules, and discovered that it would come cheaper for them, too. They had declined to split the difference on the saving thus made, but they had booked him a passage for the following week, and arranged for him to draw, on credit, from the Company's agent there.

The Martian colony in and around Port Clarke is rich in ex-spacemen who find it more comfortable to spend their rearguard years in the lesser gravity, broader morality, and greater economy obtaining there. They are great advisers. Duncan listened, but discarded most of it. Such methods of occupying oneself to preserve sanity as learning the Bible or the works of Shakespeare by heart, or copying out three pages of the Encyclopaedia every day, or building model spaceships in bottles, struck him not only as tedious, but probably of doubtful efficacy, as well. The only one which he had felt to show sound practical advantages was that which had led him to picking Lellie to share his exile, and he still fancied it was a sound one, in spite of its letting him in for £2,360.

He was well enough aware of the general opinion about it to refrain from adding a sharp retort to Wishart. Instead, he conceded:

"Maybe it'd not do to take a *real* woman to a place like that. But a Mart's kind of different . . ."

"Even a Mart—" Wishart began, but he was cut short by finding himself drift slowly across the room as the arrester tubes began to fire.

Conversation ceased as everybody turned-to on the job of securing all loose objects.

Jupiter IV/II was, by definition, a sub-moon, and probably a captured asteroid. The surface was not cratered, like Luna's: it was simply a waste of jagged, riven rocks. The satellite as a whole had the form of an irregular ovoid; it was a bleak, cheerless lump of stone splintered off some vanished planet, with nothing whatever to commend it but its situation.

There have to be way-load stations. It would be hopelessly uneconomic to build big ships capable of landing on the major planets. A few of the older and smaller ships were indeed built on Earth, and so had to be launched from there, but the very first large, moon-assembled ships. established a new practice. Ships became truly *space*ships and were no longer built to stand the strains of high gravitational pull. They began to make their voyages, carrying fuel, stores, freight, and changes of personnel, exclusively between satellites. Newer types do not put in even at Luna, but use the artificial satellite, Pseudos, exclusively as their Earth terminus.

Freight between the way-loads and their primaries is customarily consigned in powered cylinders known as crates; passengers are ferried back and forth in small rocket-ships. Stations such as Pseudos, or Deimos, the main way-load for Mars, handle enough work to keep a crew busy, but in the outlying, little-developed posts one man who is part-handler, part-watchman is enough. Ships visited them infrequently. On Jupiter IV/II one might,

Dumb Martian

according to Duncan's information, expect an average of one every eight or nine months (Earth).

The ship continued to slow, coming in on a spiral, adjusting her speed to that of the satellite. The gyros started up to give stability. The small, jagged world grew until it overflowed the watch-screens. The ship was manoeuvred into a close orbit. Miles of featureless, formidable rocks slid monotonously beneath her.

The station site came sliding on to the screen from the left; a roughly levelled area of a few acres; the first and only sign of order in the stony chaos. At the far end was a pair of hemispherical huts, one much larger than the other. At the near end, a few cylindrical crates were lined up beside a launching ramp hewn from the rock. Down each side of the area stood rows of canvas bins, some stuffed full of a conical shape; others slack, empty or half-empty. A huge parabolic mirror was perched on a crag behind the station, looking like a monstrous, formalized flower. In the whole scene there was only one sign of movement – a small, space-suited figure prancing madly about on a metal apron in front of the larger dome, waving its arms in a wild welcome.

Duncan left the screen, and went to the cabin. He found Lellie fighting off a large case which, under the influence of deceleration, seemed determined to pin her against the wall. He shoved the case aside, and pulled her out.

"We're there," he told her. "Put on your space-suit."

Her round eyes ceased to pay attention to the case, and turned towards him. There was no telling from them how she felt, what she thought. She said, simply:

"Thpace-thuit. Yith – okay."

Standing in the airlock of the dome, the outgoing Superintendent paid more attention to Lellie than to the pressure-dial. He knew from experience exactly how long equalizing took, and opened his face-plate without even a glance at the pointer.

"Wish I'd had the sense to bring one," he observed. "Could have been mighty useful on the chores, too."

379

He opened the inner door, and led through.

"Here it is — and welcome to it," he said.

The main living-room was oddly shaped by reason of the dome's architecture, but it was spacious. It was also exceedingly, sordidly untidy.

"Meant to clean it up — never got around to it, some way," he added. He looked at Lellie. There was no visible sign of what she thought of the place. "Never can tell with Marts," he said uneasily. "They kind of non-register."

Duncan agreed: "I've figured this one looked astonished at being born, and never got over it."

The other man went on looking at Lellie. His eyes strayed from her to a gallery of pinned-up terrestrial beauties, and back again.

"Sort of funny shape Marts are," he said, musingly.

"This one's reckoned a good enough looker where she comes from," Duncan told him, a trifle shortly.

"Sure. No offence, Bud. I guess they'll all seem a funny shape to me after this spell." He changed the subject. "I'd better show you the ropes around here."

Duncan signed to Lellie to open her face-plate so that she could hear him, and then told her to get out of her suit.

The dome was the usual type: double-floored, double-walled, with an insulated and evacuated space between the two; constructed as a unit, and held down by metal bars let into the rock. In the living-quarters there were three more sizable rooms, able to cope with increased personnel if trade should expand.

"The rest," the outgoing man explained, "is the regular station stores, mostly food, air cylinders, spares of one kind and another, and water — you'll need to watch her on water; most women seem to think it grows naturally in pipes."

Duncan shook his head.

"Not Marts. Living in deserts gives 'em a natural respect for water."

The other picked up a clip of store-sheets.

"We'll check and sign these later. It's a nice soft job here. Only freight now is rare metalliferous earth. Callisto's not been opened up a lot yet. Handling's easy. They tell you when a crate's on the way: you switch on the radio beacon to bring it in. On dispatch you can't go wrong if you follow the tables." He looked around the room. "All home comforts. You read? Plenty of books." He waved a hand at the packed rows which covered half the inner partition wall. Duncan said he'd never been much of a reader. "Well, it helps," said the other. "Find pretty well anything that's known in that lot. Records there. Fond of music?"

Duncan said he liked a good tune.

"H'm. Better try the other stuff. Tunes get to squirrelling inside your head. Play chess?" He pointed to a board, with men pegged into it.

Duncan shook his head.

"Pity. There's a fellow over on Callisto plays a pretty hot game. He'll be disappointed not to finish this one. Still, if I was fixed up the way you are, maybe I'd not have been interested in chess." His eyes strayed to Lellie again. "What do you reckon she's going to do here, over and above cooking and amusing you?" he asked.

It was not a question that had occurred to Duncan, but he shrugged.

"Oh, she'll be okay, I guess. There's a natural dumbness about Marts – they'll sit for hours on end, doing damn all. It's a gift they got."

"Well, it should come in handy here," said the other.

The regular ship's-call work went on. Cases were unloaded, the metalliferous earths hosed from the bins into the holds. A small ferry-rocket came up from Callisto carrying a couple of time-expired prospectors, and left again with their two replacements. The ship's engineers checked over the station's machinery, made renewals, topped up the water tanks, charged the spent air cylinders, tested, tinkered, and tested again before giving their final okay.

John Wyndham

Duncan stood outside on the metal apron where not long ago his predecessor had performed his fantastic dance of welcome, to watch the ship take off. She rose straight up, with her jets pushing her gently. The curve of her hull became an elongated crescent shining against the black sky. The main driving jets started to gush white flame edged with pink. Quickly she picked up speed. Before long she had dwindled to a speck which sank behind the ragged skyline.

Quite suddenly Duncan felt as if he, too, had dwindled. He had become a speck upon a barren mass of rock which was itself a speck in the immensity. The indifferent sky about him had no scale. It was an utterly black void wherein his mother-sun and a myriad more suns flared perpetually, without reason or purpose.

The rocks of the satellite itself, rising up in their harsh crests and ridges, were without scale, too. He could not tell which were near or far away; he could not, in the jumble of hard-lit planes and inky shadows, even make out their true form. There was nothing like them to be seen on Earth, or on Mars. Their unweathered edges were sharp as blades: they had been just as sharp as that for millions upon millions of years, and would be for as long as the satellite should last.

The unchanging millions of years seemed to stretch out before and behind him. It was not only himself, it was all life that was a speck, a briefly transitory accident, utterly unimportant to the universe. It was a queer little mote dancing for its chance moment in the light of the eternal suns. Reality was just globes of fire and balls of stone rolling on, senselessly rolling along through emptiness, through time unimaginable, for ever, and ever, and ever . . .

Within his heated suit, Duncan shivered a little. Never before had he been so alone; never so much aware of the vast, callous, futile loneliness of space. Looking out into the blackness, with light that had left a star a million years ago shining into his eyes, he wondered.

"*Why?*" he asked himself. "What the heck's it all about, anyway?"

The sound of his own unanswerable question broke up the mood. He shook his head to clear it of speculative nonsense. He turned his back on the universe, reducing it again to its proper status as a background for life in general and human life in particular, and stepped into the airlock.

The job was, as his predecessor had told him, soft. Duncan made his radio contacts with Callisto at pre-arranged times. Usually it was little more than a formal check on one another's continued existence, with perhaps an exchange of comment on the radio news. Only occasionally did they announce a dispatch and tell him when to switch on his beacon. Then, in due course, the cylinder-crate would make its appearance, and float slowly down. It was quite a simple matter to couple it up to a bin to transfer the load.

The satellite's day was too short for convenience, and its night, lit by Callisto, and sometimes by Jupiter as well, almost as bright; so they disregarded it, and lived by the calender-clock which kept Earth time on the Greenwich Meridian setting. At first much of the time had been occupied in disposing of the freight that the ship had left. Some of it into the main dome – necessities for themselves, and other items that would store better where there was warmth and air. Some into the small, airless, unheated dome. The greater part to be stowed and padded carefully into cylinders and launched off to the Callisto base. But once that work had been cleared, the job was certainly soft, too soft . . .

Duncan drew up a programme. At regular intervals he would inspect this and that, he would waft himself up to the crag and check on the sun-motor there, et cetera. But keeping to an unnecessary programme requires resolution. Sun-motors, for instance, are very necessarily built to run for long spells without attention. The only action one could take if it should stop would be to call on

Callisto for a ferry-rocket to come and take them off until a ship should call to repair it. A breakdown there, the Company had explained very clearly, was the only thing that would justify him in leaving his station, with the stores of precious earth, unmanned (and it was also conveyed that to contrive a breakdown for the sake of a change was unlikely to prove worth while). One way and another, the programme did not last long.

There were times when Duncan found himself wondering whether the bringing of Lellie had been such a good idea after all. On the purely practical side, he'd not have cooked as well as she did, and probably have pigged it quite as badly as his precessor had, but if she had not been there, the necessity of looking after himself would have given him some occupation. And even from the angle of company – well, she was that, of a sort, but she was alien, queer; kind of like a half-robot, and dumb at that; certainly no fun. There were, indeed, times – increasingly frequent times, when the very look of her irritated him intensely; so did the way she moved, *and* her gestures, *and* her silly pidgin-talk when she talked, *and* her self-contained silence when she didn't, *and* her withdrawness, *and* all her differentness, *and* the fact that he would have been £2,360 better off without her . . . Nor did she make a serious attempt to remedy her shortcomings, even where she had the means. Her face, for instance. You'd think any girl would try to make her best of that – but did she, hell! There was that left eyebrow again: made her look like a sozzled clown, but a lot she cared . . .

"For heaven's sake," he told her once more, "put the cockeyed thing straight. Don't you know how to fix 'em *yet?* And you've got your colour on wrong, too. Look at that picture – now look at yourself in the mirror: a great daub of red all in the wrong place. And your hair, too: getting all like seaweed again. You've got the things to wave it, then for crysake wave it again, and stop looking like a bloody mermaid. I know you can't help being a damn Mart, but you can at least *try* to look like a real woman."

Lellie looked at the coloured picture, and then compared her reflection with it, critically.

"Yith – okay," she said, with an equable detachment.

Duncan snorted.

"And that's another thing. Bloody baby-talk! It's not 'yith', it's 'yes'. Y-E-S, yes. So say 'yes'."

"Yith," said Lellie, obligingly.

"Oh, for – Can't you *hear* the difference? S-s-s, not th-th-th. Ye-sss."

"Yith," she said.

"No. Put your tongue further back like this—"

The lesson went on for some time. Finally he grew angry.

"Just making a monkey out of me, huh! You'd better be careful, my girl. Now, say 'yes'."

She hesitated, looking at his wrathful face.

"Go on, say it."

"Y-yeth," she said, nervously.

His hand slapped across her face harder than he had intended. The jolt broke her magnetic contact with the floor, and sent her sailing across the room in a spin of arms and legs. She struck the opposite wall, and rebounded to float helplessly, out of reach of any hold. He strode after her, turned her right way up, and set her on her feet. His left hand clutched her overall in a bunch, just below her throat, his right was raised.

"Again!" he told her.

Her eyes looked helplessly this way and that. He shook her. She tried. At the sixth attempt she managed: "Yeths."

He accepted that for the time being.

"You *can* do it, you see – when you try. What you need, my girl, is a bit of firm handling."

He let her go. She tottered across the room, holding her hands to her bruised face.

A number of times while the weeks drew out so slowly into months Duncan found himself wondering whether he was going to get through. He spun out what work there was as much as he could, but it left still too much time hanging heavy on his hands.

A middle-aged man who has read nothing longer than an occasional magazine article does not take to books. He tired very quickly, as his predecessor had prophesied, of the popular records, and could make nothing of the others. He taught himself the moves in chess from a book, and instructed Lellie in them, intending after a little practice with her to challenge the man on Callisto. Lellie, however, managed to win with such consistency that he had to decide that he had not the right kind of mind for the game. Instead, he taught her a kind of double solitaire, but that didn't last long, either; the cards seemed always to run for Lellie.

Occasionally there was some news and entertainment to be had from the radio, but with Earth somewhere round the other side of the sun just then, Mars screened off half the time by Callisto, and the rotation of the satellite itself, reception was either impossible, or badly broken up.

So mostly he sat and fretted, hating the satellite, angry with himself, and irritated by Lellie.

Just the phlegmatic way she went on with her tasks irritated him. It seemed an injustice that she could take it all better than he could simply *because* she was a dumb Mart. When his ill-temper became vocal, the look of her as she listened exasperated him still more.

"For crysake," he told her one time, "can't you make that silly face of yours *mean* something? Can't you laugh, or cry, or get mad, or something? It's enough to drive a guy nuts going on looking at a face that's fixed permanent like it was a doll just heard its first dirty story. I know you can't help being dumb, but for heaven's sake crack it up a bit, get some expression into it."

She went on looking at him without a shadow of a change.

"Go on, you heard me! Smile, damn you – Smile!"

Her mouth twitched very slightly.

"Call that a smile! Now, there's a smile!" He pointed

to a pin-up with her head split pretty much in half by a smile like a piano keyboard. "Like that! Like this!" He grinned widely.

"No," she said. "My face can't wriggle like Earth faces."

"Wriggle!" he said, incensed. "Wriggle, you call it!" He freed himself from the chair's spring-cover, and came towards her. She backed away until she fetched up against the wall. "I'll make yours wriggle, my girl. Go on, now – smile!" He lifted his hand.

Lellie put her hands up to her face.

"No!" she protested. "No-no-no!"

It was on the very day that Duncan marked off the eighth completed month that Callisto relayed news of a ship on the way. A couple of days later he was able to make contact with her himself, and confirm her arrival in about a week. He felt as if he had been given several stiff drinks. There were the preparations to make, stores to check, deficiencies to note, a string of nil-nil-nil entries to be made in the log to bring it up to date. He bustled around as he got on with it. He even hummed to himself as he worked, and ceased to be annoyed with Lellie. The effect upon her of the news was imperceptible – but then, what would you expect . . . ?

Sharp on her estimated time the ship hung above them, growing slowly larger as her upper jets pressed her down. The moment she was berthed Duncan went aboard, with the feeling that everything in sight was an old friend. The Captain received him warmly, and brought out the drinks. It was all routine – even Duncan's babbling and slightly inebriated manner was the regular thing in the circumstances. The only departure from pattern came when the Captain introduced a man beside him, and explained him.

"We've brought a surprise for you, Superintendent. This is Doctor Whint. He'll be sharing your exile for a bit."

Duncan shook hands. "Doctor . . . ?" he said, surprisedly.

"Not medicine – science," Alan Whint told him. "The Company's pushed me out here to do a geological survey – if geo isn't the wrong word to use. About a year. Hope you don't mind."

Duncan said conventionally that he'd be glad of the company, and left it at that for the moment. Later, he took him over to the dome. Alan Whint was surprised to find Lellie there; clearly nobody had told him about her. He interrupted Duncan's explanations to say:

"Won't you introduce me to your wife?"

Duncan did so, without grace. He resented the reproving tone in the man's voice; nor did he care for the way he greeted Lellie just as if she were an Earth woman. He was also aware that he had noticed the bruise on her cheek that the colour did not altogether cover. In his mind he classified Alan Whint as one of the smooth, snooty type, and hoped that there was not going to be trouble with him.

It could be, indeed, it was, a matter of opinion who made the trouble when it boiled up some three months later. There had already been several occasions when it had lurked uneasily near. Very likely it would have come into the open long before had Whint's work not taken him out of the dome so much. The moment of touch-off came when Lellie lifted her eyes from the book she was reading to ask: "What does 'female emancipation' mean?"

Alan started to explain. He was only half-way through the first sentence when Duncan broke in:

"Listen – who told you to go putting ideas into her head?"

Alan shrugged his shoulders slightly, and looked at him.

"That's a damn silly question," he said. "And, anyway, why shouldn't she have ideas? Why shouldn't anyone?"

"You know what I mean."

"I never understand you guys who apparently can't *say* what you mean. Try again."

"All right then. What I mean is this: you come here with your ritzy ways and your snazzy talk, and right from the start you start shoving your nose into things that aren't your business. You begin right off by treating her as if she was some toney dame back home."

"I hoped so. I'm glad you noticed it."

"And do you think I didn't see why?"

"I'm quite sure you didn't. You've such a well-grooved mind. You think, in your simple way, that I'm out to get your girl, and you resent that with all the weight of two thousand, three hundred and sixty pounds. But you're wrong: I'm not."

Duncan was momentarily thrown off his line, then:

"My *wife*," he corrected. "She may be only a dumb Mart, but she's legally my wife: and what I say goes."

"Yes, Lellie is a Mart, as you call it; she may even be your wife, for all I know to the contrary; but dumb, she certainly is not. For one example, look at the speed with which she's learned to read – once someone took the trouble to show her how. I don't think you'd show up any too bright yourself in a language where you only knew a few words, and which you couldn't read."

"It was none of your business to teach her. She didn't need to read. She was all right the way she was."

"The voice of the slaver down the ages. Well, if I've done nothing else, I've cracked up your ignorance racket there."

"And why? – So she'll think you're a great guy. The same reason you talk all toney and smarmy to her. So you'll get her thinking you're a better man than I am."

"I talk to her the way I'd talk to any woman anywhere – only more simply since she's not had the chance of an education. If she does think I'm a better man, then I agree with her. I'd be sorry if I couldn't."

"I'll show you who's the better man—" Duncan began.

"You don't need to. I knew when I came here that you'd be a waster, or you'd not be on this job – and it didn't take long for me to find out that you were a goddam bully, too. Do you suppose I've not noticed the bruises? Do you think I've enjoyed having to listen to you bawling out a girl whom you've deliberately kept ignorant and defenceless when she's potentially ten times the sense you have? Having to watch a *clodkopf* like you lording it over your 'dumb Mart'? You emetic!"

In the heat of the moment, Duncan could not quite remember what an emetic was, but anywhere else the man would not have got that far before he had waded in to break him up. Yet, even through his anger, twenty years of space experience held – as little more than a boy he had learnt the ludicrous futility of weightless scrapping, and that it was the angry man who always made the bigger fool of himself.

Both of them simmered, but held in. Somehow the occasion was patched up and smoothed over, and for a time things went on much as before.

Alan continued to make his expeditions in the small craft which he had brought with him. He examined and explored other parts of the satellite, returning with specimen pieces of rock which he tested, and arranged, carefully labelled, in cases. In his off times he occupied himself, as before, in teaching Lellie.

That he did it largely for his own occupation as well as from a feeling that it should be done, Duncan did not altogether deny; but he was equally sure that in continued close association one thing leads to another, sooner or later. So far, there had been nothing between them that he could put his finger on – but Alan's term had still some nine months to go, even if he were relieved to time. Lellie was already hero-worshipping. And he was spoiling her more every day by this fool business of treating her as if she were an Earth woman. One day they'd come alive to it – and the next step would be that they would see him as an obstacle that would be better removed. Prevention being better than cure, the sensible course was to see that the situation should never develop. There need not be any fuss about it . . .

There was not.

One day Alan Whint took off on a routine flight to prospect somewhere on the other side of the satellite. He simply never came back. That was all.

There was no telling what Lellie thought about it; but something seemed to happen to her.

For several days she spent almost all her time standing by the main window of the living-room, looking out into the blackness at the flaring pinpoints of light. It was not that she was waiting or hoping for Alan's return – she knew as well as Duncan himself that when thirty-six hours had gone by there was no chance of that. She said nothing. Her expression maintained its exasperating look of slight surprise, unchanged. Only in her eyes was there any perceptible difference: they looked a little less live, as if she had withdrawn herself further behind them.

Duncan could not tell whether she knew or guessed anything. And there seemed to be no way of finding out without planting the idea in her mind – *if* it were not already there. He was, without admitting it too fully to himself, nervous of her – too nervous to turn on her roundly for the time she spent vacantly mooning out of the window. He had an uncomfortable awareness of how many ways there were for even a dimwit to contrive a fatal accident in such a place. As a precaution he took to fitting new air-bottles to his suit every time he went out, and checking that they were at full pressure. He also took to placing a piece of rock so that the outer door of the airlock could not close behind him. He made a point of noticing that his food and hers came straight out of the same pot, and watched her closely as she worked. He still could not decide whether she knew, or suspected . . . After they were sure that he was gone, she never once mentioned Alan's name . . .

The mood stayed on her for perhaps a week. Then

it changed abruptly. She paid no more attention to the blackness outside. Instead, she began to read, voraciously and indiscriminately.

Duncan found it hard to understand her absorption in the books, nor did he like it, but he decided for the moment not to interfere. It did, at least, have the advantage of keeping her mind off other things.

Gradually he began to feel easier. The crisis was over. Either she had not guessed, or, if she had, she had decided to do nothing about it. Her addiction to books, however, did not abate. In spite of several reminders by Duncan that it was for *company* that he had laid out the not inconsiderable sum of £2,360, she continued, as if determined to work her way through the station's library.

By degrees the affair retreated into the background. When the next ship came Duncan watched her anxiously in case she had been biding her time to hand on her suspicions to the crew. It turned out, however, to be unnecessary. She showed no tendency to refer to the matter, and when the ship pulled out, taking the opportunity with it, he was relievedly able to tell himself that he had really been right all along – she was just a dumb Mart: she had simply forgotten the Alan Whint incident, as a child might.

And yet, as the months of his term ticked steadily away, he found that he had, bit by bit, to revise that estimate of dumbness. She was learning from books things that he did not know himself. It even had some advantages, though it put him in a position he did not care for – when she asked, as she sometimes did now, for explanations, he found it unpleasant to be stumped by a Mart. Having the practical man's suspicion of book-acquired knowledge, he felt it necessary to explain to her how much of the stuff in the books was a lot of nonsense, how they never really came to grips with the problems of life as he had lived it. He cited instances from his own affairs, gave examples from his experience, in fact, he found himself teaching her.

She learnt quickly, too; the practical as well as the book stuff. Of necessity he had to revise his opinion of Marts slightly more – it wasn't that they were altogether dumb as he had thought, just that they were normally too dumb to start using the brains they had. Once started, Lellie was a regular vacuum-cleaner for knowledge of all sorts: it didn't seem long before she knew as much about the way-load station as he did himself. Teaching her was not at all what he had intended, but it did provide an occupation much to be preferred to the boredom of the early days. Besides, it had occurred to him that she was an appreciating asset . . .

Funny thing, that. He had never before thought of education as anything but a waste of time, but now it seriously began to look as if, when he got her back to Mars, he might recover quite a bit more of the £2,360 than he had expected. Maybe she'd make quite a useful secretary to someone . . . He started to instruct her in elementary book-keeping and finance – insofar as he knew anything about it . . .

The months of service kept on piling up; going a very great deal faster now. During the later stretch, when one had acquired confidence in his ability to get through without cracking up, there was a comfortable feeling about sitting quietly out there with the knowledge of the money gradually piling up at home.

A new find opened up on Callisto, bringing a slight increase in deliveries to the satellite. Otherwise, the routine continued unchanged. The infrequent ships called in, loaded up, and went again. And then, surprisingly soon, it was possible for Duncan to say to himself: "Next ship but one, and I'll be through!" Even more surprisingly soon there came the day when he stood on the metal apron outside the dome, watching a ship lifting herself off on her under-jets and dwindling upwards into the black sky, and was able to tell himself: "That's the last time I'll see that! When the next ship lifts off this dump, I'll be aboard her, and then – boy, oh boy . . . !"

He stood watching her, one bright spark among the others, until the turn of the satellite carried her below his horizon. Then he turned back to the airlock – and found the door shut . . .

Once he had decided that there was going to be no repercussion from the Alan Whint affair he had let his habit of wedging it open with a piece of rock lapse. Whenever he emerged to do a job he left it ajar, and it stayed that way until he came back. There was no wind, or anything else on the satellite to move it. He laid hold of the latch-lever irritably, and pushed. It did not move.

Duncan swore at it for sticking. He walked to the edge of the metal apron, and then jetted himself a little round the side of the dome so that he could see in at the window. Lellie was sitting in a chair with the spring-cover fixed across it, apparently lost in thought. The inner door of the airlock was standing open, so of course the outer could not be moved. As well as the safety-locking device, there was all the dome's air pressure to hold it shut.

Forgetful for the moment, Duncan rapped on the thick glass of the double window to attract her attention; she could not have heard a sound through there, it must have been the movement that caught her eye and caused her to look up. She turned her head, and gazed at him, without moving. Duncan stared back at her. Her hair was still waved, but the eyebrows, the colour, all the other touches that he had insisted upon to make her look as much like an Earth woman as possible, were gone. Her eyes looked back at him, set hard as stones in that fixed expression of mild astonishment.

Sudden comprehension struck Duncan like a physical shock. For some seconds everything seemed to stop.

He tried to pretend to both of them that he had not understood. He made gestures to her to close the inner door of the airlock. She went on staring back at him, without moving. Then he noticed the book she was holding in her hand, and recognized it. It was not one of the books which the Company had supplied for the station's library. It was a book of verse, bound in blue. It had once belonged to Alan Whint . . .

Panic suddenly jumped out at Duncan. He looked down at the row of small dials across his chest, and then sighed with relief. She had not tampered with his air-supply: there was pressure there enough for thirty hours or so. The sweat that had started out on his brow grew cooler as he regained control of himself. A touch on the jet sent him floating back to the metal apron where he could anchor his magnetic boots, and think it over.

What a bitch! Letting him think all this time that she had forgotten all about it. Nursing it up for him. Letting him work out his time while she planned. Waiting until he was on the very last stretch before she tried her game on. Some minutes passed before his mixed anger and panic settled down and allowed him to think.

Thirty hours! Time to do quite a lot. And even if he did not succeed in getting back into the dome in twenty or so of them, there would still be the last, desperate resort of shooting himself off to Callisto in one of the cylinder-crates.

Even if Lellie were to spill over later about the Whint business, what of it? He was sure enough that she did not know *how* it had been done. It would only be the word of a Mart against his own. Very likely they'd put her down as space-crazed.

. . . All the same, some of the mud might stick; it would be better to settle with her here and now – besides, the cylinder idea was risky; only to be considered in the last extremity. There were other ways to be tried first.

Duncan reflected a few minutes longer, then he jetted himself over to the smaller dome. In there, he threw out the switches on the lines which brought power down from the main batteries charged by the sun-motor. He sat down to wait for a bit. The insulated dome would take some time to lose all its heat, but not very long for a drop in the temperature to become perceptible, and visible on the thermometers, once the heat was off. The small capacity, low voltage batteries that were in the place wouldn't be much good to her, even if she did think of lining them up.

He waited an hour, while the faraway sun set, and the arc of Callisto began to show over the horizon. Then he went back to the dome's window to observe results. He arrived just in time to see Lellie fastening herself into her space-suit by the light of a couple of emergency lamps.

He swore. A simple freezing out process wasn't going to work, then. Not only would the heated suit protect her, but her air supply would last longer than his – and there were plenty of spare bottles in there even if the free air in the dome should freeze solid.

He waited until she had put on the helmet, and then switched on the radio in his own. He saw her pause at the sound of his voice, but she did not reply. Presently she deliberately switched off her receiver. He did not; he kept his open to be ready for the moment when she should come to her senses.

Duncan returned to the apron, and reconsidered. It had been his intention to force his way into the dome without damaging it, if he could. But if she wasn't to be frozen out, that looked difficult. She had the advantage of him in air – and though it was true that in her space-suit she could neither eat nor drink, the same, unfortunately, was true for him. The only way seemed to be to tackle the dome itself.

Reluctantly, he went back to the small dome again, and connected up the electrical cutter. Its cable looped behind him as he jetted across to the main dome once more. Beside the curving metal wall, he paused to think out the job – and the consequences. Once he was through the outer shell there would be a space; then the insulating material – that was okay, it would melt away like butter, and without oxygen it could not catch fire. The more awkward part was going to come with the inner metal skin. It would be wisest to start with a few small cuts to let the air-pressure down – and stand clear of it: if it were all to come out with a whoosh he would stand a good chance in his weightless state of being blown a considerable distance by it. And what would she do? Well, she'd very likely try covering up the holes as he made them – a bit awkward if she had the sense to use asbestos packing: it'd have to be the whoosh then . . . Both shells could be welded up again before he re-aerated the place from cylinders . . . The small loss of insulating material wouldn't matter . . . Okay, better get down to it, then . . .

He made his connexions, and contrived to anchor himself enough to give some purchase. He brought the cutter up, and pressed the trigger-switch. He pressed again, and then swore, remembering that he had shut off the power.

He pulled himself back along the cable, and pushed the switches in again. Light from the dome's windows suddenly illuminated the rocks. He wondered if the restoration of power would let Lellie know what he was doing. What if it did? She'd know soon enough, anyway.

He settled himself down beside the dome once more. This time the cutter worked. It took only a few minutes to slice out a rough, two-foot circle. He pulled the piece out of the way, and inspected the opening. Then, as he levelled the cutter again, there came a click in his receiver: Lellie's voice spoke in his ear:

"Better not try to break in. I'm ready for that."

He hesitated, checking himself with his finger on the switch, wondering what counter-move she could have thought up. The threat in her voice made him uneasy. He decided to go round to the window, and see what her game was, if she had one.

She was standing by the table, still dressed in her space-suit, fiddling with some apparatus she had set up there. For a moment or two he did not grasp the purpose of it.

There was a plastic food-bag, half-inflated, and attached in some way to the table top. She was adjusting a metal plate over it to a small clearance. There was a wire, scotch-taped to the upper side of the bag. Duncan's eye ran back along the wire to a battery, a coil, and on to a detonator attached to a bundle of half a dozen blasting-sticks . . .

He was uncomfortably enlightened. It was very simple – ought to be perfectly effective. If the air-pressure in the room should fall, the bag would expand: the wire would make contact with the plate: up would go the dome . . .

Lellie finished her adjustment, and connected the second wire to the battery. She turned to look at him through the window. It was infuriatingly difficult to believe that behind that silly surprise frozen on her face she could be properly aware what she was doing.

Duncan tried to speak to her, but she had switched off, and made no attempt to switch on again. She simply stood looking steadily back at him as he blustered and raged. After some minutes she moved across to a chair, fastened the spring-cover across herself, and sat waiting.

"All right then," Duncan shouted inside his helmet. "But you'll go up with it, damn you!" Which was, of course, nonsense since he had no intention whatever of destroying either the dome or himself.

He had never learnt to tell what went on behind that silly face – she might be coldly determined, or she might not. If it had been a matter of a switch which she must press to destroy the place he might have risked her nerve failing her. But this way, it would be he who operated the switch, just as soon as he should make a hole to let the air out.

Once more he retreated to anchor himself on the apron. There must be *some* way round, some way of getting into the dome without letting the pressure down . . . He thought hard for some minutes, but if there was such a way, he could not find it – besides, there was

no guarantee that she'd not set the explosive off herself
if she got scared . . .

No – there was no way that he could think of. It would
have to be the cylinder-crate to Callisto.

He looked up at Callisto, hanging huge in the sky now,
with Jupiter smaller, but brighter, beyond. It wasn't so
much the flight, it was the landing there. Perhaps if he
were to cram it with all the padding he could find . . .
Later on, he could get the Callisto fellows to ferry him
back, and they'd find some way to get into the dome, and
Lellie would be a mighty sorry girl – *mighty* sorry . . .

Across the levelling there were three cylinders lined
up, charged and ready for use. He didn't mind admitting
he was scared of that landing: but, scared or not, if she
wouldn't even turn on her radio to listen to him, that
would be his only chance. And delay would do nothing
for him but narrow the margin of his air-supply.

He made up his mind, and stepped off the metal apron.
A touch on the jets sent him floating across the levelling
towards the cylinders. Practice made it an easy thing for
him to manoeuvre the nearest one on to the ramp. Another
glance at Callisto's inclination helped to reassure him; at
least he would reach it all right. If their beacon there was
not switched on to bring him in, he ought to be able to
call them on the communication radio in his suit when
he got closer.

There was not a lot of padding in the cylinder. He
fetched more from the others, and packed the stuff in.
It was while he paused to figure out a way of triggering
the thing off with himself inside, that he realized he
was beginning to feel cold. As he turned the knob up
a notch, he glanced down at the meter on his chest – in
an instant he knew . . . She had known that he would fit
fresh air-bottles and test them; so it had been the battery,
or more likely, the circuit, she had tampered with. The
voltage was down to a point where the needle barely
kicked. The suit must have been losing heat for some
time already.

He knew that he would not be able to last long – perhaps not more than a few minutes. After its first stab, the fear abruptly left him, giving way to an impotent fury. She'd tricked him out of his last chance, but, by God, he could make sure she didn't get away with it. He'd be going, but just one small hole in the dome, and he'd not be going alone . . .

The cold was creeping into him, it seemed to come lapping at him icily through the suit. He pressed the jet control, and sent himself scudding back towards the dome. The cold was gnawing in at him. His feet and fingers were going first. Only by an immense effort was he able to operate the jet which stopped him by the side of the dome. But it needed one more effort, for he hung there, a yard or so above the ground. The cutter lay where he had left it, a few feet beyond his reach. He struggled desperately to press the control that would let him down to it, but his fingers would no longer move. He wept and gasped at the attempt to make them work, and with the anguish of the cold creeping up his arms. Of a sudden, there was an agonizing, searing pain in his chest. It made him cry out. He gasped – and the unheated air rushed into his lungs, and froze them . . .

In the dome's living-room Lellie stood waiting. She had seen the space-suited figure come sweeping across the levelling at an abnormal speed. She understood what it meant. Her explosive device was already disconnected; now she stood alert, with a thick rubber mat in her hand, ready to clap it over any hole that might appear. She waited one minute, two minutes . . . When five minutes had passed she went to the window. By putting her face close to the pane and looking sideways she was able to see the whole of one space-suited leg and part of another. They hung there horizontally, a few feet off the ground. She watched them for several minutes. Their gradual downward drift was barely perceptible.

She left the window, and pushed the mat out of her

hand so that it floated away across the room. For a moment or two she stood thinking. Then she went to the bookshelves and pulled out the last volume of the encyclopaedia. She turned the pages, and satisfied herself on the exact status and claims which are connoted by the word 'widow'.

She found a pad of paper and a pencil. For a minute she hesitated, trying to remember the method she had been taught, then she started to write down figures, and became absorbed in them. At last she lifted her head, and contemplated the result: £5,000 per annum for five years, at 6 per cent compound interest, worked out at a nice little sum – quite a small fortune for a Martian.

But then she hesitated again. Very likely a face that was not set for ever in a mould of slightly surprised innocence would have frowned a little at that point, because, of course, there was a deduction that had to be made – a matter of £2,360.

DOCTOR WHO

(BBC TV, 1963–?)
Starring: William Hartnell, Roslyn de Winter
& Martin Jarvis
Directed by Richard Martin
Story 'The Lair of the Zarbi' by Bill Strutton

The phenomenon of *Doctor Who* is almost without precedent in television history. Although off the screen at the time of writing – only temporarily, its countless millions of fans around the world hope – this SF series which was devised in 1963 by the BBC's new Head of Drama, Sydney Newman (recently recruited from ABC where he had also been instrumental in the success of *Armchair Theatre*), embodies a concept that literally gives it an indefinite life. The idea of a Time Lord who can travel wherever he pleases and 'regenerate' at will, allows any producer to recast his leading actor without destroying the audience's identification with the central character. Hence there have been seven actors so far playing the man known only as the Doctor from the planet Gallifrey who journeys in his space vehicle, the TARDIS – which resembles an old-fashioned London police call box – confronting the enemies of interplanetary law and order: crotchety William Hartnell; the cosmic hobo Patrick Troughton; flamboyant Jon Pertwee; exhuberant Tom Baker; youthful Peter Davison; the brash Colin Baker; and comical Sylvester McCoy. All, of course, have had their companions ranging from leggy beauties given to screaming at any oportunity to streetwise, independently-minded young women.

The fame of the series was, of course, established very early on with the advent of the Daleks who frightened a whole generation of children behind their armchairs. Other favourite monsters have included the Cybermen, the Ice Warriors, the Sea Devils and many more: several of whom have generated the kind of public outcry and newspaper headlines which have given *Doctor Who* its special place in TV legend. The series has not only been well served by its scriptwriters such as the now famous Terry Nation, Kit Pedlar, Gerry Davis, Robert Holmes and Douglas Adams, but has attracted a host of guest stars, too – too numerous, in fact, to list. And to date, there have been almost 700 episodes of the Doctor's adventures . . .

'The Lair of the Zarbi' is based on the characters created by Bill Strutton (1931–) in his memorable adventure in the second season of the programme, 'The Web Planet' (1965), about a world inhabited by the hostile, ant-like Zarbi who are forever persecuting the gentle, moth-shaped Menoptra. The production was a landmark in the history of the series because of the huge cost of costuming every actor and actress from head to foot in layers of make-up plus building a set to resemble a planet with a surface like that of the Moon, all within the confines of the BBC studios. Although the first episode attracted the largest viewing figures for any of William Hartnell's apearances as the Doctor – over ten million – the overheads were so high that the experiment was never repeated. Here, though, as a reminder of that story which helped to establish one of the most famous of all TV Science Fiction series is another of the Doctor's adventure on the planet Vortis . . .

The shock of hearing the voice was so great that Dr Who had barely time to complete the materialisation processes. But old habit was strong, and smoothly and efficiently the *Tardis* slid in through the transdimensional flux and fitted its rearranged atoms into the new sphere. By all the doctor's co-ordinates and calculations this world should be the planet Vortis but just *where* on the planet, or *when* in the time-scale of that world, he could not as yet know. He drove home the last lever and, with hands on the edges of the control panel, panted with excitement. The voice through his radio had been talking in modern English!

He strapped the walkie-talkie apparatus on his shoulders, already clad in the Atmospheric Density Jacket he remembered having needed on his previous visit to this ill-omened world. Then, activating the great door, he stood waiting for it to open, fidgeting with impatience.

This was not at all like the Vortis he remembered, was his first thought as he peered out through the open portals. True, there were several moons in the sky, two of them so close to the planet that they could be seen in daylight. The sparkles he remembered were in the sky also, but the mists were not there, nor the white basaltic needle-like spires. Quite evidently, his *Tardis* had landed him in an entirely different part of the planet. He walked steadily through the doorway, the voice from the radio still murmuring in his ears.

He had first heard it during the materialisation of his ship from intra-dimensional non-space into the real space in which Vortis swam. The voice sounded low and weary and consisted of but few words. It was as though the effort to dredge the words out was almost too much for the throat uttering them. "Help, Help," the voice was muttering. "Beware Zarbi Supremo. Warn Earth. Warn Earth." That was all. It was so tantalisingly obscure that Dr Who was almost dancing with impatience as he set foot outside his ship. But what he saw when he looked round the landscape momentarily drove all else from his mind.

He was on a low plateau, overlooking a broad plain. At least it should have been a plain, for the ground itself seemed flat enough. It was the structures that reared themselves up from that plain that made the eyes almost start from his head. On every side and outwards as far as the horizon, there reared up from the ground a multitude of cone-like structures like dunces' caps, like sugar-loaves, like – and now he knew for certain that he was back on Vortis – just like ant hills. He darted back inside his ship and re-emerged with binoculars.

He trained the glasses on the cones nearest to him and his gaze roamed over the surface, confirming that his first deduction was only too true. These monstrous hills of maybe a hundred feet high were the counterparts of the ant hills or termitaries to be seen in the Southern Hemisphere of Earth and . . . crawling all over them, in and out of their holes, were hordes of the hideous inhabitants of Vortis, the huge ants or termites known as the Zarbi.

Fascinated, he allowed the glasses to lead his gaze over first one immense hill and then another. There they crawled, hundreds, thousands, perhaps millions of them. Those noxious mindless creatures, controlled from a distance by some unknown intelligence, who preyed upon the likeable innocent Butterfly people, the Menoptera, the other species native to Vortis, whom he had encountered on his last visit. He had seen but little of the Zarbi themselves then, but he had heard enough to know that they were to be dreaded.

"Help. Help. Beware Zarbi Supremo!" the voice in his earphone droned on. "Warn Earth. Warn Earth." He started as the voice again penetrated into his consciousness. Somewhere, not too far away from him, was a man of Earth. He seemed to be weak and was perhaps wounded or a prisoner – somewhere in that veritable maze of termitaries. The doctor stared sombrely at the forest of cones and lowered the glasses. On his walkie-talkie there was, of course, a directional aerial and he began to twist the knob, listening as the sound of the voice sank or grew louder.

At last he determined roughly the quarter where the

sound originated. He turned his face in that direction. It looked no different from any other part of the plain of ant hills; but somewhere out there must be the owner of that tired voice, that voice that cried out hopelessly on an alien planet for a rescue of which it had lost all hope. But Dr Who had made up his mind that rescue he would attempt, no matter where it led him or through what perils. That his first greeting on Vortis should be the sound of a human voice, speaking in his own native tongue, was so extraordinary a thing that the doctor knew that fate had directed his hands as they had locked home the controls which had precipitated the *Tardis* into the sphere of Vortis at this precise place and at this precise time.

As he approached the termitaries he was almost deafened by the shrill chirping of the millions of Zarbi as they crawled about their mysterious business. On Earth ants and termites have no real voices, they communicate by rubbing their back legs together. Dr Who reflected that he could very well be mightily in error if he was to assume that these Zarbi were just very large ants or termites. These loathsome creatures could very well be some entirely different type of creature from the ants and termites which had evolved on Earth, even though they were insectile.

They seemed to take no notice of him as he passed, trembling, close to their hills. Of course he avoided getting too close to any of them, for he could see that most of these Zarbi were of the soldier class. This was evident from their powerful huge mandibles, which in a creature of that size could tear the limbs from a man, just as a man might tear apart a roasted chicken.

The voice over the radio was stronger now so that the doctor felt that he was getting very close to its source. Walking as warily as he could and avoiding contact with any of the Zarbi, he trod softly on the sandy surface of the ground, his gaze moving constantly about. Now he switched on his sender and spoke urgently into the microphone. "Help is here," he said. "Direct me to where you are. Give me some landmark to go by. I am coming to you."

But the radio gave him back no reply, only the monotonous low repetition of the message he had first heard. Baffled he glowered round him at the jungle of termitaries and shuddered to think of his own position, one feeble, weaponless Earthman, alone amongst these hordes of malevolent giant insects, searching for the owner of a voice which could not hear him.

Looking for a needle in a haystack would be simplicity itself compared to his task, he told himself irritably. But, he reflected grimly, a needle would glitter, wouldn't it? That was just what he could see ahead of him now . . . a dull glitter that lay athwart two ant hills relatively close to each other. Excitedly now he pressed on until he came to the thing. It was circular and was half buried in the sandy soil. On every side rose the gigantic ant hills and here it lay, like a child's lost ball, unspied by the Zarbi, many of whom were even then crawling over the sand that had gathered on the top. Dr Who sensed that he had reached his objective. He was convinced that inside this sphere was the owner of the voice, now sounding much louder in his earphone. He squatted down on the sand and for five minutes he spoke urgently into his microphone.

But it was soon obvious that whoever was inside the sphere – if indeed there was anyone inside it – either had no receiver or else one that was out of order. He leaned forward and rapped sharply on the metal surface. There was no reaction. He felt in his pocket and producing a torch he began a tattoo on the same place as before. Then he moved on and around, speculating that the hull of a space-ship must be very thick and searching for a thinner place. Thus it was that he came upon the door, half buried in the sand. The hollowness of his knocking told him there was emptiness behind it. Getting to his knees he began to scoop away the sand and soon uncovered the door, a small circle just about large enough for a normal man to wriggle through. In his excitement he leaned against it and the next moment he had fallen in through the doorway and into an open space. The door closed behind him, evidently on powerful springs.

It was hot and close and dark and he reflected that it must be an airlock, now broken, and that there would be another door into the ship proper. His torch soon revealed it and he put his shoulder against the panel. It needed all his strength to force it open against extremely powerful springs, but finally, with a mighty heave, he was inside the ship. Breathing hard through the breathing apparatus necessary for the thin air of Vortis, he got to his feet and smoothed down his clothes. "My goodness," he murmured to himself. "Now here is a very fine thing. Not a soul to greet me. Upon my word—"

Then he stopped, for the voice he had been hearing in his radio was now coming directly to his ear, and it was coming from a cabinet on the opposite wall of the room. He went closer and saw the reels of the recorder going slowly round and round, while the voice seeped hopelessly and monotonously from the speaker, repeating over and over again the appeal for help and the warning. He stared round him bitterly. So this was the end of his search. A tape recorder, endlessly sending out its message while no one lived and breathed here. He was as much alone as he had been before. Exasperated, he stared round him at what was evidently the control cabin of a space-ship. Compared to his *Tardis* it was, of course, a very primitive space-ship but he could recognise many of the principles which in his own ship were so refined that only an expert could have seen the resemblance. A ship like this would require quite a crew. Where were they? Was this ship like the *Marie Celeste*, which was found drifting crewless on the sea of Earth? Just so this space-craft lay, marooned and crewless on this cruel planet of Vortis, so far from where men lived and laughed under the bright sun.

Then it was as though the heavens opened. He heard a voice. Something in him told him this was a human voice and no electronic reproduction. It was calling for help and the sound came from a round port. He struggled and fought with the unfamiliar mechanism and at last the door opened. He put his head through and his heart lightened. There were two people in there, a man and a boy. Both lay on mattresses and the man looked as though he was dead. His eyes were closed and his head had fallen sideways. But the boy was very much alive. He was sitting up on the mattress and crying out to the rescuer. Earth was the boy's original birthplace, the doctor decided. And the Twentieth Century was his period, that was obvious. His name was Gordon Hamilton and he was the son of the man who lay motionless on the mattress.

"All the others have gone," the boy told him. "Father was ill so they left us with food and water and went out to explore. You see we didn't know where we were. We crash-landed and father was injured. The others left us here and went off to get help. We could hear noises outside which told us the planet wasn't uninhabited and so—"

"The voice in the recorder?" asked the doctor. "What is that?"

"Father made that recording before he lost consciousness," Gordon said. "By that time we'd given up all hope that the others would ever return and also we'd seen through the other window those things out there. Dad said they must be for an invasion of Earth – there aren't any other planets inhabited in the Solar System. You should see them, hundreds and hundreds of them—"

"Now, sonny, wait a minute," Dr Who protested. "Not so fast. You talk of the Solar System. Why, this planet is nowhere near – tell me, how long had your ship been travelling? What is her motive-power?"

"Oh, we've been in space for two years," the boy said. "Father's ship moves by anti-gravity and can travel many times the speed of light."

The doctor reflected. This boy quite evidently had not the least notion that Vortis was not even in the Milky

Way. A space-ship travelling even at many times the speed of light would need millions of Earth-years to traverse the waste space between galaxies. There was a mystery here. But this was scarcely the time to argue, he must see what could be done for the poor fellow lying on the mattress.

In spite of all his ministrations, however, he could get no response at all from the unconscious man, although his breathing was even enough. He was bearded, but evidently not old. There seemed to be no injury to the body and, baffled, the doctor got up from his knees and looked round.

"How many were in the crew?" he asked, staring round the small cabin shaped like the segment of a circle, which he judged to be one of the living quarters.

"There were six," Gordon told him. "All scientists, like Father. They took weapons and food and they've been gone five days now. I looked through both ports and saw the space-ships on one side and the big hills on the other. There are things crawling about on the hills. You came from outside – what are they? And where did you come from? Have you a ship here?"

Which question should he answer first, the doctor wondered. The boy did not seem to be aware that the Zarbi he had seen outside were one of the dominant species on this planet. He was evidently thinking in terms of human beings living on this world and assuming that the six crewmen had been captured or killed outside. What a position to find himself in. He went to the other window and looked out. At first, all he could see was a continuation of the multitudes of termitaries.

Then a gleam caught his eye. The things were so superficially like the termitaries that he could see why he had not recognised them before. Now he found he could see scarcely anything else. The things were space-ships of the archair torpedo shape. They were almost as tall as the ant hills but, as he looked, he discerned that their outline was smooth and regular and that they gave out a deceptive gleam. He turned to the boy. "You said they were space-ships, my boy. How did you know that?"

"They couldn't very well be anything else, could they?" and the boy gave a youthful grin. "They're like the rockets they used on Earth in the first half of the century. They must travel by chemical explosions. They'll be slow enough and if we could get the *Solar Queen* repaired we could get back to Earth and warn them of the invasion."

"Bless my soul, boy," snapped Dr Who. "What nonsense are you talking? Warn Earth, indeed! Why, we are millions and millions of miles from Earth. We are in a different space and a different time. And what's this talk of invasion? Who is going to invade Earth?"

"I'm only telling you what Father told me," said the boy stubbornly. "Before he went unconscious he used to lie still as though he was listening. He said there were messages sort of drifting into his mind. He said it was almost like eavesdropping on someone else talking by radio or telephone. But it wasn't either of those because there wasn't any apparatus. He said there was a force on this world which was intent on invading Earth. Water was what they wanted, water and vegetation. There were millions of them but always the talk seemed to be about just one individual, Dad said. He didn't get many details, most of the images that came into his mind didn't have any meaning for him. But the parts about the space-ships were very clear – Father knows about things like that. He'll be very interested in your ship."

"I shouldn't be surprised at that," said the doctor dryly. "Well, all you tell me is very interesting, Gordon, but we are wasting time. I am a scientist. I came here by a-ahem – rather different route than you did. My ship is outside, in a safe place, I hope. What we must do now is to work out some plan of campaign."

"We've time enough," said the boy in a matter-of-fact tone. "Dad says Earth is at present on the other side of the system and it'll be months before this

411

world is in a position, you see, for the space-ships to travel there."

Dr Who looked at him curiously. "Did your father tell you any more about his ideas as to where this planet is?" he asked.

"Oh, yes," said the boy brightly. "It's a rogue planet," he said. "Not one of the Sun's real family. Those moons we can see, he said, are the outer moons of Jupiter, some of them. All the other planets are in the plane of the ecliptic but this one isn't. He said it's been driven into the Solar System under power. He said that if we could get out into the open at night we'd see the Solar System from an angle no other people have ever seen it from."

Dr Who reflected within himself without answering. It sounded all very wild and unlikely and, he told himself, irritably, downright impossible. But then, many of his own voyages would sound impossible to other ordinary people. This boy sounded tough and strong. He had not seemed frightened when the doctor had come upon him, marooned on an alien world, his father motionless and speechless and all his friends vanished. The doctor realised that Gordon would be his only helper in what he had decided must be done.

"We've got to follow your friends," he said tersely. "No use cowering in here. I've got a feeling they won't come back without our help."

The boy caught in his breath. "You mean, they've been captured?" he muttered. "But they all had weapons, they were scientists . . . they . . ."

The doctor looked at him. The boy looked frightened enough now that the situation was put coldly to him. But this was no time for squeamishness.

"We've got to go and find them," he said as he got up. "Your father is as comfortable as we can make him. We'll take food and weapons and we'll secure your ship. And we've got to hurry. Five days, you say. We haven't a moment to lose."

After five days of confinement, the boy seemed glad

enough to go outside the marooned ship once the doctor had convinced him that his father would be in no greater danger alone and unconscious than with his son there, powerless to help him. They emerged from the broken airlock and the boy stood still, thunderstruck, staring round him.

"I saw it from the window," he stammered. "But I couldn't really believe. Why, they're insects – they're ants. They must be all as big as men. How can that be? Where are the *people* of this world?"

"These are the people of this world, which is called Vortis, Gordon," said Dr Who firmly. "They are named the Zarbi and they are one of two dominant races on this planet. I've met the others, a gentle, peaceful race, almost like Earth butterflies with great wings. They talk and they, too, are as big as men. But here I see none of the Menoptera, this is all Zarbi territory."

They stood looking in wonder round them. The crawling busy Zarbi seemed to be taking no more notice of them than they had of the doctor when he had passed them alone before finding the *Solar Queen*. Busily and furiously they crawled hither and thither about their mysterious business, each one seeming to be furiously intent on some unknown and urgent task. It was this furious haste that directed the doctor's attention to several of the creatures lying motionless on the sand between two of the hills. Maybe half a dozen in number they lay as still as stones. He cautiously led the way and they both stood looking down on them.

"Are they dead?" asked Gordon with a little shudder.

Dr Who gave the nearest Zarbi form a touch with the toe of his boot. It gave out a metallic ring and he started. "They're not dead, my boy," he said. "They've never even been alive. These are dummies, Gordon, dummies, or should I say robots? I wonder what is inside them."

Gordon looked round fearfully. It was evidently very strange to him that these hordes of loathsome huge insects appeared quite unaware of the existence amongst them of the humans. But Dr Who was not taking any notice at all of the creatures, he was too intent on this find.

"Upon my soul," he muttered. "It is only too true, these really are robots. Look, they are made of metal and they can be opened up and, do you know, a most ingenious idea occurs to me. Quick, lend a hand here. If we can use two of these things, we can follow the trail of your friends and see where it leads to and what has happened to them. Help me with this plate, it lifts off and inside . . . oh, my goodness gracious, what have we here?"

Inside the robot Zarbi there was indeed an inhabitant and Dr Who's memory went back to his previous visit to Vortis. It had then been in another galaxy but now it had crossed intergalactic space and was in the Milky Way. How many ages had passed since then? And yet these Earth people were of the modern era; time was indeed filled with paradoxes.

It was a dead Menoptera that lay inside the robot Zarbi and, with a certain amount of reverence, Dr Who removed the body from its case. "Quick, quick," he directed the boy. "That other one there, open it up, remove the body and get inside. We'll then lie still and talk and try to investigate the controls of these things. Without them we wouldn't get very far among those millions of brutes out there."

"But they aren't taking any notice of us," Gordon objected. "I don't like the idea of being cooped up in that dark thing. Can't we just leave them and go on and trust to luck? The Zarbi aren't interfering with us at all."

"That can't last," said the doctor testily. "Do as I say, boy. It's our best chance." He was mollified to see that Gordon at last gave way. As they lay inside the great metal replicas of the Zarbi, with the thorax plates half-open, Dr Who looked at anything that might be thought of as a control of these awkward creatures. In the dim light he could see levers which might move the legs and the feelers, the thorax and the abdomen.

The eyes, though seeming compound from outside, were clear enough vision-plates from inside. As he tried a few tentative experiments he heard a frightened squeal from Gordon. The great Zarbi robot, with the doctor inside, stood up on six legs and waved its feelers about. Inside the doctor chuckled.

"It looks so real," said the boy, "that I was scared. How did you do it? Oh, I can feel now, these levers and handles. It isn't too hard, is it? I say, this is a bit of fun, isn't it? We can go anywhere in these things."

"Yes, yes, anywhere," said the doctor. "The trouble will be to determine which way we *shall* go. There'll be no trails in this soft sand and these forests of ant hills are so confusing."

"I say," came Gordon's excited voice. "I've just thought of something. All the men had walkie-talkies, like that one of yours. If you send out a signal, at least some of them might hear it and reply."

"Now, why didn't I think of that?" mused Dr Who to himself as he switched on his radio. With the metal antenna protruding through the half-open thorax plate of his robot he sent out a powerful wave-band, designed to radiate to the outermost limit of the range of his set. The result of his action was astonishing in the extreme and was a total surprise to both of them. A sudden dead silence descended on the whole scene around them. Through the eye-plates the doctor saw that every one of the Zarbi in his view had stopped in its tracks as still as a stone. The sounds of their myriad cricket chirpings died away into utter silence, and on the surface of every termitary the hordes of Zarbi lay motionless, as though dead. The reason came to him like a thunderclap and feverishly he switched off his set and stayed trembling and sweating inside his metal prison.

"Can you hear me, Gordon?" he whispered after a while, and there came a muffled murmured reply. "I won't be able to use the radio, after all. You can see what has happened. There is something not too far away from us that is receiving our wave. Did you notice how all the Zarbi out there stopped moving and trilling as soon as I switched on? They're still motionless and silent. If I switch on again whatever it is will be able to get our location."

"The others have been captured then," came Gordon's hoarse reply. "Each of them had a walkie-talkie receiver but we've never heard any signal from any of them for four days. The last signal was cut off in the middle of a sentence."

"What did the message say?" asked Dr Who urgently.

Gordon considered a moment. "Something about being very dark and very hot – I didn't really pay much attention."

"Tut, tut," snapped the doctor angrily. "That might have told us quite a lot. Now, listen carefully, Gordon. Stay absolutely still where you are. Don't touch any of those controls at all. We'll have to wait and see. It's obvious that all the Zarbi out there are controlled at a distance in some weird way. These robot Zarbi were operated by Menoptera who were killed in some unknown way. I can't think when I've ever been in such hideous danger – there must be millions of those beasts out there."

"They're moving again, look," came an excited murmur from Gordon.

It was true. The Zarbi hordes had come to life and were moving. But now there was none of the haphazard zigzagging about they had seen before. Now their movement was like a surge of the sea, all in one direction. The sounds of their shrill trilling note rose in crescendo all around them and the thunder of those millions of feet and feelers made the ground tremble. The doctor operated his controls quickly and turned. A vast wave of the creatures was approaching them from the rear. On every side they were surrounded by approaching Zarbi. They would be swept along by a tidal wave of the hurrying Zarbi unless they could do something to avoid it. But escape proved impossible. He called out sharply to Gordon.

"Close the plate and hang on, boy, we're going to be swept along wherever these monsters are going. It's like a landslide, an avalanche."

His words were swept away as the robot moved along with the multitude of Zarbi. Like corks on a turbulent sea they were carried along, over sandy ground, through and around the ant hills, past the great forest of torpedo ships.

Then Dr Who saw what was obviously their destination. It towered up over twice the height of all the other ant hills. It was squatter than the others too and there was only one entrance, not a number of holes like all the others, but a great black gaping hole at the base of the conical mountain. Within minutes the doctor and Gordon, inside their robot Zarbi, were swept along with the hordes into the darkness inside. By some miracle they were not separated and as soon as the doctor could manage it he manipulated his levers so that one of the robot feelers was round the cleft between the thorax and the abdomen of Gordon's steed. It locked there and he quickly locked the lever. Together they had a chance, but if they were separated their plight would be hopeless indeed.

The heat and the smells were almost overpowering and the doctor felt as though he would faint at any moment. But he knew he must hang on to consciousness as long as possible. Once let either of them lose control of their robot and they would be trampled to a sticky paste by the myriads of scurrying feet.

The Zarbi were being impelled in their head-long rush by some remote, but imperative call, he decided, for this was so obviously different from the previous random crawlings of the things. This great termitary must be the haunt of their ruler, or controller, great queen or whatever thing dominated these hordes of mindless creatures. Willy nilly, they were being swept along towards that thing. In reality this was just what he had wanted, the doctor thought wryly, and he shuddered. What sort of a mess had he landed himself in now? But the plight of this ill-fated expedition from Earth could not have been ignored. That he knew very well.

How did the Menoptera fit into all this? Was it an attempt by them to invade Zarbi territory by penetrating into it disguised as the native Zarbi? Or were the few they had seen merely spies? In that case why had they been killed, and how? There had been no time to examine the body he had hauled from the robot.

The air grew closer and hotter and now, through his vision-plates in the huge eyes of the thing, the doctor could see dim lights. What they were he could not discern: whether they were natural lights, such as fireflies or phosphorescence, or whether they were mechanical. By now he was a little lightheaded and he was ready to credit the mysterious something, towards which they were obviously being carried, with miraculous powers and unheard-of technology. But the Zarbi were after all, he told himself, merely huge insects, weren't they? But were they merely insects? What about that forest of torpedo space-craft outside? What about the radio? And what, to crown it all, about the mysterious control under which all these myriads of Zarbi were moving?

It was a nightmare journey. Afterwards, Dr Who scarcely knew whether he had dreamed it all; whether he had really seen and heard all he remembered or whether he had imagined it all. At the time it all seemed real enough but dreams sometimes have a quality of reality. There were caverns in which there was machinery, of that he was certain, *at the time*. He saw and heard great engines and vast furnaces with hordes of the Zarbi working round them. These would be the worker Zarbi, while the host in the midst of which they were being swept would be the soldiers.

He remembered the great mandibles of the robot in which he was imprisoned. Could it be possible that these monsters practised engineering? The idea was so fantastic that at first he scouted it. But then who or what had built those space-ships? And he was quite sure that the forms he saw working round the fires and at the machines were Zarbi.

They passed great galleries in which hung suspended, like sides of meat in a cold-store, thousands and thousands of grey shrouded forms. Of course, these would be the larvae of these creatures, the nurseries where the young ones were raised to make way for the dead Zarbi. Like grey unmoving spectres the rows and rows of larvae hung and the doctor shuddered violently.

A great opening to one side revealed, in a lightning glimpse, what he had suspected from the beginning. Perhaps two or three hundred feet in length she lay, a bloated queen with a host of workers feeding her and stroking her and attending to her wants. He saw and then it was gone and he felt very sick. There would be many of these queens in a termitary as large as this and from them had come the countless hordes of the Zarbi from outside.

Now the pace was slackening and Dr Who found a little more opportunity to see where they were being taken. Also the passages and the galleries were opening out. He felt certain that they were by now far underground, judging by the heat and the rising pressure. There came a time when the tide that bore them on stopped completely and they were at rest. Dazedly the doctor hung in his robot and then, moving gently, he knocked against the thing that held Gordon. An answering knock told him that the boy was at least alive. There had been no chance for them to communicate during that headlong flight.

It was like a vast amphitheatre, the doctor saw as he moved the great metal head from side to side, peering through the huge eye-plates. Rank upon rank of the Zarbi were there in great semi-circular rows, their number almost countless and all of them very still. Almost against his will his gaze was slowly, inexorably, drawn towards the middle of the great throng, where something sat upon a raised dais, with a glowing light shining down upon it from a roof that was almost out of sight. As the doctor's eyes reluctantly reached it, he recoiled in horror and downright disbelief.

That it was a Zarbi was obvious enough, for its form was the same as that of all the others crowding round him motionless on all sides.

But its size! It towered perhaps twenty feet tall standing on its dais, three times the height of a normal Zarbi and completely motionless on its pedestal.

The doctor tore away his eyes to gaze in startled astonishment at another scene. In a cleared space in front of the gigantic Zarbi were two parties of creatures, and one party was human. There were six of them and they were standing like marble statues in a tight group. Opposite them was another party and Dr Who knew that these were Menoptera, although they were wingless and as motionless as the human beings. He heard the hoarse voice of Gordon close by. "They're down there. They're still alive, all of them. How are we going to escape with them from here?"

"A very good question, my boy," muttered the doctor grimly. "If you have any ideas, now is the time to express them. I confess that at this very moment I must admit myself totally baffled. We got in easily enough, but I fancy it's going to be mightily harder to get out, hm?"

He could see now that all the members of each of the two parties, evidently all prisoners, were quite still as if made of stone. He tried to remember all he knew about the insect world of Earth, which was indeed remarkably little. Anyway, why try to relate these Zarbi to Earth ants or termites, or whatever? The conclusions would be quite mistaken. He went on examining the scene closely and saw that all the prisoners wore something that looked like a loose collar or ring round their necks. It shone a little and fitted very loosely. He watched as one of the Zarbi attendants on the Zarbi Supremo, for that is what the doctor had called the creature in his own mind, moved forward. The creature's mandibles hovered above the head of one of the motionless Menoptera prisoners and the ring was lifted from the Menoptera's neck. In the silence the doctor could just hear the voice of the Menoptera speaking to Zarbi Supremo up on its dais.

It was really most exasperating, the doctor thought irritably. He could hear the voice but not the words. From the giant Zarbi there came no sound at all. How it was replying he could get no idea unless perhaps it was through some electronic translator invisible to the doctor from where he stood.

They must somehow get closer to the centre of operations. His robot nudged Gordon's and pushed it forward through the massed ranks of motionless Zarbi. None of them took any notice and gradually inch by inch the two robots edged their way forward until at last they were on the rim of the cleared space. Now Dr Who found that he could hear what the Menoptera was saying.

"You will have to kill every one of the Menoptera on Vortis before we will agree to help you," the soft voice was saying. "We have watched you over the generations as your mighty engines have moved this planet into this alien system. You are transgressing the paths of Nature. Vortis can be made such a world as you want. A very little of the powers you have spent would have done this. But you cannot invade a peaceful world as you plan. First you would have to slaughter all of the creatures that live there. They are not insects, they are mammals and their world is suited to their needs. Vortis can be made suitable to beings of our own species. You say that you need us of the Menoptera as your ambassadors to the humans, because we speak as they do. You would have us speak to them as though we came in peace because you know they would kill you as soon as they saw what you were. Then, when their suspicions were lulled by us, you would turn on them all and exterminate them. We will not help you to do this."

There was a silence and the great Zarbi on the dais moved. A limb angled out and the doctor saw it manipulate a dial on an instrument board beside it. Almost dancing with rage the doctor knew that it was replying to the speaker. But not one sound could he hear. It was obvious, however, that the Menoptera was hearing something. That instrument must be some means by which the Zarbi brainwaves were translated into speech in the brain of the Menoptera.

"You must kill us all then," came the reply from the Menoptera. "It will be war between us as has never happened before. On our hemisphere we are building weapons which will give you pause. We who speak to you now are doomed, that we well know. These humans also will die, for we recognise that in you has arisen a new spirit among the Zarbi, the spirit of cruelty and destruction. We cannot halt you now, we are too few. But later you will not find your task easy, I promise you that."

A limb shot out from the great Zarbi body and hovered above the head of the Menoptera. Like a moth caught in a flame the creature shrivelled and was gone. Dr Who writhed in his excitement and his robot knocked against that of Gordon.

"The mandibles, boy," he cried, discretion now gone. "Operate the mandibles and lift those collars from round the necks of your men. I'll do the same. These creatures round us are all hypnotised. If we are quick enough we may bring it off."

His robot angled forward awkwardly and the mandibles, operated by inside levers, went up over the heads of the human prisoners. First one, then two, then three. Gordon by that time having found the right controls, freed the last three. Dr Who could feel the crackling and surging of electric waves as he worked and it seemed obvious that the great Zarbi was fighting them with its only weapons, weapons which, thank heaven, were proving ineffectual against human organisms.

Then the doctor was out of his robot and dragging Gordon out.

"Your guns," he yelled to the released prisoners, still dazed. "That thing up there. Fire anywhere. Empty your magazines. The head, the thorax, the abdomen, anywhere. We don't know where the brain and nerve centres of that thing are—"

Around them the vast hordes of the Zarbi were awakening as the hypnotic control of the giant creature took hold of them. Their trilling sound grew and grew into a crescendo and drowned the noise of the shots as the six crewmen and the doctor emptied their revolvers into the giant form above them. Many of the shots ricochetted from the hard carapace, but many found their way through chinks in that chitinous armour. The doctor saw the creature stagger, its limbs and feelers thrashing about as though in agony. The great expressionless compound eyes brooded downwards over these lilliputian creatures who were intent on thwarting its dreams of world conquest.

It was like a great building falling when at last death came to it. Even above the shrill chirpings of the Zarbi, the crash of that downfall could be heard. It lay still, a fallen hulk of insectile ambition, while all around it surged the myriads of its fellow-creatures which it had dominated.

While they had been attacking it, all eight humans had felt the thrusting limbs and feelers of the Zarbi striving to overcome them, but they had taken no heed but kept on pumping lead into the giant menace above.

Now the Zarbi were leaving them alone and milling about in the haphazard fashion that seemed to be their natural life. The little group stayed in a tight circle, watching with apprehension; but they were not attacked. Dr Who heaved a sigh of relief, and going over to the group of Menoptera prisoners who were still standing motionless, he released them by lifting from their necks the rings which in some odd way must have hypnotised them. Voices began to speak to him. Not human voices, but the soft furry voices of the folk he remembered from his previous meetings on Vortis with the peaceful Menoptera. But he took no notice. He wanted to be with his own kind again.

"Your father, Gordon, how is he?" asked one of the men. "And you, sir, how in heaven's name did you come in the nick of time? We'd given ourselves up for lost. You're from Earth. Where is your ship? When did you land?"

Dr Who chuckled. "One thing at a time, my friend. First, we've got to get out of here, you know. Even with these Zarbi uncontrolled it's going to be hard."

"Zarbi? Zarbi?" said another crewman. "Are these creatures, these bugs, the Zarbi, then? Are they intelligent?"

"They are no more intelligent than their needs demand," came a soft voice and one of the Menoptera stood at their shoulders. "For many years we and the Zarbi shared this world and lived in peace. They were our servants, our workmen and our cattle. We and the Zarbi gave to each other what the other lacked. But, over the generations, evolution has evolved a mighty intelligence in that creature who dominated them and dreamed of world conquest, even of universe conquest. We had no weapons but we are building some and we came as an expedition to see what they were planning and if we could stop them. Look, there are our people emerging from their robots."

All around them from recumbent Zarbi were emerging many of the Menoptera. These were full-grown magnificent specimens, who spread and shook their wings after their confinement. There were many hundreds of them and at once they began to shepherd the now docile Zarbi and leave a path for the exit of the released prisoners. Wonderingly, the humans followed the first Menoptera party, the wingless ones, no doubt elders among them. Their path led upwards through the galleries and passages, out to the world of day.

Gordon's father still lay unconscious but he was breathing better. The rescued men crowded into their ship in great excitement for they had given up all hope of ever seeing it again.

"If you agree, doctor," one of them said. "We can use your ship to ferry us across to Earth to get equipment to repair our ship. In time we could do it ourselves but with Earth being so relatively near—"

"That's what puzzles me about the whole thing," said Dr Who. "By my calculations this planet should be in another galaxy altogether. But Gordon kept telling me about the moons of Jupiter and all such nonsense as that."

"Not nonsense," laughed a crewman. "We found this planet when we were headed for the moons of Jupiter in fact. How it got here and how long it has been here we don't know. How it's been missed by Earth observers beats me."

"The evil Zarbi intelligence devised mighty engines which drove our planet out of its orbit many, many millions of miles away," explained one of the Menoptera. "It was searching for a green, damp world such as yours. We have only just arrived in your skies but before very long we will leave you and will sweep out of your system to find whatever fate has in store for us."

"Not so fast," said one of the men belligerently. "Those engines of the Big Bug we killed will come in mighty handy for humanity, I can tell you. There'll be many things that creature invented that we can use and profit by."

"What profit can be made out of evil?" came the soft voice. "No, we will use the engines to drive our world on a new orbit out of your sky and then we will destroy them and seal them off. It is not given to creatures to do what Zarbi Supremo was trying to do."

"I heartily agree," said Dr Who enthusiastically. "Now, you men must realise that this planet belongs to the Menoptera and the Zarbi, so long as they keep their places, of course. There must be no thought of using the powers that creature developed to dominate other beings."

"You're crazy, old man," said the other coldly. "And what in thunder do you think we're doing exploring the universe? We're looking for just such set-ups as this, inhabited by weak, unintelligent creatures. The natural resources of this world alone, even without the powers that Big Bug down there developed, will put Earth technology millions of years into the future."

There was a stirring of Menoptera wings and the crewman drew his revolver. The doctor was glad to see that the others hung back, while Gordon remained at his father's side in the globular space-ship. He lifted an arm and felt himself clasped by a pair of tiny furry clawlike hands. He was lifted into the air and he saw that all the Menoptera were rising, those wingless ones being lifted by their flying fellows. He looked down. Angrily, the man was firing his empty revolver up at them and then the scene faded from his sight.

Gently and easily they dropped him beside his *Tardis*. "We have legends in our world," said one of the Menoptera, "of you and your strange vessel. We know we have nothing to fear from you, strange immortal human who can flit in and out of all the ages. We will watch those others and will ensure that they bring no harm to us. It was good that you came to our rescue, for how else could Zarbi Supremo have been toppled from his lofty height?"

The doctor beamed at them. Sheer human ingenuity and refusal to admit defeat had won again, he thought, as he turned and went through the great doorway. Activating the controls that would close it, he wondered just what would be the future of the strange world of Vortis.

THE OUTER LIMITS

(United Artists TV, 1963–5 & 1995–)
Starring: Adam West, Rudy Solari & Peter Marko
Directed by Byron Haskin
Story 'The Invisible Enemy' by Jerry Sohl

According to SF historian **John Baxter**, the original Sixties series, *The Outer Limits* "contained the best science fiction ever to be presented on television." This was despite the fact that the series was ill-fated and misunderstood, he says, and although it was loved by teenage audiences, when it was moved to a late evening slot only confused adult audiences with its odd plots and unconventional narrative style which sealed its fate. The *Encyclopedia of Science Fiction* has gone even further and declared it to be 'more imaginative and intelligent than its more famous competitor on CBS, *The Twilight Zone*.' Now, in 1995, the series has returned to the small screen with all the benefits of colour and digital special effects, but the same basic concept brought up to date. Like *The Twilight Zone*, *Outer Limits* also has its own opening address to viewers. "There is nothing wrong with your television set," the disembodied voice of the announcer declares. "Do not attempt to adjust the picture. We are controling transmission. You are about to experience the awe and mystery which reaches from the inner mind to THE OUTER LIMITS." Despite its sad demise, 49 of the fifty-minute episodes of the series have survived and it has been due in no small measure to the successful reshowing of these stories which have gathered a whole new generation of admirers that the series has at last been revived. The programme was originally created by the playwright Leslie Stevens, but owed much of its originality to producer Joseph Stefano, the man who had written the screenplay for Alfred Hitchcock's most famous movie, *Psycho*. Although Stefano had a tendency to feature monsters as bizarre as anything seen in Doctor Who – and just as likely to terrify viewers – the first series was highlighted by the imagination of its scripts by such fine writers are Harlan Ellison, Jerry Sohl, David Duncan and Meyer Dolinsky, plus the inovative visual style of the major directors, Gerd Oswald, Charles Haas, Leonard Horn and, especially, Byron Haskin the veteran of several famous Hollywood SF movies including *War of the Worlds* (1953), *Conquest of Space* (1955) and *From Earth To The Moon* (1959). The special effects created by the Ray Mercer Company and Projects Unlimited were also way ahead of anything seen on the small screen; as was the bizarre make-up for many of the alien beings which was the handiwork of Wah Chang, Fred Phillips and John Chambers. Once again a number of 'unknown' actors got their early breaks in *Outer Limits* including Robert Culp, Bruce Dern, Martin Landau and David McCallum. The new 1995 series has so far shown itself to be more provocative in its stories, although the quality of the scriptwriting and acting is similarly high. One intriguing episode, 'I, Robot' cleverly linked the past and present by being based on a story by Isaac Asimov and directed by Adam Nimoy, son of the famous Leonard!

Another of the debutants in the original *Outer Limits* was Adam West – two years before he would become famous as TV's Batman – who starred in the chilling drama of 'The Invisible Enemy' about a four-man mission to Mars charged with discovering what has apparently been gobbling up astronauts who land on the planet. The script was by Jerry Sohl (1913–), based on his own short story, and

was yet another example of the ingenious plots that have been a hallmark of his work as a contributor to SF magazines, a novelist (*The Transcendent Man*, 1953; *Costigan's Needle*, 1953; *Point Ultimate*, 1955 & etc.) and writer for television and the movies. Sohl's teleplays for *The Outer Limits* were certainly amongst his very best and also contributed substantially to the programme's enduring legend.

For an hour they had been circling the spot at 25,000 feet while technicians weighed and measured the planet and electronic fingers probed where no eye could see.

And for an hour Harley Allison had sat in the computer room accepting the information and recording it on magnetic tapes and readying them for insertion into the machine, knowing already what the answer would be and resenting what the commander was trying to do.

It was quiet in the ship except for the occasional twitter of a speaker that recited bits of information which Allison dutifully recorded. It was a relief from the past few days of alarm bells and alerts and flashing lights and the drone of the commander's voice over the intercom, even as that had been a relief from the lethargy and mindlessness that comes with covering enormous stellar distances, for it was wonderful to see faces awaken to interest in things when the star drive went off and to become aware of a changing direction and the lessening velocity. Then had eyes turned from books and letters and other faces to the growing pinpoints of the Hyades on the scanners.

Then had Allison punched the key that had released the ship from computer control and gave it to manual, and in the ensuing lull the men of the *Nesbitt* were read the official orders by Commander William Warrick. Then they sat down to controls unmanned for so long to seek out the star among the hundreds in the system, then its fourth planet and, a few hours ago, the small space ship that lay on its side on the desert surface of the planet.

*   *   *

There was laughter and the scrape of feet in the hall and Allison looked up to see Wendell Hallom enter the computer room, followed by several others.

"Well, looks like the rumors were right," Hallom said, eyes squinting up at the live screen above the control panel. The slowly rotating picture showed the half-buried space ship and the four pillars of the force field about it tilted at ridiculous angles. "I suppose you knew all about this, Allison."

"I didn't know any more than you, except we were headed for the Hyades," Allison said. "I just work here, too, you know."

"I wish I was home," Tony Lazzari said, rolling his eyes. "I don't like the looks of that yellow sand. I don't know why I ever joined this man's army."

"It was either join or go to jail," Gordon Bacon said.

"I ought to punch you right in the nose." Lazzari moved toward Bacon who thumbed his nose at him. "In fact, I got a good mind to turn it inside out."

Allison put a big hand on his shoulder, pulled him back. "Not in here you don't. I got enough troubles. That's all I'd need."

"Yeah," Hallom said. "Relax, kid. Save your strength. You're going to need it. See that pretty ship up there with nobody on it?"

"You and the commander," Bacon said. "Why's he got it in for you, Allison?"

"I wouldn't know," Allison said smiling thinly. "I've got a wonderful personality, don't you think?"

Hallom grunted. "Allison's in the Computer Corps, ain't he? The commander thinks that's just like being a passenger along for the ride. And he don't like it."

"That's what happens when you get an old line skipper and try to help him out with a guy with a gadget," Bacon observed.

"It wouldn't be so bad," Homer Petry said at the door, "if it had been tried before."

"Mr Allison," a speaker blared.

"All right, you guys," Allison said. "Clear out." He depressed a toggle. "Yes, Lieutenant?"

"You have everything now, Allison. Might as well run it through."

"The commander can't think of anything else?"

There was a cough. "The commander's standing right here. Shall I ask him?"

"I'll run this right through, Lieutenant."

Commander William Warrick was a fine figure of a man: tall, militant, greying, hatchet-nosed. He was a man who hewed so close to the line that he let little humanity get between, a man who would be perpetually young, for even at fifty there was an absence of paunch, though his eyes held a look of a man who had many things to remember.

He stood for a while at one end of the control room without saying anything, his never-absent map pointer in his right hand, the end of it slapping the open palm of his left hand. His cold eyes surveyed the men who stood crowded shoulder-to-shoulder facing him.

"Men," he said, and his deep voice was resonant in the room, "take a good look at the screen up there." And the eyes of nearly fifty men shifted to the giant screen beside and above him. "That's the *Esther*." The ship was on gyro, circling the spot, and the screen showed a rotation ship on the sand.

"We'll be going down soon and we'll get a better look. But I want you to look at her now because you might be looking at the *Nesbitt* if you're not careful."

The commander turned to look at the ship himself before going on. "The *Esther* is a smaller ship. It had a complement of only eight men. Remember the tense there. *Had*. They disappeared just as the men in the two ships before them did, each carrying eight men

– the *Mordite* and the *Halcyon*. All three ships were sent to look for Traveen Abbott and Lew Gesell, two explorers for the Federation who had to their credit successful landings on more than ninety worlds. They were cautious, experienced and wise. Yet this planet swallowed them up. as it did the men of the three ships that followed."

Commander Warrick paused and looked at them severely. "We're fifty men and I think we have a better chance than an eight-man crew, not just because there are more of us but because we have the advantage of knowing we're against something really deadly. In case you haven't deduced our mission, it is simply to find out what it is and destroy it."

The insignia on the commander's collar and sleeve glittered in the light from the ever-changing screen as the ship circled the site of the *Esther*.

"This is a war ship. We are armed with the latest weapons. And—" his eyes caught Allison's "– we even have a man from the Computer Corps with us, if that can be counted as an advantage."

Allison who stood at the rear of the room behind the assembled soldier-technicians, reddened. "The tapes got us here, Commander."

"We could have made it without them," the commander said without ire. "But we're here with or without tape. But just because we are we're not rushing down there. We know the atmosphere is breathable, the gravity is close to Earth's and there are no unusually dangerous bacteria. All this came from the *Esther* prior to the . . . incident, whatever it was. But we checked again just to make sure. The gravity is nine-tenths that of Earth's, there is a day of twenty-four and a half hours, temperature and humidity tropical at this parallel, the atmosphere slightly less rich in oxygen, though not harmfully so – God only knows how a desert planet like this can have any oxygen at all with so little vegetation and no evident animal life. There is no dangerous radiation from the surface or from the sun. Mr Allison has run the assembled data through his machine – would you care to tell the men what the machine had to say, Allison?"

Allison cleared his throat and wondered what the commander was driving at. "The planet could sustain life, if that's what you mean, Commander."

"But what did the machine say about the inhabitants, Mr Allison?"

"There wasn't enough data for an assumption."

"Thank you. You men can get some idea of how the Computer Corps helps out in situations like this."

"That's hardly fair, Commander," Allison protested. "With more data—"

"We'll try to furnish you with armsful of data." The commander smiled broadly. "Perhaps we might let you collect a little data yourself."

There was laughter at this. "So much for the Computer Corps. We could go down now, but we're circling for eighteen more hours for observation. Then we're going down. Slowly."

The ship came out of the deep blue sky in the early morning and the commander was a man of his word. The *Nesbitt* moved down slowly, beginning at sun-up and ending in the sand within a few hundred feet of the *Esther* in an hour.

"You'd think," Lazzari said as the men filed back into the control room for another briefing, "that the commander has an idea he can talk this thing to death."

"I'd rather be talked to death by the commander than by you," Hallom said. "He has a pleasanter voice."

"I just don't like it, all that sand down there and nothing else."

"We passed over a few green places," Allison corrected. "A few rocky places, too. It's not all sand."

"But why do we have to go down in the middle of it?" Lazzari insisted.

"That's where the other ships went down. Whatever it is attacked them on the sand."

"If it was up to me, I'd say: Let the thing be, whatever it is. Live and let live. That's my motto."

"You're just lazy," said Petry, the thin-faced oldster from Chicago. "If we was pickin' apples you'd be askin' why. If you had your way you'd spend the rest of your life in a bunk."

"Lazy, hell!" Lazzari snorted. "I just don't think we should go poking our nose in where somebody's going to bite it off."

"That's not all they'll bite off, Buster," said Gar Caldwell, a radar and sonics man from Tennessee.

Wang Lee, force field expert, raised his thin oriental eyebrows and said, "It is obvious we know more than our commander. We know, for example, *it* bites. It follows then that it has teeth. We ought to report that to the commander."

The commander strode into the room, map pointer under his arm, bearing erect, shoulders back, head high. Someone called attention and every man stiffened but Allison, who leaned against the door. Commander Warrick surveyed them coldly for a moment before putting them at ease.

"We're dividing into five teams," he said. "Four in the field and the command team here. The rosters will be read shortly and duplicate equipment issued. The lieutenants know the plans and they'll explain them to you. Each unit will have a g-car, force field screen, television and radio for constant communication with the command team. There will be a blaster for each man, nuclear bombardment equipment for the weapons man, and so on."

He put his hands on his hips and eyed them all severely. "It's going to be no picnic. It's hot as hell out there. A hundred degrees in the daytime and no shade. It's eighty at night and the humidity's high. But I want you to find out what it is before it finds out what you are. I don't want any missing men. The Federation's lost three small ships and twenty-four men already. And Mr Allison—"

Allison jerked from the wall at the unexpected calling of his name. "Yes, Commander?"

"You understand this is an emergency situation?"

"Well, yes, Commander."

The commander smiled slyly and Allison could read something other than humor behind his eyes.

"Then you must be aware that, under Federation regulations governing ships in space, the commander exercises unusual privileges regarding his crew and civilians who may be aboard."

"I haven't read the regulation, Commander, but I'll take your word for it that it exists."

"Thank you, Mr Allison." The lip curled ever so slightly. "I'd be glad to read it to you in my quarters immediately after this meeting, except there isn't time. For your information in an emergency situation, though you are merely attached to a ship in an advisory capacity, you come under the jurisdiction of the ship's commander. Since we're short of men, I'm afraid I'll have to make use of you."

Allison balled two big, brown hands and put them behind his back. They had told him at Computer Corps school he might meet men like Commander Warrick – men who did not yet trust the maze of computer equipment that only a few months ago had been made mandatory on all ships of the *Nesbitt* class. It was natural that men who had fought through campaigns with the old logistics and slide-rule tactics were not going to feel immediately at home with computers and the men that went with them. It wasn't easy trusting the courses of their ships or questions of attack and defense to magnetized tape.

"I understand, Commander," Allison said. "I'll be glad to help out in whatever way you think best."

"Good of you, I'm sure." The Commander turned to

one of the lieutenants near him. "Lieutenant Cheevers, break out a blaster for Mr Allison, He may need it."

When the great port was opened, the roasting air that rushed in blasted the faces of the men loading the treadwagons. Allison, the unaccustomed weight of the blaster making him conscious of it, went with several of them down the ramp to look out at the yellow sand.

Viewing it from the surface was different from looking at it through a scanner from above. He squinted his eyes as he followed the expanse to the horizon and found there were tiny carpets of vegetation here and there, a few larger grass islands, a wooded area on a rise far away on the right, mountains in the distance on the left. And above it all was a deep blue sky with a blazing white sun. The air had a burned smell.

A tall lieutenant – Cork Rogers who would lead the first contingent – moved down the ramp into the broiling sun and gingerly stepped into the sand. He sank into it up to his ankles. He came back up, shaking his head. "Even the sand's hot."

Allison went down, the sun feeling like a hot iron on his back, bent over and picked up a handful of sand. It was yellower than Earth sand and he was surprised to find it had very little weight. It was more like sawdust, yet it was granular. He looked at several tiny grains closely, saw that they were hollow. They were easily crushed.

"Why was I born?" Lazzari asked no one in particular, his arms loaded with electrical equipment for the wagon. "And since I was, how come I ever got in this lousy outfit?"

"Better save your breath," Allison said, coming up the ramp and wiping his hands on his trousers.

"Yeah, I know. I'm going to need it." He stuck his nose up and sniffed. "They call that air!"

In a few minutes, the first treadwagon loaded with its equipment and men purred down the ramp on its tracks and into the sand. It waited there, its eye tube already revolving slowly high on its mast above the weapons bridge. The soldier on the bridge was at ready, his tinted visor pulled down. He was actually in the small g-car which could be catapulted at an instant's notice.

Not much later there were four treadwagons in the sand and the commander came down the ramp, a faint breeze tugging at his sleeves and collar.

He took the salute of each of the officers in turn – Lieutenant Cork Rogers of Unit North, Lieutenant Vicky Noromak of Unit East, Lieutenant Glen Foster of Unit West and Lieutenant Carl Quartz of Unit South. They raised the green and gold of the Federation flag as he and the command team stood at attention behind him.

Then the commander's hand whipped down and immediately the purrs of the wagons became almost deafening as they veered from one another and started off through the sand, moving gracefully over the rises, churning powder wakes and leaving dusty clouds.

It was quiet and cool in the control room. Commander Warrick watched the four television panels as they showed the terrain in panorama from out-positions a mile in each direction from the ship. On all of them there were these same things: the endless, drifting yellow sand with its frequent carpets of grass, the space ship a mile away, the distant mountain, the green area to the right.

Bacon sat at the controls for the panels, Petry at his side. Once every fifteen seconds a radio message was received from one of the treadwagon units: "Unit West reporting nothing at 12:18:15." The reports droned out over the speaker system with monotonous regularity. Petry checked off the quarter minutes and the units reporting.

Because he had nothing better to do, Allison had been sitting in the control room for four hours and all he had seen were the television panels and all he had heard were the reports – except when Lieutenant Cheevers and three other men returned from an inspection of the *Esther*.

"Pile not taken, eh?" The commander pursed his lips and ran a forefinger along his jaw. "Anything above median level would have taken the pile. I can't see it being ignored."

The lieutenant shook his head. "The *Esther* was relatively new. That would have made her pile pretty valuable."

"I can't figure out why the eight men on the Esther couldn't handle the situation. They had the *Mordite* and the *Halcyon* as object lessons. They must have been taken by surprise. No sign of a struggle, eh, Cheevers?"

"None, sir. We went over everything from stem to stern. Force field was still working, though it had fallen out of line. We turned it off."

"No blood stains? No hair? No bones?"

"No, sir."

"That's odd, don't you think? Where could they have gone?" The commander sighed. "I expect we'll know soon enough. As it is, unless something is done, the *Esther* will sink farther into this sand until she's sunk out of sight with the other two ships." He frowned. "Lieutenant, how would you like to assume command of the *Esther* on our return? It must still be in working order if the pile is there. I'll give you a crew."

"We're not through here yet, sir." Cheevers grinned. "But I'd like it."

"Look good on your service records, eh, Corvin?" The commander then saw Allison sitting at the rear of the room watching the panels. "What do you make of all this, Allison?"

"I hardly know what to think, Commander."

"Why don't you run a tape on it?"

"I wish I could, but with what little we know so far it wouldn't do any good."

"Come, now, Allison, surely a good, man like you — you're a computer man, remember? — surely you could do something. I've heard of the wonders of those little machines. I'll bet you could run that through the machine and it will tell us exactly what we want to know."

"There's not enough data. I'd just get an ID — Insufficient Data — response as I did before."

"It's too bad, Allison, that the computer people haven't considered that angle of it — that someone has to get the data to feed the machine, that the Federation must still rely on guts and horse sense and the average soldier-technician. I'll begin thinking computers are a good thing when they can go out and get their own data."

That had been two hours ago. Two hours for Allison to cool off in. Two hours to convince himself it had been best not to answer the commander. And now they all sat, stony-faced and quiet, watching the never-ending sweep of the eye-tubes that never showed anything different except the changing shadows as the planet's only sun moved across the sky. Yellow sand and carpets of green, the ship, the mountain, the wooded area . . .

It was the same on the next four-hour watch. The eye-tubes turned and the watchers in the ship watched and saw nothing new, and radio reports droned on every fifteen seconds until the men in the room were scarcely conscious of them.

And the sun went down.

Two moons, smaller than Earth's single moon, rode high in the sky, but they didn't help as much, infrared beams from the treadwagons rendered the panel pictures as plain as day. And there was nothing new.

The commander ordered the units moved a mile farther away the second day. When the action was completed, the waiting started all over again.

It would not be fair to say *nothing* was new. There was one thing — tension. Nerves that had been held ready for action began demanding it. And with the ache of taut nerves came impatience and an overexercising of the imagination. The quiet, heat, humidity and monotony of nothing the second day and night erupted in a blast from Unit East early on the morning of the third day. The nuclear weapons man in the g-car had fired at something he saw moving out on the sand.

At the site Technician Gar Caldwell reported by radio while Lieutenant Noromak and another man went through the temporarily damped force field to investigate. There was nothing at the target but some badly burned and fused sand.

Things went back to normal again.

Time dragged through the third day and night, and the hot breezes and high humidity and the waiting grated already raw nerves.

On the morning of the fourth day Homer Petry, who had been checking off the radio reports as they came in, suddenly announced: "No radio report from Unit West at 8:14:45!"

Instantly all eyes went to the Unit West panel.

The screen showed a revolving panorama of shimmering yellow sand and blue sky.

Lieutenant Cheevers opened the switch. "Unit West! Calling Unit West!"

No answer.

"What the hell's the matter with you, Unit West!"

The commander yelled, "Never mind, Lieutenant! Get two men and shoot over there. I'll alert the other units."

Lieutenant Cheevers picked up Allison, who happened to be in the control room at the time, and Hallom, and in a matter of moments the port dropped open and with the lieutenant at the controls and the two men digging their feet in the side stirrups and their hands clasping the rings for this purpose on either side, the small g-car soared out into the sweltering air and screamed toward Unit West.

The terrain rushed by below them as the car picked up still more speed and Allison, not daring to move his head too far from the protective streamlining lest it get caught in the hot airstream, saw the grass-dotted, sun-baked sand blur by.

Then the speed slackened and, raising his head, he saw

the treadwagon and the four force-field pillars they were approaching.

But he saw no men.

The lieutenant put the car in a tight turn and landed it near the wagon. The three grabbed their weapons, jumped from the car and ran with difficulty through the sand to the site.

The force field blocked them.

"What the hell!" Cheevers kicked at the inflexible, impenetrable shield and swore some more.

The treadwagon was there in the middle of the square formed by the force field posts, and there was no one in it. The eye-tube was still rotating slowly and noiselessly, weapons on the bridge beneath still pointed menacingly at the empty desert, the g-car was still in its place, and the Federation flag fluttered in the slight breeze.

But there was nothing living inside the square. The sand was oddly smooth in many places where there should have been footprints and Allison wondered if the slight breeze had already started its work of moving the sand to obliterate them. There were no bodies, no blood, no signs of a struggle.

Since they couldn't get through the barrier, they went back to the g-car and went over it, landing inside the invisible enclosure, still alert for any emergency.

But nothing attacked because there was nothing there. Only the sand, the empty treadwagons, the weapons, the stores.

"Poor Quartz," Cheevers said.

"What, sir?" Hallom asked.

"Lieutenant Quartz. I knew him better than any of the others." He picked up a handful of sand and threw it angrily at the wagon's treads.

Allison saw it hit, watched it fall, then noticed the tread prints were obliterated inside the big square. But as he looked out across the waste to the ship he noticed the tread prints there were quite clear.

He shivered in the hot sun.

The lieutenant reported by the wagon's radio, and after they had collected and packed all the gear, Allison and Hallom drove the treadwagons back to the ship.

"I tell you it's impossible!" The commander's eyes were red-rimmed and bloodshot and he ran sweating hands through wisps of uncombed grey hair. "There must have been *something!*"

"But there wasn't, sir," Cheevers said with anguish. "And nothing was overlooked, believe me."

"But how can that be?" The commander raised his arms angrily, let them fall. "And how will it look in the record? Ten men gone. Just like that." He snapped his fingers. "The Federation won't like it – especially since it is exactly what happened to the others. If only there had been a fight! If there were a chance for reprisal! But this—" he waved an arm to include the whole planet. "It's maddening!"

It was night before the commander could contain himself enough to talk rationally about what had happened and to think creatively of possible action.

"I'm not blaming you, Lieutenant Cheevers, or anybody," he said slouched in his desk chair and idly eyeing the three remaining television screens that revealed an endless, turning desert scene. "I have only myself to blame for what happened." He grunted. "I only wish I knew what happened." He turned to Cheevers, Allison and Hallom, who sat on the other side of the desk. "I've done nothing but think about this thing all day. I don't know what to tell those fellows out there, how they can protect themselves from this. I've examined the facts from every angle, but I always end up where I started." He stared at Cheevers. "Let's hear your idea again, Cheevers."

"It's like I say, sir. The attack could have come from the air."

"Carried away like eagles, eh? You've still got that idea?"

"The sand was smooth, Commander. That would support the idea of wings of birds setting the air in motion so the sand would cover up the footprints."

The commander bit his lower lip, drummed on the desk with his fingers and stared hard at Cheevers. "It *is* possible. Barely possible. But it still doesn't explain why we see no birds, why we saw no birds on the other viewers during the incident, why the other teams saw no birds in flight. We've asked, remember? Nobody has seen a living thing. Where then are we going to get enough birds to carry off ten men? And how does this happen with no bloodshed? Surely one of our men could have got off one shot, could have wounded *one* bird."

"The birds could have been invisible, sir," Hallom said hesitantly.

"Invisible birds!" The commander glared. Then he shrugged. "Hell I suppose anything is possible."

"That's what Allison's machine says."

"I ran the stuff through the computer," Allison said.

"I forgot there was such a thing . . . So that's what came out, eh?"

"Not exactly, Commander." Allison withdrew a roll of facsimile tape. "I sent through what we had. There are quite a few possibilities." He unrolled a little of it. "The men could still exist at the site, though rendered invisible—"

"Nuts!" the commander said. "How the hell—!"

"The data," Allison went on calmly, "was pretty weird itself and the machine lists only the possibilities, taking into consideration everything no matter how absurd. Other possibilities are that we are victims of hypnosis and that we are to see only what *they* – whoever *they* are – want us to see; that the men were surprised and spirited away by something invisible, which would mean none of the other units would have seen or reported it; or that the men themselves would not have seen the – let's say 'invisible birds'; that the men sank into the sand somehow by some change in the composition of the ground itself, or were taken there by something, that there was a change in time or space—"

"That's enough," the commander snapped. He rose, eyes blazing. "I can see we're going to get nothing worthwhile from the Computer Corps. 'Change in Time' hell! I want a straight answer, not a bunch of fancies or something straight from a fairy tale. The only thing you've said so far I'd put any stock in is the idea of the birds. And the lieutenant had that idea first. But as far as their being invisible is concerned, I hardly think that's likely."

"But if it had been just birds," Allison said, putting away the roll of tape, "there would have been resistance and blood would have been spilled somewhere."

Commander Warrick snorted. "If there'd been a fight we'd have seen some evidence of it. It was too quick for a fight, that's all. And I'm warning the other units of birds and of attack without warning."

As a result, the three remaining units altered the mechanism of their eye-tubes to include a sweep of the sky after each 360 degree pan of the horizon.

The fourth night passed and the blazing sun burst forth the morning of the fifth day with the situation unchanged except that anxiety and tension were more in evidence among the men than ever before. The commander ordered sedatives for all men coming off watches so they could sleep.

The fifth night passed without incident.

It was nearly noon on the sixth day when Wang Lee, who was with Lieutenant Glenn Foster's Unit West, reported that one of the men had gone out of his head.

The commander said he'd send over a couple men to get him in a g-car.

But before Petry and Hollam left, Lee was on the radio again. "It's Prince, the man I told you about," he said. "Maybe you can see him in the screen. He's got his blaster out and insists we turn off the force field."

The television screen showed the sky in a long sweep past the sun down to the sand and around, sweeping past the figure of a man, obviously Prince, as it panned the horizon.

"Lieutenant Foster's got a blaster on him," Lee went on.

"Damn it!" Sweat popped out on the commander's forehead as he looked at the screen. "Not enough trouble without that." He turned to Cheevers. "Tell Foster to blast him before he endangers the whole outfit."

But the words were not swift enough. The screen went black and the speaker emitted a harsh click.

It was late afternoon when the treadwagon from Unit West purred to a stop beside the wagon from Unit South and Petry and Bacon stepped out of it.

"There she is," Cheevers told the commander at his side on the ramp. "Prince blasted her but didn't put her out of commission. Only the radio – you can see the mast has been snapped off. No telling how many men he got in that blast before . . ."

"And now they're all gone. Twenty men." The commander stared dumbly at the wagon and his shoulders slouched a little now. He looked from the wagon to the horizon and followed it along toward the sun, shading his squinting red eyes. "What is it out there, Cheevers? What are we up against?"

"I wish I knew, sir."

They walked down the ramp to the sand and waded through it out to the treadwagon. They examined it from all sides.

"Not a goddam bloodstain anywhere," the commander said, wiping his neck with his handkerchief. "If Prince really blasted the men there ought to be stains and hair and remains and stench and – well, *something*."

"Did Rogers or Noromak report anything while I was gone?"

"Nothing. Not a damned thing . . . Scene look the same as before?"

"Just like before. Smooth sand inside the force field and no traces, though we did find Prince's blaster. At least I think it's his. Found it half-buried in the sand where he was supposed to be standing. We can check his serial number on it."

"Twenty men!" the commander breathed. He stared at the smooth sweep of sand again. "Twenty men swallowed up by nothing again." He looked up at the cloudless sky. "No birds, no life, no nothing. Yet something big enough to . . ." He shook his fist at the nothingness. "Why don't you show yourself, whoever you are – whatever you are! Why do you sneak and steal men!"

"Easy, Commander," Cheevers said, alarmed at the commander's red face, wide eyes and rising voice.

The commander relaxed, turned to the lieutenant with a wry face. "You'll have a command some day, Corvin. Then you'll know how it is."

"I think I know, sir," he said quietly.

"You only think you know. Come on, let's go in and get a drink. I need one. I've got to send in another report."

If it had been up to Allison, he would have called in the two remaining units – Unit East, Lieutenant Noromak's outfit, and Unit North, Lieutenant Rogers' group – because in the face of what had twice proved so undetectable and unpredictable, there was no sense in throwing good men after those who had already gone. He could not bear to think of how the men felt who manned the remaining outposts. Sitting ducks.

But it was not up to him. He could only run the computer and advise. And even his advice need not be heeded by the commanding officer whose will and determination to discover the planet's threat had become something more to pity than admire because he was willing to sacrifice the remaining two units rather than withdraw and consider some other method of attack.

Allison saw a man who no longer looked like a soldier, a man in soiled uniform, unshaven, an irritable man who had spurned eating and sleeping and had come to taking his nourishment from the bottle, a man who now barked his orders in a raucous voice, a man who could stand no sudden noises and, above all, could not tolerate any questions of his decisions. And so he became a lonely man because no one wanted to be near him, and he was left alone to stare with fascination at the two remaining TV panels and listen to the half-minute reports . . . and take a drink once in a while.

Allison was no different from the others. He did not want to face the commander. But he did not want to join the muttering soldiers in crew quarters either. So he kept to the computer room and, for something to do, spliced the tapes he had made from flight technician's information for their homeward flight. It took him more than three hours and when he was finished he put the reels in the flight compartment and, for what he thought surely must have been the hundredth time, took out the tapes he had already made on conditions and factors involved in the current emergency. He rearranged them and fed them into the machine again, then tapped out on the keys a request for a single factor that might emerge and prove helpful.

He watched the last of the tape whip into the machine, heard the gentle hum, the click of relays and watched the current indicators in the three different stages of the machine, knew that inside memory circuits were giving information, exchanging data, that other devices were examining results, probing for other related information, extracting useful bits, adding this to the stream, to be rejected or passed, depending upon whether it fitted the conditions.

At last the delivery section was energized, the soft ding of the response bell and the lighted green bar preceded a moment when the answer facsimile tape whirred out and even as he looked at it he knew, by its length, that it was as evasive and generalized as the information he had asked it to examine.

He had left the door to the computer room open and through it suddenly came the sound of hoarse voices. He jumped to his feet and ran out and down the hall to the control room.

The two television panels showed nothing new, but there was an excited radio voice that he recognized as Lieutenant Rogers'.

"He's violent, Commander, and there's nothing we can do," the lieutenant was saying. "He keeps running and trying to break through the force field – oh, my God!"

"What is it?" the commander cried, getting to his feet.

"He's got his blaster out and he's saying something."

The commander rushed to the microphone and tore it from Cheever's hands. "Don't force him to shoot and don't you shoot, Lieutenant. Remember what happened to Unit West."

"But he's coming up to the wagon now—"

"Don't lose your head, Rogers! Try to knock him out – *but don't use your blaster!*"

"He's entering the wagon now, Commander."

There was a moment's silence.

"He's getting into the g-car, Commander! We can't let him do that!"

"Knock him out!"

"I think we've got him – they're tangling – several men – he's knocked one away – he's got the damned thing going!"

There was a sound of clinking metal, a rasp and scrape and the obvious roar of the little g-car.

"He got away in it! Maybe you can pick it up on the screen . . ."

The TV screen moved slowly across the sky and swept by a g-car that loomed large on it.

"Let him go," the commander said. "We'll send you another. Anybody get hurt?"

"Yes, sir. One of the men got a bad cut. They're still working on him on the sand. Got knocked off the wagon and fell into the sand. I saw his head was pretty bloody a moment ago before the men gathered around him and . . . *my God! No! No!*"

"What!"

"They're coming out of the ground—"

"What?"

There were audible hisses and clanks and screams and . . . and suddenly it was quiet.

"Lieutenant! Lieutenant Rogers!" The commander's face was white. "Answer me, Lieutenant, do you hear? Answer me! You – you can't do this to me!"

But the radio was quiet.

But above, the television screen showed a panorama of endless desert illuminated by infrared and as it swept by one spot Allison caught sight of the horrified face of Tony Lazzari as the g-car soared by.

Allison pushed the shovel deep into the sand, lifted as much of it as he could get in it, deposited it on the conveyor. There were ten of them digging in the soft yellow sand in the early morning sun, sweat rolling off their backs and chins – not because the sand was heavy or that the work was hard but because the day was already unbearable hot – digging a hole that couldn't be dug. The sand kept slipping into the very place they were digging. They had only made a shallow depression two or three feet deep at the most and more than twenty feet wide.

They had found nothing.

Commander Warrick, who stood in the g-car atop Unit North's treadwagon, with Lieutenant Noromak and Lieutenant Cheevers at his side, had first ordered Unit East to return to the ship, which Allison considered the smartest thing he had done in the past five days. Then a group of ten, mostly men who had not been in the field, were dispatched in Unit South's old wagon, with the officers in the g-car accompanying them, to Unit North.

There was no sign of a struggle, just the smooth sand around the wagon, the force field still intact and functioning.

Then the ten men had started digging . . .

"All right," the commander called from the wagon. "Everybody out. We'll blast."

They got out of the hole and on the other side of the wagon while the commander ordered Cheevers to aim at the depression.

The shot was deafening, but when the clouds of sand had settled, the depression was still there with a coating of fused sand covering it.

Later, when the group returned to the ship, three g-car parties were sent out to look for Lazzari. They found him unconscious in the sun in his g-car in the sand. They brought him back to the ship where he was revived.

"What did you see?" the commander asked when Lazzari regained consciousness.

Lazzari just stared.

Allison had seen men like this before. "Commander," he said, "this man's in a catatonic state. He'd better be watched because he can have periods of violence."

The commander glared. "You go punch your goddamn computer, Mr Allison. I'll handle Lazzari."

And as the commander questioned the man, Lazzari suddenly started to cry, then jerked and, wild-eyed, leaped for the commander.

They put Lazzari in a small room.

Allison could have told the commander that was a mistake, too, but he didn't dare.

And, as the commander was planning his next moves against the planet's peril, Lazzari dashed his head against a bulkhead, fractured his skull, and died.

The funeral for Lazzari the commander said, was to be a military one – as military as was possible on a planet revolving around a remote star in the far Hyades. Since rites were not possible for the twenty-nine others of the *Nesbitt* who had vanished, the commander said Lazzari's would make up for the rest.

Then for the first time in a week men had something else to think about besides the nature of things on the planet of the yellow sand that had done away with two explorers, the crews of three ships and twenty-nine Federation soldier-technicians who had come to do battle.

New uniforms were issued, each man showered and shaved, Lieutenant Cheevers read up on the burial service, Gordon Bacon practiced *Taps* on his bugle, Homer Petry gathered some desert flowers in a g-car, and Wendell Hallom washed and prepared Lazzari for the final rites which were to be held within a few hundred feet of the ship.

Though Allison complied with the directives, he felt uneasy about a funeral on the sand. He spent the hour before the afternoon services in the computer room, running tapes through the machine again, seeking the factor responsible for what had occurred.

He reasoned that persons on the sand were safe as long as the onslaught of the *things* out of the ground was not triggered by some action of men in the parties.

He did not know what the Unit South provocation had been – the radio signals had just stopped. He did know the assault on Unit West occurred after Prince's blast at the men on the treadwagon (though the blast in the sand at Unit North had brought nothing to the surface – if one were to believe Lieutenant Roger's final words about *things* coming out of the ground). And the attack at Unit North was fomented by Lazzari's taking off in the g-car and throwing those battling him to the sand.

Allison went so far as to cut new tapes for each incident, adding every possible detail he could think of. Then he inserted these into the machine and tapped out a question of the advisability of men further exposing themselves by holding a burial service for Lazzari in the sand.

In a few moments the response whirred out.

He caught his breath because the message was so short. Printed on the facsimile tape were these words:

Not advised.

Heartened by the brevity of the message and the absence of all the ifs, ands and buts of previous responses, he tapped out another question: Was there danger to life?

Agonizing minutes. Then:

Yes.

Whose life?

All.

Do you know the factor responsible for the deaths?

Yes.

He cursed himself for not realizing the machine knew the factor and wished he had asked for it instead. With his heart tripping like a jackhammer, Allison tapped out: What is the triggering factor?

When the answer came he found it ridiculously simple and wondered why no one had thought of it before. He stood staring at the tape for a long time knowing there could now be no funeral for Tony Lazzari.

He left the computer room, found the commander talking to Lieutenant Cheevers in the control room. Commander Warrick seemed something of his old self, attired in a natty tropical, clean shaven and with a military bearing and a freshness about him that had been missing for days.

"Commander," Allison said. "I don't mean to interrupt, but – we can't have the funeral."

The commander turned to him with a look full of suspicion. Then he said, "Allison, this is the one and only trip you will ever make with me. When we get back it will be either you or me who gets off this ship for the last time. If you want to run a ship you have to go to another school besides the one for Computer Corps men."

"I've known how you feel, Commander," Allison said, "and—"

"The General Staff ought to know that you can't mix army and civilian. I shall make it a point to register my feelings on the matter when we return."

"You can tell them what you wish, Commander, but it so happens that I've found out the factor responsible for all the attacks."

"And it so happens," the commander said icily, "that the lieutenant and I are reviewing the burial rites. A strict military burial has certain formalities which cannot be overlooked, though I don't expect you to understand that. There is too little time to go into any of your fancy theories now."

"This is no theory, Commander. It's a certainty."

"Did your computer have anything to do with it?"

"It had everything to do with it. I'd been feeding the tapes for days—"

"While we're on the subject, Allison, we're not using computer tapes for our home journey. We're going the whole way manually. I'm awaiting orders now to move off this God-forsaken world, in case you want to know. I'm recommending it as out-of-bounds for all ships of the Federation. And I'm also recommending that computer units be removed from the *Nesbitt* and from all other ships."

"You'll never leave this planet if you have the funeral," Allison said heatedly. "It will be death for all of us."

"Is that so?" The commander smiled thinly. "Courtesy of your computer, no doubt. Or is it that you're afraid to go out on the sand again?"

"I'm not afraid of the sand, Commander. I'll go out any time. But it's the others I'm thinking of. I won't go out to see Lazzari buried because of the blood on his head and neither should anyone else. You see, the missing factor – the thing that caused all the attacks – is blood."

"Blood?" The commander laughed, looked at Cheevers,

who was not laughing, then back at Allison. "Sure you feel all right?"

"The blood on Lazzari, Commander. It will trigger another attack."

"What about the blood that's in us, Allison? That should have prevented us from stepping out to the sand without being attacked in the first place. Your reasoning – or rather your computer's reasoning – is ridiculous."

"It's fresh blood. Blood spilled on the sand."

"It seems to me you've got blood on the brain. Lazzari was a friend of yours, wasn't he, Allison?"

"That has nothing to do with it."

The commander looked at him hard and long, then turned to the lieutenant. "Cheevers, Allison doesn't feel very well. I think he'd better be locked up in the computer room until after the funeral."

Allison was stunned. "Commander—!"

"Will you please take him away at once, Lieutenant? I've heard all I want from him."

Sick at heart, Allison watched the commander walk out of the control room.

"You coming along, Allison?" Cheevers asked.

Allison looked at the lieutenant. "Do you know what will happen if you go out there?" But there was no sympathy or understanding in the eyes of the officer. He turned and walked down the hall to the computer room and went in.

"It doesn't make any difference what I think," Cheevers said, his hand on the knob of the door, his face not unkind. "You're not in the service. I am. I have to do what the commander says. Some day I may have a command of my own. Then I'll have a right to my own opinion."

"You'll never have a command of your own . . . after today."

"Think so?" It seemed to Allison that the lieutenant sighed a little. "Goodbye, Allison."

It was an odd way to put it. Allison saw the door close

454

and click shut. Then he heard the lieutenant walk away. It was quiet.

Anguish in every fiber, Allison clicked on the small screen above the computer, turned a knurled knob until he saw the area of the intended burial. He hated to look at what he was going to see. The eye of the wide, shallow grave stared at him from the viewplate.

In a few minutes he saw Bacon carrying a Federation flag move slowly into view, followed by six men with blasters at raise, then Hallom and his bugle, Lieutenant Cheevers and his book, the stretcher bearing Lazzari with three pall-bearers on either side, and the rest of the men in double ranks, the officers leading them.

Go ahead Commander. Have your military field day because it's one thing you know how to do well. It's men like you who need a computer . . .

The procession approached the depression, Bacon moving to one side, the firing party at the far side of the shallow, Lieutenant Cheevers at the near end, making room for the pallbearers who moved into the depression and deposited their load there. The others moved to either side of the slope in single file.

Make it slick, Commander. By the numbers, straight and strong, because it's the last thing you'll ever do . . .

The men suddenly stiffened to attention, uncovering and holding their dress hats over their left breasts.

Bacon removed the Federation flag from its staff, draped it neatly over Lazzari. Cheevers then moved to the front and conducted the services, which lasted for several minutes.

This is the end, Commander . . .

Allison could see Commander Warrick facing the firing party, saw the blast volleys. But he was more interested in Lazzari. Two soldiers were shoveling the loose sand over him. Hallom raised his bugle to his lips.

Then *they* came.

Large, heavy, white porpoise-like creatures they were,
swimming up out of the sand as if it were water, and
snatching men in their powerful jaws, rending and tearing
– clothes and all – as they rose in a fury of attacks that
whipped up sand to nearly hide the scene. There were
twenty or more and then more than a hundred rising
and sinking and snapping and slashing, sun glistening
on their shiny sides, flippers working furiously to stay
atop the sand.

This, then, was the sea and these were the fish in it,
fish normally disinterested in ordinary sweating men and
machines and treadwagons, but hungry for men's blood
or anything smeared with it – so hungry that a drop of
it on the sand must have been a signal conducted to the
depths to attract them all.

And when the men were gone there were still fish-like
creatures burrowing into the sand, moving through it
swiftly half in and out like sharks, seeking every last
vestige of – blood.

Then as suddenly as they had come, the things were
gone.

Then there was nothing but smooth sand where before
it had been covered by twenty men with bowed heads . . .
except one spot which maximum magnification showed
to be a bugle half-buried in the sand.

Allison did not know how long he sat there looking at
the screen, but it must have been been an hour because
when he finally moved he could only do so with effort.

He alone had survived out of fifty men and he – the
computer man. He was struck with the wonder of it.

He rose to leave the room. He needed a drink.

Only then did he remember that Cheevers had locked
him in.

He tried the door.

It opened!

Cheevers *had* believed him, then. Somehow, this made
the whole thing more tragic . . . there might have been

others who would have believed, too, if the commander had not stood in the way . . .

The first thing Allison did was close the great port. Then he hunted until he found the bottle he was looking for. He took it to the computer room with him, opened the flight compartment, withdrew the tapes, set them in their proper slots and started them on their way.

Only when he heard the ship tremble alive did he take a drink . . . A long drink.

There would have to be other bottles after this one. There *had* to be. It was going to be a long, lonely ride home.

And there was much to forget.

OUT OF THE UNKNOWN

(BBC TV, 1965–1971)
Starring: Ian Ogilvy, Hamilton Dyce &
Wendy Gifford
Directed by Gerald Blake
Story 'Liar!' by Isaac Asimov

Out of the Unknown **was the BBC's answer to the
success of Independent Television's** *Out of This World.*
**What both had in common was Irene Shubik as
producer, for in the interim she had moved channels
with Sydney Newman and in her new role had been
allowed to indulge her obvious penchant for SF with
a fresh series which also drew on the work of the very
best writers in the genre including John Wyndham,
Ray Bradbury, Frederick Pohl and Isaac Asimov. On
the BBC, however, after two seasons in black and
white, the rest of the series was in colour. Once again
a Martian story by John Wyndham, 'No Place Like
Earth' heralded the start of** *Out of the Unknown's*
**first season in October 1965; but it was to be a group
of stories by Isaac Asimov and several contributions
from Terry Nation, Leon Griffiths, Hugh Whitemore
and Nigel Kneale that would have the biggest impact
on audiences. The series was also well served by
its team of directors including Peter Sasdy, Alan
Bridges and Philip Saville, while working amongst
the design team was a young man who would later
take Hollywood by storm as the director of** *Alien* **and**
Blade Runner, **Ridley Scott. In all, 49 episodes of** *Out of
the Unknown* **were produced by Irene Shubik and her
successor, Alan Bromly, and among the many leading**

guest actors were stars such as David Hemmings, Warren Mitchell, Rachel Roberts and even George 'Minder' Cole!

For a quite considerable number of viewers the most fascinating episodes were those about robots based on short stories by Isaac Asimov (1920–1992), the prodigeously gifted professor of biochemistry who turned SF writer and is now widely acknowledged as one of the major influences on the genre this century. It was in 1940 that he wrote the first of his robot stories, 'Strange Playfellow', and then a year later followed it with, 'Liar!' which introduced what have been described as the 'Three Laws of Robotics' and once and for all confined the clanking mental monsters of so much earlier SF to oblivion. Of the six Asimov stories that *Out of the Unknown* adapted for television, three were specifically about robots and all featured Dr Susan Calvin, a robot psychologist, with 'Liar!' perhaps the best adaptation of all. From the apprently unexceptional situation of a robot being demonstrated to the press in order to quieten public unrest about possible dangers from the growing number of these machines, director Gerald Blake and his actors – in particular Wendy Gifford as Dr Calvin and Ian Ogilvy as robot RB–34 – produced an engrossing and thought-provoking hour of television which remained remarkably faithful to Asimov's original landmark story. It is reprinted here as a reminder of yet another piece of television's SF history . . .

Alfred Lanning lit his cigar carefully, but the tips of his fingers were trembling slightly. His gray eyebrows hunched low as he spoke between puffs.

"It reads minds all right – damn little doubt about that! But why?" He looked at Mathematician Peter Bogert, "Well?"

Bogert flattened his black hair down with both hands,

"That was the thirty-fourth RB model we've turned out, Lanning. All the others were strictly orthodox."

The third man at the table frowned. Milton Ashe was the youngest officer of U.S. Robot & Mechanical Men, Inc., and proud of his post.

"Listen, Bogert. There wasn't a hitch in the assembly from start to finish. I guarantee that."

Bogert's thick lips spread in a patronizing smile, "Do you? If you can answer for the entire assembly line, I recommend your promotion. By exact count, there are seventy-five thousand, two hundred and thirty-four operations necessary for the manufacture of a single positronic brain, each separate operation depending for successful completion upon any number of factors, from five to a hundred and five. If any one of them goes seriously wrong, the 'brain' is ruined. I quote our own information folder, Ashe."

Milton Ashe flushed, but a fourth voice cut off his reply.

"If we're going to start by trying to fix the blame on one another, I'm leaving." Susan Calvin's hands were folded tightly in her lap, and the little lines about her thin, pale lips deepened, "We've got a mind-reading robot on our hands and it strikes me as rather important that we find out just why it reads minds. We're not going to do that by saying, 'Your fault! My fault!'"

Her cold gray eyes fastened upon Ashe, and he grinned.

Lanning grinned too, and, as always at such times, his long white hair and shrewd little eyes made him the picture of a biblical patriarch. "True for you, Dr Calvin."

His voice became suddenly crisp, "Here's everything in pill-concentrate form. We've produced a positronic brain of supposedly ordinary vintage that's got the remarkable property of being able to tune in on thought waves. It would mark the most important advance in robotics in decades, if we knew how it happened. We don't, and we have to find out. Is that clear?"

"May I make a suggestion?" asked Bogert.

"Go ahead!"

"I'd say that until we do figure out the mess – and as a mathematician I expect it to be a very devil of a mess – we keep the existence of RB-34 a secret. I mean even from the other members of the staff. As heads of the departments, we ought not to find it an insoluble problem, and the fewer know about it—"

"Bogert is right," said Dr Calvin. "Ever since the Interplanetary Code was modified to allow robot models to be tested in the plants before being shipped out to space, anti-robot propaganda has increased. If any word leaks out about a robot being able to read minds before we can announce complete control of the phenomenon, pretty effective capital could be made out of it."

Lanning sucked at his cigar and nodded gravely. He turned to Ashe, "I think you said you were alone when you first stumbled on this thought-reading business."

"I'll say I was alone – I got the scare of my life. RB-34 had just been taken off the assembly table and they sent him down to me. Obermann was off somewheres, so I took him down to the testing rooms myself – at least I started to take him down." Ashe paused, and a tiny smile tugged at his lips, "Say, did any of you ever carry on a thought conversation without knowing it?"

No one bothered to answer, and he continued, "You don't realize it at first, you know. He just spoke to me – as logically and sensibly as you can imagine – and it was only when I was most of the way down to the testing rooms that I realized that I hadn't said anything. Sure, I thought lots, but that isn't the same thing, is it? I locked that thing up and ran for Lanning. Having it walking beside me, calmly peering into my thoughts and picking and choosing among them gave me the willies."

"I imagine it would," said Susan Calvin thoughtfully. Her eyes fixed themselves upon Ashe in an oddly intent manner. "We are so accustomed to considering our own thoughts private."

Lanning broke in impatiently, "Then only the four of us know. All right! We've got to go about this systematically. Ashe, I want you to check over the assembly line from beginning to end everything. You're to eliminate all operations in which there was no possible chance of an error, and list all those where there were, together with its nature and possible magnitude."

"Tall order," grunted Ashe.

"Naturally! Of course, you're to put the men under you to work on this – every single one if you have to, and I don't care if we go behind schedule, either. But they're not to know why, you understand."

"Hm-m-m, yes!" The young technician grinned wryly. "It's still a lulu of a job."

Lanning swiveled about in his chair and faced Calvin, "You'll have to tackle the job from the other direction. You're the robopsychologist of the plant, so you're to study the robot itself and work backward. Try to find out how he ticks. See what else is tied up with his telepathic powers, how far they extend, how they warp his outlook, and just exactly what harm it has done to his ordinary RB properties. You've got that?"

Lanning didn't wait for Dr Calvin to answer.

"I'll co-ordinate the work and interpret the findings mathematically." He puffed violently at his cigar and mumbled the rest through the smoke, "Bogert will help me there, of course."

Bogert polished the nails of one pudgy hand with the other and said blandly, "I dare say. I know a little in the line."

"Well! I'll get started." Ashe shoved his chair back and rose. His pleasantly youthful face crinkled in a grin, "I've got the darnedest job of any of us, so I'm getting out of here and to work."

He left with a slurred, "B' seein' ye!"

Susan Calvin answered with a barely perceptible nod,

but her eyes followed him out of sight and she did not answer when Lanning grunted and said, "Do you want to go up and see RB-34 now, Dr Calvin?"

RB-34's photoelectric eyes lifted from the book at the muffled sound of hinges turning and he was upon his feet when Susan Calvin entered.

She paused to readjust the huge 'No Entrance' sign upon the door and then approached the robot.

"I've brought you the texts upon hyperatomic motors, Herbie – a few anyway. Would you care to look at them?"

RB-34 – otherwise known as Herbie – lifted the three heavy books from her arms and opened to the title page of one:

"Hm-m-m! 'Theory of Hyperatomics.'" He mumbled inarticulately to himself as he flipped the pages and then spoke with an abstracted air, "Sit down, Dr Calvin! This will take me a few minutes."

The psychologist seated herself and watched Herbie narrowly as he took a chair at the other side of the table and went through the three books systematically.

At the end of half an hour, he put them down, "Of course, I know why you brought these."

The corner of Dr Calvin's lip twitched, "I was afraid you would. It's difficult to work with you, Herbie. You're always a step ahead of me."

"It's the same with these books, you know, as with the others. They just don't interest me. There's nothing to your textbooks. Your science is just a mass of collected data plastered together by make-shift theory – and all so incredibly simple, that it's scarcely worth bothering about.

"It's your fiction that interests me. Your studies of the interplay of human motives and emotions" – his mighty hand gestured vaguely as he sought the proper words.

Dr Calvin whispered, "I think I understand."

"I see into minds, you see," the robot continued, "and

you have no idea how complicated they are. I can't begin to understand everything because my own mind has so little in common with them – but I try, and your novels help."

"Yes, but I'm afraid that after going through some of the harrowing emotional experiences of our present-day sentimental novel" – there was a tinge of bitterness in her voice – "you find real minds like ours dull and colorless."

"But I don't!"

The sudden energy in the response brought the other to her feet. She felt herself reddening, and thought wildly, "He must know!"

Herbie subsided suddenly, and muttered in a low voice from which the metallic timbre departed almost entirely. "But, of course, I know about it, Dr Calvin. You think of it always, so how can I help but know?"

Her face was hard. "Have you – told anyone?"

"Of course not!" This, with genuine surprise. "No one has asked me."

"Well, then," she flung out, "I suppose you think I am a fool."

"No! It is a normal emotion."

"Perhaps that is why it is so foolish." The wistfulness in her voice drowned out everything else. Some of the woman peered through the layer of doctorhood. "I am not what you would call – attractive."

"If you are referring to mere physical attraction, I couldn't judge. But I know, in any case, that there are other types of attraction."

"Nor young." Dr Calvin had scarcely heard the robot.

"You are not yet forty." An anxious insistence had crept into Herbie's voice.

"Thirty-eight as you count the years; a shriveled sixty as far as my emotional outlook on life is concerned. Am I a psychologist for nothing?"

She drove on with bitter breathlessness, "And he's barely thirty-five and looks and acts younger. Do you suppose he ever sees me as anything but . . . but what I am?"

"You are wrong!" Herbie's steel fist struck the plastic-topped table with a strident clang. "Listen to me—"

But Susan Calvin whirled on him now and the hunted pain in her eyes became a blaze, "Why should I? What do you know about it all, anyway, you . . . you machine. I'm just a specimen to you; an interesting bug with a peculiar mind spread-eagled for inspection. It's a wonderful example of frustration, isn't it? Almost as good as your books." Her voice, emerging in dry sobs, choked into silence.

The robot cowered at the outburst. He shook his head pleadingly. "Won't you listen to me, please? I could help you if you would let me."

"How?" Her lips curled. "By giving me good advice?"

"No, not that. It's just that I know what other people think – Milton Ashe, for instance."

There was a long silence, and Susan Calvin's eyes dropped. "I don't want to know what he thinks," she gasped. "Keep quiet."

"I think you would want to know what he thinks."

Her head remained bent, but her breath came more quickly. "You are talking nonsense," she whispered.

"Why should I? I am trying to help. Milton Ashe's thoughts of you—" he paused.

And then the psychologist raised her head, "Well?"

The robot said quietly, "He loves you."

For a full minute, Dr Calvin did not speak. She merely stared. Then, "You are mistaken! You must be. Why should he?"

"But he does. A thing like that cannot be hidden, not from me."

"But I am so . . . so—" she stammered to a halt.

"He looks deeper than the skin, and admires intellect in others. Milton Ashe is not the type to marry a head of hair and a pair of eyes."

Susan Calvin found herself blinking rapidly and waited

before speaking. Even then her voice trembled, "Yet he certainly never in any way indicated—"

"Have you ever given him a chance?"

"How could I? I never thought that—"

"Exactly!"

The psychologist paused in thought and then looked up suddenly. "A girl visited him here at the plant half a year ago. She was pretty, I suppose – blond and slim. And, of course, could scarcely add two and two. He spent all day puffing out his chest, trying to explain how a robot was put together." The hardness had returned, "Not that she understood! Who was she?"

Herbie answered without hesitation, "I know the person you are referring to. She is his first cousin, and there is no romantic interest there, I assure you."

Susan Calvin rose to her feet with a vivacity almost girlish. "Now isn't that strange? That's exactly what I used to pretend to myself sometimes, though I never really thought so. Then it all must be true."

She ran to Herbie and seized his cold, heavy hand in both hers. "Thank you, Herbie." Her voice was an urgent, husky whisper. "Don't tell anyone about this. Let it be our secret – and thank you again." With that, and a convulsive squeeze of Herbie's unresponsive metal fingers, she left.

Herbie turned slowly to his neglected novel, but there was no one to read *his* thoughts.

Milton Ashe stretched slowly and magnificently, to the tune of cracking joints and a chorus of grunts, and then glared at Peter Bogert, Ph.D.

"Say," he said, "I've been at this for a week now with just about no sleep. How long do I have to keep it up? I thought you said the positronic bombardment in Vac Chamber D was the solution."

Bogert yawned delicately and regarded his white hands with interest. "It is. I'm on the track."

"I know what *that* means when a mathematician says it. How near the end are you?"

"It all depends."

"On what?" Ashe dropped into a chair and stretched his long legs out before him.

"On Lanning. The old fellow disagrees with me." He sighed, "A bit behind the times, that's the trouble with him. He clings to matrix mechanics as the all in all, and this problem calls for more powerful mathematical tools. He's so stubborn."

Ashe muttered sleepily, "Why not ask Herbie and settle the whole affair?"

"Ask the robot?" Bogert's eyebrows climbed.

"Why not? Didn't the old girl tell you?"

"You mean Calvin?"

"Yeah! Susie herself. That robot's a mathematical wiz. He knows all about everything plus a bit on the side. He does triple integrals in his head and eats up tensor analysis for dessert."

The mathematician stared skeptically, "Are you serious?"

"So help me! The catch is that the dope doesn't like math. He would rather read slushy novels. Honest! You should see the tripe Susie keeps feeding him: 'Purple Passion' and 'Love in Space.'"

"Dr Calvin hasn't said a word of this to us."

"Well, she hasn't finished studying him. You know how she is. She likes to have everything just so before letting out the big secret."

"She's told *you*."

"We sort of got to talking. I have been seeing a lot of her lately." He opened his eyes wide and frowned, "Say, Bogie, have you been noticing anything queer about the lady lately?"

Bogert relaxed into an undignified grin, "She's using lipstick, if that's what you mean."

"Hell, I know that. Rouge, powder and eye shadow, too. She's a sight. But it's not that. I can't put my finger on it. It's the way she talks – as if she were happy about something." He thought a little, and then shrugged.

The other allowed himself a leer, which, for a scientist past fifty, was not a bad job, "Maybe she's in love."

Ashe allowed his eyes to close again, "You're nuts, Bogie. You go speak to Herbie; I want to stay here and go to sleep."

"Right! Not that I particularly like having a robot tell me my job, nor that I think he can do it!"

A soft snore was his only answer.

Herbie listened carefully as Peter Bogert, hands in pockets, spoke with elaborate indifference.

"So there you are. I've been told you understand these things, and I am asking you more in curiosity than anything else. My line of reasoning, as I have outlined it, involves a few doubtful steps, I admit, which Dr Lanning refuses to accept, and the picture is still rather incomplete."

The robot didn't answer, and Bogert said, "Well?"

"I see no mistake," Herbie studied the scribbled figures.

"I don't suppose you can go any further than that?"

"I daren't try. You are a better mathematician than I, and – well, I'd hate to commit myself."

There was a shade of complacency in Bogert's smile, "I rather thought that would be the case. It is deep. We'll forget it." He crumpled the sheets, tossed them down the waste shaft, turned to leave, and then thought better of it.

"By the way—"

The robot waited.

Bogert seemed to have difficulty. "There is something – that is, perhaps you can—" He stopped.

Herbie spoke quietly. "Your thoughts are confused, but there is no doubt at all that they concern Dr Lanning. It is silly to hesitate, for as soon as you compose yourself, I'll know what it is you want to ask."

The mathematician's hand went to his sleek hair in the familiar smoothing gesture. "Lanning is nudging seventy," he said, as if that explained everything.

"I know that."

"And he's been director of the plant for almost thirty years." Herbie nodded.

"Well, now," Bogert's voice became ingratiating, "you would know whether . . . whether he's thinking of resigning. Health, perhaps, or some other—"

"Quite," said Herbie, and that was all.

"Well, do you know?"

"Certainly."

"Then – uh – could you tell me?"

"Since you ask, yes." The robot was quite matter-of-fact about it. "He has already resigned!"

"What!" The exclamation was an explosive, almost inarticulate, sound. The scientist's large head hunched forward, "Say that again!"

"He has already resigned," came the quiet repetition, "but it has not yet taken effect. He is waiting, you see, to solve the problem of – er – myself. That finished, he is quite ready to turn the office of director over to his successor."

Bogert expelled his breath sharply, "And this successor? Who is he?" He was quite close to Herbie now, eyes fixed fascinatedly on those unreadable dull-red photoelectric cells that were the robot's eyes.

Words came slowly, "You are the next director."

And Bogert relaxed into a tight smile, "This is good to know. I've been hoping and waiting for this. Thanks, Herbie."

Peter Bogert was at his desk until five that morning and he was back at nine. The shelf just over the desk emptied of its row of reference books and tables, as he referred to one after the other. The pages of calculations before him increased microscopically and the crumpled sheets at his feet mounted into a hill of scribbled paper.

At precisely noon, he stared at the final page, rubbed a blood-shot eye, yawned and shrugged. "This is getting worse each minute. Damn!"

He turned at the sound of the opening door and nodded at Lanning, who entered, cracking the knuckles of one gnarled hand with the other.

The director took in the disorder of the room and his eyebrows furrowed together.

"New lead?" he asked.

"No," came the defiant answer. "What's wrong with the old one?"

Lanning did not trouble to answer, nor to do more than bestow a single cursory glance at the top sheet upon Bogert's desk. He spoke through the flare of a match as he lit a cigar.

"Has Calvin told you about the robot? It's a mathematical genius. Really remarkable."

The other snorted loudly, "So I've heard. But Calvin had better stick to robopsychology. I've checked Herbie on math, and he can scarcely struggle through calculus."

"Calvin didn't find it so."

"She's crazy."

"And I don't find it so." The director's eyes narrowed dangerously.

"You!" Bogert's voice hardened. "What are you talking about?"

"I've been putting Herbie through his paces all morning, and he can do tricks you never heard of."

"Is that so?"

"You sound skeptical!" Lanning flipped a sheet of paper out of his vest pocket and unfolded it. "That's not my handwriting, is it?"

Bogert studied the large angular notation covering the sheet, "Herbie did this?"

"Right! And if you'll notice, he's been working on your time integration of Equation 22. It comes" – Lanning tapped a yellow fingernail upon the last step – "to the identical conclusion I did, and in a quarter the time. You had no right to neglect the Linger Effect in positronic bombardment."

"I didn't neglect it. For Heaven's sake, Lanning, get it through your head that it would cancel out—"

"Oh, sure, you explained that. You used the Mitchell Translation Equation, didn't you? Well – it doesn't apply."

"Why not?"

"Because you've been using hyper-imaginaries, for one thing."

"What's that to do with?"

"Mitchell's Equation won't hold when—"

"Are you crazy? If you'll reread Mitchell's original paper in the *Transactions of the Far*—"

"I don't have to. I told you in the beginning that I didn't like his reasoning, and Herbie backs me in that."

"Well, then," Bogert shouted, "let that clockwork contraption solve the entire problem for you. Why bother with nonessentials?"

"That's exactly the point. Herbie can't solve the problem. And if he can't, we can't – alone. I'm submitting the entire question to the National Board. It's gotten beyond us."

Bogert's chair went over backward as he jumped up a-snarl, face crimson. "You're doing nothing of the sort."

Lanning flushed in his turn, "Are you telling me what I can't do?"

"Exactly," was the gritted response. "I've got the problem beaten and you're not to take it out of my hands, understand? Don't think I don't see through you, you desiccated fossil. You'd cut your own nose off before you'd let me get the credit for solving robotic telepathy."

"You're a damned idiot, Bogert, and in one second I'll have you suspended for insubordination" – Lanning's lower lip trembled with passion.

"Which is one thing you won't do, Lanning. You haven't any secrets with a mind-reading robot around, so don't forget that I know all about your resignation."

The ash on Lanning's cigar trembled and fell, and the cigar itself followed, "What . . . what—"

Bogert chuckled nastily, "And I'm the new director, be it understood. I'm very aware of that; don't think I'm not. Damn your eyes, Lanning, I'm going to give the orders about here or there will be the sweetest mess that you've ever been in."

Lanning found his voice and let it out with a roar. "You're suspended, d'ye hear? You're relieved of all duties. You're broken, do you understand?"

The smile on the other's face broadened, "Now, what's the use of that? You're getting nowhere. I'm holding the trumps. I know you've resigned. Herbie told me, and he got it straight from you."

Lanning forced himself to speak quietly. He looked an old, old man, with tired eyes peering from a face in which the red had disappeared, leaving the pasty yellow of age behind, "I want to speak to Herbie. He can't have told you anything of the sort. You're playing a deep game, Bogert, but I'm calling your bluff. Come with me."

Bogert shrugged, "To see Herbie? Good! Damned good!"

It was also precisely at noon that Milton Ashe looked up from his clumsy sketch and said, "You get the idea? I'm not too good at getting this down, but that's about how it looks. It's a honey of a house, and I can get it for next to nothing."

Susan Calvin gazed across at him with melting eyes. "It's really beautiful," she sighed. "I've often thought that I'd like to—" Her voice trailed away.

"Of course," Ashe continued briskly, putting away his pencil, "I've got to wait for my vacation. It's only two weeks off, but this Herbie business has everything up in the air." His eyes dropped to his fingernails, "Besides, there's another point – but it's a secret."

"Then don't tell me."

"Oh, I'd just as soon, I'm just busting to tell someone

– and you're just about the best – er – confidante I could find here." He grinned sheepishly.

Susan Calvin's heart bounded, but she did not trust herself to speak.

"Frankly," Ashe scraped his chair closer and lowered his voice into a confidential whisper, "the house isn't to be only for myself. I'm getting married!"

And then he jumped out of his seat, "What's the matter?"

"Nothing!" The horrible spinning sensation had vanished, but it was hard to get words out. "Married? You mean—"

"Why, sure! About time, isn't it? You remember that girl who was here last summer. That's she! But you *are* sick. You—"

"Headache!" Susan Calvin motioned him away weakly. "I've . . . I've been subject to them lately. I want to . . . to congratulate you, of course. I'm very glad—" The inexpertly applied rouge made a pair of nasty red splotches upon her chalk-white face. Things had begun spinning again. "Pardon me – please—"

The words were a mumble, as she stumbled blindly out the door. It had happened with the sudden catastrophe of a dream – and with all the unreal horror of a dream.

But how could it be? Herbie had said—

And Herbie knew! He could see into minds!

She found herself leaning breathlessly against the door jamb, staring into Herbie's metal face. She must have climbed the two flights of stairs, but she had no memory of it. The distance had been covered in an instant, as in a dream.

As in a dream!

And still Herbie's unblinking eyes stared into hers and their dull red seemed to expand into dimly shining nightmarish globes.

He was speaking, and she felt the cold glass pressing against her lips. She swallowed and shuddered into a certain awareness of her surroundings.

Still Herbie spoke, and there was agitation in his voice – as if he were hurt and frightened and pleading.

The words were beginning to make sense. "This is a dream," he was saying, "and you mustn't believe in it. You'll wake into the real world soon and laugh at yourself. He loves you, I tell you. He does, he does! But not here! Not now! This is an illusion."

Susan Calvin nodded, her voice a whisper, "Yes! Yes!" She was clutching Herbie's arm, clinging to it, repeating over and over, "It isn't true, is it? It isn't, is it?"

Just how she came to her senses, she never knew – but it was like passing from a world of misty unreality to one of harsh sunlight. She pushed him away from her, pushed hard against that steely arm, and her eyes were wide.

"What are you trying to do?" Her voice rose to a harsh scream. "What are you trying to do?"

Herbie backed away, "I want to help."

The psychologist stared, "Help? By telling me this is a dream? By trying to push me into schizophrenia?" A hysterical tenseness seized her, "This is no dream! I wish it were!"

She drew her breath sharply, "Wait! Why . . . why, I understand. Merciful Heavens, it's so obvious."

There was horror in the robot's voice, "I had to!"

"And I believed you! I never thought—"

Loud voices outside the door brought her to a halt. She turned away, fists clenching spasmodically, and when Bogert and Lanning entered, she was at the far window. Neither of the men paid her the slightest attention.

They approached Herbie simultaneously; Lanning angry and impatient, Bogert, coolly sardonic. The director spoke first.

"Here now, Herbie. Listen to me!"

The robot brought his eyes sharply down upon the aged director, "Yes, Dr Lanning."

"Have you discussed me with Dr Bogert?"

"No, sir." The answer came slowly, and the smile on Bogert's face flashed off.

"What's that?" Bogert shoved in ahead of his superior and straddled the ground before the robot. "Repeat what you told me yesterday."

"I said that—" Herbie fell silent. Deep within him his metallic diaphragm vibrated in soft discords.

"Didn't you say he had resigned?" roared Bogert. "Answer me!"

Bogert raised his arm frantically, but Lanning pushed him aside, "Are you trying to bully him into lying?"

"You heard him, Lanning. He began to say 'Yes' and stopped. Get out of my way! I want the truth out of him, understand!"

"I'll ask him!" Lanning turned to the robot. "All right, Herbie, take it easy. Have I resigned?"

Herbie stared, and Lanning repeated anxiously, "Have I resigned?" There was the faintest trace of a negative shake of the robot's head. A long wait produced nothing further.

The two men looked at each other and the hostility in their eyes was all but tangible.

"What the devil," blurted Bogert, "has the robot gone mute? Can't you speak, you monstrosity?"

"I can speak," came the ready answer.

"Then answer the question. Didn't you tell me Lanning had resigned? Hasn't he resigned?"

And again there was nothing but dull silence, until from the end of the room, Susan Calvin's laugh rang out suddenly, high-pitched and semi-hysterical.

The two mathematicians jumped, and Bogert's eyes narrowed, "You here? What's so funny?"

"Nothing's funny." Her voice was not quite natural. "It's just that I'm not the only one that's been caught. There's irony in three of the greatest experts in robotics in the world falling into the same elementary trap, isn't there?" Her voice faded, and she put a pale hand to her forehead, "But it isn't funny!"

This time the look that passed between the two men

was one of raised eyebrows. "What trap are you talking about?" asked Lanning stiffly. "Is something wrong with Herbie?"

"No," she approached them slowly, "nothing is wrong with him – only with us." She whirled suddenly and shrieked at the robot, "Get away from me! Go to the other end of the room and don't let me look at you."

Herbie cringed before the fury of her eyes and stumbled away in a clattering trot.

Lanning's voice was hostile, "What is all this, Dr Calvin?"

She faced them and spoke sarcastically, "Surely you know the fundamental First Law of Robotics."

The other two nodded together. "Certainly," said Bogert, irritably, "a robot may not injure a human being or, through inaction, allow him to come to harm."

"How nicely put," sneered Calvin. "But what kind of harm?"

"Why – any kind."

"Exactly! Any kind! But what about hurt feelings? What about deflation of one's ego? What about the blasting of one's hopes? Is that injury?"

Lanning frowned, "What would a robot know about—" And then he caught himself with a gasp.

"You've caught on, have you? *This* robot reads minds. Do you suppose it doesn't know everything about mental injury? Do you suppose that if asked a question, it wouldn't give exactly that answer that one wants to hear? Wouldn't any other answer hurt us, and wouldn't Herbie know that?"

"Good Heavens!" muttered Bogert.

The psychologist cast a sardonic glance at him, "I take it you asked him whether Lanning had resigned. You wanted to hear that he had resigned and so that's what Herbie told you."

"And I suppose that is why," said Lanning, tonelessly, "it would not answer a little while ago. It couldn't answer either way without hurting one of us."

There was a short pause in which the men looked thoughtfully across the room at the robot, crouching in the chair by the bookcase, head resting in one hand.

Susan Calvin stared steadfastly at the floor, "He knew of all this. That . . . that devil knows everything – including what went wrong in his assembly." Her eyes were dark and brooding.

Lanning looked up, "You're wrong there, Dr Calvin. He doesn't know what went wrong. I asked him."

"What does that mean?" cried Calvin. "Only that you didn't want him to give you the solution. It would puncture your ego to have a machine do what you couldn't. Did you ask him?" she shot at Bogert.

"In a way." Bogert coughed and reddened. "He told me he knew very little about mathematics."

Lanning laughed, not very loudly and the psychologist smiled caustically. She said, "I'll ask him! A solution by him won't hurt my ego." She raised her voice into a cold, imperative, "Come here!"

Herbie rose and approached with hesitant steps.

"You know, I suppose," she continued, "just exactly at what point in the assembly an extraneous factor was introduced or an essential one left out."

"Yes," said Herbie, in tones barely heard.

"Hold on," broke in Bogert angrily. "That's not necessarily true. You want to hear that, that's all."

"Don't be a fool," replied Calvin. "He certainly knows as much math as you and Lanning together, since he can read minds. Give him his chance."

The mathematician subsided, and Calvin continued, "All right, then, Herbie, give! We're waiting." And in an aside, "Get pencils and paper, gentlemen."

But Herbie remained silent, and there was triumph in the psychologist's voice, "Why don't you answer, Herbie?"

The robot blurted out suddenly, "I cannot. You know I cannot! Dr Bogert and Dr Lanning don't want me to."

"They want the solution."

"But not from me."

Lanning broke in, speaking slowly and distinctly, "Don't be foolish, Herbie. We do want you to tell us."

Bogert nodded curtly.

Herbie's voice rose to wild heights, "What's the use of saying that? Don't you suppose that I can see past the superficial skin of your mind? Down below, you don't want me to. I'm a machine, given the imitation of life only by virtue of the positronic interplay in my brain – which is man's device. You can't lose face to me without being hurt. That is deep in your mind and won't be erased. I can't give the solution."

"We'll leave," said Dr Lanning. "Tell Calvin."

"That would make no difference," cried Herbie, "since you would know anyway that it was I that was supplying the answer."

Calvin resumed, "But you understand, Herbie, that despite that, Drs Lanning and Bogert want that solution."

"By their own efforts!" insisted Herbie.

"But they want it, and the fact that you have it and won't give it hurts them. You see that, don't you?"

"Yes! Yes!"

"And if you tell them that will hurt them, too."

"Yes! Yes!" Herbie was retreating slowly, and step by step Susan Calvin advanced. The two men watched in frozen bewilderment.

"You can't tell them," droned the psychologist slowly, "because that would hurt and you mustn't hurt. But if you don't tell them, you hurt, so you must tell them. And if you do, you will hurt and you mustn't, so you can't tell them; but if you don't, you hurt, so you must; but if you do, you hurt, so you mustn't; but if you don't, you hurt, so you must; but if you do, you—"

Herbie was up against the wall, and here he dropped to his knees. "Stop!" he shrieked. "Close your mind! It is full of pain and frustration and hate! I didn't mean it,

478

I tell you! I tried to help! I told you what you wanted to hear. I had to!"

The psychologist paid no attention. "You must tell them, but if you do, you hurt, so you mustn't; but if you don't, you hurt, so you must; but—"

And Herbie screamed!

It was like the whistling of a piccolo many times magnified – shrill and shriller till it keened with the terror of a lost soul and filled the room with the piercingness of itself.

And when it died into nothingness, Herbie collapsed into a huddled heap of motionless metal.

Bogert's face was bloodless, "He's dead!"

"No!" Susan Calvin burst into body-racking gusts of wild laughter, "not dead – merely insane. I confronted him with the insoluble dilemma, and he broke down. You can scrap him now – because he'll never speak again."

Lanning was on his knees beside the thing that had been Herbie. His fingers touched the cold, unresponsive metal face and he shuddered. "You did that on purpose." He rose and faced her, face contorted.

"What if I did? You can't help it now." And in a sudden access of bitterness, "He deserved it."

The director seized the paralysed, motionless Bogert by the wrist, "What's the difference. Come, Peter." He sighed, "A thinking robot of this type is worthless anyway." His eyes were old and tired, and he repeated, "Come, Peter!"

It was minutes after the two scientists left that Dr Susan Calvin regained part of her mental equilibrium. Slowly, her eyes turned to the living-dead Herbie and the tightness returned to her face. Long she stared while the triumph faded and the helpless frustration returned – and of all her turbulent thoughts only one infinitely bitter word passed her lips.

"*Liar!*"

*   *   *

That finished it for then, naturally. I knew I couldn't get any more out of her after that. She just sat there behind her desk, her white face cold and – remembering.

I said, "Thank you, Dr Calvin!" but she didn't answer. It was two days before I could get to see her again.

THE MARTIAN CHRONICLES

> (BBC TV, 1980)
> Starring: Rock Hudson, Gayle Hunnicutt &
> Roddy McDowall
> Directed by Michael Anderson
> Story 'I'll Not Look For Wine' by Ray Bradbury

The Martian Chronicles **has, to date, been the most ambitious and faithful adaptation of one of Ray Bradbury's stories for television. Ray, who is one of the most respected names in contempory SF, has had a considerable number of his tales brought to the small screen during the past forty years ever since Alfred Hitchcock first used his story 'Touched With Fire' (retitiled 'Shopping For Death') on his CBS show** *Alfred Hitchcock Presents* **in January 1956. Bradbury's highly individual work has also been seen on other anthology shows including Jane Wyman's Fireside Theatre ('The Marked Bullet', 1956), Rendezvous ('The Wonderful Ice Cream Suit', 1958), The Twilight Zone ('I Sing The Body Electric', 1962), Movie of the Week ('The Screaming Woman', 1972) and so on almost** *ad infinitum.* **But it is his famous novel about the experiences of the first astronauts on an alien planet,** *The Martian Chronicles* **(1950), which was adapted as a big budget, three part special in 1980 which remains the most memorable.**

Ray Bradbury (1920–) was a science fiction fan – producing his own magazine, *Futuria Fantasia* **– before becoming a published writer in the pages of the legendary pulp magazine,** *Weird Tales,* **in the early Forties. Always fascinated by the cinema, two of his**

early SF stories were adapted for the screen – *It Came From Outer Space* (1953) and *The Beast From 20,000 Fathoms* (1953) – before he made his break-through as a scriptwriter when John Houston took him to Ireland in 1956 to work on his epic version of *Moby Dick*, starring Gregory Peck. Although the series of stories which make up *The Martian Chronicles* were among some of the earliest written by Ray, the gestation of the film was one of the longest on record. "The book had been optioned time and time again over thirty years, but never actually made it to the screen until 1980," Ray recalls. "John Houseman, Kirk Douglas, Alan Pakula and Robert Mulligan were all seriously interested in putting the *Chronicles* on either film or television. I actually spent a year off and on writing a script for Pakula and Mulligan, and then when I finished it was the summer we first circumnavigated Mars and photographed the surface. There obviously wasn't anything there, or supposedly there wasn't, and all the studios said, 'Oh, my god, there's no life on Mars – we don't want to make *that* film!'" It was, however, at the time of the Viking landing on Mars that Ray was approached for the rights once again by producer Charles Fried who said he was particularly keen to be faithful to Ray's story of man's intrusion onto an alien planet. Now, with considerably more optimism, Ray gave his blessing. The all-star cast, headed by Rock Hudson as the leader of the Zeus III Mars Expedition, was well-served by the special effects department – but especially by the acting of James Faulkner, as the humanoid-like Martian, Mr K, and his wife, Ylla, played by Maggie Wright. Their subtle and elegant portrayal of two planet dwellers waiting fearfully for the impact of men in silver rockets was a particular delight to Ray because this part of the drama was based on one of his favourite short stories, 'I'll Not Look For Wine': first published in the Canadian magazine, *Maclean's* in January, 1950

and later retitled 'Ylla' for book publication. It is this magical tale which represents another landmark of SF on TV . . .

They had a house of crystal pillars on the planet Mars by the edge of an empty sea, and every morning you could see Mrs K eating the golden fruits that grew from the crystal walls, or cleaning the house with handfuls of magnetic dust which, taking all dirt with it, blew away on the hot wind. Afternoons, when the fossil sea was warm and motionless, and the wine trees stood stiff in the yard, and the little distant Martian bone town was all enclosed, and no one drifted out their doors, you could see Mr K himself in his room, reading from a metal book with raised hieroglyphs over which he brushed his hand, as one might play a harp. And from the book, as his fingers stroked, a voice sang, a soft ancient voice, which told tales of when the sea was red steam on the shore and ancient men had carried clouds of metal insects and electric spiders into battle.

Mr and Mrs K had lived by the dead sea for twenty years, and their ancestors had lived in the same house, which turned and followed the sun, flower-like, for ten centuries.

Mr and Mrs K were not old. They had the fair, brownish skin of the true Martian, the yellow coin eyes, the soft musical voices. Once they had liked painting pictures with chemical fire, swimming in the canals in the seasons when the wine trees filled them with green liquors, and talking into the dawn together by the blue phosphorous portraits in the speaking-room.

They were not happy now.

This morning Mrs K stood between the pillars, listening to the desert sands heat, melt into yellow wax, and seemingly run on the horizon.

Something was going to happen.

She waited.

She watched the blue sky of Mars as if it might at any moment grip in on itself, contract, and expel a shining miracle down upon the sand.

Nothing happened.

Tired of waiting, she walked through the misting pillars. A gentle rain sprang from the fluted pillar-tops, cooling the scorched air, falling gently on her. On hot days it was like walking in a creek. The floors of the house glittered with cool streams. In the distance she heard her husband playing his book steadily, his fingers never tired of the old songs. Quietly she wished he might one day again spend as much time holding and touching her like a little harp as he did his incredible books.

But no. She shook her head, an imperceptible, forgiving shrug. Her eyelids closed softly down upon her golden eyes. Marriage made people old and familiar, while still young.

She lay back in a chair that moved to take her shape even as she moved. She closed her eyes tightly and nervously.

The dream occurred.

Her brown fingers trembled, came up, grasped at the air. A moment later she sat up, startled, gasping.

She glanced about swiftly, as if expecting someone there before her. She seemed disappointed; the space between the pillars was empty.

Her husband appeared in a triangular door. "Did you call?" he asked irritably.

"No!" she cried.

"I thought I heard you cry out."

"Did I? I was almost asleep and had a dream!"

"In the daytime? You don't often do that."

She sat as if struck in the face by the dream. "How strange, how very strange," she murmured. "The dream."

"Oh?" He evidently wished to return to his book.

"I dreamed about a man."

"A man?"

"A tall man, six feet one inch tall."

"How absurd; a giant, a misshapen giant."

"Somehow" – she tried the words – "he looked all right. In spite of being tall. And he had – oh, I know you'll think it silly – he had *blue* eyes!"

"Blue eyes! Gods!" cried Mr K. "What'll you dream next? I suppose he had *black* hair?"

"How did you *guess*?" She was excited.

"I picked the most unlikely colour," he replied coldly.

"Well, black it was!" she cried. "And he had a very white skin; oh, he was *most* unusual! He was dressed in a strange uniform and he came down out of the sky and spoke pleasantly to me." She smiled.

"Out of the sky; what nonsense!"

"He came in a metal thing that glittered in the sun," she remembered. She closed her eyes to shape it again. "I dreamed there was the sky and something sparkled like a coin thrown into the air, and suddenly it grew large and fell down softly to land, a long silver craft, round and alien. And a door opened in the side of the silver object and this tall man stepped out."

"If you worked harder you wouldn't have these silly dreams."

"I rather enjoyed it," she replied, lying back. "I never suspected myself of such an imagination. Black hair, blue eyes, and white skin! What a strange man, and yet – quite handsome."

"Wishful thinking."

"You're unkind. I didn't think him up on purpose; he just came in my mind while I drowsed. It wasn't like a dream. It was so unexpected and different. He looked at me and he said, 'I've come from the third planet in my ship. My name is Nathaniel York—'"

"A stupid name; it's no name at all," objected the husband.

"Of course it's stupid, because it's a dream," she explained softly. "And he said, 'This is the first trip across space. There are only two of us in our ship, myself and my friend Bert.'"

"*Another* stupid name."

"And he said, 'We're from a city on *Earth*; that's the name of our planet,'" continued Mrs K. "That's what he said. 'Earth' was the name he spoke. And he used another language. Somehow I understood him. With my mind. Telepathy, I suppose."

Mr K turned away. She stopped him with a word. "Yll?" she called quietly. "Do you ever wonder if – well, if there *are* people living on the third planet?"

"The third planet is incapable of supporting life," stated the husband patiently. "Our scientists have said there's far too much oxygen in their atmosphere."

"But wouldn't it be fascinating if there were people? And they travelled through space in some sort of ship?"

"Really, Ylla, you know how I hate this emotional wailing. Let's get on with our work."

It was late in the day when she began singing the song as she moved among the whispering pillars of rain. She sang it over and over again.

"What's that song?" snapped her husband at last, walking in to sit at the fire table.

"I don't know." She looked up, surprised at herself. She put her hand to her mouth, unbelieving. The sun was setting. The house was closing itself in, like a giant flower, with the passing of light. A wind blew among the pillars; the fire table bubbled its fierce pool of silver lava. The wind stirred her russet hair, crooning softly in her ears. She stood silently looking out into the great sallow distances of sea bottom, as if recalling something, her yellow eyes soft and moist. "'Drink to me only with thine eyes, and I will pledge with mine,'" she sang, softly, quietly, slowly. "'Or leave a kiss but in the cup, and I'll not look for wine.'" She hummed now, moving her hands in the wind ever so lightly, her eyes shut. She finished the song.

It was very beautiful.

"Never heard that song before. Did you compose it?" he inquired, his eyes sharp.

"No. Yes. No, I don't know, really!" She hesitated wildly. "I don't even know what the words are; they're another language!"

"What language?"

She dropped portions of meat numbly into the simmering lava. "I don't know." She drew the meat forth a moment later, cooked, served on a plate for him. "It's just a crazy thing I made up, I guess. I don't know why."

He said nothing. He watched her drown meats in the hissing fire pool. The sun was gone. Slowly, slowly the night came in to fill the room, swallowing the pillars and both of them, like a dark wine poured to the ceiling. Only the silver lava's glow lit their faces.

She hummed the strange song again.

Instantly he leaped from his chair and stalked angrily from the room.

Later, in isolation, he finished supper.

When he arose he stretched, glanced at her, and suggested, yawning, "Let's take the flame birds to town tonight to see an entertainment."

"You don't *mean* it?" she said. "Are you feeling well?"

"What's so strange about that?"

"But we haven't gone for an entertainment in six months!"

"I think it's a good idea."

"Suddenly you're so solicitous," she said.

"Don't talk that way," he replied peevishly. "Do you or do you not want to go?"

She looked out at the pale desert. The twin white moons were rising. Cool water ran softly about her toes. She began to tremble just the least bit. She wanted very much to sit quietly here, soundless, not moving until this thing occurred, this thing expected all day, this thing that could not occur but might. A drift of song brushed through her mind.

"I—"

"Do you good," he urged. "Come along now."

"I'm tired," she said. "Some other night."

"Here's your scarf." He handed her a phial. "We haven't gone anywhere in months."

"Except you, twice a week to Xi City." She wouldn't look at him.

"Business," he said.

"Oh?" She whispered to herself.

From the phial a liquid poured, turned to blue mist, settled about her neck, quivering.

The flame birds waited, like a bed of coals, glowing on the cool smooth sands. The white canopy ballooned on the night wind, flapping softly, tied by a thousand green ribbons to the birds.

Ylla laid herself back in the canopy and, at a word from her husband, the birds leaped, burning, towards the dark sky. The ribbons tautened, the canopy lifted. The sand slid whining under; the blue hills drifted by, drifted by, leaving their home behind, the raining pillars, the caged flowers, the singing books, the whispering floor creeks. She did not look at her husband. She heard him crying out to the birds as they rose higher, like ten thousand hot sparkles, so many red-yellow fireworks in the heavens, tugging the canopy like a flower petal, burning through the wind.

She didn't watch the dead, ancient bone-chess cities slide under, or the old canals filled with emptiness and dreams. Past dry rivers and dry lakes they flew, like a shadow of the moon, like a torch burning.

She watched only the sky.

The husband spoke.

She watched the sky.

"Did you hear what I said?"

"What?"

He exhaled. "You might pay attention."

"I was thinking."

"I never thought you were a nature-lover, but you're certainly interested in the sky tonight," he said.

"It's very beautiful."

"I was figuring," said the husband slowly. "I thought I'd call Hulle tonight. I'd like to talk to him about us spending some time, oh, only a week or so, in the Blue Mountains. It's just an idea—"

"The Blue Mountains!" She held to the canopy rim with one hand, turning swiftly towards him.

"Oh, it's just a suggestion."

"When do you want to go?" she asked, trembling.

"I thought we might leave tomorrow morning. You know, an early start and all that," he said very casually.

"But we *never* go this early in the year!"

"Just this once, I thought—" He smiled. "Do us good to get away. Some peace and quiet. You know. You haven't anything *else* planned? We'll go, won't we?"

She took a breath, waited, and then replied, "No."

"What?" His cry startled the birds. The canopy jerked.

"No," she said firmly. "It's settled. I won't go."

He looked at her. They did not speak after that. She turned away.

The birds flew on, ten thousand firebrands down the wind.

In the dawn the sun, through the crystal pillars, melted the fog that supported Ylla as she slept. All night she had hung above the floor, buoyed by the soft carpeting of mist that poured from the walls when she lay down to rest. All night she had slept on this silent river, like a boat upon a soundless tide. Now the fog burned away, the mist level lowered until she was deposited upon the shore of wakening.

She opened her eyes.

Her husband stood over her. He looked as if he had stood there for hours, watching. She did not know why, but she could not look him in the face.

"You've been dreaming again!" he said. "You spoke out and kept me awake. I *really* think you should see a doctor."

"I'll be all right."

"You talked a lot in your sleep!"

"Did I?" She started up.

Dawn was cold in the room. A grey light filled her as she lay there.

"What was your dream?"

She had to think a moment to remember. "The ship. It came from the sky again, landed, and the tall man stepped out and talked with me, telling me little jokes, laughing, and it was pleasant."

Mr K touched a pillar. Founts of warm water leaped up, steaming; the chill vanished from the room. Mr K's face was impassive.

"And then," she said, "this man, who said his strange name was Nathaniel York, told me I was beautiful and – and kissed me."

"Ha!" cried the husband, turning violently away, his jaw working.

"It's only a dream." She was amused.

"Keep your silly, feminine dreams to yourself!"

"You're acting like a child." She lapsed back upon the few remaining remnants of chemical mist. After a moment she laughed softly. "I thought of some *more* of the dream," she confessed.

"Well, what is it, what *is* it?" he shouted.

"Yll, you're so bad-tempered."

"Tell me!" he demanded. "You can't keep secrets from me!" His face was dark and rigid as he stood over her.

"I've never seen you this way," she replied, half shocked, half entertained. "All that happened was this Nathaniel York person told me – well, he told me that he'd take me away into his ship, into the sky with him, and take me back to his planet with him. It's really quite ridiculous."

"Ridiculous, is it!" he almost screamed. "You should

have heard yourself, fawning on him, talking to him, singing with him, oh gods, all night; you should have *heard* yourself!"

"Yll!"

"When's he landing? Where's he coming down with his damned ship?"

"Yll, lower your voice."

"Voice be damned!" He bent stiffly over her. "And *in* this dream" – he seized her wrist – "didn't the ship land over in Green Valley, *didn't* it? Answer me!"

"Why, yes—"

"And it landed this afternoon, didn't it?" he kept at her.

"Yes, yes, I think so, yes, but only in a dream!"

"Well" – he flung her hand away stiffly – "it's good you're truthful! I heard every word you said in your sleep. You mentioned the valley and the time." Breathing hard, he walked between the pillars like a man blinded by a lightning bolt. Slowly his breath returned. She watched him as if he were quite insane. She arose finally and went to him. "Yll," she whispered.

"I'm all right."

"You're sick."

"No." He forced a tired smile. "Just childish. Forgive me, darling." He gave her a rough pat. "Too much work lately. I'm sorry. I think I'll lie down awhile—"

"You were so excited."

"I'm all right now. Fine." He exhaled. "Let's forget it. Say, I heard a joke about Uel yesterday, I meant to tell you. What do you say you fix breakfast, I'll tell the joke, and let's not talk about all this."

"It was only a dream."

"Of course." He kissed her cheek mechanically. "Only a dream."

At noon the sun was high and hot and the hills shimmered in the light.

"Aren't you going to town?" asked Ylla.

"Town?" He raised his brows faintly.

"This is the day you *always* go." She adjusted a flowercage on its pedestal. The flowers stirred, opening their hungry yellow mouths.

He closed his book. "No. It's too hot, and it's late."

"Oh." She finished her task and moved towards the door. "Well, I'll be back soon."

"Wait a minute! Where are you going?"

She was in the door swiftly. "Over to Pao's. She invited me!"

"Today?"

"I haven't seen her in a long time. It's only a little way."

"Over in Green Valley, isn't it?"

"Yes, just a walk, not far, I thought I'd—" She hurried.

"I'm sorry, really sorry," he said, running to fetch her back, looking very concerned about his forgetfulness. "It slipped my mind. I invited Dr Nlle out this afternoon."

"Dr Nlle!" She edged towards the door.

He caught her elbow and drew her steadily in. "Yes."

"But Pao—"

"Pao can wait, Ylla. We must entertain Nlle."

"Just for a few minutes—"

"No, Ylla."

"No?"

He shook his head. "No. Besides, it's a terribly long walk to Pao's. All the way over through Green Valley and then past the big canal and down, isn't it? And it'll be very, very hot, and Dr Nlle would be delighted to see you. Well?"

She did not answer. She wanted to break and run. She wanted to cry out. But she only sat in the chair, turning her fingers over slowly, staring at them expressionlessly, trapped.

"Ylla?" he murmured. "You *will* be here, won't you?"

"Yes," she said after a long time. "I'll be here."

"All afternoon?"

Her voice was dull. "All afternoon."

Late in the day Dr Nlle had not put in an appearance. Ylla's husband did not seem overly surprised. When it was quite late he murmured something, went to a closet, and drew forth an evil weapon, a long yellowish tube ending in a bellows and a trigger. He turned, and upon his face was a mask, hammered from silver metal, expressionless, the mask that he always wore when he wished to hide his feelings, the mask which curved and hollowed so exquisitely to his thin cheeks and chin and brow. The mask glinted, and he held the evil weapon in his hands, considering it. It hummed constantly, an insect hum. From it hordes of golden bees could be flung out with a high shriek. Golden, horrid bees that stung, poisoned, and fell lifeless, like seeds on the sand.

"Where are you going?" she asked.

"What?" He listened to the bellows, to the evil hum. "If Dr Nlle is late, I'll be damned if I'll wait. I'm going out to hunt a bit. I'll be back. You be sure to stay right here now, won't you?" The silver mask glimmered.

"Yes."

"And tell Dr Nlle I'll return. Just hunting."

The triangular door closed. His footsteps faded down the hill.

She watched him walking through the sunlight until he was gone. Then she resumed her tasks with the magnetic dusts and the new fruits to be plucked from the crystal walls. She worked with energy and dispatch, but on occasion a numbness took hold of her and she caught herself singing that odd and memorable song and looking out beyond the crystal pillars at the sky.

She held her breath and stood very still, waiting.

It was coming nearer.

At any moment it might happen.

It was like those days when you heard a thunderstorm coming and there was the waiting silence and then the faintest pressure of the atmosphere as the climate blew over the land in shifts and shadows and vapours. And the change pressed at your ears and you were suspended in the waiting time of the coming storm. You began to tremble. The sky was stained and coloured; the clouds were thickened; the mountains took on an iron taint. The caged flowers blew with faint sighs of warning. You felt your hair stir softly. Somewhere in the house the voice-clock sang. "Time, time, time, time . . ." ever so gently, no more than water tapping on velvet.

And then the storm. The electric illumination, the engulfments of dark wash and sounding black fell down, shutting in, forever.

That's how it was now. A storm gathered, yet the sky was clear. Lightning was expected, yet there was no cloud.

Ylla moved through the breathless summer-house. Lightning would strike from the sky any instant; there would be a thunder-clap, a boll of smoke, a silence, footsteps on the path, a rap on the crystalline door, and her *running* to answer . . .

Crazy Ylla! she scoffed. Why think these wild things with your idle mind?

And then it happened.

There was a warmth as of a great fire passing in the air. A whirling, rushing sound. A gleam in the sky, of metal.

Ylla cried out.

Running through the pillars, she flung wide a door. She faced the hills. But by this time there was nothing.

She was about to race down the hill when she stopped herself. She was supposed to stay here, go nowhere. The doctor was coming to visit, and her husband would be angry if she ran off.

She waited in the door, breathing rapidly, her hand out.

She strained to see over towards Green Valley, but saw nothing.

Silly woman. She went inside. You and your imagination, she thought. That was nothing but a bird, a leaf, the wind, or a fish in the canal. Sit down. Rest.

She sat down.

A shot sounded.

Very clearly, sharply, the sound of the evil insect weapon.

Her body jerked with it.

It came from a long way off. One shot. The swift humming distant bees. One shot. And then a second shot, precise and cold, and far away.

Her body winced again and for some reason she started up, screaming, and screaming, and never wanting to stop screaming. She ran violently through the house and once more threw wide the door.

The echoes were dying away, away.

Gone.

She waited in the yard, her face pale, for five minutes.

Finally, with slow steps, her head down, she wandered about the pillared rooms, laying her hand to things, her lips quivering, until finally she sat alone in the darkening wine-room, waiting. She began to wipe an amber glass with the hem of her scarf.

And then, from far off, the sound of footsteps crunching on the thin, small rocks.

She rose up to stand in the centre of the quiet room. The glass fell from her fingers, smashing to bits.

The footsteps hesitated outside the door.

Should she speak? Should she cry out, "Come in, oh, come in"?

She went forward a few paces.

The footsteps walked up the ramp. A hand twisted the door latch.

She smiled at the door.

The door opened. She stopped smiling.

It was her husband. His silver mask glowed dully.

He entered the room and looked at her for only a

moment. Then he snapped the weapon bellows open, cracked out two dead bees, heard them spat on the floor as they fell, stepped on them, and placed the empty bellows-gun in the corner of the room as Ylla bent down and tried, over and over, with no success, to pick up the pieces of the shattered glass. "What were you doing?" she asked.

"Nothing," he said with his back turned. He removed the mask.

"But the gun – I heard you fire it. Twice."

"Just hunting. Once in a while you like to hunt. Did Dr Nlle arrive?"

"No."

"Wait a minute." He snapped his fingers disgustedly. "Why, I remember now. He was supposed to visit us *tomorrow* afternoon. How stupid of me."

They sat down to eat. She looked at her food and did not move her hands. "What's wrong?" he asked, not looking up from dipping his meat in the bubbling lava.

"I don't know. I'm not hungry," she said.

"Why not?"

"I don't know; I'm just not."

The wind was rising across the sky; the sun was going down. The room was small and suddenly cold.

"I've been trying to remember," she said in the silent room, across from her cold, erect, golden-eyed husband.

"Remember what?" He sipped his wine.

"That song. That fine and beautiful song." She closed her eyes and hummed, but it was not the song. "I've forgotten it. And, somehow, I don't want to forget it. It's something I want always to remember." She moved her hands as if the rhythm might help her to remember all of it. Then she lay back in her chair. "I can't remember." She began to cry.

"Why are you crying?" he asked.

"I don't know, I don't know, but I can't help it. I'm sad and I don't know why, I cry and I don't know why, but I'm crying."

Her head was in her hands; her shoulders moved again and again.

"You'll be all right tomorrow," he said.

She did not look up at him; she looked only at the empty desert and the very bright stars coming out now on the black sky, and far away there was a sound of wind rising and canal waters stirring cold in the long canals. She shut her eyes, trembling.

"Yes," she said. "I'll be all right tomorrow."

DISCWORLD

> (Granada TV, 1996)
> Produced by Andy Harries
> Story 'Final Reward' by Terry Pratchett

The comic fantasy novels by Terry Pratchett have
become a phenomenonal success story, earning the
author lavish praise in the press – *The Mail on
Sunday* declaring him to be, 'This country's greatest
living novelist . . . the Dickens of the 20th Century.'
Such praise leaves the bearded, unassuming Terry
rather amused, although he takes considerable pride
at having reached such a vast and appreciative read-
ership: his famous series of Discworld novels alone
have already sold more than 4 million copies in the
UK. And having conquered the literary world – each
new novel from his pen invariably reaches the top of
the best seller lists – Terry has already had two of
his other stories made into television programmes:
Truckers (1991) an animated film about a family
of tiny Nomes stowed away on a truck, which was
filmed by Cosgrove Hall; and *Johnny and the Dead*
(1995) featuring a schoolboy (Andrew Falvey) who can
walk through a cemetery and talk to the occupants –
even resurecting some of them for a chat including a
Victorian worthy (George Baker), an old Communist
(Brian Blessed) and a sufragette (Jane Lapotaire).
Now Granada TV have bought the rights to the
Discworld books – stories of a world dominated
by magic travelling through space on the back of
a giant turtle being slowly turned by four elephants –
and producer Andy Harries is planning an ambitious

two-hour pilot film to be followed by a series of hour long episodes. The project has already been described, somewhat tongue-in-cheek, by one TV critic as 'Star Trek meets Monty Python'.

Terry Pratchett (1948–), who was born in Beaconsfield, has admitted that the Kenneth Grahame classic, *Wind in the Willows*, was one of his earliest influences, and such was his natural skill as a storyteller that he sold his first story, 'The Hades Business' to *Science Fantasy Magazine* when he was just 13 years old. After leaving school, Terry became a reporter on the *Bucks Free Press* and, working in his spare time, wrote his first novel for children, *The Carpet People* in 1971. Later he became a press officer with the Central Electricity Generating Board and in 1976 published his first adult novel, *The Dark Side of the Sun*, which some critics have seen as a 'stepping stone' to the Discworld series which was launched seven years later with *The Colour of Magic*. The elements of fantasy mixed with satirical wit that have made the subsequent 18 books in the series so successful was evident from the very start, as the US trade magazine *Publishers Weekly* spotted in its review: 'Heroic barbarians, chthonic monsters, beautiful princesses and fiery dragons; they're all here, but none of them is doing business as usual.' Hereunder is one of Terry's rare short stories about an equally out-of-the-ordinary barbarian hero which he wrote for *Games Magazine* in 1988. It is appearing in book form for the first time and will no doubt be as welcome to Terry's huge army of fans as the thought of his mad and magical world becoming the latest in the continuing series of space movies on television . . .

Final Reward

Dogger answered the door when he was still in his dressing gown. Something unbelievable was on the doorstep.

"There's a simple explanation," thought Dogger, "I've gone mad."

This seemed a satisfactory enough rationalisation at seven o'clock in the morning. He shut the door again and shuffled down the passage, while outside the kitchen window the Northern Line rattled with carriages full of people who weren't mad, despite appearances.

There is a blissful period of existence which the Yen Buddhists* call *plinki*. It is defined quite precisely as that interval between waking up and being hit on the back of the head by all the problems that kept you awake the night before; it ends when you realise that this was the morning everything was going to look better in, and it doesn't.

He remembered the row with Nicky. Well, not exactly *row*. More a kind of angry silence on her part, and an increasingly exasperated burbling on his, and he wasn't quite sure how it had started anyway. He recalled saying something about some of her friends looking as though they wove their own bread and baked their own goats, and then it has escalated to the level where he'd probably said things like *Since you ask, I do think green 2CVs have the anti-nuclear sticker laminated into their rear window before they leave the factory*. If he had been on the usual form he achieved after a pint of white wine he'd probably passed a remark about dungarees on women, too. It had been one of those rows where every jocular attempt to extract himself had opened another chasm under his feet.

And then she'd broken, no, shattered the silence with all those comments about Erdan *macho wish-fulfillment for adolescents*, and there'd been comments about Rambo, and then he'd found himself arguing the case for people who, in cold sobriety, he detested as much as she did.

And then he'd come home and written the last chapter of *Erdan and the Serpent of the Rim*, and out of pique, alcohol and rebellion he'd killed his hero off on the

* Like Zen Buddish only bigger begging bowls.

last page. Crushed under an avalanche. The fans were going to hate him, but he'd felt better afterwards, freed of something that had held him back all these years. And had made him quite rich, incidentally. That was because of computers, because half the fans he met now worked in computers, and of course in computers they gave you a wheelbarrow to take your wages home; science fiction fans might break out in pointy ears from time to time, but they bought books by the shovelful and read them round the clock.

Now he'd have to think of something else for them, write proper science fiction, learn about black holes and quantums . . .

There was another point nagging his mind as he yawned his way back to the kitchen.

Oh, yes. Erdan the Barbarian had been standing on his doorstep.

Funny, that.

This time the hammering made small bits of plaster detach themselves from the wall around the door, which was an unusual special effect in a hallucination. Dogger opened the door again.

Erdan was standing patiently next to his milk. The milk was white, and in bottles. Erdan was seven feet tall and in a tiny chain mail loincloth; his torso looked like a sack full of footballs. In one hand he held what Dogger knew for certainty was Skung, the Sword of the Ice Gods.

Dogger was certain about this because he had described it thousands of times. But he wasn't going to describe it again.

Erdan broke the silence.

"I have come," he said, "to meet my Maker."

"Pardon?"

"I have come," said the barbarian hero, "to receive my Final Reward." He peered down Dogger's hall expectantly and rippled his torso.

"You're a fan, right?" said Dogger. "Pretty good costume . . ."

501

"What," said Erdan, "is fan?"

"I want to drink your blood," said Skung, conversationally.

Over the giant's shoulder – metaphorically speaking, although under his massive armpit in real life – Dogger saw the postman coming up the path. The man walked around Erdan, humming, pushed a couple of bills into Dogger's unresisting hand, opined against all the evidence that it looked like being a nice day, and strolled back down the path.

"I want to drink his blood, too," said Skung.

Erdan stood impassively, making it quite clear that he was going to stay there until the Snow Mammoths of Hy-Kooli came home.

History records a great many foolish comments, such as "It looks perfectly safe", or "Indians? What Indians?" and Dogger added to the list with an old favourite which has caused more encyclopedias and life insurance policies to be sold than you would have thought possible.

"I suppose," he said, "that you'd better come in."

No one could look that much like Erdan. His leather jerkin looked as though it had been stored in a compost heap. His fingernails were purple, his hands calloused, his chest a trelliswork of scars. Something with a mouth the size of an armchair appeared to had got a grip on his arm at some time, but couldn't have liked the taste.

What it is, Dogger said, is I'm externalising my fantasies. Or I'm probably still asleep. The important thing is to act natural.

"Well, well," he said.

Erdan ducked into what Dogger liked to call his study, which was just like any other living room but had his wordprocessor on the table, and sat down in the armchair. The springs gave a threatening creak.

Then he gave Dogger an expectant look.

Of course, Dogger told himself, he may just be your everyday homicidal maniac.

"Your final reward?" he said weakly.

Erdan nodded.

"Er. What form does this take, exactly?"

Erdan shrugged. Several muscles had to move out of the way to allow the huge shoulders to rise and fall.

"It is said," he said, "that those who die in combat will feast and carouse in your hall forever."

"Oh." Dogger hovered uncertainly in the doorway. "My hall?"

Erdan nodded again. Dogger look around him. What with the telephone and the coatrack it was already pretty crowded. Opportunities for carouse looked limited.

"And, er," he said, "how long is forever, exactly?"

"Until the stars die and the Great Ice covers the world," said Erdan.

"Ah. I thought it might be something like that."

Cobham's voice crackled in the earpiece.

"You've what?" it said.

"I said I've given him a lager and a chicken leg and put him in the front of the television," said Dogger. "You know what? It was the fridge that really impressed him. He says I've got the next Ice Age shut in a prison, what do you think of that? And the TV is how I spy on the world, he says. He's watching *Neighbours* and he's laughing."

"Well, what do you expect me to do about it?"

"Look, no one could act that much like Erdan! It'd take weeks just to get the stink right! I mean, it's him. Really him. Just as I always imagined him. And he's sitting in my study watching soaps! You're my agent, what do I do next?"

"Just calm down." Cobham's voice sounded soothing. "Erdan is your creation. You've lived with him for years."

"Years is okay! Years was in my head. It's right now in my house that's on my mind!"

". . . and he's very popular and it's only to be expected that, when you take a big step like killing him off . . ."

"You know I had to do it! I mean, twenty-six books!"

The sound of Erdan's laughter boomed through the wall.

"Okay, so it's preyed on your mind. I can tell. He's not really there. You said the milkman couldn't see him.

"The postman. Yes, but he walked around him! Ron, I created him! He thinks I'm God! And now I've killed him off, he's come to meet me!"

"Kevin?"

"Yes? What?"

"Take a few tablets or something. He's bound to go away. These things do."

Dogger put the phone down carefully.

"Thanks a lot," he said bitterly.

In fact, he gave it a try. He went down to the hypermarket and pretended that the hulking figure that followed him wasn't really there.

It wasn't that Erdan was invisible to other people. Their eyes saw him all right, but somehow their brains seemed to edit him out before he impinged on any higher centres.

That is, they could walk around him and even apologised automatically if they bumped into him, but afterwards they would be at loss to explain what they had walked around and who they had apologised to.

Dogger left him behind in the maze of shelves, working on a desperate theory that if Erdan was out of his sight for a while he might evaporate, like smoke. He grabbed a few items, scurried through a blessed clear checkout, and was back on the pavement before a cheerful shout made him stiffen and turn around slowly, as though on castors.

Erdan had mastered shopping trolleys. Of course, he was really quite bright. He'd worked out the Maze of the Mad God in a matter of hours, after all, so a wire box on wheels was a doddle.

He'd even come to terms with the freezer cabinets. Of course, Dogger thought. *Erdan and the Top of the World*,

Chapter Four: he'd survived on 10,000 year old woolly mammoth, fortuitously discovered in the frozen tundra. Dogger had actually done some research about that. It had told him it wasn't in fact possible, but what the hell. As far as Erdan was concerned, the wizard Tesco had simply prepared these mammoths in handy portion packs.

"I watch everyone," said Erdan proudly. "I like being dead."

Dogger crept up to the trolley. "But it's not yours!"

Erdan looked puzzled.

"It is now," he said. "I took it. Much easy. No fighting. I have drink, I have meat, I have My-Name-Is-TRACEY-How-May-I-Help-You, I have small nuts in bag."

Dogger pulled aside most of a cow in small polystyrene boxes and Tracey's mad, terrified eyes looked up at him from the depths of the trolley. She extended a sticker gun in both hands, like Dirty Harry about to have his made, and priced his nose at 98p a lb. "Soap," said Dogger. "It's called soap. Not like *Neighbours*, this one is useful. You wash with it." He sighed. "Vigorous movements of the wet flannel over parts of your body," he went on, "It's a novel idea, I know."

"And this is the bath," he added. "And this is the sink. And this is called a lavatory. I explained about it before."

"It is smaller than the bath," Erdan complained mildly.

"Yes. *Nevertheless*. And these are towels, to dry you. And this is a toothbrush, and this is a razor." He hesitated. "You remember," he said, "When I put you in the seraglio of the Emir of the White Mountain? I'm pretty certain you had a wash and shave then. This is just like that."

"Where are the houris?"

"There are no houris. You have to do it yourself."

A train screamed past, rattling the scrubbing brush into the washbasin. Erdan growled.

"It's just a train," said Dogger. "A box to travel in. It won't hurt you. Just don't try to kill one."

Ten minutes later Dogger sat listening to Erdan singing, although that in itself wasn't the problem; it was a sound you could imagine floating across sunset taiga. Water dripped off the light fitting, but that wasn't the problem.

The problem was Nicky. It usually was. He was going to meet her after work at the House of Tofu. He was horribly afraid that Erdan would come with him. This was not likely to be good news. His stock with Nicky was bumping on the bottom even before last night, owing to an ill-chosen remark about black stockings last week, when he was still on probation for what he said ought to be done with mime-artists. Nicky liked New Men, although the term was probably out of date now. Jesus, he'd taken the *Guardian* to keep up with her and got another black mark when he said its children's page read exactly like someone would write if they set out to do a spoof *Guardian* children's page . . . Erdan wasn't a New Man. She was bound to notice him. She had a sort of radar for things like that.

He had to find a way to sent him back.

"I want to drink your blood," said Skung, from behind the sofa.

"Oh, shut up."

He tried some positive thinking again.

It is absolutely impossible that a fictional character I created is having a bath upstairs. It's overwork, caused by hallucinations. Of course I don't feel mad, but I wouldn't, would I? He's . . . he's a projection. That's right. I've, I've being going through a bad patch lately, basically since I was about ten, and Erdan is just a projection of the sort of macho thingy I secretly want to be. Nicky said I wrote the books because of that, she said. I can't cope with the real world, so I turned all the problems into monsters and invented a character that could handle them. Erdan is how I cope with the world. I never realised it myself. So all I need do be positive, and he won't exist.

He eyed the pile of manuscript on the table.

I wonder if Conan Doyle had this sort of problem?

Perhaps he was just sitting down to tea when Sherlock Holmes knocked at the door, still dripping wet from the Richtofen Falls or whatever, and then started hanging around the house making clever remarks until Doyle trapped him between pages again.

He half rose from his chair. That was it. All he had to do was rewrite the . . .

Erdan pushed open the door.

"Ho!" he said, and then stuck his little, relatively little finger in one wet ear and made a noise like a cork coming out of a bottle. He was wearing a bath towel. Somehow he looked neat, less scared. Amazing what hot water could do, Dogger decided.

"All my clothes they prickle," he said cheerfully.

"Did you try washing them?" said Dogger weakly.

"They dry all solid like wood," said Erdan. "I pray for clothes like gods, mighty Kevin."

"None of mine would fit," said Dogger. He looked at Erdan's shoulders. "None of mine would half fit," he added, "Anyway, you're not going anywhere. I give in. I'll rewrite the last chapter. You can go home."

He beamed. This was exactly the right way. By taking the madness seriously he could make it consume itself. All he need do was change the last page, he didn't even need to write another Erdan book, all he needed to do was to make it clear that Erdan was still alive somewhere.

"I'll write you some new clothes, too," he said. "Silly, isn't it," he went on, "A big lad like you dying in an avalanche! You've survived much worse."

He pulled the manuscript towards him.

"I mean," he burbled happily, "Don't you remember when you had to cross the Grebor Desert without water, and you . . ."

A hand like closed over his wrist, gently but firmly. Dogger remembered one of those science films which had showed an industrial robot, capable of putting two tons of pressure on a point an eighth of an inch across, gently picking up an egg. Now his wrist knew how the egg felt.

507

"I like it here," said Erdan.

He made him leave Skung behind. Skung was a sword of few words, and none of them would go down well in a wholefood restaurant where even the beansprouts were free-range. Erdan wasn't going to be left behind, though. Where does a seven foot barbarian hero go? Dogger thought. Wherever he likes.

He also tried writing Erdan a new suit of clothes. It was only partially successful. Erdan was not cut out by nature, by him, to wear a sports jacket. He ended up looking as Dogger had always pictured him, like a large and over-enthusiastic Motorhead fan.

Erdan seemed to be becoming more obvious. Maybe whatever kind of mental antibodies prevented people from seeing him wore away after a while. He certainly got a few odd looks.

"Who is tofu?" said Erdan, as they walked to the bus-stop.

"Ah. Not a who, an it. It's a sort of food and tiling grout combined. It's . . . it's something like . . . well, sometimes it's green, other times it isn't," said Dogger. This didn't help much. "Well," he said, "remember when you went to fight for help Doge of Tenitti? I was pretty sure I wrote you eating pasta."

"Yes."

"Compared to tofu, pasta is a taste explosion. Two to the centre please," Dogger added, to the conductor.

The man squinted at Erdan. "Rock concert on, is there? he said.

"And you carouse in this tofu?" said Erdan, as they alighted.

"You can't carouse organically. My girl . . . a young lady I know works there. She believes in things. And, look, I don't want you spoiling it, okay? My romantic life isn't exactly straightforward at the moment." A thought struck him. "And don't let's have any advice from you about how to straighten it. Throwing women over your pommel and riding off into the night isn't approved around here. It's probably an ism," he added gloomily.

"It works for me," said Erdan.

"Yes," muttered Dogger. "It always did. Funny, that. You never had any trouble, I saw to that. Twenty-six books without a change of clothes and no girl ever said she was washing her hair."

"Not my fault, they just throw . . ."

"I'm not saying it was. I'm just saying a chap has only got so much of it, and I gave mine to you."

Erdan's brow wrinkled mightily with the effort of thought. His lips moved as he repeated the sentence to himself, once or twice. Then he appeared to reach a conclusion.

"What?" he said.

"And you go back in the morning."

"I like it here. You have picture television, sweet food, soft seats."

"You enjoyed it in Chimera! The snowfields, the bracing wind, the endless taiga . . ."

Erdan gave him a sidelong glance.

"Didn't you?" said Dogger, uncertainly.

"If you say so," said Erdan.

"And you watch too much far-seeing box."

"Television," corrected Erdan. "Can I take it back?"

"What, to Chimera?"

"It get lonely on the endless taiga between books."

"You found the Channel Four button, I see." Dogger turned the idea over in his mind. It had certain charm. Erdan the Barbarian with his blood-drinking sword, chain-mail kilt, portable television and thermal blanket.

No, it wouldn't work. It wasn't as if there were many channels in Chimera, and probably one of the few things you couldn't buy in the mysterious souks of Ak-Terezical was a set of decent ni-cads.

He shivered. What was he thinking about? He really was going mad. The fans would kill him.

And he knew he'd never been able to send Erdan

back. Not now. Something had changed, he'd never be able to do it again. He'd enjoyed creating Chimera. He only had to close his eyes and he could see the Shemark mountains, every lofty peak trailing its pennant of snow. He knew the Prades delta like the back of his hand. *Better*. And now it was all going, ebbing like the tide. Leaving Erdan.

Who was evolving.

"Here it say 'House of Tofu'," said Erdan.

Who had learnt to read.

Whose clothes somehow looked less hairy, whose walk was less of a shamble.

And Dogger knew that, when they walked through that door, Erdan and Nicky would hit it off. She'd see him all right. She always seemed to look right through Dogger, but she'd see Erdan.

His hair was shorter. His clothes looked merely stylish. Erdan had achieved in a short walk from the bus-stop what it had taken most barbarians ten thousand years to accomplish. Logical, really. After all, Erdan was basically your total hero type. Put him in any environment and he'd change to fit. Two hours with Nicky and he'd be torpedoing whaling ships and shutting down nuclear power stations single-handledly.

"You go on in," he said.

"Problems?" said Erdan.

"Just got something to sort out. I'll join you later. Remember, though. I made you what you are."

"Thank you," said Erdan.

"Here's the spare key to the flat in case I'm not back. You know. Get held up or something."

Erdan took it gravely.

"You go ahead. Don't worry, I won't send you back to Chimera."

Erdan gave him a look in which surprise was leavened with just the hint of amusement.

"Chimera?" he said.

* * *

The wordprocessor clicked into life.

And the monitor was without form, and void, and darkness was upon the screen, with of course the exception of the beckoning flicker of the cursor.

Dogger's hand moved upon the face of the keyboard.

It ought to work both ways. If belief was the engine of it all, it ought to be possible to hitch a ride if you really were mad enough to try it.

Where to start?

A short story would be enough, just to create the character. Chimera already existed, in a little bubble of fractal reality created by these ten fingers.

He began to type, hesitantly at first, and then speeding up as the ideas began to crystallise out.

After a little while he opened the kitchen window. Behind him, in the darkness, the printer started up.

The key turned in the lock.

The cursor pulsed gently as the two of them came in, talked, made coffee, talked again in the body language of people finding they really have a lot in common. Words like "holistic approach" floated past its uncritical beacon.

"He's always doing things like this," she said. "It's the drinking and smoking. It's not a healthy life. He doesn't know how to look after himself."

Erdan paused. He found the printed output cascading down the table, and now he put down the short MS half read. Outside a siren wailed, dopplered closer, shut off.

"I'm sorry?" he said.

"I said he doesn't look after himself."

"I think he may have to learn," he said. He picked up a pencil, regarded the end of it thoughtfully until the necessary skills clicked precisely in his head, and made a few insertions. The idiot hadn't even specified what kind of clothing he was wearing. If you're really going to write first person, you might as well keep warm. It got damn cold out on the steppes.

"You've known him a long time, then?"

"Years."

"You don't look like most of his friends."

"We were quite close at one time. I expect I'd better see to the place until he comes back." He pencilled in *but the welcoming firelight of a Skryling encampment showed through the freezing trees.* Skrylings were okay, they considered that crazy people were great shamen, Kevin should be all right there.

Nicky stood up. "Well, I'd better be going," she said. The tone and pitch of her voice turned tumblers in his head.

"You needn't," he said. "It's entirely up to you, of course."

There was a long pause. She walked up behind him and looked over his shoulder, her manner a little awkward.

"What's this?" she said, in an attempt to turn the conversation away from its logical conclusions.

"Just a story of his. I'd better mail it in the morning."

"Oh. Are you a writer, too?"

Erdan glanced at the wordprocessor. Compared to the Bronze Hordes of Merkle it didn't look too fearsome. A whole new life was waiting for him, he could feel it, he could flow out into it. And change to suit.

"Just breaking into it," he said.

"I mean, I quite like Kevin," she said quickly. "He just never seemed to relate to the real world." She turned away to hide her embarrassment, and peered out of the window.

"There's a lot of blue lights down on the railway line," she said.

Erdan made a few more alterations. "Are there?" he said.

"And there's people milling about."

"Oh." Erdan changed the title to *The Traveller of the*

Falconsong. What was needed was more development, he could see that. He'd write about what he knew.

After a bit of thought he added *Book One in the Chronicles of Kevin the Bardsinger*.

It was the least he could do.